SOP[illegible]

At twenty-e[illegible]ucky to have achieved sup[illegible]er, she remained firmly convince[illegible] was a fluke, one she owed to the fact [illegible] lied as easily and often as men on the make. [illegible]racle her hormones had wrought in her teens had come too late to change her self-image. Deep down, she was still the too tall, all elbows and knees, unloved girl who had wandered the Pride ranch in tattered jeans and down-at-the-heels boots.

And now she was going back home.

Her heart constricted at the thought. Her father had transformed her first trip to New York into a walk on a tightrope without a net. A decade later, he wanted her back. Why? she mused. Did he really want her at his bedside – or could his motive be more Machiavellian?

Also by Alexandra Thorne

CREATIVE URGES
PAST FORGETTING

About the author

Alexander Thorne lives in Texas, USA.
She is currently working on her fourth novel.

Sophisticated Savages

Alexandra Thorne

NEW ENGLISH LIBRARY
Hodder and Stoughton

To my husband, Bill –
for the armadillo and for Texas.

Copyright © 1994 Alexandra Thorne

The right of Alexandra Thorne to be identified as the Author of the Work has been asserted by her in accordance with the Copyright, Designs and Patents Act 1988.

First published in 1994 by Hodder and Stoughton
A division of Hodder Headline PLC.

10 9 8 7 6 5 4 3 2 1

All rights reserved. No part of this publication may be reproduced, stored in a retrieval system, or transmitted, in any form or by any means without the prior written permission of the publisher, nor be otherwise circulated in any form of binding or cover other than that in which it is published and without a similar condition being imposed on the subsequent purchaser.

All characters in this publication are fictitious and any resemblance to real persons, living or dead is purely coincidental.

British Library Cataloguing in Publication Data
A Catalogue record for this book is available from the British Library.

ISBN 0 340 59711 9

Typeset by
Letterpart Limited, Reigate, Surrey
Printed and bound in Great Britain by
Cox & Wyman Ltd, Reading

Hodder and Stoughton Ltd
A division of Hodder Headline PLC
338 Euston Road
London NW1 3BH

Men honour property above all else;
it has the greatest power in human life.
Euripides, *The Phoenician Woman*

. . . and no man but feels more of a man in the world if he have a bit of ground that he can call his own.
Charles Dudley Warren, *My Summer in a Garden*

What you do to the earth, you do to the sons of the earth.
American Indian Proverb

AUTHOR'S NOTE

I first fell in love with the Texas Hill Country in the seventies when I travelled there as a sculptress, exhibiting my work in galleries in Austin and San Antonio. In 1991, prior to moving from California to Texas, I happened to tell screen writer, Steve Shearin, about the hundreds of Texas Hill Country ranchers who were raising exotic animals in a last ditch effort at wresting a profit from their land. Steve suggested I consider doing a book about them. So began *Sophisticated Savages*.

I am indebted to Nancy Thorleifson, Shirley and Jamie Estes, John Grub, Laura Taylor, Christina Dodd, Dolores Roberts, Evelyn Hubbard, Milton Baker, Terry Dobson D.V.M., the Foothills Safari Camp, the *Houston Chronicle*, and the YO Ranch, for generously sharing their information and expertise.

Although places similar to Pride's Outback can be found in the Hill Country, and many of the incidents in the book were inspired by the items in the *Houston Chronicle*, the characters exist only in my imagination.

PROLOGUE

DECEMBER 1993

The lioness was hungry, thirsty, tired. Her muscles ached from long confinement. Her golden fur had been matted, her sleek beauty diminished by the difficulty of her journey.

She flared her nostrils, breathing in the melange of strange scents carried on the wind. Bewildered, disoriented, she knew only one thing. To survive she must claim this alien territory for her own. The need for land was as deeply engraved on her brain as the need for food or sleep.

As she padded down a dry watercourse, birds warned of her coming and smaller animals fled in terror. The foliage grew thicker overhead, creating pools of light and shadow. She lay down under a tree and groomed, taking comfort in the familiar ritual. Exhausted by her journey, shivering in the unaccustomed chill, she dozed fitfully.

When she woke she took the measure of this new place, her great yellow eyes searching the terrain. She tested the air again and smelled animals nearby, vivid reminders of her hunger. She panted with desire, remembering the sweetness of fresh blood and warm flesh. She must kill and eat soon.

Growling deep in her throat, she got to her feet. Then she caught a familiar, disturbing scent – the scent of people – and moved away from it. But no matter how cannily she chose her path or how swiftly she travelled, the odour grew ever closer until she could hear the sounds the beings made when they opened their mouths.

She hid in the scrub, her fear intensifying, every muscle tense, her lips drawn back in a silent snarl as they drew nearer still. Gazing at the humans with fearful purpose, she absorbed every detail of their physical beings. The larger two smelled slightly musky. The smaller one had a sweeter, more tempting aroma.

The lioness concentrated on the smaller one, envisioning her attack. She would try to strike a killing blow and failing that, would go for a lethal, smothering hold on her victim's throat.

Instinct told her when to launch her assault. Muscles bunching, quivering with anticipation, she exploded into motion.

1

JUNE 1993

From the instant Caitlin Pride saw Mims Pauling at the La Guardia arrival gate, she knew something was wrong. Mims had never come to the airport to meet her before, not even ten years earlier when Cait arrived from Texas to launch her modelling career, as scared and green as any immigrant from another country.

What was Mims doing here now? Cait fretted as she made her way through the crowd. Had an important booking been cancelled, her apartment been robbed, or had *Vogue* decided not to use her for the November cover?

"Something tells me you didn't drive all the way out here to ask how things went on the Yucatan shoot," she said when she reached Mims' side. "What's up?"

The sympathy in Mims' china blue eyes increased Cait's apprehension.

"I have bad news. Your father is sick – very sick."

The words reverberated in the air, seeming to expand until they drowned out all other sound.

"Very sick?" Cait repeated, blinking owlishly. She was unaware that her mouth gaped open, or that the colour had drained from her face.

She hadn't heard from her father in ten years and the last time she saw him, he'd been as hale and hearty as a mustang in high clover. He was the strongest man she had ever known, as tough and durable as rawhide. The Hanks of the world were impervious to everything – love, hate, despair, loneliness, illness – everything but the force of their own indomitable wills.

Mims took one of Cait's hands in her own and gave it a comforting squeeze. "I'm sorry. I didn't mean to blurt it out like that. But we don't have much time. I've booked you on the next plane to San Antonio. I stopped at your place to pack a bag on my way here. It's already checked through. The ranch foreman will meet you when you land."

While she talked, Mims attempted to tug Cait away from the arrival gate. But Cait was a good seven inches taller than five-foot-three-inch Mims. Cait simply planted her feet and refused to budge as anger, dismay, and concern battled for supremacy over her emotions.

"For heaven's sake, Mims. You know how I feel about Hank. More important, you know how he feels about me." Cait's voice rasped with emotion. She stared into Mims' eyes, willing the older woman to understand, even though she suspected no one could unless they had endured her childhood. Just thinking about the past made her feel as if the earth had dropped out from under her feet. Hank had rejected her so often and in so many ways that he had destroyed her self-confidence. And, despite her success, she'd never really got it back.

Mims tugged even harder. "You're going to miss the flight. This may be your last chance to make things up with your father. He needs you."

Cait could feel an angry flush staining her cheeks. "Hank Pride hasn't needed anyone since my mother died – least of all me."

Mims stopped tugging on Cait's arm and turned to face her. "He has cancer – terminal cancer."

The heart-wrenching words sounded incongruous when uttered in Mims' breathy, sexy voice. It took a moment for their meaning to sink in.

"Who told you?"

"Your father's housekeeper, Delta Boudreaux. She telephoned the agency when she wasn't able to reach you. I talked to her myself."

"What kind of cancer does Hank have?" Even now, Cait couldn't bring herself to use the word, "father". God knew, Hank had never been a real father to her.

"I don't know. I never asked. What difference does it make? He's very sick and he wants to see you."

Reluctantly, Cait allowed herself to be led, like a lamb to the slaughter, to the San Antonio departure gate. Although she dreaded returning to Pride's Passion and reopening old wounds, she couldn't turn her back on Hank's request.

Mims Pauling watched with concern as Cait headed down the jetway. She wondered if Cait would resolve her long-standing differences with her father, or if her visit to the ranch would make things worse for them both.

Despite Mims' high gloss exterior, the Ungaro draping her diminutive figure and the Judith Lieberman purse on her arm, she was a mother hen driven by a fierce need to nurture, to comfort, to care.

She had never been able to maintain a professional distance from her models, and she dispensed help in the form of advice, money, and affection, with profligate largesse. This time, however, she couldn't help wondering if she had gone too far. She had the urge to call Cait back and say, "hey, never mind me, do what you think best".

She and Cait may have started out as employer and employee, mentor and mentee, teacher and pupil, but they had become best friends. Their relationship had been honed during the ten years Mims had spent helping Cait to metamorphose from a teenage beauty into a breathtakingly lovely woman. That didn't give her the right to play God, Mims thought. She began the long, lonely walk to her waiting limousine.

No one knew better than she the disastrous sequence of events that had preceded Cait's arrival in Manhattan all those years ago – or the even more unfortunate consequences. In some ways, Cait had yet to grow up. She still lived from day to day, going from one modelling assignment to another – and from one man to another – just letting life happen, never coming to grips with what she had already achieved, let alone who she wanted to be.

She was a philosopher in search of a philosophy, an activist in search of a cause – a woman in search of her soul. As Mims left the terminal, she couldn't help wondering if Cait would find any of those things in Texas.

Cait felt completely disoriented as she stared out the airplane window at the swiftly receding landscape. After the exhausting five days she had just spent in the Yucatan, modelling bathing suits that were smaller than some of the local insect life, she had been happily anticipating a quiet afternoon and evening in her own apartment. She had it all planned – luxuriating in a bubble-filled tub while Vivaldi's *Four Seasons* played on the stereo, catching up on her mail, answering the calls that had come in during her absence.

And yet here she was taking another flight.

She still couldn't bring herself to consider the reason for her unexpected journey, let alone deal with the words Mims had uttered just minutes ago. Besides, there was so much doctors could do to cure cancer these days.

Surgery, radiation, chemotherapy; Cait quickly ran the list of possible treatments through her mind. Hank's cancer couldn't be terminal. He was probably using his illness to get her back to the ranch. What was it he had said all those years ago?

"You're the last of the Prides and you'll damn well do your duty to your family."

The words had been spoken so harshly that she could still feel the answering fury they aroused in her. Just thinking about their last confrontation long ago made her head ache. She leaned back into the cushioned comfort of her first-class seat.

"Miss Pride, would you like a glass of champagne?"

She looked up to find a handsome, clean-cut flight attendant gazing down at her.

Although her face had adorned magazine covers from New York to Paris to Tokyo for years, she still hadn't become accustomed to being recognized by strangers.

"Not now, thank you."

"If you need anything at all, just let me know." The attendant's smile seemed friendly, but lust flared in his eyes.

That was something she had never got used to. She hated being regarded as a sex object. It still shocked her that the camera created a sun-streaked golden mane from her own brindle hair, wide-set green eyes from her myopic gaze and sensually curved lips from a mouth that had earned her the junior high school soubriquet of "Blubber Lips".

At twenty-eight, she felt incredibly lucky to have achieved such success as a model. However, she remained firmly convinced that her success was a fluke, one she owed to the fact that cameras lied as easily and often as men on the make. The miracle her hormones had wrought in her teens had come too late to change her self-image. Deep down, she was still the too tall, all elbows and knees, unloved girl who had wandered the Pride ranch in tattered jeans and down-at-the-heels boots.

And now she was going back home.

Her heart constricted at the thought. Hank had transformed her first trip to New York into a walk on a tightrope without a net. A decade later, he wanted her back. Why? she mused. Did he really want her at his bedside – or could his motive be more Machiavellian?

James Killian, "Comanche" to his friends, rode into the

corral at a gallop, reined his mount to a stop and jumped down from the saddle with unconscious grace. He had spent the morning checking fences, doing it the old-fashioned way, on horseback, instead of safely tucked inside an air-conditioned four-wheel-drive vehicle or aboard a dirt bike. Nothing eased his mind like spending time in the saddle with nothing between him and his Maker except the shirt on his back and a Hill Country sky. And his mind needed considerable easing these days.

Sweat trickled down his chest as he gathered the reins and led his horse into the barn's shadowed interior. He had broken the sorrel himself and there were times when he swore it could read his mind. That silent communion had come in handy on those occasions when he had to chase a wild steer into a thorny, mesquite-filled draw.

He liked horses, trusted them more than he trusted most people. Jim Dandy was one of his favourites and he talked to him soothingly while he curried dried sweat from the gelding's hide. Comanche had the sort of voice, rich and husky, and the type of hands, strong and knowing, that women and animals responded to instinctively.

He'd had very good luck with both. He'd accumulated a six-figure bank account on the rodeo circuit, and he never had to worry about having an empty bed at the end of the day if he was in the mood for companionship. But he could recall the broncs and bulls he had ridden a lot better than the women he had slept with.

With a single exception.

This afternoon the one woman he couldn't forget was coming back into his life – and it scared the hell out of him. Cait Pride. The boss's daughter. The girl he had rejected in the most heartless way.

He led the sorrel to a stall, carried his saddle and bridle into the tack room and put them away. Then he stopped to check Cait's gear. He'd kept it in prime condition himself, as if that one small act could erase what he'd done. Would Cait stay long enough to use it? Christ, he hoped not.

He walked out of the barn into the relentless July sunshine and checked his watch. He had time to eat lunch, visit a spell with Hank and catch up on some of the ranch's paperwork before he left for the San Antonio airport.

Up until Hank got sick, Delta had served Hank and Comanche in the dining room. Now Hank ate off a tray in his room most of the time, and Comanche and Delta ate in the kitchen together. But she wasn't there when he walked in. The gentle hum of the refrigerator was the only sound in the room. Delta had said something about driving to Kerrville to buy groceries for Cait's homecoming. She had left a couple of thick wax-paper-wrapped sandwiches on the table for him.

Comanche soaped and rinsed his hands at the sink before retrieving a beer from the refrigerator. He sat down and took a long swallow, letting the chilled liquid wash the morning's dust from his throat. The mouth-watering aroma of sharp mustard and rare roast beef rose from the first sandwich he unwrapped. He bit into it eagerly and chewed, but it seemed to turn into sawdust in his mouth. Despite the beer, his throat felt dry. His nerves were raw, his gut as taut as it used to be before an important rodeo.

Cait. The name rocketed into his mind again. He dreaded seeing her, and yet he couldn't concentrate on anything else. Did she ever think of him in the quiet of the night the way he thought of her? Did she hate him, or would she treat him with indifference? And what would she do about the ranch, Pride's Passion?

Hank Pride shifted his gaunt frame, trying to find a more comfortable position in bed, husbanding his strength in anticipation of Cait's arrival. He didn't want her to see him flat on his back. Sympathy had always come easy to Cait. However, he wanted much more from her, even though he had no right to ask. Damn. He'd made a mess of things.

He pushed the button that elevated the head of the bed and gazed out the window, seeking solace from the view. The ranch house sat on the crest of a hill overlooking the Guadalupe River. He could just catch the distant metallic glint of water through a stand of oak and cedar. A herd of stockers – cows, calves and steers – grazed in the distance. A decade ago such a herd would have been an asset. Now they represented a mounting debit. The cost of raising beef had never been higher.

He should have reacted to the changing times sooner instead of continuing to run the ranch according to rules that no longer applied. The enormity of his failure was as much a part of him as his cancer. He clenched the covers in his fists, closing his eyes in a futile attempt to escape the prison of his mind.

Things would be different if he had his health. Now it was all up to Cait. He needed her. The ranch needed her. But he wouldn't blame her if she told him to go straight to hell.

He wasn't aware of dozing off. He had no idea how long he'd slept when the sound of boot-shod feet woke him. He opened his eyes to see Comanche poised in the doorway.

"Shouldn't you be on your way to the airport, son?" he said. He'd used the filial term for years, and there had been lots of times when he wished the foreman was his son. He'd always been at ease with Comanche and able to speak his mind. If only he'd had that sort of relationship with Cait. Instead, he'd held her at emotional arm's length.

"Not for a couple of hours. I thought I'd catch up on some paperwork before I left."

"Paperwork!" Hank's mouth thinned in a bitter smile. "I remember when I could keep track of every man, every piece of equipment, every animal on the ranch in my head. Now you need to be a goddamn computer whiz like the sons-of-bitches who have been buying up Hill Country land. Most of those boys wouldn't know one end of a steer from the other. *Businessmen*!" He spat out the word as if it was the worst epithet in his vocabulary. "You can't tell those bastards that ranching is more than dollars and cents, that it's a way of life, a trust passed from one generation to the next. All they care about is the bottom line, the . . ."

He stopped in mid-sentence as pain knifed through his gut. Forcing himself to lie still, he breathed deeply. So far he had managed to deal with his physical pain. The mental anguish was unbearable. His illness had forced him to face the truth. He had lost the two people he cared about most, his wife and daughter, and now he was in danger of losing the ranch that had been in his family for a hundred and fifty years. Death held no terror for him. He'd learned there were worse disasters.

Comanche hated watching Hank suffer. But he knew Hank was trying to tough out his illness without resorting to pain pills. Had Hank been another sort of man, Comanche might have verbalized his concern or even put an arm around Hank's shoulder in a rough gesture of sympathy. But Hank was about as approachable as a thicket of prickly pear cactus. You touched him at your own risk. So Comanche settled for waiting quietly until the spasm passed.

Hank's features finally returned to their customary, weather-beaten arrangement. He reached for the glass of water on the nightstand and took a sip. "Oh hell," he said, "you know how I feel about what's happening to ranching."

"Yes, sir." Comanche knew Hank's views all too well, not that it had done either of them much good. He shuffled from one boot-shod foot to another. He wasn't accustomed to Hank's semi-invalidism and had yet to figure out how to exit the sick room gracefully.

He cleared his throat nervously, then said, "Well, you're not paying me to stand around passing the time. I'd better get to that paperwork."

"Don't forget to meet Cait."

"Don't worry. It won't slip my mind." Comanche managed a weak grin. Talk about understatements. He'd been able to think of little else.

He turned on his heel as smartly as a drill sergeant, headed to the foreman's office at the other end of the house, sat down behind his desk and sorted the day's mail. He couldn't keep his mind on business, though. After reading the same circular twice without absorbing a word, he rocked back in his chair and gazed out the window.

He felt desperately sorry for Hank. Still, Hank's problems had opened a door of opportunity. Pride's Passion would soon be up for grabs. The bank or the Resolution Trust Corporation would take it over if someone didn't beat them to it. He had made up his mind to be that someone until he'd heard that Cait, the prodigal daughter, was maybe coming home. Recalling what had happened between them before he left for college still had the capacity to quicken his pulse and send a rush of blood to his groin.

He jumped and shook himself like a wet dog. Propinquity, that's all it had been – one misguided night of passion. They had lived very different lives since then. Considering the poor start he'd had in life, he was damn proud of his accomplishments. Getting a college degree, becoming a respected member of the community, being the foreman of the ranch where his daddy and granddaddy had been hired hands, those had to count for something.

Although the office was spacious, he crossed the floor in a couple of long-legged strides, turned and crossed it again. He had more than proven himself as a man. Could Cait say the same? Had she proven herself as a woman?

Not if he believed all the things the tabloids had written about her. The list of her former fiancés – a movie star, a rock musician, a race-car driver and an up-and-coming politician – read like a stud book. Cait had been too fickle to stick with any of them, though.

No, Comanche thought. From everything he'd read, she was still a spoiled brat, a girl who had everything except the common sense to count her blessings. She hadn't proven herself as a woman unless you counted her success as a model. And how hard did she have to work at it, considering she had the face of an angel – and a body made for sin?

They had indeed lived different lives. All he had to do was concentrate on those differences and he'd have no problem when he saw her again. He'd be a fool to let her stand in the way of his dreams.

2

Ten minutes before touchdown, Cait went to the lavatory to try to exorcise the effects of ten hours spent travelling. Her suit was wrinkled beyond redemption. Reapplying eyeliner and mascara couldn't erase the worry in her eyes any more than blush and lipstick could conceal her pallor.

She stared at her reflection in the mirror over the tiny metal sink, trying to rein in her runaway emotions. Seeing Hank was bound to be traumatic. Mims had been right, though; she'd never forgive herself if she didn't see him. She'd spend a couple of days visiting his bedside before returning to her own life in New York. Her fists were clenched as she returned to her seat. She might look and feel like hell, but she was determined to get through this.

When she left the flight in San Antonio, the invasive heat was a vivid reminder of her childhood. By the time she walked through the departure ramp and into the airport, a trickle of perspiration was rolling down her cleavage and her underarms felt damp. Frowning, she searched the waiting crowd for Bert McClain, her father's grizzled, veteran foreman.

One by one, people stepped forward to greet other passengers until she was enveloped by kissing, hugging, handshaking strangers. She continued waiting, still hoping to see Bert, while the knots of humanity unravelled in different directions. And then she was alone. A fine welcome home, she thought, her suspicion and distrust multiplying.

Knowing Bert would expect to find her by the arrival gate, she collapsed into the nearest seat. She had never been a patient person and now it took considerable willpower to stay put while the minutes ticked by. She drummed her fingers on the arms of her chair, picked up a magazine someone had left on an adjacent seat, and thumbed through it without really absorbing any of the contents. Every time she felt someone draw near, she looked up anxiously.

A teen-aged girl finally took the seat next to her. Cait could feel the girl's gaze boring into her even though she kept her own fixed on the magazine.

"Are you someone famous?" the girl abruptly asked.

Still keeping her glance lowered, Cait shook her head, no, hoping her swirling hair would conceal her face.

Her ruse didn't work. The teenager gave a sudden yelp and loudly declared, "You are too famous! You're that model, Cait what's-her-name."

This time Cait looked up, giving the girl the full benefit of her travel-ravaged appearance. "That's very flattering," she said, "but Caitlin Pride is much better-looking than I am."

The girl studied Cait's face for a moment. "Yeah, she is," she agreed before getting to her feet and drifting off.

Cait stayed put until she was sure the girl had gone. Then she got to her feet, searching the area for Bert McClain one last time while her indignation threatened to bubble over. A tiny voice in the back of her mind told her some emergency must have delayed the foreman. She ignored it in favour of a louder one hotly declaring she had been played for a fool.

To think she had actually been worried about Hank. He had probably exaggerated his illness to insure her return. And then he had taken the opportunity to humiliate her by letting her cool her heels. She could spend the rest of her life in the San Antonio airport, put down roots and sprout leaves before the foreman put in an appearance.

★ ★ ★

If only he hadn't spent so much time deciding what to wear – putting on a suit and tie that made him look about as natural as a department-store mannequin, then changing into slacks and a leather jacket that made him sweat so much he needed to take another shower – Comanche Killian would have made it to the airport before Cait's plane touched down.

It wasn't like him, fussing over his appearance that way. The last thing he wanted was to give Cait the impression that he had dressed up for the occasion. So he finally settled on a pair of well-washed jeans and his second-best boots and stetson.

Now he pulled into an airport parking space and brought the huge GMC Surburban to a stop with a squeal of brakes accompanied by the unmistakable aroma of burning rubber. Damn. He was late. He hadn't counted on the paving project on Route 27 or the traffic jam on 410. Cait, who had always made a fetish of being prompt, was probably seething.

He raced into the terminal with a juggernaut's disregard for everything in his path and reached the Continental gate to find it deserted. The sign over the check-in desk indicated Cait's flight had arrived some twenty minutes earlier. Consternation at missing her mingled with relief as he realized he'd been granted a last-minute reprieve. He didn't have to face her just yet.

A decade earlier one of his college professors had suggested that there was no such thing as an accident, that a person's lifestyle and/or state of mind predisposed them to most of the things they attributed to happenstance.

If the theory was correct, he had missed Cait's flight on purpose. But now, unless he wanted to upset a sick old man, he had better find her.

Delta Boudreaux's heart spasmed the way it did every time she walked into Hank's sick room. She was an attractive middle-aged woman whose dark hair, olive complexion, and expressive brown eyes, spoke of her Cajun ancestry. The last few months had engraved an habitual expression of sadness on her face.

Despite the tightness in her chest, she managed a cheerful smile as she looked at Hank. "Miss Caitlin should be here in an hour. Do you need any help getting ready?"

"I may be sick but I can still dress myself." The warmth in his eyes belied the gruffness of his tone.

Delta knew, better than anyone else, how he despised his growing weakness. He had always been so vigorous. If only he had gone to Doc Williams years ago at the first sign of trouble. But Hank hated doctoring even more than most men. So he'd ignored his symptoms and now it was too late.

Made mute by her own sorrow, she watched while he got out of bed cautiously, as if any uncontrolled motion was likely to arouse the beast of pain in his gut. He unbuttoned his pyjama top, folded it with his habitual neatness, put it on the bed and began to take off the bottom, so preoccupied by the effort of doing even the simplest task that he didn't seem to realize she hadn't left the room.

When he turned around and saw her still standing there, he gave her the grin that never failed to arrow straight into her heart. "So you still like to watch, do you?" he asked.

She rewarded him with a throaty chuckle. "Some things never change, Hank."

Knowing it would please him, she continued her quiet observation as he finished undressing. Although he was dreadfully thin, his bones and musculature were still pleasing to her eyes. Her glance lowered to his penis and testicles. How dreadful to realize that what had once been a source of so much pleasure to them both, was going to kill him.

She longed to hold his angularity against the plump cushion of her body, to kiss away the weariness and the hurt she read so plainly on his face. But kisses were no cure for what ailed Hank.

She continued watching as he walked into the bathroom and shut the door. Only then did she collapse on the bed and give in to tears. The last two months had been the hardest of her life. She would carry to her own grave the memory of Hank coming back from the hospital and telling her he was dying.

It had been a terrible shock. Just a year earlier he had looked lots younger than others his age. And strong. Lord. He could outwork men in their twenties. Then, without explanation, he had started to fade like a Polaroid photograph left out in the sun. Now, at sixty-five, he looked a decade older.

She began making the bed, working automatically as she struggled to face a future without Hank, a future made even more uncertain by Cait's impending arrival.

The baggage claim area was almost empty when Cait walked in. A few people stood around arranging their luggage on flimsy carts. One young mother, seemingly overwhelmed by the logistics of carrying a diaper bag, a baby, and a couple of suitcases, stood near one of the carousels weeping quietly.

Cait was about to go over and offer to help when a skycap diverted her attention. "Can I fetch your bags, ma'am?" he asked.

She took a moment to consider the inequity that made skycaps hurry to her own well-dressed side while the young mother so obviously needed assistance. Instead of giving the man a lecture on social injustice, she pressed a ten dollar bill into his hand and sent him to the weeping woman's aid. Then she began searching for her own belongings.

None of the carousels was moving. The lighted signs over them, announcing which held bags from which flight, were all dark. Considering the sort of day she'd had so far, it would be just her luck to have lost her luggage.

Frowning fiercely, she walked towards a cluster of bags against a far wall. As she drew nearer she saw her own Vuittons, the two pieces she had taken to Mexico plus the larger one Mims had mentioned packing. They made a formidable pile. Feeling a twinge of regret for having summarily sent the skycap on his way, she bent over, taking the handle of the largest piece in her right hand.

Its weight tugged on her arm and shoulder. Good lord! What in the world had Mims put in it? Cait's frown deepened when she thought of making her way to the cab stand in the heat, loaded down like a pack mule.

As she reached for the second bag, she heard a vibrant masculine voice say, "I'll take that for you, Cait."

Her physical response was instantaneous – and thoroughly unpleasant. Her heart constricted, her mouth dried, her palms dampened and her stomach found its way into her throat. She would have known that voice anywhere – any place – any time. She spun around to confront its owner, the last man on earth she wanted to see again. God. Of all the despicable, no account . . .

"What the hell are you doing here?" she asked, her tone as cold as winter's first frost.

A tall woman, Cait was accustomed to looking down on most men. Enjoyed it, too! She hated having to look up at this one.

Cowboy boots enhanced his six-feet-four-inch height. His gold-flecked brown eyes were surrounded by laugh lines that hinted at good times. His cheekbones, jaw and brow, gave evidence of his exotic, black-Irish-Indian heritage. A stetson failed to conceal a luxuriant growth of jet black hair tied back in a neat ponytail.

His chest and shoulders were broader than she remembered, defining the shirt that covered them. Her heart pounded even harder as her gaze drifted downward. Tight jeans advertised his sex rather than concealing it, cupping the source of his palpable masculinity.

When her gaze returned to his face he gave her the lazy, knowing grin that had always infuriated her when they were kids. Still did, for that matter. Only now, a blatantly sexual component made it even more insufferable. James Comanche Killian had been a handsome young man. Mature, he was utterly devastating – a woman-trap who radiated the sort of instant physical impact that is normally the province of film idols or rock stars.

"You're looking good, Cait," he said. His grin deepened as his insolent gaze meandered over her body, pausing at her breasts before returning to her face.

"What the hell are you doing here?" she repeated, furious because she couldn't control the tremor in her voice or the flush staining her cheeks.

"Didn't Miss Pauling tell you I'd be there?"

"She said the foreman . . ." Cait couldn't complete the sentence. She was having difficulty getting her breath.

The prospect of seeing her father had been painful enough. Had she known James Comanche Killian would be part of the package, no power on earth could have forced her to return to the ranch.

The last she'd heard about him from Delta, he had graduated from college and gone on the rodeo circuit. Five years ago she ran across a photo of him in *People* magazine, holding a huge trophy in one arm and a bleached blonde with a boob job in the other. At the time she had fervently wished he would break his neck the next time he rode a bronc.

Her feelings hadn't changed.

"I was expecting Bert McClain," she said, spitting the words out as if they had a foul taste.

"If you had stayed in touch with your father, you would have known Bert retired two years ago. I've been the foreman of Pride's ever since."

Although he spoke in the most matter-of-fact way as if he were commenting on something as trivial as the weather, Cait took instant offence. "How dare you – you of all people – talk about staying in touch?"

The fury in her voice whiplashed through Comanche. Who the hell did she think she was, using that tone on him? True, he hadn't been a perfect gentleman where she was concerned. But she hadn't exactly been a lady either. He turned his back on her so she wouldn't see the anger in his eyes and pretended total preoccupation with her luggage.

"The car's this way," he said, glancing over his shoulder just once to make sure she followed.

Damn, she certainly filled a man's eyes. From the way other men's heads turned as she walked by, no male in viewing distance was immune to her charms. Having her around wasn't going to be easy.

He consoled himself with the thought that a woman who looked, acted, and dressed like Cait Pride, would be bored stiff on a remote Hill Country ranch. She'd soon be back in New York and he could go ahead with his plan.

After stowing her bags in the back of the Suburban, he walked around the car and took her hand to help her up into the high front seat – and her touch shimmered through him like a meteor shower. The women he had known, and there had been many, worked for a living. Their reddened hands suffered from it. Cait's hands reminded him of warm satin, the pearly nails tapered and womanly. He clenched his jaws as memories of those hands touching him, exploring his body in the most intimate way, sizzled through his mind.

Cait was buckling her seat belt when he opened the driver's door and slid behind the wheel. Opening her purse, she removed a pack of cigarettes. "Do you mind?"

Comanche shook his head. How could he object, considering he was the one who had dared Cait to smoke her first cigarette when they were barely in their teens?

She put the cigarette in her mouth and lit up, seeming to relax a little when the nicotine hit her blood stream. The cigarette was long, slim and elegant, an echo of her new persona. He detested seeing most women smoke but Cait made the simple act look sophisticated and mysterious, the way Lauren Bacall had in her movies with Bogart. Come to think of it, Cait reminded him a lot of the youthful Bacall he had come to admire after seeing her movies on late-night television. Cait had the same leggy good looks, the same aura of mystery – and the same cool arrogance.

He stole an occasional glance at her as he drove away from the airport. A homely child, she hadn't grown into her features until her teens. Now her beauty was as glorious as a summer storm – and as potentially dangerous, he cautioned himself, steeling his heart against her presence and the memories she provoked.

Although Cait was aware of Comanche's occasional appraisal while he threaded the huge Suburban through the thick airport traffic, she kept her own gaze straight ahead, pretending an interest in the scenery. She had spent a lot of lonely nights fantasizing about what she would say to him if she ever had the chance, had pictured herself inventing new and clever names to castigate him with because "bastard" simply didn't say it all. She still carried the anguish he had caused her deep inside. Now it threatened to break free. But she'd be damned if she'd give him the satisfaction.

The years seemed to have been good to him, better than he deserved. He had an aura of authority – a self-assurance that set her teeth on edge. He was the Marlboro man come to life, more handsome and decidedly more masculine than any of the male models she worked with in New York.

Try as she might to resist his appeal, those broad shoulders, slim hips, arrogant cheekbones and smouldering eyes were undoubtedly sending her oestrogen level through the roof. Thank heaven she wasn't a hormone-driven, hero-worshipping teenager any more. She was a mature woman who had long since learned that this particular idol had feet of clay.

"Mims wasn't able to tell me very much about Hank's condition," she said, pleased that her voice sounded level again, "but she made it sound urgent. What kind of cancer does he have, and how far has it advanced?"

"I wish I could give you better news, Katydid."

"Don't call me that!" she snapped. *Katydid* had been his nickname for her when they were kids. She didn't like it now any more than she did then. "Just tell me about Hank."

"He's a very sick man, and he has a lot of pain to deal with."

The scald of tears at the back of her eyes took her by surprise. "What hospital is he in?"

"You know Hank. The only thing he hates more than doctors is hospitals. He's at the ranch."

"What about treatment? Isn't he getting chemotherapy? Or radiation"

Comanche finally turned and looked her squarely in the eyes. She read sympathy in his gaze and something she would have interpreted as tenderness in another man. "It's too late for a cure, Cait. Your father, well, you know how he used to be, working from dawn to dusk. When he started slowing down it was so gradual, no one noticed at first. He kept up a front for a long time. Every now and then he'd get a look on his face like he'd seen something that scared the hell out of him. I couldn't figure it out because Hank Pride isn't scared of anything. But I finally got the picture. He wasn't afraid. He was hurting. Bad."

Cait fiddled with her purse, nervously unsnapping and snapping the clasp. Hearing about Hank's pain made her almost as uneasy as if she had seen him in the nude. He had raised her to believe that pain was private and best suffered in silence. If he actually let his pain show on his face, he must have been in agony.

"What did you do?"

"I asked him if he was sick. He told me he had a touch

of arthritis, nothing to worry about. When Delta asked if he was ailing, he told her the same thing."

"How did you find out he had cancer?"

"Two months ago, Hank collapsed during the branding. Hit his head when he fell off his horse. By the time he came to, we were halfway to the hospital in Kerrville. I damn near had to hog-tie him before we made it all the way. After Doc Williams examined him and saw the condition Hank was in, he chewed him up one side and down the other. I never heard anyone talk to Hank like that before – and I expect I never will again."

Despite Comanche's limited skills as a storyteller, Cait had a vivid mental picture of Hank sitting on an examining table in stoic silence while Dr Williams read him the riot act. "How long did Hank stay in the hospital?"

"Long enough for a bunch of tests and a diagnosis. He came home a couple of days later. There wasn't anything anybody could do by then except pray, and I don't have to tell you Hank isn't a religious man."

"And that's it? That's all any of you did for my father?" As Cait's pent-up emotions burst free, she was too shaken to realize she had actually called Hank, "Father".

The word wasn't lost on Comanche, though. He hated being the bearer of bad news. But he didn't have any choice. Cait needed to be prepared for seeing her father and fate had chosen him to do the job.

"There wasn't anything more to be done," he said with all the gentleness he could muster. "Testicular cancer can be cured if it's caught in time. Hank waited too long. Much too long. His cancer has metastisized."

"But surely chemotherapy . . .?"

"It would just make him suffer needlessly."

"How long does he have?"

"Doc Williams can't say for certain. Six months, maybe a year. Hank is a strong man and he's always been a fighter. I guess it depends on what he's fighting for." Comanche couldn't bring himself to tell Cait the rest of the story. Besides, that was Hank's right.

Fortunately Cait didn't ask any more questions. She lapsed into silence, her spine poker-straight, her expression inscrutable. But her pallor, the way she kept on snapping and unsnapping her purse, told him how hard she was taking it.

Senator John "Blackjack" Morgan was an imposing man rather than a handsome one. His carefully put together aura of power was abetted by the perfect fit of his suits, by the impression of height created by his custom-made cowboy boots and by the internalized certainty that he was a man to be reckoned with. He carried his fifty-two years well, seeming to offer proof that, like a fine wine, a successful man improved with age.

Blackjack had a florid complexion, a leonine mane of silvering hair, a square jaw grown a bit jowly and a prominent nose. This afternoon an expression of displeasure rode his features as he sat behind his desk in his suite of offices on the fiftieth floor of the Allen Center. Houston, the city he regarded as his fiefdom – his by *droit de seigneur* – lay outside the walls of glass surrounding him, shimmering in the late afternoon sun.

He loved the place for its raw power, its implicit promise that anything was acceptable except failure. From his high eyrie he could see the banks of Buffalo Bayou where the Allen brothers had first platted a town a century and a half earlier. To the south, the downtown's glittering glass skyscrapers thrust their phallic spires into the sky. The massive Transco Tower and the wealth of the Galleria area with its glitzy stores and trendy restaurants lay to the west.

Riveted by the scene, Blackjack rose, walked across the plush emerald carpet and gazed down. From this height it was impossible to see the decaying infrastructure, the poorly paved streets and cracked sidewalks, the half-empty strip malls and office buildings that offered visible proof of Texas's economic troubles. The once proud state had fallen to its financial knees in the mid-eighties and had yet to regain its feet.

As he gazed out the window, he unconsciously squared his stance and clasped his hands behind his back, a habit born of his military service. Damn Regan and Bush for their inability to set a course and hold to it, for creating the shifting sands of deregulation. Damn his fellow Congressmen for whistle-blowing in public while privately milking pork barrel projects and getting in bed with lobbyists.

Blackjack's frown deepened. The last decade had seen his beloved Texas raped by the quick money boys. Now, instead of cleaning up the mess created by the multitude of failed Savings and Loans, the Resolution Trust Corporation – which was, in his opinion, neither resolute or trustworthy – compounded the problem.

Today his own fortune was in danger. But he'd be damned if he would go down the tubes like former Governor John Connally. Connally had the sympathy of the world the day he got shot along with President Kennedy.

That hadn't stopped the media from pouncing on Connally's financial problems like a cat on a mouse, televising pictures of John and Nellie talking to potential buyers the day their belongings were auctioned right off their front lawn. Empathy made him tremble as he recalled the public humiliation that had undoubtedly hastened Connally's death.

Thank God his own money problems weren't as deep-seated as Connally's had been. Although Blackjack's vast holdings had diminished in value since the Texas crash, he had survived the worst. All he needed was a little luck, some quick money to prop up his cash flow, and he would be home free.

Despite the air conditioning's steady drone, a sheen of perspiration slicked his forehead. He pulled a pristine white monogrammed handkerchief from his jacket pocket and mopped his brow. He had always been lucky, from the day his first wildcat well made him an overnight millionaire at the age of twenty-three, to his tour in Vietnam.

He could have avoided the draft but he'd had political aspirations even then. And you didn't have to be a Rhodes scholar to figure out a draft dodger might have a problem getting elected to the halls of power in Washington. So he'd served his time and returned to the States unscathed. Yes, indeed, he'd been very, very lucky, right down to winning his first Congressional seat by a landslide. He saw no reason for that bitch goddess, Lady Luck, to desert him now.

He had just returned to his massive rosewood desk, settled in the deep leather chair behind it and started signing the letters his secretary had brought in half an hour earlier, when the intercom buzzed.

"The delegation from Nishida Corporation is here, Senator," his secretary said.

Blackjack checked his desk calendar and then his watch. The Japanese executives were predictably prompt. He had met them in Tokyo on a vacation thinly disguised as a Congressional fact-finding junket. Being a prudent man, he had stayed in touch as he stayed in touch with anyone whose acquaintance might prove of future benefit. He'd dictated a letter thanking them for their hospitality, issuing an open invitation to visit him, either in Washington or Houston. That they had chosen Houston aroused his curiosity.

"Send them right in," he said.

As a political conservative and self-styled patriot, he had no fondness for Chinks, gooks, spics, ragheads, or any of the other minorities who were contributing to what he thought of as "the mongrelization of America". Someday when he sat in the Oval Office, he intended to do something about it.

In the meantime, though, circumstances had forced him to accept the fact that money has no colour. So he welcomed the Nishida delegation with a big smile and a hearty handshake and endured the traditional bowing and scraping which were the price of doing business with men who took great stock in ritual. It would undoubtedly take hours of wining and dining before the Japs revealed the reason for their presence.

He could only hope it would be worth the wait.

3

Cait stared out the car window, too shaken to do anything but watch the miles roll by. To hear about the seriousness of Hank's condition from Mims had been one thing; Mims' information was second-hand at best. Hearing it from Comanche made it all too real.

"Hank waited too long," Comanche had said with a finality that left her feeling hollow, helpless, and finally – angry. She wanted to grab and shake Comanche until he took the words back. She wanted to make him turn the Suburban round and head straight back to the airport so she wouldn't have to deal with the truth.

She and Hank may not have spoken for years but the fact of his existence had anchored her. Although he had never been much of a father, he was her only family. Now he had found the ultimate way to abandon her. To her surprise, the child inside her wasn't ready to face the world alone.

She bit her lip and clenched her fists until her nails dug deep into her palms. She ought to be worrying about Hank instead of herself. She wanted to break down and weep, to wash away her feelings of guilt, betrayal, and loss in a sea of tears. But a decade of schooling herself not to give away her emotions, of smiling for the camera no matter what was happening in her private life, stood her in good stead now. Determined not to reveal any vulnerability in Comanche's presence, she forced her features into a semblance of composure, sat back and tried to relax.

At first the scenery was nothing more than an on-rushing kaleidoscope of colour. Ever so slowly, she found herself absorbed by it. She had forgotten the rugged beauty of the Hill Country with its limestone cliffs and pink granite outcroppings, its green valleys studded with oak and cedar. Now it awakened an almost atavistic response inside her, a primal sense of homecoming. She was able to see it with eyes washed clean by ten years spent in other places and perceptions heightened by her current turmoil. Born to this place, she surrendered her aching heart to it. She was a Pride, after all.

Comanche continued to watch Cait covertly as he took the interstate toward Kerrville. But for a brief outburst, she hadn't said a word since she asked how long Hank would live. Her continued silence bothered him. *A lot.* Time was when he could read every emotional nuance on her mobile features. He had no idea what Cait was thinking or feeling this afternoon.

His own emotions were attested to by the pounding of his pulse, the dryness of his mouth and the surging warmth in his groin. Cait was even lovelier than he had expected.

Over the years, he'd got dozens of glimpses of her gazing seductively out at the world from the covers of magazines as he walked past newspaper stands in countless little towns on the rodeo circuit. Each time his breath had caught in his throat.

He had rationalized his response by telling himself it was due to the shock of seeing a familiar face in unfamiliar circumstances. Now, seeing her in person – close enough to touch – was electrifying. A man would have to be a blind eunuch, or made of stone, not to want a woman like Cait – and he didn't fit either of those categories.

He could have dealt with lust, though. The thing that stole his breath away was a totally unexpected sense of lost love. He must be out of his mind. Although he and Cait had grown up together, they had been rivals at best – but for that one night. Now, keeping his gaze on the road, he let memory sweep him back to that night, his last on the ranch before leaving for his freshman year at the University of Oklahoma.

Hank Pride had hosted a farewell dinner with Delta, Bert McClain and his own father, Orry, in attendance. Delta had outdone herself, fixing shrimp étouffée, dirty rice, and a melt-in-your-mouth pecan pie.

He had barely tasted the food, though. Cait, newly returned from Houston where she had just graduated from Kinkaid, an ultra-exclusive private school, had captured and held his attention from the moment she walked into the room. Come to think of it, walked didn't half do justice to the way she moved. Neither did words like stroll or saunter. Just watching her put one foot in front of the other had been riveting.

Although they'd been classmates through eighth grade, he'd seen very little of her since she went off to private school. Lord, had she changed! No one in their right mind would call her "bean pole" now. Instead of her habitual jeans and shirt, she was wearing a sweater that clung to her breasts and a skirt that exposed the longest, shapeliest legs he'd ever seen. Her ponytail had metamorphosed into a silky drift of golden hair that fell below her shoulders. To his amazement, he realized she was even prettier than Bobby Rae Seeley – and everyone said Bobby Rae was the prettiest girl at Tivy High.

He broke out into a clammy sweat every time their eyes met. And yet he kept on trying to capture her gaze, expecting to see the old resentment and finding something very different. Had she been any other girl, he would have been certain she was coming on to him.

After dinner he had reluctantly followed Orry back to the bunkhouse for another farewell party with the hands. But his mind had been on Cait the whole time. At midnight, with the room reverberating with the sounds tired men make in their sleep, he'd slipped out and strolled down to the swimming hole on the Guadalupe hoping a quick plunge would cool his fevered libido.

Despite the lingering warmth of late summer, his skin goosebumped when he saw Cait sitting on the river bank, her skirt hiked up to her thighs, her bare feet danging in the water. He tried to think of something devastatingly clever and sophisticated to say, opening and closing his mouth a time or two like some damn guppy before producing a strangled, "Hi".

He expected a disdain-filled glance at his lack of cool. Instead, she looked up and gave him an alluring, wet-lipped smile that sent his pulse into the stratosphere.

"I guess you couldn't sleep either," she said. "Hot, isn't it?"

Hot didn't begin to do it justice. He felt as if he'd caught fire. Unable to use a tongue that had suddenly gone dry as the desert, he nodded and sat down, glancing at her sidelong and trying to gauge her mood.

She continued to look straight ahead, idly swinging one slender foot to and fro in the water. "It's going to be strange here without you."

Startled, he turned to face her. "I doubt you'll miss me. We haven't exactly hit it off over the years." And that was putting it nicely.

She sighed. "I'm afraid that was only natural. Brothers and sisters fight, and we were raised like siblings."

"Yeah, I guess you're right," he conceded. At the moment, though, he was feeling far from brotherly. And it surprised the hell out him. Thank God the flow of the river drowned out the thud of his heart and scudding clouds kept the moonlight from revealing the flush on his cheeks. He couldn't equate the lovely young woman by his side with the spoiled, argumentative girl he used to take such pleasure in teasing.

The ranch's isolation had forced them to spend a lot of time together when they were kids but he hadn't enjoyed it much. She'd had everything he desperately wanted – a home, a rock solid place in society, and a father other men respected. She also had a poor-me-I-never-knew-my-mother-and-my-daddy-doesn't-love-me attitude that drove him up the wall.

"Have you picked a major yet?" she asked.

He never much cared what she thought of him in the past. Now though, he found himself wanting to impress her. "I'm planning a double major," he replied with a touch of braggadocio, "business and agriculture. I intend to make a lot of money ranching one of these days."

"You sound as if you have it all thought out."

"Considering the way things are with my father and all, I can't afford to leave things to chance."

"You know, I can't help envying you. You've always been so sure of yourself," she said in a surprisingly wistful voice. "You're smart, popular, and everyone thinks the world of you – including my father."

He could have told her she would have been popular too if she hadn't always been so standoffish. But he didn't want to rile her when they were getting along so well. "What do you think of me?" he couldn't resist asking, although he was half afraid to hear the answer.

"I used to think you were a jerk."

"And now?"

She finally turned to face him. "Now, I'd like to kiss you goodbye."

Her eyes locked with his. He felt as if he were drowning in her gaze. He couldn't believe what he was feeling. About Cait Pride, for God's sake.

She tilted her face up to his. She's trouble, he thought as, with a groan, he pulled her into his arms and claimed her lips. He half expected her to pull away. Instead she deepened their kiss, opening her mouth to welcome his tongue. He'd been on the knife-edge of arousal before they embraced. As he reached down to caress her breasts, cupping their warmth in his hands, his erection pressed against his jeans like a steel rod.

He kept expecting her to put an abrupt end to the

encounter. When she didn't, he lowered her to the sandy river bank and pulled the sweater over her head.

She was naked underneath. He gazed at the splendour of her strong young body, his fingers tracing the full moon of her breasts and the arc of her ribs. Then he took one of her nipples in his mouth.

She moaned at the contact. It was the most erotic sound he'd ever heard. A tumultuous wave of ecstasy rippled through his body. He'd never felt so needy, so desirous. And yet, somehow, he found the strength to break away. "If you want me to stop, you'd better say so now."

The stars hung motionless in the sky and the night stilled as he waited for her reply. He felt as if he was on the brink of something momentous, something that could change the course of his life. It took all his willpower to keep his hands at his side, to give her time to consider what she really wanted.

She closed her eyes and, with a cry, reached for him. "Please don't stop. I want you to make love to me."

"Are you sure?" he asked through clenched teeth. Although he'd been with other girls, he wanted this one so badly that it frightened him.

"I'm sure," she said throatily.

Not giving her a chance to change her mind, he brought her face to his and plunged his tongue between her lips again, drinking in her unique taste while desire heated his blood and throbbed in his groin. He hurt with the need to bury himself deep inside her, to thrust his erection into the slick, tight sheath between her legs. But he schooled himself to patience, hoping to make her want it as much as he did.

She offered herself up to him with a shyness that touched the deepest core of his manhood, responding to his most intimate caresses with a rapture that inflamed his innate sensuality. Her body was his to plunder, to touch and taste. He battled for control, wanting to spin the exquisite agony of their foreplay into an eternity.

But his greedy body would not obey. Unable to wait another second, he positioned himself between her thighs.

By the time he felt the internal barrier and realized she was too tight to have made love before, no power on earth could have prevented him from burying his arousal as deep as the hardest thrust could reach. He caught her soft cry in his mouth, inhaling her pain and then kissing it away. When they were fully joined, he had the strangest sensation of having arrived at a destination he'd been seeking all his life.

He continued to hold her long after he had spent himself. Shaken by the power of his newly awakened feelings, he had one question.

"Why? Why me?" he whispered in her ear.

She gazed into his eyes as if searching for something. Then, seeming to find it, she replied, "Because I always knew it would be like this."

He'd spent many a long, lonely night since then puzzling over her cryptic answer, trying to decipher its true meaning. But it remained as much an enigma now as it had been then.

He glanced at her sidelong, wondering if he would ever know the truth – and more than a little fearful that he would. Some things, he mused, tearing his gaze from Cait, are best buried in the past.

Cait was grateful Comanche had the good sense not to keep up a meaningless stream of chitchat as he drove. She continued gazing out the window, noting familiar landmarks as he turned off the interstate at Kerrville. They covered the miles between town and the ranch all too quickly. And then, before she was really ready, the massive stone pillars and wrought-iron gates of Pride's Passion loomed straight ahead.

Home. The word leapt into her mind. A lump coalesced in her throat. Her eyes sheened. In her ten-year absence she had forgotten its beauty and only remembered her pain.

She took a deep breath and looked up the winding oak-lined drive to the main house. It sat on the crest of a hill, its buttermilk-coloured limestone gleaming in the late afternoon sun. The pink and white of crepe myrtles in full bloom softened its rectangular lines.

The building, in the shape of an H, had grown according to five generations' differing needs. Despite the lack of a long-range master plan, they had achieved something that the most accomplished architects can only aspire to. The house looked as if it belonged to the land, as if some elemental force of nature had set it in just the right place.

The litany of her ancestors' names and accomplishments reverberated through her mind. They had always seemed larger than life to her. The men had all been heroes, the women all heroines. She had grown up convinced she could never live up to the precedent they had set.

The central portion of the house, with its deep porch made from cedar trees that grew on the ranch, had been erected by Patrick Pride one hundred and fifty years ago. It contained a wide hall that ran from the front door to the back. In the days before air conditioning, it had served as a breezeway. The formal parlour and family room were to the left, the dining, kitchen, and breakfast rooms to the right.

The east wing had been built by Patrick's son, Ulysses. The ground floor contained Hank's office, a library and the music room. A series of bedrooms including her own were on the second storey.

Garth Pride had added the west wing. The ground floor was devoted to a den, a playroom and maids' quarters. The master suite and a nursery were on the second floor.

All told, the house contained eighteen rooms, five and a half baths, seven fireplaces, two staircases and enough nooks and crannies to delight the most adventurous child.

She and Comanche had used every square foot in daredevil games.

Frowning, Cait retreated from the memory. The last thing she needed was to get sentimental over the things she and Comanche had done.

She continued to study the house, wondering if Hank was watching from behind one of the windows, while Comanche brought the Suburban to a stop in the circular drive. Without saying a word, he opened the driver's door, got out and hurried to her side of the car while she silently cursed herself for sitting there like a helpless fool.

Racked by emotion at this unexpected homecoming, she knew her legs wouldn't hold her if she tried to get out of the car unaided.

Delta Boudreaux was in the parlour waiting for Comanche and Cait, when she saw the silver Suburban coming up the drive. She patted her hair into place and smoothed the new print dress she'd bought at Beall's, feeling dowdy compared to the sophisticatd-looking woman who stepped from the car. *Mon dieu*. How Cait had changed!

Although Delta had urged Hank to get in touch with Cait, she had been dreading this moment. She'd had Hank to herself for ten years and wasn't sure she could bear to share him with another woman during his remaining days, even if that woman was his daughter.

If the reunion went well, Cait and Hank would resolve their differences. But there was always the possibility that the divisions between them would grow even wider. While Delta's heart had gone out to Cait from the day she came to work at the ranch twenty-five years ago, Delta was in love with Hank. If events forced her to choose between the two, he would come out the winner.

Conquering her apprehension, she opened the front door, walked across the wide porch and greeted Cait warmly. "Aren't you a sight for sore eyes. Welcome home, *cher*. I never thought I'd see this day."

"Neither did I," Cait replied, an anxious smile on her lips.

"Are you all right? How was your flight? Are you tired?"

"I'm fine," Cait said.

But she looked far from fine. The skin around her eyes was white and drawn. Delta couldn't help feeling sorry for her. The Prides certainly had a talent for complicating the simplest things – like this homecoming. It should have happened years ago.

"Where's Hank?" Cait asked.

"He's waiting for you in the music room. We converted it into a bedroom when he came home from the hospital. It's real convenient because he doesn't have to climb the stairs. And he can look out the windows and keep an eye on the ranch. Comanche helped me rearrange the furniture to make room for one of those beds you can raise and lower."

Delta knew that nervousness had turned her into a chatterbox. But Cait didn't seem to notice. As she reached the porch steps, she turned and looked back towards the car. She had such a peculiar expression on her face that Delta couldn't help looking back too.

There wasn't anything to see except Comanche unloading the Suburban. "Be with you in a minute," he called. His voice sounded normal enough, though there was something tight and guarded about the set of his mouth that matched the set of Cait's.

Not another complication, Delta thought, as if things weren't complicated enough already. Looking from one to the other, she had a vivid memory of two lonely seven-year-old children meeting for the first time. They'd taken each other's measure with careful solemnity. Seeing as how they were both motherless and the same age, they should have been friends. They had been antagonists from the get go. The fact that Hank had quickly taken to the boy hadn't helped matters one bit.

From the look of things they were still a combustible pair. Under other circumstances, Delta would have been sympathetic. But her heart and mind were too full of Hank's problems to begin dealing with Cait's and Comanche's.

Leading the way inside the house, she turned to Comanche. "I'd appreciate it if you'd take Miss Caitlin's things up to her old room." To Cait, she explained, "I thought about putting you in one of the guest rooms but I figured you'd be more comfortable with your own things around."

"I hope you didn't go to any trouble," Cait replied politely, as if she were any old guest instead of Hank's only child.

"Oh, honey, that's the kind of trouble I love," Delta said.

Delta's loving words almost shattered Cait's rigid control. She longed to embrace the woman who had been like a mother to her. Butt the sound of someone playing a piano froze Cait in place. That someone could only be her father.

The familiar music had run through her childhood like a Wagnerian leitmotif. Hank had played Rachmaninov's *Rhapsody on a theme of Paganini* to the exclusion of all other compositions. He played it loud, played it soft, played it angry – played it until she wanted to slam the piano lid on his hands.

Now as she gazed around, thc melodic theme sent a chill racing along her spine.

Comanche disappeared up the stairs, leaving Cait and Delta alone in the echoing entry hall.

"Would you like to wash up?" Delta asked.

"No, thank you. I just travelled two thousand miles to see Hank. I don't see any point in putting it off."

"Good. I know he's anxious."

Cait square her weary shoulders. "Is there anything I need to know before I go in there?"

"*Cher*, your father's had a very hard time. He hates being dependent on others, and he's nervous about seeing you. Be kind to him." Without another word, Delta left Cait alone.

The house seemed to settle around her as if it, too, had been awaiting her arrival. She hesitated a moment before taking the hall that led to the music room. The door was open and she caught a glimpse of an empty hospital bed before she entered.

Hank was seated at the old Chickering piano, lost in his music. *He's changed*, she thought, *God, how he's changed*. His once ruddy skin had paled and his rugged frame seemed shrunken so that he looked as if he were wearing a larger man's clothes. Her breath caught in her throat, seeming to expand into an amorphous, choking lump.

She had spent the last ten years convincing herself she didn't love or need her father. Just one look told her how wrong she had been.

Suddenly Hank glanced her way and she saw that, despite his illness, the indomitable light she remembered so well still shone in his eyes.

"So you still play the Rachmaninov," she blurted out.

"I'm not fit for much else." His gaunt features relaxed in a smile. "Thank you for coming. I wasn't sure you would."

When he got to his feet Cait froze, wondering if he intended to embrace her. Instead he walked the few feet to the leather armchair positioned in front of the window, took a magazine off the seat and cautiously lowered himself. Then he gestured at the adjacent chair. "Sit down and make yourself at home."

Cait did as he asked, crossing her long legs, smoothing her skirt, wondering what to say. Nothing in the past had prepared her for this meeting. Simple good manners had got her through awkward situations before. But the rules of etiquette didn't cover what to do in situations like this.

Hank's continued silence reinforced her uncertainty. The ticking of an antique Regulator clock reverberated through the quiet while he studied her face. "You look just like your mother when she was your age," he finally said, surprise and pleasure lighting his eyes.

The comment caught Cait off guard. "That's the last thing I expected you to say."

"I should have talked to you about your mother a long time ago."

"Yes – you should have." Although she tried to fight it, Cait was helpless to control the resentment bubbling inside her like a witch's brew.

One of the many unhappy days she had spent in this house, leapt into her mind. It was the day she realized she was different from other children – so different that her father would never be able to love her.

Newly enrolled in kindergarten, she'd just learned that other children celebrated the day of their birth. The revelation had come as such a surprise that she could hardly wait to get home from school to ask Hank if she could have a birthday party of her own.

He had turned scarlet and then white, his eyes seeming to sink in his head. "While you live in this house," he'd said, "you'd be well advised to forget such foolish notions. Nothing on earth could make me celebrate the day your mother died. You're old enough now to know it was your fault."

Cait didn't realize she was scowling until the sound of Hank's voice brought her back to the present. "You're angry, aren't you?" he asked.

"I'm very sorry you're sick, but yes, I am angry." She bit her lower lip to keep it from trembling. She felt as if every nerve ending had suddenly been exposed.

To her astonishment, Hank leaned forward and patted her knee. His hand looked bony, the skin mottled with age. The magazine that had been on his lap spilled to the floor. Cait looked down, expecting to see the latest issue of *Progressive Farmer*. Instead her own face looked up at her from the cover of *Elle*.

Her rioting emotions escaped in an hysterical laugh. "When did you start buying women's magazines?" she sputtered.

Hank bent over, retrieved the magazine, put it back on his lap and gently smoothed the cover. Then he looked her squarely in the eyes. "Since you became so successful that I saw your picture everywhere. Before I got sick I used to ride out to your mother's grave with the magazines. It was the only way I could think of to be with the two of you."

The admission was so startling that Cait's lower jaw dropped. "I don't know what to say."

"You don't have to say anything. But I do, Cait. Beginning with an apology. I'm sorrier than I can say for the way I treated you before you left – for the way I always treated you. I've been a terrible father. I used to tell myself the ranch kept me too busy to spend time with you. There was always some emergency, a downed fence, a sick herd, a sudden storm. I used all those reasons and lots more I can't even remember to avoid being with you. Then when you got older, I didn't know how to talk to you – my own daugher and I didn't know how to talk to you. I don't expect you'll ever be able to forgive me."

Cait couldn't help being suspicious of his seeming reformation. Was he trying to manipulate her? Logic told her to hold him at an emotional distance. Her yearning female heart commanded her to hear him out.

"When I think of all the years I wasted . . ." Hunching his shoulders like a turtle retreating into its shell, he gazed out the window so all she could see was his profile.

There could be no mistaking the sheen of tears in his eyes. She had never seen him even close to tears before, had never been permitted to see beyond the stoic mask he showed the world. It frightened her, embarrassed her, touched her. "You said you would tell me about my mother."

Hank's answering smile made him look years younger, as if the mere mention of Elizabeth could hold his illness at bay. "Your mother was a wonderful woman. I didn't half deserve her." He looked around. "This was her music room. She brought the Chickering with her when we got married."

"I didn't know that."

"If she hadn't made up her mind to be a teacher, I think she could have been a concert pianist, she was that talented." He chuckled, laughing at a private joke, then explained. "She's the one who taught me to play the Rachmaninov – note by note. It became a joke between us. I'd play it at parties and then, pretending to be a temperamental artist, refuse to play anything else. After she died, playing it made me feel closer to her. There are times at the piano when I can almost hear her laughter."

Cait was having a hard time equating the dour father of her childhood with the man who had played party pranks. She sat still, totally absorbed, while Hank told the story of how he and Elizabeth – he called her Lizzie – met the year he served on the school board and she came to Kerrville to teach music. The daughter of a Fredericksburg lawyer, she had been the sweetest, prettiest woman in the Hill Country.

"I knew Lizzie was the woman for me from the first," he said, his eyes firmly locked on a vision only he could see, "but I'd have sworn she didn't feel the same way. I pursued her slowly, only throwing caution to the winds when I couldn't count my rivals on the fingers of both hands. The day I worked up the nerve to propose, I'd already thought of a dozen different reasons why Lizzie would turn me down. I was too old, too set in my ways, not sociable enough.' The list of his faults came far easier than any recital of his virtues.

"Lizzie confounded all my fears by saying yes. We both wanted a child, but after Lizzie's third pregnancy ended in a miscarriage, Doc Williams warned us to stop trying. I was scared to death of losing Lizzie so I agreed at once."

"Why didn't you tell me any of this before?" Cait demanded.

Hank gazed off into the distance as if he had just seen something fascinating outside his bedroom window. Don't stop talking now, Cait silently urged. Once again she became aware of the clock ticking in the silence. When Hank closed his eyes, she thought he had dozed off.

"I was ashamed," he said softly.

"What did you have to be ashamed of?"

"I should have asked your mother what she was doing to prevent getting pregnant. My only excuse is in those days most men thought birth control was a woman's responsibility."

Cait could have said "they still do", but she didn't dare interrupt the flow of his words.

"Your mother knew how much having an heir – someone to inherit the ranch – meant to me. To her, too. She was a city girl but she loved the land as much as I did. Maybe more. When she got pregnant again she was so excited, I didn't have the heart to tell her how worried I was. And when she made it through the fifth month without any problems, even Doc Williams stopped worrying." While he talked the colour washed from his face until he looked even greyer than he had when Cait first saw him.

"I'd gone to Dallas to a livestock auction the day Lizzie went into labour. She wasn't due for five more weeks or I'd never have left like that. Bert McClain drove her to the hospital. She died before I got there." His voice cracked. "She had haemorrhaged after every one of her miscarriages. This time Doc Williams couldn't stop the bleeding." He seemed unaware of the tears leaving watery tracks on his withered cheeks. "If I hadn't been so set on having an heir, your mother would never have attempted another pregnancy. I'm the reason she died. No one else. I was half out of my mind afterwards. When the doctor told me you would have to stay in an incubator for a few weeks, I was relieved. I couldn't deal with anything but Lizzie's death."

Cait didn't know what to say to comfort him. He seemed almost unaware of her presence as he began speaking again.

"By the time you came home, I didn't want anything to do with you. I couldn't live with my part in what had happened. It was easier to blame you instead. So I left your care to a nurse and then later, to Delta."

"Why didn't you tell me any of this sooner?" Cait couldn't help thinking of all the years she and Hank had lost. She felt desperately sorry for the grieving widower he had been, but she couldn't deny her own anger. Fate had cheated her of a mother's love. Hank had cheated her of a father's.

"It isn't the sort of thing a man can talk about easily. At least not a man like me. By the time I admitted the truth, I'd built such a high wall between us that I didn't know how to break it down. The day you told me about the modelling contest, I knew you'd win. You were the prettiest thing in the world even then. But I couldn't let you leave Pride's Passion because it would be like admitting your mother died for nothing."

Cait felt acutely uncomfortable. She wrapped her arms around herself in an unconsciously protective gesture. "I'm so sorry," she said, "for both of us. But I'm glad you finally told me the truth."

Hank's eyes searched her own. "Do you think we can make a new start?"

Cait's mouth gaped open. Her heart stopped. She couldn't believe her ears. Hank had rejected her time and again. Apparently now she was rich and famous, he had decided he had fatherly feelings towards her after all.

Wondering if his illness could have affected his brain, she burst out, "You want what?"

4

Blackjack pushed his plate away and looked around the dinner table at his guests. He had only eaten half of the generous cut of beef for which Brenner's, a landmark Houston restaurant, was famous. His guests, the four Nishida executives, seemed determined to finish theirs.

They concentrated on their steaks with the same single-minded attention they undoubtedly gave to balance sheets, cutting and chewing with the precision of a drill team. It was all he could do not to show his impatience.

He had made a reservation at the restaurant because he was aware of the Japanese preference for fine beef. While other Houston steak houses had either gone out of business or changed their menus in response to the public's growing concern about cholesterol, Brenner's had gone right on serving big juicy prime cuts.

Satisfied that he had chosen well, Blackjack continued to study his guests. No matter how hard he tried, he couldn't tell them apart. If he hadn't placed the CEO, Sato Tochigi, to his right, he wouldn't have been able to address the man by name.

"Thank you for a wonderful meal, Senator." Tochigi said, finally pushing his own plate aside.

Tochigi spoke perfect English. He had undoubtedly been one of the thousands of Japanese who enrolled in American universities every year, crowding out American students.

"It's my pleasure," Blackjack replied graciously,

although he was privately wondering when the hell the man would finally get down to business. "I'm glad you enjoyed it."

"Ah, yes, the steak was very fine indeed. Such a dinner would be prohibitively expensive in one of Tokyo's better restaurants. We Japanese are proud of the quality of our cattle. But meat is far more expensive in my country than it is in yours."

"The Japanese price is understandable, considering how little land you have for ranching."

Tochigi responded with a toothy grin. "I'm glad you understand our problem." He turned to his companions, reeled off a jumble of words in Japanese and waited until they nodded their heads before turning back to Blackjack.

Lowering his voice to a conspiratorial level, he said, "Are you aware that Japanese companies have purchased large ranches in California, Montana and Oregon?"

"I'd heard something about it."

Blackjack's answer was a half truth. His senatorial office had been flooded with complaints about how foreigners – Japs, ragheads, and gooks – were buying up America. To the best of his knowledge they had restricted their acquisitions to glamour properties – skyscrapers, electronics companies, movie studios. But Tochigi was too knowledgeable to have made a mistake. If he said Japanese conglomerates were buying ranches, you could make a book on it.

Tochigi leaned closer. "When Japanese insurance companies purchased controlling interests in Rockefeller Center, the Citicorp Tower and the Exxon building, they paid twenty per cent above the fair market value. The price of real estate has been dropping ever since and now, as you Americans would say," Tochigi impaled Blackjack with his shrewd gaze, "they are holding the bag.

"Japanese companies also own ninety major golf courses in the United States. My countryman, Minoru Isutani, paid a record $800 million dollars for the master's course at Pebble Beach, considerably more than it was worth according to our own experts. He borrowed part of the purchase price from the Mitsubishi Bank and Trust and now that noble establishment faces the most grave consequences."

Blackjack was wearying of Tochigi's self-important lecture. Cut to the chase, he silently implored.

"I also have it on the best authority that Sony and Matsushita will be unable to run Columbia Pictures and MCA at a profit because they grossly overpaid for those properties," Tochigi continued. "A reasonable man may conclude that Japanese corporations will eventually be forced to sell their American holdings at a considerable loss. While I understand the enthusiasm that leads to such rash investments, I do not intend to allow Nishida to travel the same road."

The bastard really does his homework, Blackjack thought. There had been such a public hue and cry over Japanese investors buying American trophy properties that no one had taken the trouble to assess whether their purchases had been fiscally sound. But the sale of land always had a way of arousing intense emotions.

Tochigi stopped speaking long enough to take a pack of cigarettes from inside his suit jacket. One of his underlings immediately produced a light. He inhaled deeply before continuing in the same conspiratorial tone he had used before. "Nishida plans to buy ranch land in Texas. We can raise cattle here, ship the beef to our own country, and sell at a greater profit than we could if we raised them in Japan."

So that's why Tochigi had looked him up, Blackjack thought. It was crazy. "Why don't you just buy American cattle and ship them back home?"

Tochigi gave him a toothy smile in response, as if Blackjack had just asked the dumbest question in the world. "My dear Senator, they wouldn't be Japanese.

"I see." Blackjack felt like a fool. He should have

realized the Japanese would never allow American beef growers to undercut the Japanese market the way America had allowed the Japanese to undercut American-made steel, automobiles, electronics – the list went on and on.

Blackjack cleared his throat. He sensed that Tochigi was very close to getting down to the nitty-gritty. Since Blackjack had already paid the price of admission, he might as well hear the little fucker out.

"May I be of help? I'd be happy to refer you to a top notch ranch broker."

"This is a matter of some embarrassment to businessmen such as ourselves, for whom the world of commerce has few boundaries. But I'm sure you're aware of the wave of anti-Japanese sentiment sweeping your country. Should your fellow Texans become aware of our intention, we fear they might attempt to block such a purchase."

Not fucking likely, Blackjack thought considering the state's financial difficulties. He didn't tell Tochigi that, though. He continued to sit quietly, his fingers pyramided, his expression thoughtful, biding his time.

Tochigi's toothy grin had vanished. He looked every inch the hard-as-nails businessman when he spoke again. "And that brings me to the heart of our purpose in visiting you in Houston. Specifically, we hoped to prevail on your good offices to act for us. Nishida would like to buy the land through a dummy Texas corporation whose board of directors, hand-picked by you, would loyally serve our interests without question or equivocation. Of course, we are prepared to show our gratitude."

"That's a very interesting proposal. I admit to a certain curiosity concerning your definition of gratitude." Having neatly returned the ball to Tochigi's court, Blackjack sat back and folded his arms across his chest.

Tochigi snapped his fingers, one of his henchmen produced a notepad and pen and he quickly scribbled something. Then he passed the pad to Blackjack.

The figure written there made Blackjack swallow hard. It would certainly solve his temporary cash flow problems. He'd have time to restructure a few critical loans, saving himself the public embarrassment that estate entrepreneurs like Donald Trump had suffered.

While accepting a gratuity – hell, why not call a spade a spade? – accepting a bribe was occasionally part of doing business in Japan and the United States, it was against the law. He looked at the figure again, his pulse accelerating. Legality be damned, he decided. If other Senators could do favours for men like Charles Keating and the infamous Bank of Credit and Commerce, he could certainly do one favour for a reputable businessman like Sato Tochigi.

"I think I can be of service," he said. "But I'd like more specific information about the type of property you want. Texas is a big state. Do you have any particular location in mind?"

"The ranch must be near major modes of transportation – highway, rail, and more specifically, an airport. We understand there are ranches in Texas that are bigger than some of your eastern states."

Blackjack finally cracked a genuine smile. "We like to do things big here."

"Our ambitions are not quite so lofty. We would like to acquire between fifty and one hundred thousand acres, with a variety of terrains including fields where we can raise our own feed. A reliable source of water is important too. My experts tell me you Texans have gone to war over water rights."

"I'm afraid your experts have seen too many Hollywood movies," Blackjack said dryly. Tochigi had just eliminated all of west Texas where a ten-year drought held sway.

"Perhaps so. We are all great fans of Western heroes like John Wayne. And that brings up another point. We would like the property to include a large ranch house, a place with a true Western ambience similar to the one in Mr Wayne's movie, *Big Jake*. In addition to raising cattle, it is our intention to use the ranch as a corporate retreat where we can experience the American West first hand."

Although Tochigi continued talking, waxing enthusiastic about his vision of life in the West, Blackjack had stopped paying attention. Worry tugged at his mind. Tochigi wasn't going to settle for just any ranch, any more than Sony had settled for any old movie studio.

The Nishida CEO wanted a trophy property that would glisten on the corporate crown like a prize jewel. No wonder he wanted to keep the purchase secret. Texans had a way of getting riled up when it came to parting with pieces of their heritage. The son-of-a-bitch was inviting a second Alamo.

Still, Blackjack couldn't repress a small smile. The Jap certainly had a case of Texas fever. He could picture Tochigi and his slant-eyed associates striding around in chaps, boots and stetsons, playing cowboys.

"Do you know of such a ranch?" Tochigi asked.

"I think something in the Hill Country might fill the bill."

Tochigi's brows elevated. "I'm not familiar with this Hill Country."

"It's the heart of Texas," Blackjack began in the sonorous tones he used when speaking in the Senate. "The place where the state was born – twenty counties of the prettiest ranch land the good Lord ever created, with San Antonio and Austin to serve your transportation needs. The Pedernales river, the Guadalupe and the Colorado cut across it. There are several lakes with good fishing and the hunting is the best in the state. President Johnson had a ranch in the area and his wife, Ladybird, still lives there."

Blackjack continued talking about the virtues of the Hill Country, unaware of the genuine enthusiasm colouring his voice. But Sato Tochigi didn't miss it. By the time

Blackjack stopped speaking, Tochigi had made up his mind that the Nishida ranch must be in this fabled Hill Country.

"We will be returning to Japan in a few days. Will you be able to find a suitable Hill Country ranch before we leave?" he asked.

The bastard was unusually direct for a Jap. He was also in one hell of a hurry, Blackjack mused, uncomfortably aware that Tochigi radiated a power and purpose that equalled his own. If he didn't take control of the situation now, Tochigi would try to call the shots long distance. And Blackjack would be damned if he'd be led around by the nose like a prize bull, and especially not by some fucking slant-eye.

"We Americans have a saying, Mr Tochigi. Act in haste, repent at leisure. Finding a ranch that fulfils your requirements, and then convincing the owners to sell, will take time."

"How much time?"

"I won't be sure until I do a preliminary investigation. Perhaps a year. Maybe more. There are a number of steps to be concluded first, not the least of which is setting up the Texas corporation and choosing a trustworthy board of directors."

Blackjack stopped talking long enough to run a list of possible candidates through his mind. He had a feeling he was going to have to call in a lot of markers before this was over. "The legal end of things will take a few months."

Tochigi nodded. "All right, you have a year. But no more. We want to buy at the bottom of the market, Senator. Not the top."

Despite the warning implicit in his words, he picked up his wine glass, gave Blackjack another toothy grin and offered a toast. "To the successful conclusion of our business."

5

"Can we make a new start?" Hank repeated anxiously.

Cait felt intensely uncomfortable. She couldn't lie to him. Their reconciliation was too new, too fragile, too foreign for her to trust. "I'll try to meet you halfway – but that's all I can promise."

"All I ask is that you try. I always loved you, Cait. I just didn't know how to show it. But I swear I won't fail you again." And I hope you won't fail me, he silently added.

The chill that had crept into his bones during the last few months seemed to relax its icy grip as he looked at Cait. She had Lizzie's beauty and goodness. Did she have her courage, her spirit, her loyalty? How little he knew his daughter.

"Tell me about your life," he said. "I know you're successful. Are you happy?"

"Happy enough."

He had expected a more enthusiastic response. "Do you like it? Modelling, I mean."

"Most of the time. I love working with Mims Pauling. I hope you'll meet her one day soon. She's a brilliant businesswoman. I owe my success to her."

"Have you ever thought about marriage, kids, raising a family? I would love to have grandchildren someday." In his happiness at their reconciliation, he momentarily forgot his illness.

Cait hadn't, though. The misery in her eyes clearly said she knew he wouldn't live long enough to see his grandchildren, even if she found the right man to father them tomorrow.

"I have thought about marriage. If you had read the tabloids, you'd know I was engaged four times." Her gaze danced away from his. The admission seemed to embarrass her.

"A father always feels no man is good enough for his daughter, but surely one of those fellas . . .?" Hank's voice trailed off. Who the hell was he to judge Cait, considering how miserably he had failed at being her father? "I'm sorry. I have no business asking these things."

"You aren't asking anything I haven't asked myself. The only answer I can give is that I truly believed I was in love with each one. In the end, though, I always felt as if something was missing, something I couldn't even define."

She looked so sad and bewildered that he had an urge to hold her close. How awful it was not to be able to touch his own daughter. But children learned to love by being loved and he'd been a very poor teacher. Except for Lizzie, he'd never been at ease giving physical expression to his feelings.

He had lost the art of compassion, if not the feeling, the day his beloved Lizzie died. By example, he'd taught his daughter to judge harshly, to be unforgiving, and to flee at the first sign of affection.

Cait was looking across the room at the old clock hanging on the wall. "I don't want to tire you. It's getting late. Should I tell Delta you're ready for supper?"

"Sit with me a while longer," he replied, stalling for time. It was near the dinner hour. Any minute now Delta would come bustling in with her unfailing good cheer, insisting he had to eat to keep up his strength. Sometimes he wished she would break down and cry, or get angry – do anything except pretend he wasn't dying.

Hellfire. He had made so many wrong decisions

concerning Cait and Delta and the ranch. He prayed he wouldn't make another one now. Out with it, he ordered himself. Tell Cait the truth.

She was snuggling deeper into her chair, looking surprisingly content. "It's good to be home," she said. "I never admitted it to anyone including myself, but I missed you and Delta and the ranch."

Home, Hank thought, she had actually referred to the ranch as "home". He couldn't have asked for a more hopeful sign. "I have something to ask you," he said.

What now? Cait thought. She'd been braced for the worst – bitterness, anger, recriminations – when she walked into the room. Instead, Hank had given her a glimpse of the man behind the stoic mask. He had reached out to her. She was trying to reach back. But she wouldn't be pushed.

"We're both tired. Can't it wait until tomorrow?"

"No, it can't. I don't want you to spend the night here under false pretences. You and I would have had this talk long ago if I hadn't been such a stubborn fool. I picked up the phone to call you dozens of times over the years, but I always lost my nerve. I'll do it tomorrow or the next day, I told myself. Now I'm just about out of tomorrows." He paused, gathering his courage. "Cait, I want you to come home for good. Deep inside, I think you love the ranch. Pride women have always been this land's heart and soul. It's more than just a piece of land or a way to make a living. It's our birthright. It's who we are."

Cait almost said it might be who he was, but it had nothing to do with her. Somehow the angry retort stayed locked in her throat. She had been deeply moved by the story of her own birth, and the sacrifice her mother had made to give Hank and the ranch an heir.

"The thought of strangers in this house," Hank continued, "the thought that no one will take care of your mother's grave – it's killing me, Cait, as surely as the cancer. I want to be buried next to Lizzie, and I want to know you'll watch over her resting place after I'm gone."

Cait was incredulous. "I can understand your feeling that way. But do you have any idea what you're asking me to give up?"

"Yes – I think I do. But I'm asking just the same." He managed a lopsided grin. "If you can't see your way clear to doing it, though, I'll understand. I don't want to go back to the way things were between us. I couldn't stand that."

Had he shouted, blustered, demanded like he used to, she would have been able to deny his request without giving it a second thought. But she couldn't walk out on this new Hank, or the desperation she saw in his eyes.

"You've taken my by surprise," she said. "The truth is, I don't know what to say."

"Then don't say anything. Not yet. I haven't told you everything. The ranch is in financial trouble. We're barely keeping our head above water."

"I've got some money, if that's what you need." Was that why he asked her to come home? To borrow money? If money rather than love proved to be his motive, she'd write him a cheque, leave in the morning, and never look back. She felt as if she'd been riding an emotional seesaw that had stopped in midair.

The sound of Hank's voice interrupted her grim musing. "I appreciate your offer more than I can say. The ranch does need new capital. But it needs new life even more. If you take over you can write your own ticket, run the spread any way you see fit."

Cait didn't know whether to laugh or cry. "I've been living in a city for the last ten years. And I didn't know that much about ranching when I lived here."

"In view of the mess I made of things, that's probably an asset. At least you won't be set in your ways like me. And I know you can count on Comanche. He's a fine person, the best foreman I ever had, and he cares about this place as much as I do."

At the mention of Comanche's name, Cait's stomach soured. "I couldn't possibly work with him."

"I don't understand. You two grew up together. I thought you'd be pleased he was here."

All her distrust of Comanche came rushing back. All her jealousy too. Obviously he was still Hank's favourite.

She wanted to tell Hank he'd been wrong to place his faith in a man like Comanche, that neither of them could or should count on Comanche for anything. But if she did she'd have to tell her father why she felt that way. And she hadn't sorted out the Pandora's box of emotions that seeing Comanche again had opened.

Besides, the idea of her taking over the ranch was preposterous. She wouldn't know where to begin. More to the point, she had her own life two thousand miles away.

Hank was looking at her, his eyes as eager as a young man's. "I know I've given you a lot to think about. And I don't expect you to give me your answer tonight. I was hoping you would stay on for a few days – spend a little time getting to know the place again, getting to know me. Will you do that much?"

She took a deep breath and then another as her racing heart demanded oxygen. "All right, I'll stay for a few days. After that, well, we'll see."

She excused herself a few minutes later and went up to her room. Her Vuittons were by the closet where Comanche had left them, their elegance a reminder of her life in Manhattan and everything that went with it. Mims had already booked her for the November runway shows in New York and Paris when the designers launched their spring lines. Her personal calendar was full of engagements – dinner parties, openings, fund raisers. Could she turn her back on all that?

Like the rest of the house, her room hadn't changed since the day she left. The floral wallpaper with its pattern of Texas bluebonnets had barely faded. The bird's-eye-maple canopy bed with its matching marble-topped dressing table had been in the family for generations. Faded bride's boxes were stacked by the *Kleiderschrank*, a German armoire. The entire set had belonged to her great-great-grandmother Elke, and had been handed down for generations.

In her teens she had badgered Hank to buy a modern bedroom set and been furious when he turned her down. Now she was glad. The antique pieces had a gentle grace she had never appreciated before, a patinaed warmth that seemed to say "welcome home".

If only she and Hank had made the effort to understand one another years ago. She sighed heavily. They couldn't go back. All they could do was go forward into a problematical future.

Sunshine filled Cait's room with a buttercup glow when she woke the next morning. She stretched languorously, and checked the clock on the night table, surprised to see how long she had slept. She had gone to bed convinced she'd spend the night tossing and turning. But her sleep had been deep and restful.

It must be the quiet, she thought. New York nights were full of intrusive sounds, honking horns, neighbours coming and going at all hours, wailing sirens that dragged her from slumber.

She got out of bed, padded to the closet and took out a pair of expensive designer jeans, a Mercedes-Adrienne blouse with leather appliqués and custom-made boots that had been in the suitcase Mims packed. In a Manhattan boutique they had seemed the epitome of western chic. Here they looked just plain silly.

Grimacing, she hung them back up and instead chose an old pair of Levis and a cotton shirt she had left behind when she went to New York. To her pleasure, they seemed to have been recently laundered. She would have to remember to thank Delta.

After two cups of coffee, one with Delta and another

with Hank, Cait opened the front door, stepped out onto the shaded porch and gazed around. Pride's Passion, sixty thousand prime acres straddling the Guadalupe river, stretched as far as she could see in any direction.

She and Comanche had ridden over every square foot as children. Of all the places he had been in the years since, why had he chosen to come back here? With his college degree, his riveting looks, his rodeo success, he must have had other offers. What could he hope to gain by being Hank's foreman? She would give a great deal to know the answer to that particular question.

Hank had suggested she spend the day riding, getting to know the place again. Striding purposefully, she walked down the porch steps and across the acre of lawn that separated the old stone barn from the main house.

The interior smelled of maure and hay, a pungent aroma that always made her sneeze. Rubbing her nose – unaware of the grin on her face – she glanced around. Although the building was as old as the house, the shafts of light slanting down from the hayloft didn't reveal any deterioration.

Suddenly she felt as if a vice had tightened around her heart. She and Comanche had played in the loft as children, pretending to be pirates – he always wanted her to be the slave girl – fighting it out as cowboys and Indians, constantly trying to best one another.

It had been a shock yesterday, seeing him. No wonder she had reacted so strongly. The next time, she swore she would be as cool, as coldly analytical as an FBI agent investigating a case. She mustn't permit her past or present feelings for him to interfere with her decision about Hank and the ranch.

Hank had told her to saddle any horse that took her fancy. She walked from stall to stall, taking the measure of the occupants before settling on a trim chestnut mare. Her own saddle was still in its accustomed place in the tack room. The leather looked as supple and clean as if she had just ridden yesterday. Delta had laundered her old clothes. Who had taken such loving care of her rig?

She hadn't saddled a horse in a decade but her hands remembered the task. The mare easily accepted a bridle and followed her from the barn. The saddle was heavy enough to make her grunt as she lifted it. The physical effort felt great, though, uncomplicated and honest, the antithesis of the artifice modelling required.

Sighing, she leaned her head against the mare's side and shut her eyes. So much had happened in the last twenty-four hours; hearing about Hank's illness, returning to Pride's Passion, feeling a closeness to her father she had longed for when she was little. And then his astonishing request that she take over the ranch, a request complicated by Comanche's position as the foreman. She could hardly believe that only yesterday morning she had been in the Yucatan impatiently waiting for her Manhattan-bound flight.

Mounting up, she rode out of the corral and gave the chestnut her head. Over the years she had become expert at shutting out the past. Now it came clamouring back, and all the old hurt feelings with it. She and Hank had never understood one another. Could she get past her bitterness?

Her last night at home had been typical of the rancour between them. It had been the end of August, 1983. Comanche had left for college a few days earlier and Pride's Passion seemed empty without him.

She had just sat down to supper when Hank walked into the cavernous dining room. Without so much as saying, "Hello, how are you, did you have a nice day?" he dropped an envelope by her plate on the way to his own seat at the head of the table.

Cait looked down, hoping it was from Comanche, and saw a letterhead reading *Mims' Models* with a New York city address beneath it. What can this be? she wondered. She began reading the contents while absent-mindedly taking a bite of Delta's chicken-fried steak.

Dear Miss Pride, the letter began, *We are delighted to inform you that you have been chosen as one of the twelve finalists in our annual Face of the Future talent search.*

She must have gasped because Hank looked up from his newspaper. "Are you all right?" he asked.

"I'm fine," she quickly replied.

Aside from ensuring she was in good health, well fed and properly educated, Hank had never shown the slightest interest in her activities. He'd even sent her off to high school in Houston to get her out of the way. She wasn't about to share this deliciously weird letter with him until she knew what it was all about.

But for the fact that the letter was clearly addressed to her right down to the correct Farm Route, she would have been certain the whole thing was a mistake. She read it all the way through to Mims Pauling's boldly scrawled signature and then read it again, her eyes widening with confused delight. She'd been marking time, wondering what to do with the rest of the summer. Now, out of the blue, Mims Pauling, the owner of Mims' Models, was offering her an all-expenses-paid trip to New York.

Mims' Models. Mims Pauling. The names tugged at her memory. Six months earlier at Kinkaid, Avery Morgan had urged her to enter a modelling competition. Mims' Models. Yes. That was the name Avery had mentioned.

Too agitated to eat another bite, Cait pushed the food around on her plate until Hank rose, signalling the end of the meal. Five minutes later, alone in her room, she dialled the Morgans' Houston number. To her relief, Avery answered on the second ring.

"It's me," Cait said. "Am I ever glad you're home. Guess what just came in the mail." She read the letter, then said, "I figured you would know how Mims Pauling happened to get my pictures."

"Now that's what I call brilliant deductive reasoning," Avery replied gleefully.

"So you did enter me in the contest."

"Damn right. I knew you'd win. Oh, Cait, aren't you just thrilled to itty-bitty pieces?"

Cait had no problem resisting Avery's excitement. "I haven't won yet."

"Don't be a *wuss*. I know you think you're still an ugly duckling. But damn you, girl, you're a swan. You'll knock 'em dead in the Big Apple. When do you leave?"

Cait would have given anything to be able to match Avery, squeal for exuberant squeal. However bile rose in her throat at the thought of being compared to eleven truly beautiful girls. Making the finals had to be a fluke. Mims Pauling would undoubtedly have a first-class hissy the minute she saw Cait in the flesh. "I haven't decided to go."

"What do you mean, you haven't decided? Have you lost your mind, girl? Now you listen to me and listen good. This is the chance of a lifetime. Sure you're nervous. But a modelling contest in New York beats the devil out of anything you've got planned now."

Avery continued proselytizing with all the fervour of an early Christian seeking a convert until she overcame Cait's reservations. Fifteen minutes later, a bemused Cait found herself sitting in the parlour telling Hank how she just happened to have won a trip to New York. She watched with growing concern as his chiselled features hardened.

"Of all the damn foolishness," he grumbled. "I won't have any daughter of mine parading up and down in front of a bunch of strangers like a heifer being auctioned to the highest bidder. You're not going to New York – not next week, next month or next year."

His anger took Cait by surprise. "But, Dad, it won't cost you a penny."

Hank's grey eyes narrowed under the fierce thrust of his brow, his habitual glower deepening as he impaled her with his gaze. "It's not the money, Caitlin. You belong on the ranch. I expect you to stay here, to marry someone suitable and raise a family like all the other generations of Prides. You're the last of us, and you'll damn well do your duty to your family."

He turned to the family protraits hanging on the walls, then back to Cait. "Pride women have always been special. Your Great-Great-Grandmother Elke, was an abolitionist. Your Great-Great-Grandmother Reina, helped revolutionize the cattle industry. Her daughter Philippa, was a famous suffragette. Your picture will hang with theirs one day and I'll be damned if it will say 'model' underneath."

Her entire life, Cait had felt as if Hank was measuring her against her ancestors – redoubtable women like Elke and Philippa and her own mother. And she was damn sure she had never measured up.

"Family?" she burst out. "Don't make me laugh. You don't know the meaning of the word. You and I have never been a family! I have the chance to do something exciting, to have some fun and I'm not about to let being a Pride stand in my way."

Hank's ruddy skin paled. His voice was as cold as a blue norther when he finally spoke into the silence filling the room. "You do what you think best, Caitlin. But while you're thinking on it, you had better remember this. I have never put up with defiance in my dogs, my horses or my hired hands. I certainly will not tolerate it in my daughter. If you leave the ranch, you won't be welcome back."

Now, as she followed a well-beaten path to the banks of the Guadalupe, Cait finally knew why he had been so dictatorial. He had been lonely and afraid. She understood the way those emotions warped people. God knew, they had warped her.

The river was straight ahead. She dismounted, looped the reins around a nearby sapling and left the horse to graze. Then she took off her boots and went wading the way she had a thousand times when she was little. The water felt deliciously cool. As she waded deeper, a bold minnow nibbled on her toes, bringing a smile to her lips. You can take the girl out of the country, she thought, rolling up her jeans even further, but you can't take the country out of the girl.

She couldn't remember the last time she breathed such pure air. The stuff she took into her lungs in New York seemed to be composed of exhaust fumes, carbon by-products and particulate matter. There were winter days when the sun never made its way between the monolithic skyscrapers and into her apartment. The crowds, the dirt, the noise could be overwhelming.

When she first moved to the city, she had worked hard at convincing herself that the obvious drawbacks were a small price to pay for living on the cutting edge. With Mims' help, she had developed a veneer of sophistication. She had learned where to shop, what labels to buy, where to be seen and who to be seen with. But she had never felt completely at ease in Manhattan the way she did at this very moment.

She returned to the river bank, sat down on the sand and turned her face up to the sun, shaking her head in amazement as she realized her current thought process could only lead to one conclusion. She was actually considering saying yes to Hank's request.

She must be out of her mind. What in the world made her think she could run the biggest spread in the Hill Country, let alone make it profitable again? She might as well try to reinvent the wheel.

6

All the way back to Manhattan, Cait tried to forget the bleak look in Hank's eyes when she said goodbye. Although she had promised to visit often, his disappointment had been palpable. Now, as the taxi pulled up in front of the brownstone where she lived, the memory soured her homecoming. She had always loved this section of Sixty-fourth, with its gracious turn-of-the-century homes and mature trees. Today however, the trees looked sickly and the brownstones shoddy.

Giving the driver a generous tip, she manhandled her bags into the building's minuscule lobby, then pushed the button to summon the ancient elevator. Home at last, she thought a few minutes later, opening the series of locks that secured her front door.

She struggled her bags inside and began turning on lights as she made her way to the living room. When she was in residence the apartment always smelled of fresh flowers, Tex-Mex cooking and her favourite perfume.

Today, however, there was no pot of green chilli stew simmering on the stove, dead flowers filled the vases and the air felt stale and close.

She had fallen in love with the place the first time the real estate agent showed it to her. Its four rooms boasted high ceilings, crown mouldings, a working fireplace and a view of a tiny garden from her bedroom. Rather than hiring the high-priced decorator Mims recommended, Cait had done the place over herself, bleaching the oak floors until they were the colour of home-churned butter, painting the walls a matching shade and doing the kitchen and bathroom with Saltillo tiles from Mexico. It had been a labour of love.

This afternoon as she opened the drapes and gazed around, she felt a vague sense of dissatisfaction. She had assembled the furnishings – a blend of Ralph Lauren western chic and turn-of-the-century antiques – with patience and care. With sudden clarity, she realized she had achieved a pale imitation of her childhood home. Why hadn't she seen it before?

The ringing of the telephone brought an abrupt end to her introspection.

"Cait Pride," she answered.

"Is that you?" came the sound of Mims' voice, "or is it your machine?"

Cait let go an exhausted sigh. "It's me."

"Is something wrong? You sound awful."

"I'm just a little tired."

"Not too tired to go back to work, I hope. You're booked straight through the week."

"Let me get a pen and paper and you can fill me in," Cait replied.

They talked shop for ten minutes, then made a dinner date for Friday. After saying goodbye, Cait played back her messages before carrying her bags to her bedroom and unpacking.

The designer clothes in her closet seemed strangely unfamiliar, as if she'd bought and worn them in another lifetime. She felt trapped in a limbo that only existed in the terrain of her mind, a never-never land halfway between Manhattan and the Hill Country.

On her way back from the Yucatan, she had been anxious for a long soak in a bubble-filled tub. As she finally fulfilled that desire, all she could think about was Hank. She hadn't wanted to leave him, and yet she didn't really have a choice. She'd made a life in New York – a rich, full life, she reminded herself.

Lowering her body into the tub and closing her eyes, she tried to concentrate on the coming week, the modelling assignments, the dates with friends and found herself searching her heart instead.

Did she really want to go on living a life where her biggest worry was gaining a few pounds, having a bad hair day or, God forbid, showing signs of age? Did she want to go on being treated as if her looks were the most important thing about her?

Her career had been an accident, a gift from Avery and Mims. While she worked hard at it, she had never been genuinely fulfilled by it. She had always yearned to be more, to do more, to make a difference.

Despite its aura of glamour, there were times when modelling was dehumanizing. At the beginning of her career, photographers and designers had treated her like a collection of body parts – hair, face, breasts, legs and ass – rather than a human being.

If Mims hadn't been there to prop her up, to soothe away the thousand and one wounds to her fragile ego, she would have given up. But returning to the ranch hadn't seemed like the answer ten years ago any more than it did now.

Hank. Comanche. Pride's Passion. Each name carried a burden of memories.

Hank had given her an ultimatum ten years ago that cut the slender tenuous tie that bound them together. But she loved him in spite of their differences – both past and present. He needed her now as no one ever had. That need tugged at her like an anchor beneath the surface of the sea.

Her feelings for Comanche were even more complex. He had hurt her terribly, breaking her spirit as well as her heart. She could never forgive him for that. She couldn't stop wanting him either.

Last, there was the land itself. Pride's Passion. Five

generations had given their all to the ranch. Now her father wanted her to do the same thing. She shuddered at the thought.

The bubbles dissipated and the water grew cold as unruly thoughts windmilled through her mind, spinning in useless circles. She had to stop torturing herself. Her decision had been made.

And yet she couldn't put Hank and the ranch out of her mind.

Cait arrived at the Russian Tea Room on Friday night to find Mims already seated on one of the red leather banquettes. Wearing a perfectly accessorized peach linen Chanel suit, with every one of her pale blonde hairs in place, Mims looked chic and utterly at ease.

No matter how much trouble Cait took over her own appearance, she never quite equalled Mims' panache. She had long ago decided that the difference was due to the fact that Mims had grown up in the city and had imbibed a dose of sophistication along with her mother's milk.

"Rough week?" Mims asked, looking up as Cait joined her.

"Rough enough."

"Under the circumstances, I thought you'd rather be busy. Have you talked to your father since you came home?"

"Of course. I know you never expected to hear me say this – but I miss him."

Mims' brow elevated. "That's a switch."

The appearance of their waiter cut the conversation short. The next few minutes were taken up with the business of ordering drinks and dinner. After the waiter left, Mims launched into a recap of everything that had happened at the agency during Cait's absence.

Cait tried to nod and smile in all the appropriate places, however she couldn't concentrate on the conversation. She kept on flashing back to that dreadful look on Hank's face the day she left and hating herself for having caused it.

"Of course, we'll be staying at the Georges Cinq for the Paris shows in November," Mims was saying. "I've booked the usual suite. I thought I might go to Santorini for a few days of R and R afterwards and I was hoping you'd join me."

"I don't think I can," Cait replied. "In fact, I was going to ask you to replace me for the runway shows too."

Mims' china blue eyes widened. "But why? You've always loved doing those shows."

"I don't want to be away that long. I promised Hank I'd visit him every few weeks."

"I practically had to shanghai you to get you to see your father in the first place. What happened to change your mind?"

Cait shifted on the banquette seat, her nerves taut. How could she explain what she herself didn't understand?

She felt as if some mysterious power was reshaping her from the inside out. Her thought patterns seemed to be exploding like so many supernova. The status quo had suddenly become quo vadis. The things she accepted as givens just two weeks ago no longer held true in the new universe she inhabited.

"I guess it is a little hard to understand," she said.

Mims stared back at her. "Try me."

"So much has happened since we last talked," she began hesitantly. "I really haven't sorted it all out."

Sitting in the baronial splendour of the Russian Tea Room, surrounded by movers and shakers whose presence used to impress her, she experienced an Epiphany that would for ever alter the course of her life. She realized that she belonged to Pride's Passion as much as any of her ancestors. The land was in her blood. Texas was in her blood.

As she recounted her stay at Pride's Passion, her newly awakened love for Hank came shining through like a beacon to guide her home. She took her first easy breath in days. The tension left her body.

"I've got to go back, Mims," she concluded, feeling the weight of indecision lift off her shoulders.

"How long will you be gone this time?"

She hesitated a moment. "I plan to stay."

"Stay? What does that mean?"

"I feel terrible about leaving you and the agency but I'm going to do what Hank wants. I'm going to run Pride's Passion."

"I'm glad that you and your father got along, but I just can't see you devoting the rest of your life to the ranch. Are you sure seeing Comanche again hasn't influenced your decision?"

Cait ignored the confusion and hurt that the mere mention of his name aroused. "My feelings for him haven't changed. Don't you see, this is my last chance to spend time with my father?"

"What about your career? You know how stiff the competition is. You're not getting any younger. If you're gone too long, you may not be able to pick up where you left off. I don't mean to play devil's advocate, but are you sure you know what you're doing? What in the world do you know about raising cattle? You don't even eat red meat!"

"I didn't know a thing about modelling when I started out either. Besides, this isn't about the ranch. It's about my father and all the things we missed. It's about who I am. All I know is I've got to go back."

Ulysses Pride had ruled over Pride's Passion at the turn of the century, an era of boundless optimism when prosperity seemed even more inevitable than death or taxes. He'd added onto the house and furnished the new rooms with a potpourri of expensive collectibles. The formal dining room still reflected his opulent lifestyle and grandiose taste.

Cait paused in the entrance, thinking the room was better suited to a banquet than dinner for two. A sixteenth-century Flemish tapestry depicting a stag hunt hung on one wall. The heads of animals Ulysses had shot on safari with Teddy Roosevelt in 1909 – kudu, oryx, hartebeest, eland and rhino – adorned another. A baronial antique table that could easily accommodate twenty people occupied the centre of the floor.

This evening a couple of lonely place settings reminded Cait of the challenge she faced. An hour earlier she had told Hank she would take over the ranch. She could almost feel the mantle of her new responsibilities dropping onto her shoulders as she walked to the place at the head of the table. It was hers now, and all the responsibilities that went with it.

She had dressed for dinner in a tailored blouse and slacks that were meant to show Comanche she regarded eating with him as a necessity – a business encounter rather than a social one. She would as soon break bread with the devil, she thought, ignoring the butterflies in her stomach.

The setting didn't improve her mood. It had been a terrifying place for a lonely child to take meals with a father who barely acknowledged her existence. The chandeliers never seemed to light the dark corners and her imagination used to create lurking monsters from the shadows cast by the trophy heads.

Now she took a reluctant inventory as she gazed around. How much would the tapestry and the table bring if she sent them to Sotheby's? The house contained other treasures as well, original Remington bronzes, paintings by William Russell and Albert Bierstadt, a beaded Comanche cradle board, a Kiowa war bonnet – museum quality art, artifacts and antiques that the family had collected over the generations.

She grimaced as she realized what she was thinking. Hank had turned the ranch over to her because he hoped she would find a way to save it. He could have sold off its assets bit by bit himself if that would have accomplished his goal.

Comanche's "good evening" interrupted her unhappy reverie. As if on cue, her pulse skipped a beat.

He had obviously taken pains with his appearance. His brush-popper shirt was bandbox fresh, his face and hands scrubbed pink, his long black hair slicked back into a neat ponytail. She read admiration in his eyes. Hunger, too – and not the kind he'd satisfy at the dinner table.

Damn him for looking at her that way. Double damn her for letting it affect her. As he crossed the floor he exuded a raw masculinity that sent her pulse into the stratosphere.

"I'm sorry I couldn't meet you at the airport," he said. "You know how busy things get on a cattle ranch in the summer."

"I remember," Cait replied in an even tone, although privately she thought Comanche had enjoyed letting her wait around a second time. She didn't add that Delta had been positively unfriendly when she picked her up, and that Delta didn't thaw until Cait said she was home to stay.

Comanche pulled out her chair with the courtliness of a medieval knight and helped her into it. However, her reaction was far from ladylike. She was almost painfully aware of the heat coming off his body, of his scent – a combination of lemony soap with an underlying note of masculine musk.

She shrugged off his hand and gestured at the chair to her right. "Won't you sit down?"

Although Comanche hadn't eaten all day and Delta had prepared one of his favourite meals – barbecued ribs, mashed potatoes and fried okra – his stomach knotted at the thought of consuming any of it. Being close to Cait was playing hell with his appetite. If she kept on popping in every few weeks, he would have to take his belt in a notch.

"What brings you back so soon?" he asked, lifting the lid from one of the serving platters and passing it to her.

"Hank," she replied succinctly, spooning food onto her plate, although Comanche's nearness thundered through her mind like tympany.

She could barely take her eyes off his hands as he held out first one serving dish and then another. His fingers were broad, the nails blunt, square, and immaculate. A light dusting of hair showed on the back of his knuckles, growing more profuse at his wrists before disappearing under pristine white cuffs.

He'd had very little body hair in his teens. Her mouth dried and her heart gave a bump as she tried to imagine what his naked torso looked like now. She wanted Comanche at some primal level she couldn't explain or understand, and was infuriated by it.

"Well, what did you think?" he asked.

"About what?" she replied, so distracted that she had no idea what they had been discussing.

"How does the ranch look to you after all these years?"

Cait reached for her water glass and took a sip. When she finally met his eyes, she felt the impact as strongly as if he had touched her. She'd heard about women who yearned for their first love, but she'd got over Comanche years ago. Her runaway libido had to be due to the fact that she hadn't been intimate with a man for a long time.

"Hank told me the ranch isn't making any money," she said, determined to keep the conversation on a strictly business basis. "Frankly, I'm confused. He says you're the best foreman he's ever had. If you're the best, why isn't the ranch profitable?"

"That's a complicated question."

"We've got all night. Fill me in, hotshot." The nickname was unbidden, and with it came another flood of memories. She reached for her water glass again and this time, in her agitation, knocked it over.

Good God, what was wrong with her? She'd had verbal duels with businessmen and politicians who didn't share her opinions. She had dined tête-à-tête with movie stars. She'd been engaged to four of the world's most eligible bachelors. After all that, you'd think she'd be able to manage a simple supper with a cowboy.

She reached across the table to pick up the spilled ice cubes as Comanche began to blot the stain with his napkin.

Their fingers touched.

The contact sent sparks shimmering along her nerve paths.

Comanche righted the glass.

She accidentally knocked it over again.

An hysterical laugh burst from her mouth before she could muster the self-control to prevent it.

Why was Cait so nervous? Comanche wondered. Despite her beauty she looked strung out, like a thoroughbred filly who'd been ridden hard and put up wet. He wished he could reassure her, tell her he understood how awkward this dinner must feel under the circumstances. But he didn't think she'd welcome so personal a comment.

"You were asking why the ranch is in financial trouble," he said after setting her water glass upright for the second time. "The truth is, it was in trouble long before I came back. If it will put your mind at ease, I'd be happy to show you the books in the morning."

"Why can't you tell me what happened right now?"

"It's not exactly a pleasant topic for the dinner table. Besides, I thought you might be tired."

"A model gets used to travelling. I'd like you to fill me in now."

He shrugged. "All right, Cait, have it your way. I'll level with you. You know your father. There are two ways to do things as far as he is concerned – his way and no way. He has some very old-fashioned ideas about raising beef that cut into his profit margin."

"What sort of ideas?"

"Unlike other ranchers, he refuses to use steroids or other chemicals that speed growth. As a result, Pride steers take too long to reach market weight. The longer we keep them on the ranch, the more money we put out in feed, in salaries, in vet bills. To compensate, Hank spent a small fortune buying bulls to improve the herd. Beefmaster, Limousin, Santa Gertrudis, Brahma, you name the breed and he bought them."

"What's wrong with that?"

"You can run into unexpected trouble, cross-breeding indiscrimately. Take Beefmaster bulls. They throw huge calves. It's damn hard on the cows."

"You make it sound as if even that is my father's fault."

The harsh sound of Comanche's laughter echoed through the room. "That's ridiculous. You know how I feel about Hank – or at least you should. Why do you always have to be so quick to assess blame? The ranch's financial problems aren't anyone's fault. A combination of things went wrong when they could just as easily have gone right. To compound our difficulties, we don't get much more for stockers today than we did twenty years ago. Meanwhile our costs have quadrupled. The bills keep rolling in. The money keeps rolling out. But our biggest problem is that Americans don't consume beef the way they used to. The market is drying up."

"You make it sound hopeless."

"Hopeless is a pretty strong word."

"Dad has asked me to stay on and take over the ranch," Cait announced out of the blue.

Comanche blinked away his surprise. "I guess he took it pretty hard when you refused."

"I didn't refuse."

"What?" He'd expected – no – he'd counted on Cait leaving Pride's Passion again in a day or two. His future depended on it.

"I'm staying," she reiterated as solemnly as a nun taking her vows.

"You don't know anything about running a ranch, Cait. It's a lot harder than posing in front of a camera. It's risky. Dirty. Dangerous. It's – it's man's work," he sputtered ineffectually.

Cait didn't know whether to laugh in his face or punch him squarely on his handsome macho nose. "I realize the Hill Country isn't exactly in the mainstream, but even you must have heard about women's liberation. There are female police officers, airline pilots, truck drivers, and I'm damn sure there are female ranchers!"

Comanche felt like a fool. He knew better than to challenge Cait. He'd gone through childhood double daring her at every turn and she had bested him more times than he cared to remember. But he didn't want her to accept this new challenge to her abilities.

"I'm aware of the women's movement. While you may not believe me, I've never quarrelled with its goals. I even voted for Ann Richards for governor. But you must admit that being a high-priced New York model is as far removed from ranching as you can get."

"If you're trying to make me change my mind, you can forget it. I've already given Hank my word. Other Hill Country ranchers are managing to get by. How are they doing it?"

"You're really serious, aren't you?"

"Dead serious."

What next? he wondered. His senses had been on overload ever since he walked into the room. How could he handle seeing her day after day when just sitting across the table from her made his heart jump in his chest like a bucking horse? Did she know her tailored blouse accented her femininity rather than obscuring it, or that it was all he could do not to stare at the way her breasts thrust against the fabric?

He had never held with the idea that the way a woman

dressed invited a man to assault her, and he would cheerfully have gelded any of the cowardly raping bastards who used their bodies as weapons. But damn! There were times when the way one special woman looked sure made a man yearn to touch her.

He wanted to reach across the table and pull Cait into his arms. He wanted to strip that gorgeous body bare – he wanted to make love to her until she moaned with pleasure. And then, he reminded himself, grateful that the tablecloth hid his arousal, he wanted her to go back to New York.

Cait was uncomfortably aware of Comanche's silent appraisal. His eyes could compel, command or dance with mischief. Now they were gazing at her with a smouldering hunger that evoked a throbbing response deep in her womb. She didn't want to feel that way – not with this man. But, to her everlasting regret, she had never felt that way with any other.

"How long can the ranch survive financially the way things are?" she asked, struggling to maintain her composure.

"That depends on what you mean by survive. Your father's in debt and I don't know how long you can stall the creditors. They sure as hell won't lend more money for a cattle operation."

"What can I do with the land besides raising cattle?"

"There isn't a foolproof recipe for success, Cait. There's always the chance you'll go under no matter how hard you try."

"Just give me some options. I'm perfectly capable of taking it from there," she replied with a certainty she was far from feeling.

"Have you given any thought to dude ranching?"

"That was my first idea. But Dad tells me the Hill Country is already saturated with dude ranches."

"There is another possibility." Comanche pushed his plate away, rocked back in his chair and gazed off into space with carefully calculated indifference. "You could sell to me."

So that's why he came back, Cait thought bitterly. Comanche wanted the ranch for himself. Well, he'd get it over her dead body! God, why couldn't Hank see through him?

"If you're honest with yourself," Comanche continued, "you'll realize it's the best solution. Hank doesn't even need to know." He hadn't meant to make the offer tonight, and certainly not to Cait. He had planned to talk to Hank after she left. But her sudden decision to take over the ranch didn't give him any alternative.

"If things are as bad as you say, why do you want Pride's Passion?"

"My father and grandfather worked this land all their lives. I grew up here. No one knows it the way I do. The place is in my blood."

"That doesn't give you squatter's rights. In case it's slipped your mind, I grew up here too. So did my father, his father and his father's father. This has been Pride land for one hundred and fifty years and I intend to see that it stays that way."

"Be reasonable, Cait. I love this ranch. And I know the cattle business. If anyone can make a success on this land, I can. I want to get married and raise a family here some day."

A cramp ripped through her stomach at the thought of his bringing a bride to Pride's Passion, rearing a bunch of squalling brats on her family's land. "And I suppose you have Miss Right waiting in the wings?"

Comanche cursed himself for a fool. He shouldn't have blurted it out like that. But he did dream of a home and a family, all the things he'd wanted desperately growing up – all the things Cait had taken for granted. He bristled every time he thought about her cavalier attitude towards her birthright. She'd walked out on Hank and the ranch ten years ago and now, on a whim, she'd marched right back.

"No. There isn't anyone waiting in the wings. But what about you? What's the point of saving the ranch if you don't plan to leave it to your heirs?"

Cait couldn't deal with that question – especially not when it was asked by this particular man. Besides, her personal life was just that – *personal*. And James Comanche Killian didn't have any part in it!

"I guess you have your reasons for wanting the place," she said, "but how do you plan to make it profitable?"

"It won't be easy. However I'm in a much better cash position than your father. You may not have heard, but I did quite well on the rodeo circuit. More important, I plan to raise a new type of cattle that could revolutionize the beef industry. A lot of ranchers are trying to produce low-fat beef. I plan to beat them to it."

"My, you are full of yourself, aren't you?"

"It's no idle boast," he said with quiet conviction. "When I was on the rodeo circuit I heard about a breed of cattle in the Mexican interior called criollos. They were supposed to be directly descended from cattle the Spaniards brought to the New World. Criollos thrive on conditions that other stock can't tolerate and they're highly resistant to disease. And here's the clincher. They store fat in their internal organs rather than their flesh. They're cheap to raise, and their meat is lower in cholesterol than turkey."

Cait was beginning to see why he seemed so sure of himself. "If what you say is true, it might be possible to reawaken the public's appetite for beef. But knowing about criollos is a long way from getting a herd to market."

"I don't just know about them, Cait. I went down to Mexico and bought a small herd a couple of years ago. Paid a fortune for them, too. Everything I'd heard about them is true."

Cait square her shoulders and stared at Comanche. He hadn't just grown hair on his chest and bigger muscles. He had grown a brain too. He sounded as knowledgeable and confident as any of the successful entrepreneurs she had met in Manhattan. Perhaps his rare cattle were the way to get the ranch out of the red, Cait thought.

A frisson raced down her spine. She'd be damned if she'd go partners with Comanche, though. If he could buy criollos, so could she. In fact, she'd take particular pleasure in beating him at his own game. "How long would it take to build a big enough herd to get some publicity and make a real impact on the market?"

"Five or six years."

Damn him. He'd been playing with her, building up her hopes only to send them crashing down. "According to Hank, we'll be broke long before then. Do you have any other brilliant ideas?"

Comanche choked down a hostile retort. Although he fervently wished Cait would take the next flight to New York, he couldn't ignore his obligation to Hank Pride. Hank had taken Orry and him in when they were flat broke and so deep in an emotional hole that they didn't know how to crawl out. He couldn't turn his back on Hank now that their roles had been reversed. He had no choice but to help Cait, no matter how her presence troubled him.

"There is another possibility," he said reluctantly.

"Don't keep me in suspense."

"Part of our current income is derived from hunting leases, selling city boys the right to shoot game on Pride land. A lot of local ranchers have taken the hunting thing a step further. They're raising exotic animals from Africa and Asia – sika, mouflon, waterbuck, barasingha, gazelle, oryx, greater kudu and the like."

"Why would they do that? Is there a market for all those animals?"

"Not the way you mean. While it's true that a few restaurants offer exotics on their menus, there's a much better way to make them pay off. Folks have taken to calling the Hill Country "Little Africa" because of what's happened here."

Intrigued, Cait leaned towards him. She had always loved animals and given generously to organizations that were devoted to keeping them in their natural environment. "What has been happening here?"

"There's almost no limit to the amount wealthy hunters will pay to shoot a trophy animal. The going rate for a blackbuck is nine hundred dollars, thirty-five hundred for an oryx. An out-of-town sportsman can collect half a dozen trophy animals in one day and be back in his office the next. And the five hundred plus ranchers who raise them make one hell of a profit."

"Apparently you've forgotten how I feel about hunting," Cait said with ill-disguised fury. The one and only time Comanche had goaded her into testing her markmanship, she'd killed a squirrel with one well-placed shot. When he brought back the bloody trophy, she had rewarded him by throwing up all over his boots.

His eyes locked with hers. "I haven't forgotten anything about you, Cait. I was just trying to be helpful."

Helpful, my ass, she thought. More likely, he was just trying to show her how poorly prepared she was to run the ranch. "I'm not interested in turning the ranch into a glorified slaughterhouse," she said, getting to her feet.

He pushed back his chair and stood too. "Don't get all riled up. It was just a suggestion. But I am serious about buying the place. Think about it Cait, and while you're at it, think about this, too.'

He closed the distance between them in one little stride, pulled her into his arms and planted his lips firmly on hers.

It happened so quickly that it took her a second to react. Then, to her horror, instead of trying to break free, she found herself returning his kiss, opening her mouth and welcoming his tongue, pressing her breasts and thighs against his muscular chest and legs as if she were a bitch in heat. Her nipples hardened, her knees went weak, her skin burned where they touched. She felt as if her entire being was concentrated on their erotic contact.

It took a determined effort to conquer her own tumultuous desire and pull away. Her right arm seemed to rise of its own volition and her hand connected with his face in an audible crack.

Comanche could still feel the imprint of Cait's hand as he walked the couple of hundred yards to the foreman's house. The fire of her kiss burned even more. Although she had stomped out of the dining room in a fit-to-bust fury, he didn't regret what he'd done. He even smiled at the thought of it. Cait Pride hadn't changed as much as she wanted the world – and him in particular – to think.

When he opened the gate in the picket fence surrounding the front yard, a shadowed hulk moved on the front porch and he heard the rhythmic sound of a bushy tail beating against the floorboards. Trouble had been gone all day, undoubtedly romancing the collie bitch on the neighbouring ranch.

"Hope you're doing better in the love department than I am, old boy," Comanche said as Trouble ambled across the yard to greet him.

He was a big dog, part red-bone hound, part St Bernard, with maybe a little lobo thrown in for added character. He had wandered into Comanche's life eight years ago when Comanche found him hanging around the stock pens at the Calgary Stampede, half-starved and looking for a hand-out.

When Comanche had decided to keep the animal – or rather the animal decided to keep him – his friends had predicted the dog would be more trouble than he was worth. The prediction proved wrong. The name stuck. Trouble was both loyal and independent, the ideal companion for a bachelor with the same traits.

Now Trouble followed Comanche into the house, wagging his hindquarters with unbridled pleasure as

Comanche headed for the kitchen. Comanche opened a couple of cans of dog food for Trouble, a beer for himself, then sat down at the kitchen table and watched the dog wolf his supper.

Apparently lust hadn't spoiled Trouble's appetite. He wished he could say the same.

Here he was, ready and willing to commit himself to helping a cantankerous woman who wanted nothing to do with him. Damn fool. He ought to have more sense. Only sense didn't count for much when a man was thinking with the organ between his legs instead of the one in his head.

He took a deep swallow but the icy liquid didn't cool him off. He kept on picturing Cait the way she had looked at the dinner table, her hair tumbled around her shoulders, the firm swell of her breasts pressing against her blouse, her fragrance wafting towards him every time she moved.

She had grown into a stunning woman, a woman who left him weak with wanting. Although she had appeared as polished as a fine gem on those magazine covers, his Katydid hadn't become a citified society lady. She was hellfire and brimstone – funny and bright and bubbling with life – and even more stubborn than he remembered.

He rose, walked into the living room and took his dog-eared copy of the *Complete Works* of Shakespeare from the coffee table. He'd come to love Shakespeare years ago. Now, the well-used volume fell open to Romeo and Juliet's balcony scene.

> Romeo, Romeo, wherefore art thou Romeo?
> Deny thy father and refuse thy name . . .

He closed the book with a thud and dropped it like a hot potato. Hell, even Shakespeare was against him tonight, he thought, grimacing. Romeo and Juliet be damned! He didn't need any romantic notions clouding his judgement when he was already having all the trouble he could handle controlling the sexual ones.

No matter how many men Cait had been with, he was her first. Women don't forget their first.

Men, neither.

But tonight he needed more than memories.

7

Bobby Rae Seeley turned off the shower and blinked a watery haze from her eyes. Still dripping, she stepped out of the tub and grabbed a towel. Then she padded across the floor, wiped the steam off the mirror over the bathroom sink and studied her naked body with a critical eye.

Perhaps her tits weren't as perky as they had been when she was named Tivy High's homecoming queen, but they still looked good enough to win a wet T-shirt contest. Thanks to the eight-hour days she spent on her feet waiting tables at the Hill Country Café, her stomach and thighs were as firm as an athlete's.

Turning around, she gazed over her shoulder. That's a great ass, sugar, she thought with satisfaction. The blonde hair hanging halfway to her waist didn't hurt the total picture either. Most men would jump at the chance to climb in her bed.

But Comanche Killian wasn't most men, she mused ruefully. She'd hankered after him for years. They'd never gone all the way when they dated in high school, and now fate had given her a chance to remedy that situation. When he appeared on her doorstep last night, her hopes had run high.

"Aren't you a sight for sore eyes?" she had said, breathing in the scent of his cologne. "You sure do clean up good."

"You don't look half bad yourself," he replied, right on cue.

She sensed his heart wasn't in the compliment, though. He looked even sadder than the old hound at his heels. She invited the two of them in, settled Trouble in the kitchen with a bowl of water and a steak bone, grabbed a six-pack from the fridge and returned to the living room.

"Make yourself to home," she said, handing Comanche an ice-cold brew.

He settled on the sofa, took a big swallow and stared into the phoney fireplace with its glowing electric log while she moved around the parlour, dimming the lights and turning on her favourite country music station, the one that played lots of Wynona and Clint Black and that darlin' Billy Ray Cyrus. Talk about achy, breaky hearts, hers was fit to bust wide open if Comanche gave her half a chance.

"What brings you into town tonight?" she asked, joining Comanche on the sofa.

"I wanted some company." He gave her a smile so sweet, it reminded her of a field full of wild flowers, he was that pretty.

"You sure came to the right place."

They had a few brews and talked about this and that while she edged closer. When he failed to make his move she made hers, putting her arms around his neck and giving him the sort of open-mouthed kiss that made both of her husbands forget what was on their minds and concentrate on what was on hers.

At first it seemed to be equally effective with Comanche. He pulled her close, his lips parted, and one of his big warm hands began caressing her left breast. It doesn't get much better than this, she thought dreamily, revelling in the feel of his solid male body.

To her consternation he suddenly broke their contact in mid-kiss. "I'm sorry, Bobby Rae," he said, jumping to his feet like a scalded cat. "This just isn't working."

Her inclination was to reply, "speak for yourself." She couldn't have been hotter if she'd just spent the day outdoors tending the grill at a fourth of July barbecue. Comanche's hangdog expression told her he was miles, or in this case several critical inches, from feeling the same way.

"Don't fret, sugar," she said soothingly. "You aren't the only man to have a little problem in the love department from time to time."

Seeing Comanche turn beet red, she was sure she had identified the source of his consternation. Thinking he was just tired and would prove more capable in the morning, she had insisted he spend the night and offered to share her bed.

At his refusal she had bustled around making up a bed on the sofa, acting all sweet and sympathetic even though she felt fit to burst with disappointment. As far as she knew, the big lummox was still snoozing in her parlour.

She tiptoed from the bathroom to her bedroom door, cracked it open and peaked out. Comanche lay curled on his side, his eyes closed, his long legs bent at the knees, his ankles and feet hanging over the edge of the upholstery. Lord, please let him sleep in the altogether, she silently implored, shutting the door again. If she played her cards right, he wouldn't be able to resist her this morning.

She opened the drawer in the night table, took out a package of condoms, the ones that tasted like peppermint, and set them down on her pillow. Humming softly, she picked up a bottle of perfume from her dressing table and annointed her cleavage, her neck, her wrists and the juncture of her thighs.

Then she put on her make-up, a fifteen-minute process that included applying false eyelashes her girlfriends swore looked real as can be. Next she pulled on a lacy black garter belt, a pair of thigh-high black stockings with seams up the back, and stiletto heels with rhinestones on the toes. Satisfied no red-blooded man could resist her, she reopened the door to the living room, making considerably more noise this time.

The sound woke Comanche. He opened his eyes and gazed around, not recognizing the parlour with its flowery chintz upholstery and fussy, knick-knack-laden tables. A couple of times after celebrating a win too vigorously on the rodeo circuit, he had wakened in a strange bed wondering where he was. This morning Bobby Rae Seeley solved the mystery by undulating into view wearing even less than a dancer in one of those titty bars. The sight jolted him wide awake.

"What the hell?" he said in a strangled voice.

He recalled arriving on her doorstep last night, hoping for sympathy and a warm bed. He'd got both. Now Bobby Rae was obviously looking for him to make good on his end of the deal.

"That's one hell of an outfit," he said, blushing from jaw to hairline as he sat bolt upright, "but you're wasting it on me."

"Let me be the judge of that."

Bobby Rae vamped across the floor with the hip-swinging walk that made her the toast of the Hill Country Café, and didn't stop until her enticing pubic mound was just inches from his face. Good Lord! He'd never known she was a natural blonde!

"I know you weren't in the mood last night. But I thought after a good rest . . .' She bent over and planted a kiss on top of his head, her bare breasts swinging just inches from his mouth.

Groaning out loud, he leaned back until the sofa prevented further escape. Then he tore the bed sheet from his body and held it out to Bobby Rae. "You better put this on."

Her eyes widened in surprise. "Are you sure? I could call in sick if . . ."

"I'm sure!" he declared miserably. Apparently his body had decided it wanted nothing to do with sex before his conscious mind agreed to go along with the plan. He could no more have made love to Bobby Rae than he could willingly put down a perfectly healthy horse.

"It's nothing to do with you, Bobby Rae. I know a dozen men who would kill to be in my place."

"Then what's the matter?" Bobby Rae's mouth pursed with disappointment as she plopped onto the sofa by his side.

"Oh, hell, Bobby Rae," he muttered, averting his eyes from where the tops of her breasts showed invitingly above the sheet. Bobby Rae had great breasts, but right now he just felt embarrassed, seeing so much of them. "I can't talk unless you cover yourself up better."

He waited until she was more modestly swathed before going on. "When you kissed me last night – and believe me, you're one hell of a good kisser – I realized I couldn't make love to you."

"That doesn't make sense."

"Like I said, it's nothing to do with you, honey. It's me. I've got some problems."

Bobby Rae's big blue eyes widened even more. "Since when did problems stop a man from having a little fun?"

"It may not stop other man, but it stopped me."

First he couldn't eat and now he couldn't perform. What other tortures would his dismay over Cait's return consign him to, he wearily wondered.

"Is Hank worse?" Bobby Rae asked.

"Not that I know."

"Then what's the matter? Jeez, Comanche, it's not like we've got any secrets from each other. We've practically known each other since we were potty-trained. I walked in here half-naked and I can see everything the good Lord gave you through your briefs. If ever there was a time when a man ought to level, this is it."

"It's Cait."

"Cait? What does she have to do with it?"

"Hank asked her to come back and take over the ranch."

"So?"

"So – she agreed."

"You're funning me!"

"I wish I was. You know how much I wanted that ranch."

"I still don't see why you're so het up, sugar. There are plenty of other spreads to choose from. Besides, the Pride place has never even been for sale."

"I know. But I didn't grow up on another spread. I grew up on Pride's Passion. My father and his father worked there. Sixty years of their blood, sweat, and tears went into that land. Damn it, Bobby Rae, I want that place bad, it hurts. I want everyone in the Hill Country to know that Killians count for something."

"That's your pride talking, sugar. You're a respected man now, not a poor boy whose mother ran off. You don't need that ranch, Comanche. Don't you realize you've already proven that you're nothing like your parents?"

He rubbed his brow pensively. "Is that what you think I'm trying to do?"

"If ever there was an overachiever, you're it. How many boys at Tivy High were captain of the football team, homecoming king and class valedictorian?" She didn't wait for his answer. "Just one, sugar, and he's sitting right in front of me looking sadder than his old hound."

She got to her feet, a move which caused the sheet to droop intriguingly. But Comanche wasn't intriguable, more's the pity, she realized. She crossed the floor to her bedroom and paused in the door. "I guess I might as well get dressed."

"I'm sorry. Maybe one of these days . . ."

"Sure hon', one of these days. I just want you to know there aren't any hard feelings." She giggled naughtily. "Maybe I shouldn't use the word, 'hard', at a time like this. You're the best in my book."

"Thanks. I can use all the friends I can get right now."

Bobby Rae shut the door behind herself, dropped the sheet and took one last look in the mirror over her dresser. Her body, all female curves and enticing shadows, gleamed in the early morning light. She looked damn good if she had to say so herself. The mirror reassured her that despite her twenty-eight years, she was still the sexiest thing in Kerr County. And she had brains, too, even if most men never noticed.

Comanche waited until Bobby Rae shut the bedroom door before getting up. His legs were cramped from spending the night on the sofa, he needed a shave and his mouth tasted of last night's beer. Even worse, he felt like the world's biggest fool.

He should have slept at his own place. But he couldn't bear the thought of being that close to Cait. He knew he'd just spend the night out on his front porch, swinging back and forth on the glider and gazing up at her window, wondering what to do about the problem she presented – imagining her all warm and sweet-smelling in her bed – and wishing she had never walked back into his life.

Staying at Bobby Rae's had seemed like the lesser of two evils. But he hadn't meant to lead Bobby Rae on. He hadn't made love with a woman in months and, considering his sorry performance last night and then again this morning, it looked like his hand was going to be his best friend from now on.

Grimacing at the thought, he pulled on yesterday's shirt and trousers, released Trouble from confinement in the kitchen, set a pot of coffee to perking on the stove and then took the dog outdoors to do his business.

When he returned to Bobby Rae's living room, she was sitting on one of the chintz-covered chairs, dressed in the mini-skirted uniform she wore to work. "Thanks for the coffee," she said, saluting him with her cup.

"I'm the one who should be thanking you. I shouldn't have taken advantage of our friendship last night."

Bobby Rae winked at him. "You can take advantage of me anytime you have a mind."

"Thanks for trying to make it easy on me. I feel like a heel just the same."

"Oh, come on, don't go getting all syrupy sweet on me. I like my men with a little spice." She put her cup down, walked over and kissed him on the cheek. "See you at the café. Breakfast's on me."

After she was gone, Comanche continued to sit on the sofa, too bewildered to move a muscle, nailed in place by the eternal, unfathomable mystery of women. Men had learned to split the atom, to harness the power of the universe, but he doubted they'd ever really know what went on in a woman's mind.

Cait had so little sleep she expected to be bone tired when she came wide awake before dawn. But she felt as energized as she used to on the first day of summer vacation when she was a kid – and as excited. Despite the things she had said to her father when she returned yesterday, she hadn't been sure of her ability to take the reins of the ranch into her own hands. Her insecurity had been strengthened by Comanche's gloomy assessment of the problems she faced.

She had mulled over the information he had given her, turning the problem of Pride's Passion around and around in her mind so she could examine the possibilities from every angle. The solution, an answer so perfect, so suited to her personal preferences that she was chomping at the bit to do more than just think about it, had come to her in the small hours of the morning.

Fifteen minutes later, her hair still damp from the shower, she hurried into the kitchen.

Delta was already at the table having a cup of coffee. "My, aren't you the early bird," she said, getting to her feet. "Can I fix you some breakfast?"

Cait walked behind Delta's chair and gently pushed her back down into it. "I don't want you waiting on me. I'm not company. I live here now."

Delta turned and gave her a big, shiny, new day smile. "Hank's so happy. He says he feels much better. Why, he was even talking about going for a drive later. I don't know how to thank you. You've given him a new lease on life, *cher*."

Near tears, Cait walked over to the stove and busied herself pouring coffee. Strange. Delta sounded more like a wife than an employee. Hank and Delta were close, but she had never wondered how close before. And she shouldn't now, she cautioned herself, not when she had so many other things on her mind.

"Hank may not be so pleased when I tell him my plan for the ranch," she said, carrying her cup to the table and taking the chair opposite the housekeeper.

She quickly outlined her idea, the words spilling out with breathless haste. "Well, what do you think?" she asked when she was done.

"I'm no expert when it comes to the ranch. But I am when it comes to your father. He's been through a lot. I wouldn't want him to go through anything more, needlessly. So before you go getting his hopes too high, you had better talk to Comanche."

"I'm perfectly capable of making this decision without consulting him," Cait hotly declared.

"Everyone needs help along the way, Cait – even a Pride. I know you and Comanche had problems in the past but you're too old to get in a fuss with each other now. He's a fine man with a good head on his shoulders. Folks around here respect him. If you're serious, you're going to need his connections, his know-how."

Cait sighed. The idea of consulting Comanche chapped her. However, she didn't seem to have any choice. "All right, all right. You win. I'll talk to Comanche before I talk to Dad. What time does he usually come in for breakfast?"

"I'm not expecting him this morning, *cher*. I heard him drive off last night and his truck isn't in front of the foreman's house."

Cait knew it wasn't reasonable, but she couldn't control her angry response. "Does he leave you and Dad alone often?" she demanded.

"*Cher*, he's the foreman, not a baby-sitter. He's entitled to his own life. He has breakfast at the Hill Country Café over to Kerrville once or twice a week."

"I'll drive into town, then."

"If you take my advice, you'll let the man have his breakfast in peace and talk to him later."

Cait pushed her chair back and got to her feet. She had no intention of letting Comanche have a peaceful breakfast. Everyone kept on telling her how wonderful, how knowledgeable he was.

This morning he'd have the opportunity to prove it.

In its one hundred and sixty years, Kerrville had attracted a variety of characters – shingle makers who were drawn by the local cedars, rustlers who ran wild during the lawless period around the Civil War, consumptives who'd heard it was a healthy place to live, and finally, tourists and retirees. Their numbers had brought prosperity to the old county seat.

Although it had grown since Cait left, at heart it remained a small town where everyone knew everyone else. Her return was bound to cause speculation, she thought as she struggled to ease the oversized Suburban into a parking space across from the Hill Country Café. She should have listened to Delta. The last thing she wanted was to give Comanche or the locals the impression she had tracked him down.

She frowned at her own perfectly groomed reflection in the Suburban's rear-view mirror, then slid from the high front seat and walked across the street to the café. The minute she opened the door she realized how overdressed she must look, even though she was wearing a simple Nicole Miller linen sheath and flats.

With its scarred wooden tables, mismatched plastic-covered chairs and patrons dressed in jeans, boots, and peaked caps with labels that read John Deere or Kerrville Feed and Seed sewn on the brims, the Hill Country Café was a down-home sort of place. Her breath caught in her throat when she spied Comanche at the far end of the restaurant. His back was towards the door – and he wasn't alone.

Cait recognized his companion at once. Bobby Rae Seeley, former homecoming queen and head cheerleader, the girl voted most popular, most likely to succeed and the cause of more wet dreams among Tivy High's male populace than any other coed before or since, was sitting across from Comanche, laughing at something he had said.

Cait had gone to school with Bobby Rae until Hank sent Cait off to Kinkaid. She had always liked and admired Bobby Rae, and not just because of her looks. Bobby Rae had never called her Blubber Lips or Bean Pole the way the other kids did. Instead, she had gone out of her way to be nice, even inviting Cait to a movie a couple of times. But all the warm feelings Cait used to have for her evaporated as she realized Bobby Rae had to be the woman Comanche was talking about when he said he hoped to marry some day.

Cait stood rooted in the entry, cursing herself for driving into town so precipitously, while Bobby Rae poured sugar in Comanche's coffee cup and then stirred it with her index finger. Either the coffee wasn't hot, or Bobby Rae was even hotter. Cait suspected the latter. She could almost see the sexual heat vaporizing the air around her former classmate. Ignoring the jealousy that spiked through her, she squared her shoulders and began threading her way past the crowded tables.

Bobby Rae looked up to see a woman silhouetted in the doorway. A quick appraisal told Bobby Rae she wasn't a local – not in that uptown outfit. Tourists seldom wandered into the café. Who can she be? Bobby

Rae wondered. She continued staring as the stranger drew closer.

Good heavens, it's Cait Pride, she realized. The café was the last place Bobby Rae expected to see her famous former classmate. There had been lots of mean-spirited gossip about Cait every time one of the tabloids reporter her on-again, off-again romances. Although Cait seemed to collect engagement rings the way other women collected eye shadow, she didn't look any the worse for wear. In fact, she looked so glamorous that she made Bobby Rae feel hand-me-down by contrast.

"Speak of the devil," Bobby Rae said, "Cait Pride just walked in."

Comanche put his cup down so forcefully that the coffee spilled. "You're kidding!"

"She's headed our way, sugar."

His brows lifted, and a lopsided grin skittered across his face. He managed to look both confused and delighted, like a newborn calf who finally finds a teat and doesn't quite know what to do with it.

Bobby Rae sighed. Comanche had sounded none too happy when he told her Cait was back. But a man didn't look the way he did right now unless he had a special feeling for a woman. Intuition told her he was more involved with Cait than he cared to admit.

Ignoring a stab of envy, she waved at Cait. "Come on over and take a load off, stranger."

"It's nice to see you again, Bobby Rae," Cait said, reaching the table.

Comanche jumped to his feet so abruptly that his chair fell over backwards. "Is something the matter with Hank?" he asked anxiously.

Cait looked Comanche up and down disdainfully. He was wearing the clothes he had worn to dinner yesterday. They weren't bandbox fresh any more. He needed a shave, too. He had obviously spent the night with Bobby Rae and didn't care who knew it. "Hank was all right when I left."

"I wasn't expecting you to – I just thought – I—' Comanche's voice stuttered to a half as he righted his chair.

"Well, isn't this like old times," Bobby Rae said into the awkward silence. "Comanche and I were just talking about that time in the sixth grade when he put a toad in Miss Barnaby's desk. You were there, weren't you, Cait?"

Neither Cait or Comanche seemed to hear a word she said.

"What are you doing here?" Comanche demanded of Cait.

"What are *you* doing here?" Cait shot back.

Hell, Bobby Rae thought. The party, or at least her share of it, was definitely over. "I've got to get back to work," she said. "Can I get you two some menus?"

"Just coffee," Comanche replied.

"I'll have the same," Cait echoed, sliding into the seat Bobby Rae had just vacated.

She felt uncomfortable, even angry, at catching Comanche with Bobby Rae. Things must have changed in Kerrville a lot for the two of them to flaunt their affair so openly.

"I reckon you didn't drive all the way into town for the pleasure of my company," Comanche said, giving her that glorious cover-boy smile that displayed his square white teeth to their best advantage.

"Of course, he was wasting the effort, she told herself, ignoring the tiny shiver that raced down her spine.

"I wouldn't be here at all if Delta hadn't insisted I talk to you." Cait paused, wondering if she would ever get used to sitting so close to Comanche – if her heart would ever beat normally when she was with him. Damn her traitorous body.

She took a deep breath, then plunged ahead. "I've come up with a plan, a new direction for the ranch. I want to raise exotic animals – but not just any exotics. I want to concentrate on threatened and endangered species, to turn Pride's Passion into a hybrid between a zoo and a resort."

She was watching Comanche carefully, studying his face for any sign of disapproval. If he had laughed, frowned, indicated by so much as a twitch of an eyebrow that he didn't think much of her idea, she would have walked out on him then and there. But he did none of those things.

"Go on," he said.

"Last night you told me sportsmen were willing to pay a fortune to shoot a trophy animal without having to take the time and trouble of going to Africa. However, most of the people who go to Africa aren't hunters these days. They're environmental tourists, wildlife enthusiasts armed with nothing more than a camera. I was up half the night thinking about it and I don't see why we can't duplicate an African photographic safari on the ranch. We have the climate and we have the land."

"You've always been overly sentimental about animals. No one objected when you insisted on bringing every last motherless creature home when you were a kid. But you're not a kid any more. This is a high stakes game, Cait." Comanche shifted to the edge of his chair, and leaned towards her. "If you're talking about a glorified animal park, other people have tried it and failed."

"I thought that's what you'd say. After all, you want the ranch yourself."

He leaned even closer, his body language so intimidating that she had to keep herself from shrinking back. "It's not a question of what I do or don't want. I know you find it hard to understand that duty and obligation matter to me. But I owe your father."

She hadn't intended to do more than sketch her idea for Comanche. Now she was determined to convince him that she knew whereof she spoke. "Will you please just shut up and give me a chance to explain before you come to any conclusions? I'm not interested in running an outdoor zoo for nickel and dime tourists because I know it won't save the ranch. I'm planning to do something far more glamorous and exciting. I want to create the sort of place my friends would patronize. They're always on the lookout for something new and different. My idea is to create a cross between a world class resort and a haven for endangered species. Jim Foley once told me the only way to save animals was to turn them into a paying proposition. And I can do it, Comanche. I know I can. I'm convinced Pride's Outback will work."

"Pride's Outback?"

"That's what I plan to call it. Don't you see, the ranch gives me a chance to do something about the environment, about the way species are disappearing." She hadn't started out to give a speech. Now she couldn't seem to stop. "I met Richard Leakey at a fund raiser in New York last year and he told me Kenya had 140,000 elephants and 60,000 black rhinoceros a decade ago. There are damn few left, but poachers continue to slaughter them, along with cheetahs, leopards and lions. Certain species of zebra and giraffe are threatened, too. And that's just the tip of the iceberg. By the time mankind catches on to the fact that we need the animals, that our own survival as a species may depend on our ability to coexist with them, it may be too late. I'm convinced that by saving them, we may be saving ourselves."

She paused to judge the effect of her words. Was he genuinely interested, or was he just giving her a chance to make a fool of herself? He continued to stare at her as if she were some damn specimen under a microscope.

"What about the cattle? Your father won't let go of his prize bulls easily, not to mention the longhorns who are descended from Patrick Pride's original herd, and I'm running my criollos on land I lease from you."

"That's the beauty of it," she replied, having anticipated the question. "We have enough land to do both if we sell off the stockers. The safari operation will support the purebred cattle. And there will still be room for your criollos. We can even feature their meat on our menus. Well, what do you think?"

"It's an ambitious, expensive plan."

"Don't keep me in suspense, hotshot. Either you're with me – or against me."

He gazed at her bleakly, weighing his choices, and picked the lesser of two evils. I'm with you," he said, "but if you fail I give you fair warning. I intend to be around to pick up the pieces."

8

Business at the Hill Country Café had reached its morning peak. But Cait paid no attention to the hubbub. She gazed at Comanche unhappily. "I'll be damned if I want to spend my time wondering if you're trying to sabotage the Outback."

His jaw firmed and his glance turned steely. "I said I'd help you and that ought to be good enough."

A flush heated her cheeks. She wanted to say she already knew how little his word meant, but she repressed the angry retort. Like it or not, she was stuck with Comanche until she could convince Hank they needed to replace him. "Look, you might as well head on back to the ranch. I have something to do in town."

"Can I help? Do you need directions to wherever you're going?"

He looked far too smug and self-confident to suit her. She would enjoy taking him down a peg or two at the first opportunity. "I won't have any trouble finding City Hall."

"City Hall?"

"I thought I'd stop by planning and zoning to see what sort of permits I'll need for the Outback."

Comanche's insolent grin had returned. "This isn't New York, honey. It's Texas."

"What does that have to do with it?"

"You don't need to fuss with all that paperwork. In Texas, a man's home is still his castle. Besides, Pride's Passion isn't in the city. It's in the county. If you're bound and determined to waste time, we can stop by the county clerk's office."

In view of Comanche's already superior attitude, she could have kicked herself for forgetting. "We? Aren't you needed at the ranch?"

He gave her that damn smile again. "The hands know what they're supposed to do. Besides, you may not realize it, but you need my help a lot more."

Half an hour later, having studied the microfiche copies of the documents that recorded ownership of Pride's Passion, she realized Comanche had been right. The title went all the way back to a land grant. There were no deed restrictions, no rules or regulations to prohibit using the land in any way the Prides saw fit. The ranch was an anachronism, a kingdom subject only to state law.

"I guess that's that," she said, scrolling the microfiche tape back to its original position. "We're home free."

To her consternation, Comanche's smile deepened. "Lady, you haven't even hit the ball yet. The game is just beginning."

He backed his words up with action hustling her out of the building while talking about an itinerary that would immediately immerse her in the esoteric world of exotic animal ranching.

They spent the day touring huge operations like the historic YO ranch with its dazzling variety of creatures – ten thousand animals from every corner of the globe – and smaller spreads that concentrated on a single species, talking to owners who seemed eager to tell of their experiences with exotics. She learned there were more bushbuck in the Hill Country than in their native India, that some growers regarded ostriches as feathered gold mines because their meat, hide and featthers brought top dollars.

Several ranchers warned of the fragility of exotics, their low tolerance for stress, the fact that some of them were so high-strung that they could literally be frightened to death. Others spoke of losses to disease, to coyotes and to accidents. One of them told her that so many fallow and axis deer had escaped from exotic ranches that they were considered a nuisance by cattle growers.

"I spend a small fortune on my fences but my neighbour is still on my case. You don't know what you're getting into, Miss Caitlin," he warned, looking at her as if she was one card shy of a full deck.

"Then why did you go into exotics?" she shot back.

"For the money," he replied just as quickly. "But I doubt you'll make a penny with what you've got planned."

As they drove away from his ranch, Cait turned to Comanche angrily. "If this is your way of telling me that the Outback doesn't stand a chance, I don't appreciate it."

"Damn it, Cait, I'm only going to say this one more time. I told you I'd help any way I could. And whether you believe it or not, my word is my bond. So quit thinking of me as the enemy. You needed to know what you're up against."

After an exhausting ten-hour day that left her longing for a hot bath and a change of clothes, Comanche insisted on driving to the YO Hilton in Kerrville to have dinner with Garner Holland, a man who had been importing and selling exotics for years.

The spacious lobby, decorated with an impressive display of the taxidermist's art, offered further proof of how important hunting exotics had become to the Hill Country economy. Holland was already at a table in the restaurant when they arrived. An unprepossessing individual in his mid-forties, he was the sort of man you would never notice unless you looked in his eyes. They burned with a fanatic light. Comanche had told her exotics were Holland's passion, and that no one knew more about them.

After the introductions and ordering their meals had

been attended to, Cait wasted no time telling Holland what she hoped to do, painting a word picture of Pride's Outback complete with luxurious accommodation for tourists and enough threatened and endangered species to make a zoo proud.

While she spoke he became increasingly agitated, drumming his fingers on the table, folding and unfolding his napkin, his strange eyes burning even brighter. "I've dreamed of having my own safari ranch since my first buying trip to Africa years ago," he burst out when she finished.

"Then why didn't you start one?" she demanded, half expecting him to add to the horror stories she had already heard that day.

He shifted in his chair, lowering his voice and his gaze. "It would take millions of dollars and thousands of acres. I'm not a rich man, Miss Pride, and I don't own a ranch." He paused and studied her, seeming to take her measure, the fire in his eyes burning brighter. "From what I know of Pride's Passion, you have all the land you could possibly need. If you're really serious, I'd consider it an honour to help you with the rest."

"I'm serious, Mr Holland."

He began pouring out information, telling her where and how to buy animals, the difficulties inherent in their care, how much land and what sort of habitat individual species required, cramming so much of his hard-won knowledge into the next ten minutes that she couldn't possibly absorb it all.

"Slow down," Comanche said when he finally stopped for breath. "This is all new to Cait."

"My apologies, ma'am," Holland replied. "I'm afraid I get carried away when I talk about exotics."

Moments later, though, he was talking just as fast. He told her about the wildlife auctions held in the Hill Country every year, took a *Houston Chronicle* classified page from his battered briefcase and showed her ads offering lions, tigers, emus, ostriches and even a giraffe for sale locally.

He rattled off figures in a mind-boggling flurry, then ticked off the things a safari ranch required – huge enclosures surrounded by specialized high fencing, holding pens where new arrivals could recover from the stress of shipping while becoming acclimatized to their new environment, a full-time veterinarian and a well-equipped hospital with a nursery. He told her that animals who coexisted peacefully on the African plains would become uneasy neighbours if they felt crowded and that zebras were especially aggressive. Rather than limiting the Outback to endangered or threatened species, he suggested she include animals who shared habitats in the wild.

Exhilarated by finally meeting someone who shared her enthusiasm for the project, Cait found herself elaborating on her original concept, coming up with plans for wildlife workshops for commercial photographers and artists, a summer camp for underprivileged children and seminars with experts like Richard Leakey, Desmond Morris and Jane Goodall as guest lecturers.

Comanche suggested she add a special area for species that were on the threatened list in Texas, and that she consider offering more traditional ranch activities as well – trail rides, chuck wagon cook-outs – in the section of the Outback that would continue as a cattle operation.

By the time Comanche asked for their check, Cait no longer thought of Garner Holland as an eccentric. Instead he seemed like the answer to her most pressing problem, the need to find an employee who would match her dedication to the Outback and who she could trust completely. "How would you like to run the Outback?" she asked impulsively.

Holland's gaze plummeted to his scuffed boots' tops. "I know animals, but you've probably figured out I'm not very good with people. I'd be happy to help behind the scenes, but you need a front man who knows exotics as well as Comanche knows cattle, and who can handle people too."

Cait thought for a moment. "What about a zoo director?"

He shook his head. "If you really want to duplicate the safari experience, what you need is a white hunter."

"A white hunter? How in the world am I going to find a white hunter in the middle of Texas?"

"You might try advertising for one," Comanche replied laconically, taking her by the elbow and easing her towards the door.

It was a perfect starlit night as they drove through town past the new mall on Sidney Baker. Instead of heading back to the Hill Country Café so he could retrieve his own truck, Comanche surprised Cait by pulling into the little park that overlooked the Guadalupe. Teenagers used to make out there when Cait and Comanche were kids.

All Cait's senses became instantly alert. "What do you think you're doing?" she demanded.

"We need to talk," he said.

Cait moved as far away from him as she could get. "We've spent the whole day talking."

She gazed across the front seat at him, wondering what game he was playing now. She didn't trust him at all. It made her even angrier to admit she didn't trust herself either. She'd given in to his sexual appeal once, to her eternal regret. She couldn't let that happen again.

"Like it or not, Cait, we're stuck with one another," he said. "I know you're not happy about it and I thought we ought to clear the air."

"Consider it cleared." She fumbled in her purse for a cigarette. "Now if you don't mind, I'd like to go home."

Before she could object, he took the unlit cigarette from her hand and tossed it out the window. "They aren't good for you."

"Since when do you care about what's good for me? You were always pushing me when we were kids, daring me to do things that any fool would have known were dangerous."

"That's just what I mean about clearing the air," he said. "You're still angry at me for things that happened years ago. I'm perfectly willing to let bygones be bygones. Why aren't you?"

Ten years of remorse welled in her chest. Her eyes burned with unshed tears. "All right. Since you seem so damned determined to clear the air I'll play along. This morning you said you were a man of your word. But you broke your word to me years ago. You were going to stay in touch when you went to college. Damn it, we had plans. In case you never figured it out, I had a terrific crush on you when we were kids. I did all those crazy things because I was too homely to get your attention any other way. The night before you left for college I even let you make love to me. But it didn't mean a damn thing to you, did it?"

"Hold on. First off, I didn't make love to you. The way I recall, we made love to each other. And if it makes you feel any better, I was half in love with you too."

"So what went wrong?" Her body was rigid with tension and she could feel a tiny nerve pulsing under one eye. "Well?" she prodded. When he continued to sit quietly, she answered herself. "Oh hell, I know what went wrong. You went off to college and fell in love with someone else faster than dogs get fleas."

"It wasn't like you think. I've waited ten years to tell you the truth. The least you can do is hear me out. My father followed me to the river that night. He saw us together."

"Oh, my God," Cait moaned. "What did he say?"

"Plenty. On our way to the airport the next morning we had our first and last father-son talk." As he spoke, Comanche closed his eyes and let memory take him back in time to what had been one of the most miserable days in his life.

He had a vivid image of Orry sitting behind the wheel of his rattle-trap truck, looking decidedly uncomfortable in his only suit. "This is a red letter day," Orry was saying, shifting his chewing tobacco from one side of his mouth to the other. "I never thought any son of mine would get a college scholarship. I just wish your mother . . ." Cracking with emotion, Orry's voice came to a halt.

Comanche knew that time had suffused Orry's memories of his wife in a golden glow. According to Orry, she had been an Indian princess whose problems stemmed from the fact that people treated her badly. Time, however, hadn't distorted Comanche's recollection. He couldn't think of his mother without shame. A few faded photographs attested to her loveliness. The princess part was pure bull.

He had inherited her high cheekbones and jet black hair, and had spent his childhood worrying that he might also have inherited some of her less admirable traits. Despite being a descendant of the great Comanche chief, Quanah Parker, she had been a faithless, falling-down drunk who ran off with another man after Orry hurt his back and couldn't rodeo any more.

"Like I said," Orry's voice broke into Comanche's troubled thoughts, "you done good. The problem is you've been doing some bad, too. I was awake when you left the bunkhouse last night. I thought I'd enjoy a little fresh air myself, so I followed you." Orry's Adam's apple bobbed up and down as he cleared his throat. "I watched you and Miss Caitlin down by the river."

Comanche reddened. The realization that his father had spied on them mortified him.

Orry's voice was surprisingly gentle as he continued. "I don't blame you, son. I was young and full of juice once too, so I know what I'm asking you to give up."

A sense of foreboding rippled through Comanche like

an autumn wind in an aspen grove. He wished he could put his hands over his ears and refuse to listen, the way he used to when his parents argued. "I don't know what you're talking about," he protested.

"You got to stop this thing with Miss Caitlin before her father finds out. Hank Pride is a hard man. He won't take it kindly if he learns you've been humping his little girl."

Orry's vulgarity filled Comanche with rage. "You don't understand. What you saw last night, well, it was the first time. I wouldn't do anything to hurt Cait – or Hank, either. It just happened. But now that it has, she means a lot to me."

"Seein' as how I only got a third-grade education, I reckon you don't hold my opinion too high. But you cain't learn everything there is to know from some damn book. You've got to have a little common sense too. And mine tells me Hank Pride will run us both off if he finds out what's happened."

Comanche had grown up knowing Killians didn't count for much in the Hill Country and had worked hard at overcoming that reputation. Now, however, he saw himself through the eyes of a successful rancher like Hank Pride, and didn't like what he saw.

He was a nothing, a nobody, the son of a hired hand with the taint of his mother's wild Comanche blood in his veins. The taste of misery was caustic in his mouth as he faced the truth. He had no right to a girl like Cait, no right at all, any more than he had a right to endanger his father's job.

Now, sitting in the Suburban, he still felt the pain of that revelation. He had spent the last ten years trying to prove himself worthy. "Before I got on the plane that day, I promised Orry I'd break up with you. That's why I wrote to tell you I had fallen in love with someone else. And it worked out for the best, didn't it? You went off to New York and became a famous model. You've had a wonderful life."

Cait had forced herself to listen without interrupting. The fury that had been building throughout his recital burst from her throat in a torrent of angry words. "A wonderful life? Is that what you think I had? Damn you to hell, Comanche. What I had was an abortion."

His complexion greyed under his tan. Shock and disapproval were evident on his face. "My God. Why didn't you tell me you were pregnant?"

"By the time I was certain, I'd already got your letter."

"But an abortion . . ."

"Don't you *dare* judge me. I was eighteen years old, alone in a strange city, and Hank wouldn't take my calls or answer my letters. So I turned to my boss, Mims Pauling, for help. Afterwards I felt so guilty, so desperate to prove I was worthy of being loved that I went to bed with any man who asked. Hell, they didn't even have to ask. All they had to do was buy me a drink, give me a smile, crook a finger. But sex didn't take away the pain. It just anaesthetized me for an hour or two. You see, the more I slept around, the more I hated myself. You may call that a wonderful life but it felt like hell to me."

"Oh, God, Cait, I'm so sorry. My only excuse is I thought our breaking up was for the best."

"Whose best? Maybe yours and Orry's. Not mine. If it hadn't been for Mims, I don't know how I would have ended up. She arranged for the abortion and pulled me through that first year."

Cait was shaking so hard, she felt as if she was going to shatter into a thousand little pieces. Gazing across the front seat at Comanche, she realized he didn't look much better. His shoulders were hunched, his complexion pale and his fists were clenched. He seemed unaware of the low groan that rumbled up from deep in his chest. When his eyes finally met hers, they were dull with pain.

"I'd give anything if I could change what happened," he said. "I never meant to hurt you. I wish I could find the words to tell you how sorry I am, but I've never been much good with words. If I had known . . ." He gazed straight ahead, his features frozen in an expression of infinite regret.

There was no denying his sincerity, although, God knew, she would have liked to. She had despised Comanche for ten years and had grown comfortable with the feeling. It had helped to fill the emptiness inside her. Now, knowing the truth, she couldn't blame the boy Comanche had been, a boy driven by forces beyond his control.

She drew in a deep breath as her anger slowly seeped away, leaving a hollow ache where all that ugliness had dwelled. Deep inside, she might still rail at the cosmic bullet that had shattered their relationship. But the long open wound had already begun to scab over.

She gazed at him, trying to see him the way a stranger would, someone who didn't share twenty years of sorry history. Of course, his looks were the first thing any red-blooded woman would notice. Denying his potent sex appeal would be akin to pretending the sun didn't come up every morning when all any damn fool had to do was go out and look for themselves.

Even more striking was the aura of strength he projected. He'd offered her that strength when he offered his help. She felt a great deal easier about accepting it now.

"I'm glad you told me about Orry. You were right about clearing the air," she said. "It's time we stopped locking horns and started working together."

Cait's forgiveness came as balm to Comanche's wounded soul. He'd been horrified to hear of the price she'd paid for their one night of passion. The trouble was that in the primitive part of his psyche, the part where his "me Tarzan, you Jane" masculinity dwelled, he wanted more than her forgiveness.

He wanted her.

Cait's first ten days at home had been so crammed with

activity, she'd had no time to catch her breath and reflect on everything that had happened. She'd spent hours with Garner Holland trying to absorb his knowledge, had met and talked to all the hands about the ranch's future, had gone through the house with Delta to evaluate its potential as the centrepiece of the Outback and had spent evenings with Hank refining her plans.

But the time she'd spent with Comanche dominated her thoughts as she turned the Suburban onto the Interstate. She was determined to use the five-hour drive to Avery's Houston house to put things in perspective.

Working with Comanche, coming up with a budget, a business plan and finally a prospectus had made her acutely aware of his mental acuity. They'd spent hours sitting side by side in front of the word processor in his office. His physical appeal had proven even more potent when he was so close that she drew in his scent with every breath.

Looking back, she realized how thoroughly he had insinuated himself into her new life. Only her determination to keep their relationship on a businesslike level had kept her from asking if the dinner invitation was still open.

She had seized the chance to go to Houston, to raise the capital she needed for the Outback, like a prisoner grabbing for a reprieve. And yet, as the miles unravelled, there was no reprieve from her thoughts.

Comanche intruded on every one of them.

To her dismay she wasn't able to concentrate on anything else until she saw the freeway exit Avery Morgan had told her to take. She drove south on Durham past the ugly warehouses and strip mills near the interstate, watching the neighbourhood become increasingly gentrified as she approached River Oaks.

Every city has a wealthy ghetto where the haves seclude themselves from the have nots. Fuelled by oil money, Houston did it better than most. River Oaks was an elegant example of conspicuous consumption practised as an art form. The vast lawns were as carefully manicured as golf greens – the trees, shrubs and flowers so perfectly maintained that they owed their beauty to man more than nature.

But it was the houses that gave the area its greatest claim to fame. They were a fantastic melange of every conceivable style. And all of them trumpeted, money, money, MONEY. As Cait drove along River Oaks Boulevard, she had the feeling she had come to the right place. People didn't get this rich without taking a risk or two. Surely one of the palatial homes belonged to the investor she needed.

Avery's house, with its half-timbered upper story, would have suited a Tudor blueblood. On Inwood Drive though, it was just another River Oaks home, no more imposing or noteworthy than any of its neighbours. As Cait retrieved her bag from the Suburban's front seat, Avery came running out the front door. Her unruly copper curls and the freckles splashed across her face made her look more like a teenager than a twenty six-year-old wife and mother.

The demands of their busy lives – Cait's career and Avery's commitment to her husband and daughter – had kept them from seeing as much of each other as often as they would have liked. But the bonds between them had been durably forged during the shared angst of their teen years. Closer than sisters, they were best friends.

"I've been keeping an eye out for you," Avery said, throwing her arms around Cait. "I can't believe you're finally here. It will be just like old times. Cantrell's out of town so we can talk from here to eternity the way we used to. I've been dying to hear what brings you to Houston after all these years."

"I can't wait to tell you," Cait replied. "I need your help."

Senator Morgan's estate, Belle Terre, occupied five prime

acres on Lazy Lane in the heart of River Oaks. The grounds included an Olympic-size swimming pool, stables, tennis courts and a putting green. The estate had intimidated Cait in her teens. As she parked the Suburban in the brick-paved circular drive, she was even more nervous than she had been during her first visit. So much depended on her meeting with the Senator.

"Are you sure your father doesn't mind seeing me on such short notice?" she asked.

Avery gave a reassuring smile. "Honey, no man in his right mind would object to seeing you under any circumstances."

The Senator was waiting in front of the fireplace when they walked into the panelled library. Although the midsummer night had been heavy with humid heat, a fire blazed on the hearth, its warmth offset by the steady influx of artificially chilled air. Mementos of Senator Morgan's distinguished career – photographs taken with the last four presidents and innumerable heads of state – hung on the walls, a potent reminder of his power and position.

He strode across the room and took both of Cait's hands in his. "This is a very pleasant surprise. How long has it been?"

"Much too long," Cait replied, thinking the Senator hadn't changed a bit. He still looked and sounded larger than life.

"As I told you on the phone, Dad, Cait has the most marvellous idea," Avery burst out with her habitual enthusiasm. "I know you're going to think it's the opportunity of a lifetime. Since I've already heard all about it, I'll spend some time with Mother while the two of you talk."

"Please sit down, Cait," the Senator said, after Avery had gone.

Clutching her briefcase, Cait took the chair opposite his.

"Now, what's this idea of yours?"

Clearing her throat, Cait launched into the presentation she had rehearsed in front of a mirror half a dozen times at home. When she finished she opened her briefcase, withdrew the financial plan and the prospectus and passed them to the Senator. She tried not to display any outward sign of agitation as she waited for him to read them.

He read through the material quickly, then handed it back. "This is very impressive. Someone did a very fine job on it. Why does your father want to give up raising cattle?"

"It isn't profitable. If Pride's Passion is to survive, the land must be put to another use."

A frisson of excitement made the hair on Blackjack's neck rise. "Why are you here instead of your father?"

"My father's terminally ill. He's turned the ranch over to me."

Good God. Talk about serendipity. The best broker in the Hill Country had told him it might be months, perhaps years before he found a property that fitted Nishida's special requirements. And now the heir to the ideal ranch was sitting next to him. All he had to do was convince her to sell and his deal with Nishida could be finalized.

"I'm sorry to hear that, Cait," he said, deepening his voice as evidence of his sincerity. "Your father is a fine man, a pillar of the community who will be sorely missed. How can I help you in the difficult days ahead?"

She gave him the dazzling smile that had graced so many magazine covers, then smoothed her hair away from her face. Lord, she was gorgeous. Who'd have thought a skinny kid like Cait would grow up to be . . . He didn't finish the thought. For a moment there, his resolve had weakened. However, his success was due, in part, to the fact that he always acted in enlightened self-interest. Cait Pride in all her glory couldn't deter him from his goal.

"I need an investor to put up the money for the Outback," she said.

He leaned back and pyramided his long fingers, hoping he looked thoughtful and wise despite the heat flooding his loins. "Why would a beautiful young woman want to be saddled with a huge debt and an even bigger responsibility? My advice is to sell the ranch and return to your career. Considering the advanced medical facilities in Manhattan, your father would be much better off there as well."

As if it were an afterthought, he added, "I'd be happy to help you find a buyer for Pride's Passion."

"That's very kind, but I promised my father I'd keep the ranch in the family."

Stubborn bitch, he thought, then controlled his anger. "Your loyalty is admirable. But loyalty is not the best basis for making a business decision. Consider the facts. If your venture doesn't succeed, you'll lose the property. I'm certain I could help you find a buyer who'd permit you to stay in residence until your father passed on. He needn't even know about the sale."

"But I would," Cait replied.

"How long have we known each other?" he asked, trying another tack.

"Fifteen years."

"You used to be in and out of this house all the time when you and Avery were at school together. I thought of you as a member of the family. Permit me to give you some fatherly advice. You really must sell, my dear. It's the sensible thing – the *only* thing to do under the circumstances."

"I know you mean well. But I'm convinced the Outback will be both worthwhile and profitable. I intend to go through with it, with or without your help, Senator."

It took a supreme effort of will not to grab her and shake her until her teeth rattled. "I respect your idealism. Still I can't help thinking you'll regret being tied to the ranch after your father is gone."

"This isn't my father's project. It's mine. While I will

miss him dreadfully, the success or failure of the Outback isn't riding on his shoulders."

Blackjack was accustomed to having his opinions taken seriously, especially by women. His wife, daughter and secretaries all jumped when he said jump. He hated Cait for her intransigence, but he had to go right on playing the father figure.

Leaning forward, he took her hands in his. "Believe me, Cait, I understand your attachment to the land. It's a trait we Texans share. But you'd be wrong to allow yourself to be governed by sentiment when so much is at stake."

"It's not the land, it's what I can do with it. It's important to me and, I firmly believe, to the world."

"There are other ways to show your support for wildlife."

Cait extricated her hands, sat back and squared her shoulders. "I already donate to organizations like Greenpeace and the World Wildlife Fund. The Outback gives me a chance to do much more. Ask yourself these questions, Senator. Why do handicapped children develop confidence when they learn to ride a horse? Why do autistic children respond to dolphins? Why do nursing-home residents improve when dogs and cats are regular visitors? Why does stroking a dog or cat lower blood pressure?"

She answered her own questions triumphantly. "Because animals heal the human spirit just as exposure to art sends it soaring. Whether you realize it or not, we need to be in contact with nature. That's why the Outback is going to be a success." She put her papers back in her briefcase and got to her feet. "Thank you for seeing me, and give my best to your wife."

God save him from do-gooders who didn't understand that business, like politics, was the art of the possible. Blackjack rose and put a restraining hand on her arm. "Don't be so hasty, Cait. I hope you're not angry with me for playing the devil's advocate. I needed to be sure you were completely committed to the project before referring you to a friend of mine, a venture capitalist in Houston. I'm sure I can prevail on him to hear you out."

Cait's relief was visible. "I'd be very grateful for an introduction."

"I plan to do a great deal more." Damn it all, he didn't mean Cait any harm, but she hadn't given him any choice. There was no way he could be one hundred per cent certain the Outback would fail in the time required by his Nishida deal, but he intended to do the next best thing. He could make sure the terms of her loan would be virtually impossible to meet.

In the long run, he'd be serving Cait's interests as well as his own. When the moment was right he'd ride to the rescue and produce a buyer. Cait would be free to return to her career, Tochigi would be appropriately grateful and the Hill Country would benefit from an infusion of new capital.

Like other farming-ranching communities in Texas, Elgin had fallen on hard times. The Old Tavern was typical of the town. Nothing about its appearance other than the promise of cheap booze, invited patronage. It suited Carroll Detweiler's needs. He couldn't afford ambience on his pension.

He was a huge man in his late forties. Over six feet tall and running to fat, he had a bull's neck and a temper to match. His military crew cut was a nondescript beige, his eyes a muddy brown. Aside from his size, his most memorable feature was a scar running down the left side of his face.

Carroll Detweiler was a killer by trade. It all started with his name. In grade school the other boys had assumed that a kid named Carroll had to be a sissy. After coming home with a bloody nose time and again, his mother had ordered him to stand and fight.

Her face had glowed with pride when he won. Damn, he missed her.

Having developed a taste for violence in school, he enlisted in the Marines at the age of eighteen. He'd been furious when the Vietnam war came to an ignominious end. He'd returned to the States without so much as a welcoming parade, let alone the promise of a job. After months of unemployment he'd taken a job overseas as a mercenary. For the next two decades – until the afternoon when a Lebanese sniper shattered his kneecap – he'd fought in different wars for a dozen different masters.

Despite his limp, there was still an aura of barely controlled violence about him, a don't-fuck-with-me coldness in his eyes that made people avoid him. Now, as he occupied his accustomed stool at the end of the bar, no one looked at him, let alone attempted to strike up a conversation.

He had just started his second beer when the bartender came over. "You're wanted on the phone, Detweiler."

Carroll limped across the floor and grabbed the receiver from the bartender's hand. "Yeah," he snarled.

"Det, it's Blackjack Morgan."

"How the hell are you?" Carroll asked, breaking into a rare smile.

The Senator was a hell of a good guy, the best motherfucker of them all and the only man in the world he respected or liked. They'd served in Nam together. Hell, they even got a dose of the clap from the same whore. Thank God none of their escapades had come out the first time Blackjack ran for office.

"Never better," Blackjack answered. "And you?" How're they hanging? How's the knee?"

"Fucking A on both counts."

"Glad to hear it. Look, I know you're retired, but how would you like to go active for a while? I've got a little job for you. And I'll pay cash so it won't screw up your pension."

"You don't need to pay me. Just cover my expenses. A man doesn't take money from his friends."

"That's great. Just great." Blackjack's voice radiated warmth and camaraderie. "Have you ever heard of a ranch called Pride's Passion"

"Sure. The Detweilers and the Prides go way back. My mother told me the Prides ruined my granddaddy. They're the biggest bunch of bastards in Texas."

"Are you sure you can do what I want without letting your personal feelings get in the way?"

"No problem, old buddy."

"Caitlin Pride, the owner's daughter, plans to turn the ranch into an animal refuge, a sort of safari ranch for wealthy people."

Carroll grimaced into the phone. "Hell, Senator. Taming lions isn't exactly my field."

The senator laughed appreciatively. "I just want you to keep an eye on Cait Pride for me, let me know what she does, where she goes, who she sees. For a man with your talents, it should be a piece of cake."

Mims Pauling took a frozen diet dinner out of the microwave and peeled back the clear plastic cover. It grew harder every year to keep her figure – and less worthwhile. She hadn't had sex in so long that she considered herself a born-again virgin.

In the past, she had been a sucker for a handsome face, broad shoulders and a well-filled jockstrap. But she had made up her mind to forgo the transitory pleasures of a relationship. The only man she permitted under her skirts these days was her gynaecologist. It was a hell of a lot safer that way.

She put the plastic plate on an elegant chinoiserie tray, added a crystal bud vase with a single yellow rose to cheer herself up, and carried the tray into the living room of her

Trump Tower condo. Ceiling-to-floor windows looked out onto vast canyons formed by tall buildings sparkling with lights.

Kicking off her pumps, she walked over to the mirrored wet bar, poured herself a glass of Merlot, and then returned to her supper. By the time the phone rang five minutes later, she had decided the food wasn't near as appetizing as the wine.

"Mims Pauling here," she said.

"Hi, Mims, it's me," Cait replied, sounding remarkably cheerful for a woman who had given up her career to stay with a terminally ill parent.

"It's good to hear your voice." Mims cradled the phone between her shoulder and cheek and walked over to the bar to refill her wine glass. "How's Hank?"

"No better than he was the last time we talked. No worse either, thank God. And you?"

"I wish I could say you were interrupting a cosy tête-à-tête with a gorgeous man. But I'm alone, as usual. I miss you – the agency misses you. Getting girls to fill your bookings hasn't been easy. To make matters worse, Kimberly has a terminal case of acne so I had to cancel her appointments today."

"Sounds like business as usual."

"I'm afraid so. And you? Have you decided what to do about the ranch? I still can't picture you spending the rest of your life nursemaiding a bunch of cattle."

There was a long pause at the other end of the line. "I've decided to turn the ranch into a haven for endangered species. In fact, I'm in Houston right now trying to get financing."

"You're going to open a zoo?"

"Not exactly."

Mims listened with growing surprise while Cait explained her plans for Pride's Outback. Cait had always been an animal lover. She had refused to model furs and had contributed generously to organizations that promoted the environment. However, this went far beyond a dilettante's interest. Hearing the enthusiasm in her voice, the commitment and the confidence, Mims couldn't help a twinge of envy.

She had loved running a modelling agency until AIDS invaded the fashion industry. Now it seemed another friend or acquaintance was diagnosed HIV positive every week. Halston, Willi Smith, Perry Ellis – all gone. She had already shed too many private tears for public personalities and the end was no where in sight.

"That sounds very exciting," she said after Cait finished. "One of these days, I'm going to get on an airplane and come see what you're up to."

A few minutes later she put the telephone back in its cradle, then poured her wine down the sink. Wine made her maudlin and she felt bad enough already. She missed Cait. Worse, she coveted Cait's chance at a whole new life. Blinking back tears, she returned to her chair, curled up, and gazed out over the city, feeling terribly isolated in her glamorous eyrie.

She was forty-five years old and a success by anyone's standards. But the joy had gone out of her life and she didn't know how to get it back.

9

Cait smiled as she put her suitcase in the back of the Suburban. She couldn't remember feeling so excited, not even the first time she saw her picture on the cover of a national magazine. The week she'd spent in Houston had really paid off.

"I don't know how to thank you," she said, turning to Avery.

"You don't need to. You know me. I'll use any excuse to eat out. Besides, I had a ball."

Cait's eyes misted. How like Avery it was not to want any thanks. Her support had been as steady and reliable as the tides, her enthusiasm as effervescent as champagne. Despite the demands that a daughter and a husband made on her time, she had been a one woman PR firm, arranging lunches and dinners at elegant places like the River Oaks Country Club and Tony's, or more trendy ones such as La Griglia and the Third Coast, so Cait could meet the sort of people whose patronage would guarantee the Outback's success.

"Just the same, I owe you. And your father too. I sent a dozen roses to his office. I still can't get over how he did a complete about face. One minute, he was doing his level best to talk me out of the Outback and the next he was promising to make a pitch to a venture capitalist."

"I've been trying to figure my dad out for the last twenty years without any success. I can tell you this, though. He always gets what he goes after."

"I guess I'm lucky he's on my side. He even offered to help again if I ran into any roadblocks." Cait glanced down at her watch, then back at Avery. "I better get going."

"Are you sure you won't stay for lunch?"

"I'd loved to but I'm running late as it is."

"I'm sure Hank will understand when you tell him you had to wait for the loan papers."

"He would – but you know me."

Avery burst out laughing. "I certainly do. When it comes to being on time, you're anal-retentive, obsessive-compulsive . . ."

"And a general nerd," Cait said, completing the old high school litany as she slid behind the Suburban's wheel.

"Now that we both live in the same state, don't be such a stranger."

"I won't. And Avery, thanks – for everything." Cait blinked away the tears that threatened to spill down her cheeks.

Avery responded by gleefully thrusting the middle finger of her left hand in the air. Cait drove off laughing.

This time, as she headed for the freeway, she was oblivious to the splendour of River Oaks. She could hardly wait to see Hank's face when she gave him the good news. Thanks to Senator Morgan, she had negotiated the multimillion dollar loan she needed to make Pride's Outback a reality. The documents in her briefcase only needed Hank's signature to make them legal and binding.

With the financing in place, she had been able to telephone Garner Holland and hire him as a full-time consultant. He was due at the ranch in the morning to help formulate a list of animals for acquisition, to define their habitat requirements, to specify which could be kept together and which couldn't, and then to work with a surveying crew to lay out the actual enclosures. Last but far from least, a friend who worked for Reuters in New

York had placed her ad for a wildlife manager in the appropriate African newspapers.

The sharp aroma of cordite and the even sharper scent of his own sweat made twelve-year-old Byron Neville's stomach churn. He clutched the twenty-two calibre rifle his father had given him on his birthday and gazed despairingly through the shattered living-room window to the front lawn. He had failed a crucial test of courage a week ago. The price of failing this new one would be death.

The piercing cries of Mau Mau marauders shattered the quiet night. *Uhuru, uhuru*, they chanted as if the word held a magic that could protect them from a well-aimed bullet.

From another window, Byron heard the answering boom of his father's .375 magnum. Across the room his older sister Winifred fired a double-barrelled shotgun at the attackers, looking as cool as the Queen of England at a lawn party despite the horror that threatened to engulf them. The five Rhodesian ridgebacks that were his father's pride and joy added their own guttural growls to the fearful din.

"Steady," Byron heard his father call out. "Don't shoot until you've got one of the bloody sods in your sights."

Byron's heart pronged like a startled gazelle as he peered into the darkness in search of a sure target. The raiders' black skin and dark trousers were perfect camouflage on this moonless night. Suddenly he caught a glimpse of a white shirt. Knuckling away the nervous sweat trickling into his eyes and screwing his courage to the sticking point, he took careful aim.

He pulled the trigger and saw a gout of blood blossom against the snowy cloth. Sighting and shooting again and then again as other targets presented themselves, he had no time for a man's triumpth or twelve-year-old's tears.

The acrid odour grew stronger. He cried out – and the sound of his own voice woke him.

He opened his eyes to find himself in a luxurious king-size bed in Nairobi's historic Norfolk hotel. His sleep-drugged mind had interpreted the lingering aroma of sex and stale champagne as something far more sinister. He lay still, waiting for his heart to stop thundering in his ears. The nightmare was always tough to banish.

That long-ago Mau Mau raid had been his rite of passage from youth to manhood. Small wonder the incident haunted his dreams. But for a devoted Kikuyu servant's timely warning, he and his family would have been slaughtered in their beds.

Instead he had lived to see the death of the Kenya he loved. What a bloody waste – all those lives, all those dreams ground into the dust of nationalism. And for what? For the bloody disaster that was his birthplace today, a nation torn by the demons of tribalism and political corruption, a country where *Nipe Chai* – grease my palm – was the first Swahili phrase a tourist learned.

Byron eased to his feet so as not to wake the woman who slept by his side. Rosebud Fairchild. What a ridiculous name. There was, however, nothing ridiculous about the woman. A wealthy widow in her late forties who had successfully taken control of her husband's real estate business, Rosebud epitomized the things he liked best about Yanks.

She was open, honest, funny, filled with a lively curiosity and very clear about what she wanted. When he brought her tour group back to Nairobi last night, she had made it clear she wanted him.

Women seemed to go into heat on safari, he mused, a wry grin parting his lips. It was probably due to the mystique of the "white hunter", a fantasy created by Hemingway's writing and reinforced by movies starring men like Stewart Granger and Clark Gable. Whatever the reason, most women on safari regarded the white hunter as the ultimate trophy. But few of them had been as direct about it as Rosebud.

Barefoot and bare-assed, Byron padded to the bathroom to rid himself of the morning's hard-on and the night's accumulation of champagne. He was a slender, elegantly built man with wiry muscles stretched taut over his five feet ten inches. When he was wearing his habitual garb, a perfectly tailored safari suit, he gave the impression that he would be as at ease at high tea as he was in the bush behind the sights of a gun.

At forty-seven, his hair, which had started to grey while he was at Cambridge, gleamed like sterling. His eyes, the palest blue, were set in a perpetually tanned face and stunningly framed by black brows. There was something boyish about the arrangement of his features – a slight tilt of the nose, a roundness of the chin, deep dimples when he smiled – that belied the harsh lines around his eyes and mouth, lines etched by disappointment as well as by laughter.

He stood over the toilet urinating a long golden stream, the primal pleasure of emptying his bladder almost obscured by a deeper dissatisfaction that seldom left him these days. He was tired of nurse-maiding a never-ending stream of wealthy, camera-toting tourists through the bush.

Tourists didn't want to hear that their fantasy of Africa no longer existed, that even the great reserves like Tsavo, Aberdare and Masai Mara were losing their animals in an endless bloody bacchanal. The worst of it was he didn't see any hope for change, not as long as poverty and poaching went hand in hand.

Bloody hell. What was the matter with him, thinking about Kenya's problems when a warm and willing woman was just a few feet away? A little R and R, a decent meal, a fine wine and good sex, such things used to lift his spirits. He'd had all three last night. But dissatisfaction still gnawed at him.

The Eden of his youth had vanished and all the grousing in the world wouldn't bring it back. God, he needed a change, he thought, giving his penis a final shake.

Rosebud Fairchild was awake when he returned to the bedroom. She stretched, exposing a pair of enticingly Rubenesque breasts. That's more like it, he thought. Sweet Jesus, she'd been a good fuck.

"You talked in your sleep last night," she said, giving him a seductively wet-lipped smile.

He crossed the floor and sat on the edge of the bed, grazing her mouth with his. "What did I say?"

"It sounded something like *uhuru, bloody, fucking uhuru*. Does that mean anything to you?" She retrieved a pack of cigarettes from the night table and shook one out. Long and brown, it looked like a miniature cheroot. It gave her a rakehell look when she put it between her lips.

"It does," he said, automatically reaching for his pocket lighter before he recalled that he was naked. "I'd give you a light, love, but . . ."

Rosebud laughed lustily. "You lit my fire pretty thoroughly last night. Now, tell me about *bloody, fucking uhuru*."

"I don't want to bore you."

"I doubt you could. All I know about you is you're a terrific tour guide – and an even better bedmate," she said. "I like to know more than that about the man I fuck, including why they talk in their sleep."

Byron chuckled at her verbiage. Rosebud had occasionally shocked her fellow tourists with her colourful vocabulary. But he liked a woman who called a spade a spade. "*Uhuru* was the Mau Mau rallying cry in the days before colonialism came to an end. It means freedoom. The Mau Mau claimed to have been fighting for independence. Personally, I think they were fighting for land. God knows, we whites were doing our best to hang on to it for ourselves."

"Darling, you may not know it but you're in bed with a liberal democrat who voted for Hubert Humphrey and Jimmy Carter. I believe Africans have every right to their own country. After all, they were here long before Europeans arrived."

"The blacks may have been here first," Byron explained as he had to so many other well-meaning tourists, "but they didn't do a thing with the land. It wasn't productive until men like my great-grandfather settled on it. We had rights, too."

She held her cigarette out to him as if it were a peace offering. "If there's one thing I've learned in real estate, it's that logic flies out the window when it comes to owning land. It brings out the savage in the most sophisticated people."

He inhaled, savouring her taste along with the tobacco. "You're right. What was it the hippies used to say? Make love – not war. I'm all for that."

He stubbed the cigarette out in the nearest ashtray and reached for her. To his surprise, she evaded his embrace.

"I'm sore," she said. "Good lord, Byron, I haven't done that three times in one night since my honeymoon. Besides, I can see something's troubling you. If you feel like talking, you'll find me a good listener."

"It's a long story."

"Those are usually the most interesting ones."

Surprised by the need to let go of all the things he'd felt and thought since the dream woke him, he found himself telling her about the only truly happy years he had known, growing up on Kifaru farm surrounded by a loving family. He held nothing back as he spoke of the growing nationalistic movement and the terror of the Mau Mau attack, unaware of how vividly he had conjured up the long-ago horror until he felt Rosebud shivering by his side.

"I'm sorry," he said lamely. "I didn't mean to upset you."

"Please don't stop," she urged.

He leaned back against the pillows, his mind slipping back through time. "Things were never the same after that night. My father sold Kifaru a couple of years later and we moved to England. My parents died in a motorcar accident when I was eighteen."

Rosebud's warm brown eyes brimmed with sympathy. "How awful for you."

He cleared his throat. "My sister Winnie married a civil servant a few months later and I used my share of our inheritance to read history at Cambridge. Did a little boxing while I was there. But I never felt at home in England. I came back to Kenya to visit and one of my father's friends agreed to let me apprentice with him as a white hunter. When the government made hunting illegal in 1977, I hired on with the wildlife ministry as a special game warden assigned to tracking poachers."

Byron shook his head to dispel haunting visions of magnificent animals turned into rotting carcasses so some rich man's mistress could wear a fur or some ageing oriental could still get an erection. "It's a bloody business all round. I quit last year and hired on as a tour guide with Watson's Photographic Safaris. That brings me to the day I met you. So you see, I'm just the standard issue white African misfit looking for a place to call home."

Rosebud had been listening intently, her head cocked to one side. "Do you ever see Winnie?"

"Rarely. I have no desire to go to England again. Winnie's husband retired a few years ago and bought a cottage in the Cotswolds. They raise ridgebacks."

Before he'd begun talking, Rosebud had had the mellow look of a well-fucked female. Now her features seemed harder, giving Byron an idea of how different she would appear sitting behind a desk in her office.

"Have you ever considered coming to America?" she asked.

He laughed. "Half the world dreams of settling in the States. I don't think there are many jobs there for retired white hunters."

"I might be able to find something for you in my organization . . ."

"That's very kind," he interrupted.

"But you're not interested?"

"We both know it's out of the question. I have no desire to be a kept man, and I don't think you'd like me one bit if I did. Now, why don't I order up some breakfast?" He firmly believed that a man who liked a woman well enough to bed her damn well ought to like her enough to buy her breakfast. "How do kippers sound?"

"Ugh," she replied.

An hour later, he was idly skimming the *Daily Nation*, the newspaper room service had delivered along with their meal, while he waited for Rosebud to finish her toilette. He ignored the front pages, glanced through the sports headlines and then, out of boredom, began reading the help wanted section.

Well, I'll be buggered, he thought, breaking into a wide grin. He'd been dead wrong, thinking there were no jobs for white hunters in the States. Some woman in Texas was looking for a game consultant, a sort of white hunter cum game warden to recreate the safari experience on her ranch.

Suddenly, he laughed out loud. Lions and elephants in Texas?

Why the hell not?

Carroll Detweiler leaned against a limestone outcrop at the crest of a hill, smoking a Marlboro and enjoying an unaccustomed sense of wellbeing. From his vantage point, he could see a couple of miles down the road to the gates of Pride's Passion. Although he was sitting out in the open, the cammies he wore made him virtually invisible to any but the most sharp-eyed observer. And the only observers in the vicinity were the ever-watchful turkey vultures soaring overhead in search of carrion.

He put out his cigarette and immediately lit another, his mind drifting back to Vietnam. It had been both the zenith and nadir of his existence, the brutal standard against which he measured everything that had happened since. By comparison, this op was R and R, a fucking vacation that made him feel guilty about spending the Senator's money.

He'd driven to Fredericksburg the morning after the Senator's call and checked into the Sunday House Motel using an alias, just the way Blackjack had told him. After unpacking, he'd lunched at the Alpine Inn, treating himself to a tasty meal of kraut, sausage and a deeply satisfying Pilsner beer.

Then he drove the twenty-four miles to Kerrville where he spent the remainder of the day going from one bar to another, listening to local gossip, enough of it about the Pride family – Hank's illness, Cait's return – to make it worth his while to buy a couple of rounds to encourage further conversation. The unaccustomed sociability hadn't come easy. But his mother had drilled enough manners into him so that he could get by when he had to.

The next morning he began getting to know the lie of the land. It had taken the better part of two days to find his way around the ranch's boundaries, taking side roads, then bladed dirt tracks when the paving ran out, putting his four-wheel-drive Blazer through its paces as he encountered steep hills and brush-filled draws.

Shit! The spread was as big as some of the Third World countries that had hired him over the years. However, its size could work to his advantage, he thought, stubbing his cigarette out in the dirt. The hands were spread real thin. He could keep an eye on Cait Pride and no one would be the wiser.

According to the Senator, Cait was due home this afternoon. He checked his watch, then raised his Nikon binoculars to his eyes, sitting motionless, as patient as any carnivore lying in ambush.

The muted hum of an approaching car brought him fully alert. Moments later a silver Suburban with the ranch's distinctive brand painted on the side, came barrelling into view. Bingo, he thought, adjusting his binoculars to study the driver.

Cait was on the home stretch, just a few miles from the ranch house when, with a sickening lurch, the Suburban began careening down the road in a wild skid. She hadn't owned a car in New York and her driving skills were still rusty. She pumped the brakes the way Hank had taught her so many years ago, turning in the direction of the skid, fighting for control.

The car didn't respond. It seemed to have taken on a malevolent will of its own, lurching towards the deep run-off ditch bordering the road. She continued to battle the skid, her knuckles white on the steering wheel, her arms aching from the strain as the wheels left the paving.

The Suburban's steel underbody shrieked its own bloodcurdling protest as it made contact with the macadam, leaving a trail of sparks in its wake. Forgetting everything Hank had taught her, she tramped on the brake as the car continued hurtling along the ditch. Dear God, it couldn't end like this . . . not when it had just begun.

10

Comanche's pick-up trailed a plume of dust as he sped down the long drive, over the cattle-guard and out the front gate. He had tried to conceal his concern from Hank and Delta. Now it churned in his gut. He had the sick feeling something had happened to Cait – something bad.

She was never late and couldn't tolerate people who were. Before she left for Houston last week, she had promised Hank she would telephone at nine every morning. Delta said you could set a clock by her calls.

He searched both sides of the road as the truck rocketed down FM 1340, hoping against hope to see the Suburban heading in his direction. What the hell could have happened to delay her? Certainly not the thin dinner-hour traffic. If it turned out to be some damn foolishness like a sudden urge to get her nails done, he'd turn her over his knee for all the needless worry she'd caused.

Six miles from the ranch, the road began following the Guadalupe's meandering course in a series of undulating turns. He took them with reckless speed, heedless of any danger to himself. And then he saw the Suburban far ahead. Canting into the drainage ditch by the side of the road, it listed like a sinking ship. He braked to a stop.

"Cait," he shouted, running towards the disabled vehicle, "Cait, are you there?"

"I'm stuck in the car," she called out. "The doors are jammed."

A moment later, she saw his head and shoulders through the open window. "Are you all right?" he asked, peering down at her intently. "Can you move? Should I call an ambulance?"

"I'm just a little shaken," she replied through her chattering teeth. Now that the worst seemed to be over, her legs felt as weak as branch water.

He manhandled the jammed door open with a casual strength that made a mockery of her previous efforts. And then she was in his arms.

There are times when even the most determined liberated woman has a primal need to be held by a man, to be sheltered by his strength and comforted by his concern. Cait had known such moments before when fate had won the toss of the dice and she'd been left to pick up the pieces of her life. In the past, however, she'd had no one to cling to, no one she trusted other thaan Mims.

"You're bleeding." He tried to step back to examine her wound, but she was still too shaken to let him go.

Later, alone in her room, she would tell herself that she would have reacted that way to any man. At the moment though, she wanted to be sheltered in Comanche's embrace more than she had ever wanted anything in her life.

"It's only a cut. It can wait. Please, just hold me."

Comanche didn't have to be asked twice. He pulled her closer until they touched from shoulder to thigh. He'd almost forgotten how sweet it was to feel the curves and swells of her body. She fitted against him as neatly as a missing puzzle piece. He could have gone on holding her that way for ever but he felt her tremble, and knew she might be going into shock.

"I need to get you home and into bed, Katydid," he said, sweeping her up and carrying her towards his pick-up.

He settled her in the truck, belted her in and drove back to the ranch as quickly as safety permitted. Cait let out a strangled little cry when she saw Hank and Delta waiting on the front porch. As Comanche braked to a stop, she opened the pick-up door and half stumbled, half ran straight into Hank's arms.

"I had an accident. I think the car's totalled."

"An accident?" Hank looked over Cait's head to Comanche for confirmation.

"It looked like she blew a tyre," Comanche affirmed.

"I was driving too fast because I was late," Cait moaned into Hank's shirt front.

Relieved and concerned, he mopped up her tears with his handkerchief. "Cars can be replaced, sweetheart. But I only have one daughter and you're very precious to me. Thank God you're all right."

He kept his arms firmly around her all the way to the kitchen. Right then, he regretted his illness more than he had at any time since Doc Williams gave him the news. If he had his health, Cait wouldn't have had to go traipsing around Texas by herself, trying to save the ranch.

He helped her into a chair, then sat down beside her and took both her icy hands in his. "Are you hurt?"

Her tears had stopped but her face looked white with strain. "Something cut my neck."

"Will you take a look, Delta?" he asked.

Delta hurried over with a clean dishcloth in her hand. She pulled Cait's hair away from her neck, tsking loudly.

"Is it bad?" he asked.

"She got hurt worse falling off her bike years ago," Delta reassured him.

"Just the same, I think we should call Doc Williams and have him check Cait over."

"I don't need to see a doctor!" Cait hotly declared.

Hank would have laughed out loud at how much she sounded like him if he hadn't been so worried.

"It's only a scratch," Delta confirmed. "Make yourself useful and hold this on it while I get my first-aid kit." She pressed the cloth into his hands.

Cait fidgeted while Delta bandaged her neck. She wasn't accustomed to being fussed over. The loan, she thought – in all the commotion she hadn't told them about the loan.

She squeezed Hank's hands. "There's no reason for us to be sitting around like mourners at a wake just because I screwed up on the way home. I got the loan, Dad, every last penny I asked for."

Hank's lips parted but the smile never reached his eyes. "That is good news. I wasn't optimistic, considering the trouble the Texas savings and loans have been in."

"I didn't go to a savings and loan, or a bank. Senator Morgan made an appointment for me with a venture capitalist. I left the loan documents in my briefcase back in the Suburban but the terms are fairly simple. Do you feel up to hearing them?"

"I do if you're up to telling me about them," Hank replied. He couldn't deny Cait her moment of triumph.

"It's a five-year note. We pay interest on the principal for the first twelve months. At the end of that time one fifth of the principal is due, and so on for the next four years until the principal has been repaid."

Hank quickly made some mental calculations. The numbers he came up with were staggering. "Did you use the ranch for collateral?"

"It was the only way I could get the loan. You don't need to worry though. I know I'll be able to handle the payments."

Hank had to bite his tongue to keep from saying she had made a terrible mistake.

Cait was eyeing him warily. "Do you have a problem with the terms?"

He had promised her a free hand, and he couldn't back away from that promise. "I'm sure you got the very best deal you could under the circumstances."

"You don't sound very enthusiastic."

"I'm not upset about the loan. However, I am worried sick about you. You still look pale."

"If Cait has no objections," Comanche interrupted, "I'll go over the figures when I bring her briefcase back to the ranch."

Delta got to her feet. "That's enough business talk," she declared firmly. "Please help Hank to his room, Comanche, while I take Cait upstairs."

"You won't get any objections from me," Hank said. His legs shook as he got to his feet. He put a hand on the table to steady himself and kissed the top of Cait's head. "Delta's right. Time for both of us to get a little rest."

Under normal circumstances, he would never have leaned on Comanche for support. However, this evening he was grateful for the younger man's help.

"I could use a drink," he said after he was settled in his favourite leather armchair, "a stiff one."

"So could I, sir."

Comanche went off to get a bottle of bourbon and a couple of tumblers from the bar in the game room. When he returned, he splashed a healthy dollop into both glasses and handed one to Hank. The two of them drank greedily, like parched men who have miraculously stumbled across a desert oasis.

"Things don't look very good do they?" Hank finally said, putting his empty glass down.

"They're not that bad." Comanche refilled both tumblers to the brim.

"Don't humour me, son. I may be old and sick but I've still got all my faculties. Cait could have been killed this afternoon. If that isn't enough, she tells me a son-of-a-bitch Houston money man has played her for a fool. So don't tell me things aren't *that bad*."

Comanche stopped pacing and sat down in the chair opposite Hank's. "The ranch is still in your name. You don't need to sign the loan documents."

"Damn it, Comanche, you don't understand. I promised Cait a free hand. If I go back on that promise, she'll get on the next plane to New York. So you see, son, I'm between a rock and a hard place."

"I think you're wrong about her leaving."

"God, I hope so. I know it's selfish of me, and that it won't be easy on her, but I want her with me until the end."

"We've talked about selling off the beef cattle to make room for the exotics. That's going to improve our cash flow. And I do have some money saved. Cait's more than welcome to it if she gets in a bind."

Hank had been staring into his glass as if it were a crystal ball that could foretell the future. Now he looked up, skewering Comanche with his steady gaze. "I can't ask you to use your own money to make those payments."

"You're not asking. I'm offering."

Too tired to stay up and too upset to sleep, Hank was in bed thumbing through an old issue of the *Gulf Coast Cattleman* when Delta walked into his room.

"Cait finally went to sleep,' she said.

"Did she eat any supper?"

"No more than it would take to keep a bird alive."

He patted the bed. "You look tuckered out. Come on over and rest a spell."

Delta kicked off her shoes, stretched out beside him and rested her head on his shoulder. "I've missed this," she said, sighing.

Not certain if he was giving comfort or taking it, he eased his arm around her and pulled her close. "Sometimes I forget how hard all this is on you."

"With everything else you've got on your mind, I don't want you worrying about me, *cher*."

He ran his fingers through her hair, noting how the grey

seemed to have multiplied of late. "I want you to know how sorry I am for everything, but most of all, for wasting your life."

Delta raised up on her elbow and looked at him. "It wasn't yours to waste," she said firmly. "I was where I wanted to be."

Delta was a good woman, he mused, and he had taken her for granted. Now he saw the enormity of the wrong he had done her. But some accounts, he thought with new-found wisdom, just couldn't be squared in the time he had left. "Do you hate me?"

"A little, sometimes. Mostly, I'm angry with myself. I should have insisted we marry years ago."

"It's not too late. There's still time to call a preacher if that's what you want."

"That would just complicate things. I wanted to be your wife. I have no desire to be your widow."

"Like father, like daughter," he muttered.

"What do you mean?"

"I never gave us a chance, and now Cait is doing the same thing to Comanche. Unless I'm misinterpreting the signs, he's in love with her."

Delta sat up and looked into his eyes. "You know what, *cher* you just may be right."

For the first time in months, she seemed to forget his illness. She put her arms around him and hugged him hard, then planted a firm kiss on his lips. When she finally pulled away, her smile was as warm as a summer day.

"There may be hope for you yet, Hank Pride," she declared before kissing him again.

To his joy, Hank discovered that there was more life in his ailing body than he had realized.

Carroll Detweiler shucked off his cammies, stripped to his underwear and turned up the air conditioning. Then he dialled the Senator's private number and reported what he'd seen, half expecting Blackjack to give him hell for not helping Cait.

Instead, the Senator surprised him by saying, "You did the right thing. This is just the kind of information I want. Keep up the good work."

"It's not my place to tell you how to spend your money, but are you sure you don't want me to get a little more involved?" he asked hopefully. "Spying isn't exactly my line."

"I know you have a personal grudge against the Pride family. I want your promise that you won't exceed your mission," Blackjack replied.

"You've got it, boss."

After they said goodbye, Carroll sprawled across the queen-sized bed in his room at the Sunday House, stroking his cock while images of Cait Pride swirled through his mind. He hated her for being a Pride, and yet he couldn't help wanting her.

She'd been driving with the window open, her high, full breasts clearly outlined against her wind-blown blouse. Her lips had been parted in a smile. Now he imagined those lips sliding up and down his cock, sucking him, pulling him deep inside her mouth. He'd never fucked a classy bitch like her, not even in Nam when he'd been able to afford the best-looking whores. If he just once got Cait Pride in bed, he knew he could teach her a thing or two.

His stroking increased in intensity as he imagined her sprawled beneath him, her hands and feet tied to the bed, her pussy spread wide. He'd tied up a Saigon whore that way once. They'd been drinking cheap champagne when he thought of a new use for the bottle. He'd shoved it deep inside her while she struggled against her bonds, begging him to stop.

"Hell. A little rough sex never hurt anyone," he'd told her. By then, though, she'd been screaming too loud to hear.

When Carroll came to a throbbing orgasm a few minutes later, it wasn't the whores face he saw, or her body that he violated.

It was Cait's.

11

A subdued group gathered around the kitchen table the morning after Cait's accident. Comanche's red-rimmed eyes reflected his lack of sleep, the lines in Hank's face seemed to have deepened overnight, Delta was quieter than usual and the smallest movement made Cait wince.

Comanche had already spent two hours in his office poring over the loan documents in Cait's briefcase, comparing the numbers it would take to pay off the loan to the income he and Cait had projected when they prepared the Outback's business plan. The situation, he had concluded, was grim but not hopeless.

If everything happened on schedule, if everyone performed at their optimum, if Cait hired a superbly competent game manager, if there were no unforeseen problems, if the Outback opened within a year and produced some cash flow – they had a shot.

However, experience had taught him that accidents like Cait's yesterday happened when you could least afford them, and that people tended to crumble under pressure.

"If you all don't need me," Cait said, "I think I'll ride on down to the gate to pick up the mail."

"Why don't you take my car?" Delta said.

Comanche had to choke down the urge to say he'd get the mail himself. No way did he want Cait behind the wheel until she'd recovered from the accident.

"Are you sure you don't mind?" Cait asked.

"You know what they say about getting back up on a

horse after you've been thrown. Go ahead, *cher*."

Cait returned fifteen minutes later with a bundle of mail under her arm. There were several periodicals for Hank, bills and circulars for Comanche and, at the bottom of the pile, a thick envelope addressed to her. With a swift intake of breath, she saw that it carried an African postmark.

Resuming her seat, she tore it open. It contained a four-page letter, a resumé, a half a dozen letters of recommendation and a photograph of an attractive middle-aged man in a safari suit.

She read the resumé first. Byron Neville had been born and raised outside Nairobi, Kenya. He had grown up on a farm and had a working knowledge of cattle and crops. He had spent five years in England where he studied history at Cambridge before returning to the land of his birth.

He'd been a white hunter for eight years and his client list, which read like a *Who's Who*, included people Cait knew. In addition, he had worked for the government as a game warden and had spent the last five years as a photographic safari guide for the prestigious Watson's Tours.

Byron Neville sounded like the answer to her prayers, she thought, reading on. The enclosed recommendations couldn't have been more impressive. His own letter was literate, intelligent, worldly and laced with wry humour. Best of all, Byron Neville was unabashedly enthusiastic about Pride's Outback, agreeing with the need to save the world's dwindling animal populations with a passion that transcended pen and paper.

Although he was the only applicant so far, she felt certain she need look no further. Grinning broadly, she passed the bundle to Hank. "Get a load of this," she said.

"What is it, honey?"

"A job application from a white hunter in Kenya."

Looking up from his own mail, Comanche turned to Hank. "I'd like to see it when you're done, sir."

Cait waited impatiently while the two men read through the packet. "Isn't he just perfect?" she enthused when they were done.

"He sounds fine to me," Hank responded at once.

"Don't you think you ought to wait and see how he stacks up against other applicants before you go off half-cocked?" Comanche asked.

"No, I dont," she replied more forcefully than she intended. She'd been hurt by Comanche's cool reception of her news about the loan. But she'd be damned if she turn herself inside out trying to win his approval. "I intend to look into his references today," she said in a more reasonable tone. "If they check out, I'm going to offer him the job. In case you've forgotten, we don't have the luxury of time."

"You don't have the luxury of making a mistake, either," Comanche replied.

Cait bit back an angry retort. Hank's peace of mind overshadowed every other consideration, including her need to establish her independence from Comanche. Yesterday, she had welcomed his arms as a safe haven. Today, she wanted to break them.

She had been walking a tightrope between her head and her heart ever since she laid eyes on him at the airport. Her emotions were as jumbled as alphabet soup, and a lot less palatable.

"Well, what do you think of Pride's Passion," Cait asked Garner Holland later that day. They were seated in Comanche's office but Comanche wasn't with them.

Garner perched on a chair across from Cait's place behind the desk, his burning eyes hidden by the tilt of his battered stetson. "If what I've seen so far is a fair sample, it couldn't be better suited to your purposes. But then I never thought the land would be a problem."

"What will be?" Cait asked, opening a notepad and picking up a pen in anticipation of his rapid-fire response.

"The money and the land are just the beginning, Miss Cait. We've already talked about the need for high fences, bad weather shelters and the like. I don't know a damn thing about the resort end of it, the guest quarters and the frills, but I do know animals. Acquiring them and keeping them in peak condition will be your biggest challenge."

"Let's start with acquiring them."

He nodded and settled more securely in his chair. "The most obvious way is to breed them yourself and that's going to be one of your goals. But to start with, you're going to have to buy them. It's going to be expensive. Raz's Livestock Sales over to Harper runs one of the biggest exotic auctions in the state. If you don't like what you see there, you can buy direct from other ranches like the YO. Comanche can help you with that. He knows those fellows better than I do. Or you can deal with animal brokers like me, middlemen who get their stock from a variety of sources. Lastly, you can buy direct from zoos. That's where having a man like Byron Neville on the payroll will be a big help."

"I don't understand."

"You're really lucky he wants the job. The man's a legend in Kenya. Neville will give the Outback instant credibility. Zoo directors don't like to sell their surplus animals to just anybody. They've been burned too often."

"Burned how?"

"They don't want to see their surplus animals wind up as trophies on some hunter's wall. Unfortunately, it happens a lot in the Hill Country. I've heard ranchers boast that they can walk into any zoo with cash in their pockets, talk to the right person, say they want this or that animal and have it on their property ready to hunt in a week. I've heard tell of zoo animals being so used to people that they followed a truck full of hunters. Hell, the poor things have even been known to walk right up to a man with a gun."

"But that's so unfair – so cruel. And it's hardly sporting.

Isn't there any law against hunting zoo animals?"

"Fair, sporting and legal don't come into it, Miss Cait, not when there's so much money at stake. Dealing in exotics can be a dirty business. That's why I was so happy when you told me about the Outback. I knew you were sincere about wanting to save animals."

"Don't the zoos take precautions to keep it from happening?"

"They try. But when a zoo animal has changed hands a time or two, anything can happen. There's virtually no regulation of exotics in Texas. Most folks think they're a commodity, not a resource. I give you fair warning, you're going to be swimming upstream."

Two months after she first conceived of the Outback, Cait attended an exotic auction of the YO ranch with Comanche and Garner. To her surprise it was a black-tie affair and several other celebrities were in attendance.

She enjoyed seeing the way Garner's eyes widened and his Adam's apple bobbed when she introduced him to people like Kenny Rogers and Ted Turner. But Comanche took it all in his stride.

The auction was held in a series of enclosures covered by a massive roof. The chandeliers overhead were decorated with branding irons from ranches throughout the state. The same chandeliers, Cait recalled, had hung in the lobby of the YO Hilton.

While Garner and Comanche pointed out the healthiest, most vigorous-looking nilgai, springboks and oryx, her attention was drawn to the most frightened, timid creatures.

"What's the matter with that one?" she had asked, pointing to a blackbuck who cowered in a corner, seemingly in some sort of catatonic state.

"He's scared to death," Garner replied. "I told you that exotics are vulnerable to stress. That's one reason so many of them used to die on their way from Africa. Transporting any animals, even ones as phlegmatic as cattle, can cause problems. I remember one nilgai bull who ran into a fence and broke his neck after I unloaded him from a shipping crate."

"How can we prevent disasters like that at the Outback?"

"First off, you want to buy animals in prime condition and have them checked by a vet before they're shipped," Garner replied. "Second, use a company that specializes in moving animals so the job is done right. And it sure helps if you introduce an animal to its new surroundings slow and easy. If you do all that right, you're halfway home. Then all you have to worry about is disease. Right, Comanche?" he said, turning to the other man for confirmation.

Comanche nodded. "Exotics can get hoof and mouth, anthrax and brucellosis, just like cattle. Then there are natural enemies like coyotes, screworms and insects. Fire ants kill more newborn exotics every year than hunters kill adults."

Cait's anticipatory pleasure at bidding was diminished by the realization of the problems that lay ahead. She had always taken her father's cattle for granted, never realizing that they lived in a fragile stasis with the environment, that only man's constant intervention made their survival possible. The exotics would require even closer stewardship. And that took money.

The loan was never far from her thoughts. Each day counted, each hour had to be spent wisely if she hoped to open the Outback to paying guests in time. Could she pull it off?

Comanche rode drag as half a dozen hands drove the small herd of cattle along an arroyo. Sweat mixed with the dust churned up by their hooves coated his exposed arms and face. He untied his neckerchief and mopped his dripping brow. His position at the rear of the herd was so miserable with the temperature nearing a hundred degrees that he would have felt guilty assigning it to someone else.

Other ranches the size of Pride's Passion used helicopters to drive cattle. But the price of a helicopter was far out of Hank's reach. And so Comanche had spent the last three days in the saddle from sunup to sunset, moving stockers from the far reaches of the ranch to the corrals in preparation for shipping them to market.

When they finished with this bunch, he'd head straight for the swimming hole, he decided, closing his mind to his current discomfort. How good it would feel to plunge into the Guadalupe's cool jade water.

The sun sucked a man dry and the milk of human kindness seemed to ooze out with the sweat. The hands were short-tempered, Hank kept on consulting the Farmer's Almanac to see when the weather would break and Delta had forgotten how to smile. But Cait was the worst of the lot.

Despite her promise to forget the past, she seemed determined to make his life miserable. He had to keep on reminding himself that she was under a lot of stress. He couldn't recall the last time they'd had a civil conversation.

They had fought over her impulsive hiring of Byron Neville, argued about the proposed guest facilities – she insisted on hardened tents that would carry out the safari theme while he thought log cabins would be more appropriate to the setting – and quarrelled over every expenditure.

No doubt about it, she certainly had the bit between her teeth. She'd been acting like a spoiled child in bad need of a spanking. Every time he thought about doing the job, though, he got so hot and bothered that if he once got her across his kness, he knew he'd have more on his mind than reddening her bottom.

★ ★ ★

Blackjack Morgan had just returned to his Senate offices after a roll call when his secretary buzzed on the intercom. "Sato Tochigi is on the line," she said. "Can you take it?"

Blackjack's fists clenched involuntarily as he checked his watch. It had to be two in the morning in Japan. Didn't the bastard ever sleep? He considered telling his secretary he wasn't available but he knew Tochigi would just call later. The man was nothing if not persistent. "All right. Put him on."

A moment later Tochigi's disembodied voice filled his ear. Blackjack impatiently endured the requisite "hello, how are you, how are your associates, how is the weather" chitchat before Tochigi got to the point.

"Have you made any progress on our venture?"

Blackjack gritted his teeth. "Nothing has happened since the report I faxed last week. The lawyer is preparing the articles of incorporation and I'm still interviewing candidates for the board of directors. I expect to make my final selection soon."

"Have you found a suitable ranch yet?"

"I'm working on it."

"I hope it won't take much longer. My experts tell me the Houston business downturn is coming to an end."

Blackjack fervently wished he was in a position to tell Tochigi and his experts to go to hell. However, he still needed Tochigi's money. Barely controlling his temper, he said, "There's no need to worry. Houston isn't the Hill Country."

"The clock is ticking, Senator."

Blackjack could feel his gorge rising. He would have liked to reach through the phone and strangle the son-of-a-bitch. "Things are moving along as quickly as can be expected. I have a line on several properties."

"Can you tell me about them?"

"That would be premature."

Suddenly, a wicked gleam lit his eyes. He dropped the phone on his desk, opened a drawer, took out some paper and crumpled it next to the mouth piece.

He could hear Tochigi calling out, "Are you there, Senator?"

He banged the receiver on the desk a couple of times, crumpled some more paper including two letters his secretary had just left for his signature. He was still smiling when he picked the phone up and covered the mouthpiece with his handkerchief.

"We seem to have a terrible connection," he said. "I can barely hear you. I'll send another fax as soon as I have something to report."

He broke the connection with Tochigi, his momentary pleasure at having outwitted the CEO quickly evaporating. If only he'd been able to convince Cait to sell Pride's Passion, his problems would have been over.

He'd counted on her inability to get the Outback off the ground.

Detweiler's weekly reports indicated that she was making steady progress. He ground his teeth together in frustration. Damn. There had to be a way to get her to leave the ranch.

From the way things had been going, it would take an Act of Congress. And even he didn't wield that much influence.

12

Mims left her Trump Tower condo for her office at seven every morning and rarely returned before seven at night. Today was an exception. She felt too drained, exhausted and dispirited to work.

Another friend gone from AIDS, she thought, inserting the key in the lock and letting herself into her apartment. Paul had suffered so at the end, it had taken all her courage to go on visiting him. If only his other friends had shown a little more compassion, it might have eased his passing. But lately, compassion seemed in short supply.

AIDS was taking a terrible toll on the worlds of fashion and the arts. Bad as the situation had become in the United States, it didn't touch what was happening in some Third World countries. And yet the government stubbornly refused to take meaningful measures to stop its spread.

So what else is new? She had lost faith in the government and in men at about the same time. Call it the price of growing up, she thought sourly. What was that bumper sticker? *Life's a bitch and then you die*. It seemed terribly appropriate today.

She walked into the living room, kicked off her shoes, dialled her office and told her secretary she wouldn't be coming in even though it was only three in the afternoon. Then, needing to talk to someone who would understand, who had known Paul in the old days, she telephoned Cait.

"You sound down," Cait said after they had exchanged

greetings. "Is something wrong?"

"I just came from Paul's funeral."

"Oh, God, I'm so sorry."

"Hell, it was probably a blessing. You wouldn't have recognized him. You know how much he loved beauty. He couldn't stand the sight of himself the last few months." She knuckled away a tear. "He was the first important photographer to give my models a break. It seems all the people I care about are disappearing – and that includes you. How are things in the Wild West?"

"Fairly tame since I wrecked the car."

"That's nice," Mims replied absently. She stared out the window, heedless of the stunning view. Her mind kept on returning to the cemetery, the tiny knot of mourners, the flowers wilting in the heat, the thud of dirt being shovelled onto the coffin. She'd never felt lonelier or more useless. God, how she neeed a change of scene.

"I've decided to take a vacation," she blurted out.

"That's a terrific idea. You sound like you could use one."

"At the ranch."

"You're going to a dude ranch? I thought you planned to visit Santorini after the Paris shows."

"I'm not going to a dude ranch or Santorini. I'm coming to see you if you'll have me."

"In a New York minute," Cait replied. "Hang up right now and call your travel agent."

Cait didn't waste a minute hurrying to Hank's room to give him the news. Mims' visit was sure to lift all their spirits. Mims was the smartest, most intuitive person Cait knew. She had a level head that enabled her to function in the midst of chaos, a way of seeing silver linings in almost every cloud and she was a consummate businesswoman who would bring a fresh perspective to the Outback.

Cait found Hank dozing. She paused in the doorway, studying his face. He looked younger with his features in repose. Thank heaven he'd been eating better and resting more since he got those pills from Doc Williams a couple of weeks ago.

The medication had done wonders to relieve his pain. If only she could find a way to relieve his mind. But Hank would go right on fretting until the Outback's success was assured. She'd do anything to make that happen.

Her news could wait, she decided, turning away. Hank needed his rest more than he needed to hear about Mims. Anxious to tell someone, Cait headed for the kitchen to let Delta know they would soon have company. The room was empty though, and when she looked out the window, she didn't see Delta's car in its accustomed place.

Suddenly it hit Cait. For the first time in weeks, she didn't have any appointments or urgent tasks demanding her immediate attention. She opened the kitchen door and gazed out, thinking how long it had been since she'd gone riding.

There wasn't a soul in sight. Alone. She was gloriously, deliciously alone.

It was a perfect day for a ride and a swim. She'd exercise Dulcinea, the sweet chestnut mare she'd claimed for her own that first day on the ranch, catch a few rays down by the Guadalupe and be back at her desk in an hour.

Fifteen minutes later, she finished saddling Dulcinea and mounted up. Casting one last look towards the house, she dug her heels into the mare's flanks. The horse responded instantly, breaking into a ground-covering gallop. The breeze raking Cait's hair seemed to hold the essence of freedom. She could have raced along forever. But a mile into her ride, she slowed the mare to a walk. It was far too warm to run her needlessly.

The creak of the saddle and the hum of insects proved to be a soporific. High above, a pair of black vultures spiralled ever upward like animated kites. Pink primrose and yellow coreopsis mingled with the red blossoms of cow vine to carpet the rocky soil. She rode for half an hour, letting Dulcinea choose her own pace. By the time they reached the river, Cait felt more relaxed than she had since her return from Houston.

The swimming hole nestled in a cut bank where the current had scoured a deep depression in the river's bed. A high bluff on the far side and a strand of trees growing within ten feet of the water guaranteed privacy.

Cait dismounted, tying the reins to a low branch so Dulcinea could browse in the shade. Then she made her way through the thick grove of oak, yaupon and laurel, her footsteps rendered silent by a deep mulch of fallen leaves.

She had almost reached the edge of the trees when she heard a dog barking. There was no menace in the noise, though. The animal sounded playful. She crept closer and peered through the final curtain of leaves screening the river from view. At first all she saw was Trouble cavorting in the water like a puppy.

A sideways shift of her gaze brought Comanche into view. She swallowed convulsively, running her tongue over lips that suddenly felt parched. He was naked, stark naked, his body a golden icon glistening in the sun. His face, neck, arms and shoulders were deep bronze, his chest and legs a lighter tan. A strip of white ran across his muscular buttocks and groin.

God, he was beautiful.

She knew she ought to stop acting the voyeur and leave, but no power on earth could have forced her from her hiding place. She had seen naked men before but never one who thought himself alone. There was, she realized, a certain self-conscious preening and posturing when a man stood naked in front of a woman, a tightening of the gut, a squaring of the shoulders.

Some men, having an erection, displayed it like a magic wand as if to say "Look what I can do – isn't this wonderful – it's all for you". Unaware of her presence, Comanche splashed and dived like a river otter. He made no effort to hide his genitals, or to flaunt them.

His shoulders, chest and arms had filled out since the last time they had been alone by the river. His muscles, defined by manual labour, were smoother, more elegant and infinitely more appealing than the bulging biceps, pectorals and laterals that other men achieve in a gym. Comanche didn't have to keep himself "in shape". He epitomized the words. A marble sculpture come to life couldn't have been more mesmerizing.

A fine mat of hair covered his chest, tapering to a V at his waist. Cait's eyes were inexorably drawn to the tangle of dark curls at his groin. She had never permitted herself to gape at male genitalia in the past, and had satisfied her innate feminine curiosity with discreet glances that had told her all men were not created equal.

Comanche, she thought with a quick intake of breath, was more equal than most. She flushed crimson as, utterly fascinated, she watched the way his penis moved with every step. It was a beautiful organ, symmetrical, broad and long.

The tender flesh between her legs dampened as she remembered what it felt like to have him buried inside her body. He had been a wonderful lover – ardent, as eager to give pleasure as take it. Heat – more mental than physical – made her long to strip off her clothes and join Comanche in the cool river.

She felt as if she were suffocating. Her breath came in little gasps as she undid the top buttons of her blouse.

Comanche couldn't say exactly when he realized Cait was crouching at the edge of the trees. He sensed her presence before he saw a flash of white skin between the leaves. What the hell was she doing here at this time of day, and how long had she been hiding?

Had she crept away, he would have teased her mercilessly later. The fact that she stayed hidden, a silent audience, began to take its toll. His skin warmed despite the cool current reaching to his thighs. Deep in his groin, he felt an inward spiralling warmth, a tug of desire. He moved further into the stream to conceal his burgeoning erection. Cait had looked her fill. He wanted his turn.

"It must be hot in those trees," he called out. "Come on in, Cait. The water's fine."

Cait almost bolted at the sound of his voice. She had been so sure he didn't know she was there.

"What's the matter, Katydid? Cat got your tongue?"

Comanche was looking straight at her, that lazy smile of his challenging her to leave her hiding place. Knowing he would never let her live it down if she ran away, she stood up and pushed through the screen of leaves. A thorn caught at her skin, leaving a tiny crimson smear in its wake. She didn't feel it, though. Her eyes were locked with Comanche's.

"I thought you were rounding up cattle," she said, keeping her voice steady despite her galloping pulse.

"We finished half an hour ago. Besides, you know what they say about all work and no play." His smile deepened, his eyes glittering with mischief and, heaven help her, desire.

She reached the water's edge and stood there, her arms limp at her sides, her head spinning, wishing she was somewhere else and yet utterly incapable of voluntary movement.

Comanche moved towards her, lofting a handful of water. From then on things seemed to happen in slow motion. She watched the playful splash arc through the air, the individual droplets catching the sun like diamonds. When they showered over her, they seemed to sizzle on her skin.

She tried to break free of Comanche's eyes but his gaze never wavered. It trapped her, held her, promised her things she had forgotten. Without making a conscious decision to do so, she unbuttoned her blouse, pulled it free of her jeans and dropped it on the ground. Then she stepped out of her boots and unbuckled her belt, her hands seeming to move of their own volition. And all the while Comanche's gaze held her in an inescapable embrace.

God, what eyes he had. As green as emeralds, his soul seemed to leap from them.

Her jeans quickly joined her blouse and she stood there, half naked in a sheer bra and a string bikini.

"All of it – take all of it off," he commanded in a husky voice that sent a wave of desire vibrating through her.

Comanche gasped with pleasure as she did his bidding. He had dreamed of this moment in countless erotic fantasies, but the reality of Cait exceeded all his imaginings. Gazing at her, he felt as if two images, one composed of memory, the other of reality, were superimposed over one another.

The girl he had known, the awkward duckling grown into a swan, was still present in Cait's long arms and legs. But her breasts were fuller, her hips wider, her stomach rounder than he remembered. The last time they made love, she had been half child. The naked creature facing him at the river's edge was all woman.

He moved towards her as a fever raged through him. He wanted her with a soul-searing need that would have shaken him right down to his boots had he been wearing any.

Cait never moved closer nor backed away. Her wide staring eyes never left his. She seemed to be in the grip of some emotion he couldn't fathom.

"Why are you doing this to me? What do you want?" Her words came out in a ragged gasp, as if she had been in a foot race.

"I'll tell you what I want," he replied, reaching for her shoulders and pulling her close. "I want you to stop pretending you don't feel anything when we're together. I want your tongue in my mouth, your breasts in my hands, your legs wrapped around my waist. I want to suck on your nipples and bury my face between your legs. I want to hear the sounds you make when you come. I want you to need me more than you've ever needed a man before. I want you Cait, all of you – your body, your heart, your soul."

She flowed into his arms like molten gold, moulding to him, her face turned up, her eyes closed. He kissed them first, careful of their delicacy, feeling her lashes flutter at his touch. Then his lips sought the pink shell of her ear. She shivered when his tongue darted inside. He trailed kisses down her neck, nibbling the sweet curve of her jaw, feathering the corner of her mouth before he finally claimed her lips.

An exquisite pleasure sparked through his veins as she opened her mouth. The taste of her exhilarated him more than the finest champagne. When her tongue joined with his, he groaned with pleasure. He ached to know her completely and at once, to explore her body, to claim her in the way of all men from time immemorial.

Reluctantly leaving her sweet mouth, he lowered his head to her breasts, marvelling at their perfection. Her aureoles were a wide, dusky pink, her firm nipples an invitation to suckle. He fed from one and then the other, holding her close with one hand while his knee parted her legs.

His free hand cupped her womanhood, marvelling at her heat, and then he slipped a finger deep inside the damp furnace at her centre. Love gentled his caresses even as lust drove him. In exchange for Cait's body he silently offered up his life, his soul, his last breath if need be.

She had to know how he felt, now, this very minute. He had to tell her before he took her. But when he opened his mouth to speak he saw a flash of light high on the bluff across the river – and the words died unborn.

Cait's blood moved like molten lava, thick and heavy with desire. She hadn't been with a man for a long time, and never a man so knowing and yet so tender. Comanche's touch was both familiar and foreign, a part of her past and her present blending in the most exquisite sensations.

She hadn't meant to undress, to let him touch her. But now she felt she would die if he stopped. Her hands and mouth enjoyed their own urgent exploration, plundering his body, savouring his taste, his scent, the pulsing erection that scorched her belly.

Madness. It was madness, the sweetest insanity. She wanted him inside her. Now, please now. The unspoken words cannonaded through her mind.

Suddenly, Comanche froze like a hunting dog on a point. Then without warning, he snatched her up and raced for the trees. Cait was too startled to do anything but hang on. Was this some new style of love-making, had he lost his mind, or was this his way of humiliating her?

He didn't slow his flight until he reached the place where she had left Dulcinea. Only then did he set her down. The urgent passion she had read in his gaze moments earlier had been replaced by a new expression. He seemed as alert, as wary as a hunter or a hunter's prey.

"What's wrong? Why did you run like that?" she asked.

"I saw something up on the bluff."

Her heart seemed to collide with her lungs. "Something – or someone?"

"I'm not sure. All I know is I've got to get you out of here."

"But my clothes! I can't go back to the house like this!"

A swift hiss of indrawn breath snaked through Carroll Detweiler's lips. He gazed through his binoculars, his mouth moving in a silent litany. *Do it, do it, do it. Put it to her. Screw the bitch.*

He'd been shadowing Cait Pride for weeks, trailing her into Kerrville and San Antonio, logging the names of everyone she saw – architects, decorators, contractors.

The mission was driving him up the wall.

He'd been about to pack it in for the day when Cait Pride emerged from the trees, undressed and joined the breed in the river. Now that's more like it, he thought, feeling a surge of warmth that had nothing to do with the temperature.

He was too far away to hear what Cait and her foreman were saying, not that the show they put on required any dialogue. He liked watching other people get it on – a pleasure he'd learned from Blackjack. Talk about being hung . . . If the Senator's female constituents knew what he carried between his legs, he'd get all their votes.

Ignoring the sweat trickling down his brow, Carroll kept his binoculars firmly fixed on the action below, while memory took him back to 1965.

He and the Senator – everyone called him Blackjack then – had been enjoying a little R and R in Thailand, prowling Patpong, Bangkok's infamous red-light district, going from bar to bar, sampling the booze and eyeing the women. Finally, too drunk to go any further, they'd settled in a neon-lit honky-tonk that promised a live floor show.

They continued drinking while watching a series of performers – strippers, a contortionist who could do things with her body that boggled the mind, a man and a woman who had sex on stage. Then, with a drum roll, a naked young girl was dragged into the spotlight. With her barely budded breasts and sparse pubic hair, she couldn't have been more than twelve. The master of ceremonies said she was a virgin and asked for a volunteer to come up and screw her.

"Shit," Blackjack had said. "We can't let one of these mini-pricks do it. It takes a real man to break a girl in. How 'bout it, Det?"

Carroll shook his head. "Not enough tits and ass for me."

Although Blackjack was so drunk that Carroll didn't

think he could walk, let alone fuck, he stumbled to the stage amid thunderous applause. When he shucked his pants, revealing an erection that would have done credit to a stud bull, the applause grew even louder.

A stage hand came scurrying out with a flimsy cot but Blackjack waved him off. He grabbed the girl and ran his hands over her body, pinching her breasts and buttocks so hard that tears spurted in her eyes. Grinning drunkenly, he spit-wet two fingers, thrust them inside the girl and nodded, yes, to the audience to confirm her virginity. Then he picked her up as easily as though she were a doll and rammed her down on his erection.

Carroll had never forgotten the look of panic on her face or the thin sound of her scream when Blackjack forced his full length inside her. The Senator had taught him a thing or two that night. He'd made the girl ride him for a long time while the audience roared its approval. That's when Carroll had realized that watching a great fuck was almost as enjoyable as having one.

Now, he wet his lips as he saw the breed use a knee to part the Pride woman's thighs. His own erection pressed against his cammies while he imagined himself in the breed's place. He shifted slightly and lowered his hand to his crotch, tugging at his pants to accommodate his straining penis. The binoculars shifted in his other hand.

Suddenly, the breed picked the woman up and streaked for the trees. Det dropped the binoculars as if they were on fire. Fuck. FUCK. *FUCK*! The breed must have spotted a reflection off the lens.

His dwindling erection pressed against the ground as he belly-crawled away from the bluff.

13

Cait checked the computer screen for errors, then hit the print command. The work had to go on. The first balloon payment fell due in nine and a half months. She mustn't allow anything to prevent the Outback from opening on time – and that included her rioting emotions.

While waiting for the spread sheet to print, she took another look at the bids for construction of the guest facilities, pondering the variables, trying to assess the importance of the bottom line versus the need for quality. Writing cheques, entering them in the proper ledger columns and dealing with the rest of the papers piled on the roll-top desk, occupied another hour. When she finished, she rocked back and looked around wearily.

She had managed to put Comanche out of her mind for a while. Now he came crowding back in. Everything about the office, the rodeo trophies on display, the worn stetson on the hatrack, even the way his body had contoured the chair she sat in, reminded her of him. She closed her eyes, frowning as she remembered their hasty retreat from the river yesterday.

Thank heaven no one had seen them riding double with nothing but Dulcinea's blanket to cover them. She'd been angry, embarrassed, a little frightened, and – heaven help her – very turned on.

"We wouldn't be in this mess if you hadn't decided to go for a swim," Comanche said.

"But you dared me to," she replied, half turning to face him.

He groaned. "Do you have any idea what you do to me when you wiggle like that?"

She felt his manhood stir. A moment later his erection was pressing against her buttocks. It had been her turn to groan. Riding double had proven to be erotic torture. She'd wanted him so much yesterday. Still did, for that matter.

Unconsciously squeezing her thighs together, she attempted to rationalize their encounter on the riverbank by telling herself any woman would have reacted the way she did. A hot day, cool water, a gorgeous naked man were volatile ingredients. Remembering what had happened, she didn't know whether to weep, shout the rafters down or laugh out loud.

What was that quote about those who didn't learn from past mistakes being destined to repeat them? Her determination to treat Comanche as a business associate had failed.

Where did lust end and love begin? She might as well ask how many angels could dance on the head of a pin. Did she love Comanche or just want him? How could she tell the difference? She couldn't afford to make another mistake, not when Hank's emotional wellbeing would be at risk too.

She had expected Comanche to carry her straight to his bed when he reined Dulcinea to a stop at his back door. As it turned out though, making love had been the last thing on his mind. Once they were safe from prying eyes, he hurried to his bedroom as if the hounds of hell bayed at his heels.

So much for romance, she had thought. She found one of his shirts draped over the back of a chair and put it on while Trouble looked at her quizzically, his massive head tilted to the side as if he was trying to figure out what was going on.

"Don't ask me," she said, reaching down to scratch him

behind the ears. "I just work here."

Comanche emerged from the bedroom minutes later, fully clothed, a revolver in his hand.

"Where do you think you're going with that?" she demanded.

His sensually curved mouth had thinned into a grim slash. "Back to the river."

She had never seen him in a rage before. Fearful for his safety, she grabbed his arm. "You can't leave me here like this."

"I have to know who was on the bluff – and I'll pick up your clothes on the way back. You're right about one thing. You sure as hell can't go back to the main house like that." For a second, mischief danced in his eyes. It flared out quickly, though, and he looked all business as he walked out the door.

He looked even grimmer when he returned an hour later, her clothes tucked under his arm. "Some damn Peeping Tom was spying on us."

"Could it have been an accident? Perhaps one of the women or children who live on the ranch came for a swim and got embarrassed seeing us."

"Not unless they wear size twelve army boots. I found a few cigarette butts too."

"I hope it doesn't sound paranoid but I have had the strangest feeling lately that someone was watching me."

"Why didn't you tell me before?"

"Because it was just a feeling. I didn't have anything concrete to go on."

"For God's sake, Cait, does the name Teresa Saldana ring a bell?"

"Now you're scaring me. Besides, I haven't publicly announced my retirement yet. No one knows I'm here. It must have been one of the hands."

"If it was, he'll be looking for another job by sunset."

The sound of the front door opening and closing brought Cait abruptly back to the present. Startled, she gripped the arms of her chair. They weren't expecting any one. Besides, a visitor would ring the bell.

Comanche had been gone since first light and Delta was at the market. Fear prickled her skin as she realized she and Hank were alone. If the Peeping Tom was spying on her today, he knew how vulnerable she was.

She got up and removed a twenty-two calibre rifle from the gun rack over the fireplace, her hands shaking as she checked to see if it was loaded. The sound of boot-shod feet coming ever closer, not hesitating even once as if the intruder knew exactly where to find her, made her stomach spasm.

She took a position opposite the door, shouldered the rifle, and prayed she would have the internal fortitude to use it if an intruder came through the door.

Comanche braked his pick-up to a stop in front of the ranch house and slumped behind the wheel, too weary in mind, body and soul to move. His eyes were bloodshot, a frown knit his forehead, and the lines around his mouth seemed to have deepened overnight. Hell and damnation. How could one day make such a difference?

He'd been the happiest man in creation when he held Cait in his arms yesterday. He'd even allowed himself to think they had a future. Today, he wouldn't blame her if she fired him on the spot. Steeling himself for the worst, he left the truck, took the porch steps in a single bound, opened the front door and made his way to the office.

He saw the rifle before he saw her and ducked instinctively. "For God's sake, Cait, don't shoot."

"Comanche?" Her voice sounded thin.

Taking a deep breath, he hurried to her side and took the rifle from her shaking hands. "Are you all right?"

"Oh, sure, I'm just great. I almost shot you but what the hell, I guess it's all in a day's work."

He put the rifle back where it belonged and turned to face her. "I didn't mean to frighten you."

"Of course not. You don't mean any of the things you do."

"I really am sorry, Katydid, more sorry than you'll ever know." He wanted nothing more than to take her in his arms. The angry gleam in her eyes told him he was likely to get slapped if he tried.

"Sometimes sorry doesn't cut it," she shot back angrily. She paused, then continued in a more moderate tone. "What are you doing back here at this hour?"

"I just came from the corrals. I don't know how to tell you this except just to say it straight out. The cattle are gone."

"What do you mean – gone?"

"Gone as in rustled, stolen."

"You've got to be kidding."

"I wish I was. We haven't lost cattle to rustlers in years. Someone drove four semis up to the pens last night and helped themselves. I've never seen a cleaner operation."

Cait felt sick. They'd been counting on the sale to help meet the interest payments. Now she knew why Comanche looked so defeated.

"Surely we carry insurance?" she said in a small voice.

"Hank dropped it last year. He was short of cash, and he thought the premiums were a rip-off. Hell, Cait, this whole mess is my fault."

"What's your fault?" Hank asked, appearing in the doorway. "I heard a ruckus so I thought I'd better see what it was all about."

Shivering inwardly, Cait hurried to him and took his hand, needing his warmth now more than she had when she was little. "We lost the cattle in the corrals last night," she blurted out.

Hank looked at Comanche. "Rustlers?"

"Yes, sir."

"Damn! Didn't you post a guard?"

Comanche shook his head. "We're short-handed. The

men are worn out. I planned to keep watch myself but something came up."

"The hell you say!"

"I thought my time would be better spent protecting Cait."

Hank cut a sharp glance at Comanche. "Why? What's been going on? What haven't you told me?"

"It's not Comanche's fault," Cait interrupted. "It's mine."

"Yours?" Hank looked completely baffled.

"I rode down to the river yesterday to take a swim. Thank heavens Comanche happened along because someone was on the bluff, watching. He brought me home and went back to investigate."

"What did you find?" Hank asked.

"A man had been up there long enough to leave half a dozen calling cards. Marlboros. When I told Cait, she said she'd had the feeling that someone has been watching her. Maybe I'm jumping to conclusions but it's possible she's being stalked. God knows, her picture's been on enough magazine covers to bring a crazy or two out of the woodwork. That's why I wasn't at the pens last night. I was afraid whoever was on the bluff might come back after it got dark so I kept watch on the house instead."

Hank's anger faded abruptly. "You did the right thing, son. I don't have to tell you how precious Cait is to me."

"Just the same, I plan to make your loss good."

"How?" Cait said. "Do you think you can catch the rustlers?"

"They've probably crossed the border into Mexico by now. I plan to repay you from my savings."

Cait couldn't have been more surprised. He'd boasted of having a healthy bank account. Did he really mean to make use of it to pay back their loss? Could he still afford his own ranch if she let him? Suddenly, she had the feeling that she didn't know Comanche at all. Even worse, she no longer knew herself.

14

Two weeks ago, when Mims decided to visit Cait, Mims' one thought had been to leave all that was troubling her behind. She'd had no expectation of finding anything at Pride's Passion aside from peace and quiet.

Now, after just four days at the ranch, she was in love with the place and its inhabitants. It seemed perfectly natural to receive Hank's and Delta's parting hugs as she and Cait prepared to drive to San Antonio to meet Byron Neville.

"Drive safely," Hank admonished as they got in the Suburban.

"And don't stop to eat on the way," Delta chimed in. "I'm fixin' a special dinner."

"What time will you be home?" Hank seemed reluctant to let go of Cait's hand. Love and concern shone in his eyes.

"The plane gets in at two. If it's on time, we'll be back by five." From her place in the driver's seat, Cait pointed at the newly installed car phone. "I'll call if anything goes wrong." She started the engine, gave Hank and Delta a last wave and headed down the drive.

"Are you sure you don't mind going to the airport with me?" she asked, turning her attention to Mims.

"Not at all. Besides, I'm curious about Byron Neville. His resumé made him sound fascinating."

They drove in companionable silence for a while before Mims spoke again. "I had no idea the Hill Country was this beautiful. When you told me you were giving up your career to stay here, I thought you'd lost your mind. Now I can't help wondering how you managed to stay away so long."

"You knew my reasons."

Mims lifted one brow. "I know they seemed valid to you. But Hank is nothing like the man you described."

"He's changed a lot."

"So have you."

Cait smiled. "I guess I don't look much like a supermodel any more."

"It isn't just your make-up – or lack of it. It's something much more fundamental. I always wondered what would happen when you finally figured out who you wanted to be when you grew up. Now I know. The Outback is really important to you, isn't it?"

"As important as the agency is to you."

Mims sighed. "I don't know about that. I guess I'm having some sort of mid-life crisis. Lately, I've been thinking I missed out on a lot of things other women take for granted."

"I can't picture you with a squalling baby on your hip, doing floors and windows. You're the quintessential businesswoman."

"When I graduated from Harvard with my MBA, women could have a career – or a family."

"And you wanted a career, right?"

"In those days, you couldn't have both. I envy young women today, having so many choices."

"You make it sound as if you're ancient."

"I feel ancient. But I don't want to talk about myself. You've spent the last four days telling me all about the Outback. I want to know about you. I can see things have really worked out for you and your father. How about you and Comanche?"

Cait gave Mims a tight smile. "I don't know what you mean."

"For heaven's sake, I've noticed the way you light up when he walks into a room. Have you two talked about the past yet?"

Cait nodded.

"So you're not angry at him any more?"

"It isn't easy to get over something like that. But he had his reasons for what he did."

"And you accept them?"

"No." Cait waved one hand in the air. "Yes."

Mims chuckled. "What the hell does that mean?"

"The truth is, I don't know what I'd do without Comanche. He's been a terrific help. He even insisted on paying for the cattle we lost."

"From the dreamy look on your face, my guess is you feel a lot more than gratitude. Is it possible that you're still in love with him?"

"I don't think I'd recognize love if it walked up to me and said how-do-you-do. It's sex, pure and simple."

Mims let go another of her trademark throaty chuckles. "By now you ought to realize there's nothing pure or simple about sex."

She wanted to say Cait would be a fool to let a man like Comanche get away a second time. Considering her own chequered past, though, she was in no position to throw stones, even figurative ones. She turned her attention back to the scenery.

Born and raised in Manhattan, Mims used to regard the land stretching between the two coasts as a vast wasteland inhabited by an alien culture known as Middle America. She'd never wanted to get any closer to nature than she could during a taxi ride through Central Park. She'd never ridden a horse or seen a cow up close and personal, let alone had a calf lick the salt from her skin with its rough tongue.

Since arriving at the ranch she'd done all those things and more, and loved every minute of it even though her muscles ached every night from forking a saddle. She grinned to herself. *Forking a saddle*? Talk about going native. Next she'd probably start saying things like *bidness* or *fixin' to* and referring to every female acquaintance, including the married ones, as *Miss this* or *Miss that* the way Hank and Delta did.

There was something addictive about ranch life, with its dawn to dusk rhythm of hard work and peaceful nights when only the cicadas broke the quiet. The people she'd met had an honesty, a friendliness, she'd all but forgotten existed.

The Hill Country towns reminded her of Currier and Ives prints come to life. Kerrville and Fredericksburg had a turn-of-the-century charm that made it possible to forget the harsh reality of AIDS, homelessness, soaring crime rates and all the other ills that plagued big cities. Had she known how much she was going to enjoy herself, she would have planned to stay longer.

Now she found herself thinking up good reasons to come back. She thought she knew the perfect one. "Have you thought about who you want to handle the Outback's publicity?"

"I haven't got that far. Do you have anyone in mind?"

"How about the firm I use? That way, I could oversee what they were doing. You're going to need colour brochures, a national print campaign, a preview for travel agents, and a big grand opening. I'd enjoy working on all of them – especially the opening. I'd like to help you put together a guest list that combines Hollywood, New York and Washington. You need the kind of attendance that will guarantee lots of media attention – air time on *Entertainment Tonight*, and coverage in *People*."

Cait hesitated. Mims' help would be invaluable. She had a genius for public relations. She also had a horrendous schedule of her own. "You're way ahead of me. I've been so involved with getting the construction underway, working with decorators and landscapers and all the other subcontractors, that I haven't had time to do much else. I appreciate your offer more than I can say but you've got enough to do without going to all that trouble. Besides, it would mean making several trips to the ranch."

Mims gave Cait her sweetish smile. "Sugah," she said, producing a passable Texas drawl, "it will be no trouble at all. I'm *fixin' to* come back anyway."

From the air, Texas didn't look so very different from Kenya, Byron Neville decided. He found the thought comforting as he gazed down at cities and farms huddling like so many lonely oases in all that vastness.

Rolling his shoulders and tugging at his trousers to relieve the pressure on his crotch, he looked around the cabin. What he wouldn't give for a Player's cigarette. But there'd been no smoking on board since the flight departed New York.

It was damn good of his future employer, or was the correct term employeress? to send a first-class ticket. And bloody expensive. He couldn't help wondering if the dozen or so other passengers in the forward compartment were millionaires. It felt a bit strange to be surrounded by so many white faces. He missed the sibilant murmur of Swahili. America, he decided, would take a bit of getting used to.

Half an hour later, he was the first to deplane in San Antonio. He hurried up the jetway, smoothing his trousers and settling his shoulders in his safari jacket, hoping he didn't look too travel-worn. He'd taken advantage of a six-hour lay over in New York to get a shave, have his suit pressed and his Wellingtons polished in the hope of making a good first impression. He wanted, no, needed Miss Pride's approval and acceptance.

Kenya held nothing for him any more. He'd burned all his bridges. There was something unsettling about being a man without a country.

Miss Pride had written that she'd have someone meet him in the luggage area. Following the signs, he made his way through the crush of travellers, his senses bombarded with new sights and sounds. He'd sent most of his things – his guns, his safari gear – a couple of weeks earlier. The shipping agent had promised they would arrive in Texas shortly after he did.

While waiting for his bags, he studied the polyglot crowd. There were more black faces here than on the plane, he noted. Brown and yellow ones, too. America, the melting pot, melt me, he thought, smiling at his own unaccustomed whimsy.

He looked around with lively curiosity, his gaze finally captured by two stunning women. The older of the pair, a delicate platinum blonde, was wearing a suit that had *haute couture* written all over it. The younger, an exceptionally tall ash blonde, was dressed more casually in slacks and a tailored blouse.

Wonder who the lucky chap is they've come to meet? he mused, pulling a rectangular pack of Players from his jacket pocket and lighting up. He inhaled gratefully and turned his attention back to the luggage carousel.

By the time his luggage appeared, he'd finished smoking. He gathered his belongings and turned back to the crowd. To his surprise, the two women were still there. The taller one was looking around anxiously, holding up a sign that said, BYRON NEVILLE.

So he was the lucky chap! How bloody marvellous, he thought, hurrying towards them.

Mims was standing on tiptoe the way she always did when confronted with a milling throng. "I don't see how we could have missed him," she said.

"I don't either," Cait replied. "Do you think I should have him paged?"

"Let's give him another minute."

Just then, Mims' attention was diverted by a striking-looking man in a safari suit. He had the most gorgeous silver hair, a George Hamilton tan and even at a distance there was no mistaking the brilliance of his blue eyes.

A considerable part of her income depended on her ability to find men and women with that indefinable quality that would turn an eight by ten glossy into a riveting photograph. This man had it in spades. The perfect cut of his safari suit could only be achieved by a Saville Row tailor. Who can he be? she wondered.

She nudged Cait with her elbow. "Get a load of that. I think I'll go over and give him my card. You never know. He might be interested in doing some modelling."

She was groping in her purse for her card case when she realized he was headed their way. He had a loping walk that would look terrific on a runway. Calvin would give him a job in a New York minute.

Which one is Cait Pride? Byron wondered as he approached the two women. The older one was looking right at him. He walked up to her, held out his hand and said, "Byron Neville at your service. And you must be—'

"Mims Pauling." Her breathy voice sent a tingle racing up his spine. She gestured at the tall woman by her side. "This is Cait Pride."

Late again, Comanche thought, walking up to the ranch house. He'd taken the time to shower and change for dinner. Although Cait wouldn't approve of his tardiness, she'd appreciate it even less if he came to the table smelling of male sweat and horse dander, tonight of all nights.

The sound of laughter met him in the entry hall. He followed it to the dining room and paused in the double doors, started by the unaccustomed merriment. Hank, Delta, Cait and Mims seemed unaware of his arrival. Their joint gaze was fixed on the stranger in their midst.

So that's the white hunter, Comanche thought, taking the opportunity to study the other man. Byron Neville had the sort of silver hair that older women at the Bon Ton in Kerrville would kill to duplicate, a beach boy's tan and a set of white teeth that looked too perfect to be real. He wore a tweed jacket and an old school tie with a casual disregard that made Comanche feel like a hick in his own western-cut trousers and pearl-buttoned shirt from Shepler's.

Neville was too good-looking, too much the centre of attention, too damn everything, Comanche thought, taking instant umbrage. But the thing that really chapped him was the worshipful expression in Cait's eyes.

"When I got back to camp," Neville was saying, "the duchess was still sitting on the portable loo like a queen on her throne even though the wind had blown the tent away."

"What did she do?" Cait asked between giggles.

"She held up her hand and said, 'Do you have any lavatory paper?' I suppose that's what they mean by *noblesse oblige*."

A new round of laughter rocked the table. Finally, Cait glanced Comanche's way. "Oh, there you are," she said. "We've been waiting dinner for you. I'd like you to meet our new game manager, Byron Neville. Byron, this is our foreman, Comanche Killian."

Comanche walked over to the Kenyan and dutifully offered his hand. Neville's grip was surprisingly strong.

"I say, old chap, what an interesting name. Are you tribal by any chance?"

"Tribal?" Comanche could feel himself reddening.

"Indian," Neville explained.

"I'm one half Native American if that's what you mean," he replied grudgingly. What the hell did it matter? He hadn't asked Neville to produce his own pedigree.

Hank, who had taken the opportunity to fill their wine glasses, interrupted the uncomfortable colloquy.

"Now we're all here, I'd like to propose a toast." He lifted his glass high, his eyes shining with pride as he looked at Cait. "To my lovely daughter, and to the Outback."

"To your lovely daughter," Neville echoed, accenting

the lovely, "and to the Outback." He drained his goblet in a single draught and then, to Comanche's surprise, tossed it over his shoulder into the fireplace. The others laughed even harder as they followed suit.

Comanche sat there like a stone, thinking it was a damn silly waste of glassware. He glared at Neville. "What tribe taught you that trick?"

"The English tribe," Neville replied with good-humoured equanimity. "My father served in the RAF during the war. It's an old mess custom."

"You're right about the mess part," Comanche said, looking at the splinters of glass on the hearth.

As the meal progressed, Neville seemed to have no end of amusing anecdotes, coupled with a wealth of animal lore that exceeded Garner Holland's. He monopolized the conversation from soup to dessert.

Comanche never thought he would see the day when he felt like a stranger at the Pride's table. Damn it, Neville was the interloper, not him. Cait could barely tear her eyes from Neville's face long enough to ask Comanche to pass the salt and pepper.

Although Hank and Mims made an effort to include Comanche in the conversation, he felt so out of sorts that he rebuffed their overtures. He knew he was behaving like a spoiled brat and yet he couldn't seem to stop.

He'd never been jealous of a man before, but every time Cait looked at the white hunter with that star-struck gaze or favoured him with one of her megavolt smiles, Comanche had the irrational urge to leap across the table, grab the man by the collar and throw him out on his ear.

Fuck him and the horse he rode in on.

"My compliments, Delta," Neville said when the meal ended. "I don't know when I've enjoyed a supper more."

Delta rose to clear the table, and Neville jumped to his feet like a damn jack-in-the-box. "Let me help."

"I wouldn't think of it," she said, shaking her head from side to side. "You've got a lot to learn about the way we do things in Texas. Guests aren't welcome in the kitchen."

"I hope you don't think of me as a guest."

Cait gave Neville a smile that would have melted a glacier. "You don't go on the payroll until tomorrow. You're still our guest tonight."

"Speaking of the way we do things in Texas," Hank interjected, catching Comanche's eyes, "I'd appreciate it if you showed Mims and Byron the local nightlife. How about you and Cait taking them to the South Star?"

Comanche had never turned down any of Hank's requests before. But he couldn't see himself sitting across a table from Byron Neville, shooting the breeze. Nor could he imagine a pretty boy like Neville in a place like the South Star.

Ignoring the three expectant faces turned in his direction, he kept his gaze firmly fixed on Hank. "I don't think that's a very good idea, sir. It's a good thirty miles to the South Star and I planned an early night. We're cutting hay tomorrow."

"Perhaps some other time," Neville said, making light of Comanche's refusal. "I'd be happy to escort the ladies if Cait will show me the way – with your permission of course, Hank."

The South Star was an anachronism, a nineteenth-century saloon and dance hall with a twentieth-century clientèle. It had a smoky ambience complete with a long bar that invited cowboys to belly up, a jukebox that ate quarters during the day and a small dais where local talent played country-and-western music in the evening.

Ranchers, hired hands and storekeepers accompanied by wives and girlfriends flocked to the South Star on weekends like starlings to their roost. Beer flowed and complexions glowed as the air conditioning failed to keep pace with their combined body heat.

"I didn't think places like this existed except in the movies. Talk about local colour," Mims said, following

Cait to the last empty table. She looked over her shoulder at Byron. "Do you have anything like this in Nairobi?"

He nodded. "But I'm not sure I'd take either of you there."

"It may look a bit rough," Cait said as Byron helped her and Mims into their chairs, "but most of the people are local. Everyone knows everyone else. And Sheriff Schumaker or one of his men stops by regularly. I should caution you, though," she turned to Byron, "not to ask anyone else to dance. Texans can be very possessive when it comes to their women."

"Thanks for the warning but I can't imagine wanting to dance with anyone else when I'm already with the two best-looking ladies in the place."

Just then, a jeans-clad waitress came over and took their drink order.

"My apologies for Comanche's behaviour," Cait said, after the waitress left.

"We all have bad days," Byron replied.

Bad days, my foot, Mims thought. Comanche had behaved like a jealous child who didn't want to share a favourite toy. Not that she blamed him. Byron would be a formidable rival for any man.

She sat back, content to listen while he and Cait discussed the Outback. He had a delightful English accent with an overlay of Kenya. Despite being in a foreign country and having travelled thousands of miles to get there, he seemed perfectly at ease. That sort of confidence only came from competence, the sure and certain knowledge you could handle anything life sent your way.

Occasionally though, she glimpsed an intriguing world weariness in his eyes. She couldn't remember the last time she had reacted to a man so strongly. If he were any other man she would have talked to him about his potential as a model. The fact that he was Cait's employee made it out of the question.

She didn't realize she had lost track of the conversation

until he said, "Would you like to dance, Mims?"

Although she would have liked nothing more, she hesitated to leave Cait alone.

"Go on," Cait urged. "I'll order another round while you're gone."

"Are you sure you'll be all right?"

"Of course."

"I'd love to, then," Mims said, getting to her feet.

Carroll Detweiler had already consumed a six-pack when he walked into the South Star at ten. As he made his way to the bar, people cleared a path before him as if they were the Red Sea and he was Moses.

He'd spent every Friday at the South Star since coming to the Hill Country. With its cheap drinks and the you-mind-your-business-and-I'll-mind-mine attitude of the patrons, it suited him almost as well as the Old Tavern back home in Elgin. And it sure as hell beat twiddling his thumbs, flicking through the television channels or giving himself another hand job in a lousy motel room.

He ordered a beer, drank half of it down as soon as it came, lit a Marlboro and turned around to take in the action. The dance floor was so crowded, he didn't see them at first. But then the throng parted and he got a good look. Shit! There could be no mistaking Mims Pauling and Byron Neville, the white hunter Cait and Mims had met at the airport earlier in the day. In their fancy duds, they looked about as out of place as tits on a bull.

What the fuck were they doing here so far from the ranch? And where was Miss High and Mighty? He studied the dancing couples, half expecting to see her with the breed. When he didn't, he began circling the room, his gaze darted over the tables.

Fucking A, he thought, catching sight of her unmistakable profile. She was watching her friends so intently that she seemed unaware of his approach.

He knew he had no business going up to her but he was as irresistibly drawn to her as iron filings to a magnet. He was getting hard looking at her and remembering how she'd undressed down by the river that day. The thought of dancing with her, feeling her breasts against his chest, made him even harder.

He'd run into hot-looking broads on other ops, but he'd never had a chance to do anything about it, not with some fucking officer looking over his shoulder. Tonight he was on his own and damn glad of it. Hell, what harm could one little dance do? As far as Cait was concerned, he'd just be another cowboy in town for a little fun.

They make a terrific couple, Cait thought, when a beer belly blocked her view of Mims and Byron.

"How about a dance?" the belly's owner said in a rasping voice that grated on her ears.

She gazed upward to find herself confronted by a singularly unattractive man. He was massive, at least as tall as Comanche and probably fifty pounds heavier. His crew cut topped a set of porcine features, made even uglier by a jagged scar that ran down one cheek. The stranger would have made Freddie Kruger seem lovable by comparison.

"I think not," she said in her chilliest tone.

"Oh, come on, lady. What harm is there in a little dance?" Without giving her a chance to say no again, he yanked her to her feet and propelled her to the dance floor as if she were a marionette and he her puppeteer.

Resistance was useless in the face of such overpowering force. She couldn't help wishing Comanche were there, bad manners and all. Certainly Byron was no match for this incredible hulk.

"All right then," she said, "but just one dance. My boyfriend is the jealous type and he has a terrible temper. I wouldn't want you to get in trouble with him."

The hulk seemed unimpressed. "You're that famous model, aren't you?" he asked, pulling her far too close for comfort.

"Hey, back off. I'd like to have a little breathing room." She tried for a friendly tone although she wished she had the nerve to kick him in the shins.

"What's the matter? Aren't I good enough for you?"

The stranger was gripping her so tightly that she felt his erection pressing into her abdomen. She tried to squirm away but his grip only tightened. Good God, could you get raped in full view of a hundred people? she wondered as he pulled her even closer.

She managed to free her right hand and pounded him on the shoulder. For all his reaction, she might as well have been hitting a wall.

"I like a woman with a little fight in her," he whispered, his breath hot against her face.

He easily recaptured her hand, pulled her arm down to her side and held it there while his left hand lowered to her buttocks. He kneaded one cheek and then the other, groaning in her ear with sick passion.

She thought about screaming, but she couldn't be sure how the South Star crowd would react. Besides, anyone seeing the way they were dancing was bound to think they were having a lover's quarrel.

"God damn it, let me go, you ape," she hissed.

"Admit it, you love it." His hand abandoned her buttocks, moved around her back and touched the swell of her left breast before his fingers pinched her nipple. His breath was coming faster. "I'd sure like to eat your pussy. Are you wet yet? I like 'em juicy."

Cait gagged. In desperation, she tried to knee him, but he deftly caught the blow on his thigh. The pressure on her ribs kept her from getting a deep breath. He seemed oblivious to the fact that the music had stopped, oblivious to everything but his own sick pleasure.

★ ★ ★

Mims was a terrific dancer, Byron thought, breathing in her scent. She had brains, charm, looks and a wonderful breezy American way about her. Too bad she had to leave in a couple of days.

"Do you visit Cait often?" he asked.

"This is my first trip. But I plan to come back."

"Soon, I hope."

They talked about her agency, his reasons for leaving Kenya, her friendship with Cait, his hopes for the Outback, moving closer until the length of their bodies touched. Then there was no need for words. Their bodies said it all, swaying in perfect unison as if they'd danced together all their lives.

He was enjoying the experience so much that he kept her on the floor through an entire set even though he felt a bit guilty about leaving his employeress alone. Cait had said it herself though – he didn't go on the payroll until tomorrow.

They were making their way back to the table when he saw Cait with a stranger, still dancing even though the band had taken a break. The last time he had seen such panic in a woman's eyes had been when the Mau Mau attacked Kifaru.

"Bloody hell!" he muttered, stopping dead in his tracks.

"What's the matter?" Mims asked.

"Cait seems to be in a spot of trouble."

Mims looked across the floor, her eyes widening. "Oh, my God. What are we going to do?"

"Not *we*, love. *Me*. I'm afraid I'll have to play it by ear. You wait here."

"Should I call the sheriff?"

"I don't think there's time."

Beauty and the beast, Byron thought, approaching the mismatched couple, and a very formidable beast at that. He looked as solid as a barn.

"I say, old chap," he tapped the barn politely on the

shoulder, "you may not have noticed but the music stopped."

"Fuck off," the barn replied.

Byron used both hands to grab his arm and Cait took the opportunity to break free. Good girl, he thought, never taking his eyes from his adversary.

"I told you to fuck off," the monster repeated. He certainly did have a limited vocabulary.

"Is that any way to treat a visitor to the States?" Byron placed himself between the monster and Cait's escape route. He was peripherally aware of a crowd beginning to gather around them.

"Go get him, tiger," some one called out.

Hell. It would take a tiger to intimidate this beast.

"Why don't you ladies go on out to the car," he called over his shoulder, hoping Mims and Cait would do as he said. All the while, his gaze never left the monster's eyes. Animals always signalled an attack with their eyes, and there could be no doubt this man was an animal, as dangerous as any predator.

"And what if I want the bitches to stay?"

"I'd have to do my best to change your mind."

The monster's lips parted in a grin that would have done credit to a hyena. "You and who else?"

"Just me."

"Try it, motherfucker," the monster said, swinging a fist the size of a Polish ham.

Byron read the message in his eyes before the monster moved. He ducked under the punch and kicked out with his right foot, his Wellington making vicious contact with the monster's genitals.

The behemoth let go a strangled "aaargh", clutched his privates and fell face forward like a harvested tree.

Just then, a middle-aged man in some sort of uniform came across the floor with Cait and Mims in tow.

"Are you all right?" Mims asked, her beautiful blue eyes clouded with worry.

"Never better," Byron replied.

"What happened?" the uniformed man asked.

"Nothing much. It would appear the bloody sot can't hold his drink."

Although Comanche had gone to bed early, he couldn't sleep. He kept on replaying the dinner in his mind, not certain if he felt more upset with Cait or himself. He'd acted the fool. But Cait's performance had been even worse. She'd hung on every word Neville said.

Frowning in the dark, he kicked his twisted covers aside, got out of bed, put on a robe and walked through the house to the front door. Trouble padded at his heels, whining softly as if he shared Comanche's misery.

Humidity hung heavy in the night air and a flash of heat lightning streaked across the sky as Comanche settled on the porch swing, idly pushing himself back and forth. He was so lost in thought that he didn't hear the Suburban coming up the drive until it passed his house. He hadn't expected them home this early. Could something be wrong?

Tightening his belt, he hurried after the car, painfully aware of the ludicrous sight he must be with his threadbare robe flapping around his thighs. Reaching the Suburban as it braked to a stop, he opened the driver's door. To his surprise, Cait wasn't behind the wheel.

Byron stepped out. "What's this? A greetings committee?" He bent down to pat Trouble as the dog sniffed his trousers.

Trouble was usually standoffish but he wagged his tail as if Byron were an old friend. Traitor, Comanche thought.

"You're home early," Comanche said, seeing Cait emerge from the other side of the car. "How was the South Star?"

Cait doubled over laughing, as if he'd said something extraordinarily funny.

Mims, who got out of the car next, was laughing, too. "You should have been there. This big goon asked Cait to dance and he wouldn't let her go when the music stopped."

"Big goon?" Comanche's stomach knotted.

"The biggest," Byron chimed in. "He seemed quite smitten with our Cait."

Our Cait? Comanche silently fumed. She was *his* Cait. "What happened?"

Cait and Mims were laughing so hard that they had to hold onto each other to stay upright.

"Byron came to my rescue," Cait finally managed to gasp between chortles.

Comanche turned to Byron, the knot in his stomach tightening. "You didn't happen to notice if he smoked Marlboros?"

"I didn't have time to notice much of anything. He must have weighed eighteen stones and every one of them was mean."

Comanche looked Byron up and down, wondering how he could have handled someone that size. "Did you call the sheriff?"

"There wasn't time."

"So what did you do?"

"I didn't fight him according to the Marquess of Queensbury rules, if that's what you want to know."

"What the hell does that mean?"

"I kicked him in the balls," Byron said, grinning triumphantly.

"He was wonderful." Cait came around the car and took Byron's arm. "I don't know what I'd have done without him."

"It was nothing." Byron's shoulders lifted in a self-deprecating shrug.

Nothing, my ass, Comanche thought five minutes later as he walked back to his house alone. Byron had played the hero and he hadn't even barked his knuckles doing it.

★ ★ ★

Carroll Detweiler sat on his bed breathing heavily, a Marlboro in his mouth, an ice bag held against his crotch. Fuck. Another kick like that and he'd be singing soprano. His balls hurt. His head hurt. His pride hurt most of all. He sure as hell couldn't tell the Senator how badly he'd bungled things.

He still couldn't believe he'd been dumb enough to let that little motherfucker get away with the oldest trick in the book. If it hadn't been for the Pride bitch, it would never have happened, not in a million years.

If she hadn't acted so high-and-mighty, if she'd accepted his offer to dance, he'd have copped a quick feel and no one would have been the wiser. But the cunt had looked at him as if he'd just crawled out from under a rock.

A litany of oaths ran through his mind like prayer beads. What had started out to be just another op had turned into a personal vendetta. One way or another, Cait Pride was going to pay.

15

The frigid December wind chilled Comanche to the bone as he hurried to the barn. Shivering, he turned up his jacket collar to ward off the cold. He could do nothing about the glacier sheeting his heart. What was that Shakespearean line about "the winter of our discontent"? Now he knew what it meant – in spades. He felt empty inside, as if all his hopes and dreams had vanished with the first frost.

He'd been so close to having it all, the ranch and the woman who went with it. Looking back, he couldn't recall which he had wanted more that day down by the river. No, he admitted, that wasn't true. Losing Cait was bad enough without compounding the hurt by lying to himself about how he felt.

Not so very long ago he couldn't imagine anything grander than owning Pride's Passion. Now the size and scope of his dream had nothing to do with the land. He'd have wanted Cait under any circumstances. Although he fought it with everything at his command, he fell more in love with her all the time.

He'd always been attracted by her looks, but it was her grit, her courage, and yes, even her mule-headedness that had put a hammerlock on his heart. She had changed immeasurably in the last few months. Her tenderness and devotion to Hank, her determination to do something of value touched an answering chord deep within him.

There were times when he would gladly have changed

places with Hank to have Cait look at him just once with love shining in her eyes. But he'd been relegated to the sidelines since Neville appeared on the scene.

Neville represented all the things Comanche didn't have – breeding, sophistication and charm. His worldliness made Comanche feeling like a tongue-tied dolt by comparison. Worse still, Neville stuck to Cait like burrs to a sheep. They worked together, travelled together – hell, for all Comanche knew, they even slept together.

The thought burned in his brain like acid. He felt as hopeless as he had on the long-ago day when his mother walked out. He'd been having the old nightmares about being abandoned by her. Only in his dreams, she had Cait's face. Every time he woke up drenched in sweat, he knew he wouldn't sleep any more that night.

Even more troubling was his feeling that Neville didn't deserve Cait or the ranch that was her birthright. Sure, the man knew exotic animals. And yes, he could tell one hell of a story. Sometimes Comanche couldn't help laughing at them in spite of himself.

Hank liked him, Delta liked him, Mims liked him. Even Trouble liked him. For all Comanche cared though, the entire city of Kerrville could declare a Byron Neville day and hold a parade in his honour. It wouldn't change his opinion.

Anyway he looked at it, Neville just didn't seem good enough, or man enough, for Cait.

Cait yawned, stretched, and rolled her shoulders to ease her exhaustion. Although she'd been working since sunup, her desk was still stacked with papers that needed her attention. Job applications, proposals from a dozen different vendors including food wholesalers, linen suppliers, veterinary pharmaceutical houses, farm equipment dealers and many others all needed to be evaluated. There were bills to pay, documents to review and file, the list seemed endless.

The treadmill of her existence had accelerated so quickly she barely had time for Hank and none for herself. No one would ever mistake her for a glamorous model today.

The work piled up every time she and Byron left town. She'd just get caught up and the two of them would be off to yet another zoo or wildlife auction to purchase animals.

On the plus size, the fencing crews had nearly finished. Three holding pens, each the size of a football field, circled the half-completed veterinary clinic. Half a dozen vast enclosures of a thousand acres or more had been completed, secured by tall steel fences guarded by double gates. The warming barns and the nursery would be complete by Christmas, and not a moment too soon in view of the animals she and Byron had already purchased.

This very morning, a hundred new arrivals were in the holding pens getting acclimatized. Dozens more, zebra, wildebeest, oryx, eland and gazelle – ungulates from three different continents – already roamed two of the larger enclosures. The hands reported a steady influx of local wildlife as well.

The increased numbers of white-tailed deer, coyotes, armadillos and opossums offered positive proof that the enclosures provided a healthy environment. The Outback was well on its way to becoming a haven for animals as well as a place where city dwellers could get back in touch with the natural world.

The guest rooms, dining pavilion, an Olympic-sized swimming pool, jacuzzi, saunas, tennis courts and all the other amenities sophisticated travellers regarded as their due were under way. Support facilities – an administration building and an up-to-the-minute commercial kitchen capable of preparing anything from a picnic to a banquet – were in various stages of construction. Mark Calhoun, a young hotelier just three years out of college, would be joining the staff in February to oversee their completion.

Thanks to Mims' publicity campaign, fashion photographers had begun calling to ask about using the Outback as a backdrop for their shoots. And a movie company had contacted her about doing some location work. With any luck, this time next year the Outback would be almost as well known as Club Med.

She didn't dare count on luck, though, because so far, the Outback's had all been bad.

"How's it going?" Byron's appearance at the office door interrupted her reverie.

He held a cigarette in one hand and two cups of coffee in the other. Although they had flown back from Seattle late yesterday, arriving at the ranch after midnight, his tan skin glowed with good health, every one of his distinctive silver hairs had been combed in place, and he was perfectly turned out in knife-pleated khaki trousers, a matching shirt and expensive ostrich boots.

She accepted the coffee gratefully and took a long swallow. "Thanks. How did you know that's just what I needed?"

"I wish I could take the credit, but it was Delta's idea. She said you'd been working for a couple of hours. Did you get any sleep?"

"Not much." Cait put the cup down and gestured at the folders on her desk. "I kept on thinking about all of this."

"Any replies to our search for a breeding pair of black rhinos?"

"I don't know. I haven't got through all the mail yet."

"We'd better find a pair soon. They'd be a terrific drawing card. And a couple of elephants wouldn't hurt. In Kenya, tourists weren't happy until they'd photographed the big three – rhinos, elephants and lions. The animals have to be in place at least three months before the grand opening if we hope to habituate them."

She gave a helpless shrug. "I'm doing the best I can."

"Sorry, Cait. I didn't mean to give you a difficult time.

You look exhausted. Are you still planning to inspect the enclosures this morning?"

"I wouldn't miss it for the world. Seeing the animals makes it all worthwhile." Closing her eyes, she rubbed her brow, then rolled her shoulders again in a futile attempt to unknot the muscles in her neck and back.

She heard Byron's chair scrape the floor. His first touch startled her and she pulled away reflexively. Then, as he began to massage away her tension, she leaned back and relaxed.

Comanche finished saddling Jim Dandy, Dulcinea and Randy, the spirited gelding Neville rode. In addition to everything else, the white hunter had a terrific seat on a horse.

Leading them out to the corral, Comanche looped their reins around a post and headed for the house to get Neville and Cait. Damn. He could think of lots of better ways to start his day than inspecting the enclosures with the two of them. Hell, eating ground glass would have been preferable.

When he walked into his office, a space he reluctantly shared with them until the Outback's new offices were finished, his first instinct was to turn tail and run.

Byron was standing behind Cait, rubbing her neck. Her eyes were closed, her lips parted. Her head rested against his chest. A soft sigh escaped her mouth as she lifted her hair to bare her nape.

Comanche repressed a groan, recalling how sensitive that area had been to his kisses. It felt like death, seeing another man's hands giving Cait pleasure.

"Are you ready to inspect the animals?" he said.

"Give me a minute to finish here," Byron replied.

Cait finally opened her eyes and gazed at Comanche.

His anger faded as he realized how weary she looked. Her face was pale, her eyes shadowed and new lines of worry had been etched on her forehead. Sometimes he forgot the burden of responsibility she carried. "How did things go at the Seattle Zoo?"

"Better than we hoped. We were able to buy two lionesses at a very reasonable price, thanks to Byron. I wish you could see how well he handles people."

Comanche's concern for Cait evaporated instantly. He had an all too graphic example of how well Byron "handled" people right in front of him. The man was a master manipulator in more ways than one.

"It was nothing," Byron said. "I happened to meet the zoo's director at a wildlife symposium in Nairobi a couple of years ago, invited him for a few drinks at my club, swapped stories, showed him the town – that sort of thing. He was only too happy to get rid of his excess big cats. We can count on getting more animals from him if the lions do well." He kept a proprietary hand on Cait's shoulder. "We really must do something about our girl, though. Maybe you can talk some sense into her. She's been working much too hard."

Comanche almost gagged on his impotent anger. "We're all working hard."

Byron gestured at the crowded desk top. "You're in charge of the cattle and I take care of the exotics. Cait's responsible for the whole show."

"I can manage," Cait said, getting to her feet. Suddenly the office seemed too small to contain the emotions filling it.

Although she headed for the door, Comanche made no move to follow. "Perhaps Byron's right. You do need some help," he said, a strange smile playing on his lips.

What had got into him now? she mused. The unhappiness in his emerald eyes had been superseded by a wicked gleam. She had seen that same gleam before he launched a devilish escapade when they were children.

"You sound like you have someone in mind," she said cautiously.

"Oh, I do, indeed I do." His tone was as syrupy sweet

as Delta's home made pralines. "I'm thinking about someone who knows her way around a ranch, who can type, file, use a computer and keep books too."

Byron stopped halfway to the door. "Who is this paragon?"

"An old friend of Cait's and mine. Bobby Rae Seeley." Comanche looked straight at Cait, his eyes challenging her to object.

"Bobby Rae has a job."

"If I've heard Bobby Rae say it once I've heard her say it a thousand times. She doesn't want to spend the rest of her life waitressing. You wouldn't deny an old friend a chance to better herself and to give you the help you obviously need."

A tidal wave of jealousy purged Cait's mind of reason. She had a swift mental image of Bobby Rae and Comanche laughing intimately, their heads so close that Bobby Rae's blonde locks touched his dark hair. It was the vision that had greeted her the day she walked into the Hill Country Café.

The thought of seeing that moment repeated a thousand times right here in her own home made her dizzy with anger. How dare he suggest bringing Bobby Rae to the Outback? "You know I've been trying to hold costs down."

"You can't go on burning the candle at both ends, Cait," Byron interjected. "It won't do the Outback any good if you collapse. This Bobby Rae sounds perfect. And considering she's been getting by on a waitress's wages, I don't imagine she'll expect a huge salary."

Of all the times for Byron and Comanche finally to agree on something. "All right. I'll give her a call one of these days," Cait said, stalling for time in the hope that the idea would eventually be forgotten.

Comanche's smile had become downright Mephistophelian. "Terrific. Let me jot down her number for you. Better still, I'll call her right now."

* * *

Hank stood at the window watching as Cait, Comanche and Byron rode away. When they disappeared from sight he crossed the floor to the night stand by his bed, opened a vial of pills, took one and lay down to wait for it to work. Over the last few months his consumption of painkillers had increased while their ability to give him relief steadily diminished. He could almost feel the cancer growing, robbing him of his remaining strength.

Alone at night there were times when he would have welcomed death. But dawn always renewed his determination to survive as long as possible. He couldn't let go of life until Cait's future was assured.

The drug was just beginning to take hold when Delta appeared with his breakfast tray. She set it on the night table, leaned over and kissed his forehead. "How are you today, *cher*?"

"The truth?"

"Of course. Only the truth between us."

"I felt like hell when I woke up. The pills help."

Delta kissed him again. "But not as much as they used to."

"How can you tell?"

"No matter how you smile, I see the hurt in your eyes. It might help if you talked about it. There must be times when you're scared, when you want to shout the house down."

"You're right, as usual," he replied softly. "Do you remember the trip we took to the Grand Canyon when Cait was little?"

"Certainly, *cher*."

"We drove for hours, and then when we got to the canyon it was covered with fog and we couldn't see the other side."

"Cait was so angry. You would think nature had set out to cheat her."

"Sometimes I think death is like that canyon. I know it's

out there. But no matter how hard I try, I can't see what's on the other side."

Delta's heart seemed to rise up her throat as she looked at him. Although he was doing his best to conceal his deterioration from everyone else, he couldn't conceal it from her. He reached for her hand, and she clasped it hard.

"I'm still hurting. Would you call Doc Williams and make an appointment for me? I think I need a stronger prescription."

She tried to smile but had to fight tears instead. If Hank was asking to see the doctor, he must feel worse than even she knew. Could the end be that close? "I'll call him while you eat."

"Good. And don't tell Cait."

Twenty-five years of keeping secrets ballooned in Delta's chest like bread dough that has risen too long. She brushed her tears angrily away. "I'll do no such thing! Cait has a right to know."

"She's got enough on her mind."

"If she knew, she might spend more time at home and less running around the country with Byron."

"She isn't running around. She's buying animals. You know how much the Outback means to her."

"You're afraid she's just like you, aren't you?"

"What do you mean?"

"Five months ago, you were worried Cait wouldn't stay here. Now you're worried that the Outback means more to her than you do. But you couldn't be more wrong. Don't you see, *cher*? She's still trying to earn your love. And the only way she knows to do it is to make the Outback a success."

"I'm so afraid she'll throw her life away on the Outback – and Comanche's too – the way I wasted yours and mine."

Delta shook her head. "Love is never wasted."

"But it can be blind. No one knows that better than I do."

"Then you and I will just have to find a way to open Cait's eyes," Delta replied firmly.

The sound of traffic barely penetrated the hundred and fifty-year-old brick walls of Senator Morgan's Georgetown pied-à-terre, an historic town house he regarded as a pit stop on his way to the White House.

"If you'll excuse me, dear," he said, getting up from the dinner table, "I have some work to do in my office." He walked to his wife's side, gave her a quick peck on the cheek and then, the amenities of marriage attended to, headed for his den without another word.

He had no sooner walked in and shut the door than his benign expression gave way to a fierce scowl. Damn the Democrats. Damn the recession. Damn Tochigi. Damn Detweiler. Most of all, *damn Cait Pride*.

Instead of concentrating on affairs of state, he found himself devoting more and more thought to her and Pride's Passion. Here he was, a member of the most august legislative body in the world, a man his party touted as a future presidential candidate and he hadn't been able to persuade her to sell the ranch.

Although wisdom had dictated that he stay out of the picture as much as possible, his need to know more about what was happening drove him to the telephone. Checking his watch, he took a seat behind his elegant Sheraton desk and reluctantly dialled Cait's number.

"Good evening, dear girl," he said in his most mellow baritone when she came on the line. "I've been thinking about you and your father. How are the two of you managing?"

"How kind of you to ask. I'm fine and Dad, well, he's hanging in there."

"It's not kindness at all, just an old friend's concern. I can't help thinking you've taken on too much, caring for your father and starting up a major project like the Outback, to say nothing of the financial responsibilities.

I'm afraid my friend was a bit greedy when it came to the terms of your loan."

"Considering the financial climate in Texas, I was lucky to get the capital I needed. So don't worry about greed."

"Then you aren't having second thoughts about the Outback?"

"Not at all. I wish you could have been with me when I toured the ranch this morning," she enthused. "Construction is moving right alone, but it's the animals that really make the Outback special."

"Animals? What animals?" Why hadn't he heard about them from Det?

He listened to her enthusiastic reply, his expression growing more sour by the minute. In view of her lack of business acumen, she should never have got this far. The realization that she might never sell the ranch hit him like a sucker punch.

If only the Hill Country realtor he'd been talking to would come up with an alternative property. If only Tochigi weren't in such a blasted hurry. If only his finances looked brighter. If only he'd never heard of Pride's Passion.

But all the "if onlys" in the world didn't change a thing. He was running out of time. One way or another, he would have to see to it that Cait Pride failed.

He pressed the speaker button, put down the receiver and paced his way through the rest of their conversation, then continued pacing long after Cait said goodbye, rationalizing what he was going to do.

Cait wasn't important in the grand scheme of things. The greater good had to come first. The Hill Country would benefit from Japanese money. The Senate and the nation would benefit with his ongoing participation in the affairs of state. He had to be free of the financial worries that had dogged his last few years.

At last, he dialled Det's number. "Why didn't you tell

me about the exotics on the Pride ranch?" he demanded without even saying hello.

"I didn't think it was important."

"What do you mean, not important? Cait Pride is well on her way to opening the Outback and you say it's not important. Have you lost your fucking mind?"

"I've followed your instructions to the letter. You wanted me to watch Cait Pride, and I have. You didn't tell me to report on the ranch, too." Det sounded aggrieved.

Christ, the man was an idiot.

Blackjack caught the sour scent of his own fear as he thought about the high stakes game he had been playing – and losing. It made him even more nervous, thinking Det was the only ace in his deck. He couldn't afford to alienate him.

"Sorry, Det. You're absolutely right. You've done a terrific job. As of this evening though, the mission's changed. Forget about keeping an eye on Cait Pride. I want you to do whatever it takes to insure that the Outback never opens. Do you think you can manage that for me?"

"I don't get it. Are you saying you want me to eliminate her?"

"No, damn it. I don't want you to lay a hand on her. For Christ' sake, she's my daughter's best friend. I just want you to put some stumbling blocks in her way, hit her in the pocketbook. For openers, how about getting rid of those animals. It should be a piece of cake for a man with your training, your talent. You can count on a bonus the day she leaves the ranch for good."

"I read you loud and clear, Senator."

"I'm counting on you, Det. And one more thing. Whatever you do, make sure no one can connect the two of us."

After Blackjack said goodbye, Carroll sat in his motel room waiting until the beat of his heart returned to normal. The Senator had almost tripped him up, finding out about the exotics on his own. He could hardly tell Blackjack he'd been lying low since the incident at the South Star, letting his beard and his crew cut grow out, dying his hair and even wearing mirrored sunglasses in the hope he wouldn't be recognized if he ran into the sheriff again.

The only light in the room came from the flickering image on the television. But he ignored the action on screen. His imagination ran wild as he thought about his changed mission. Plans. He had to make plans.

Since it looked like he'd be in town a little longer he'd move into an apartment. Then what? he mused, rubbing the itchy stubble on his chin. Suddenly, he broke into a smile of pure malicious glee. Fucking A! He knew just what to do.

In a couple of days, he'd be ready to rock and roll.

16

The noise woke Cait at three in the morning. It sounds like firecrackers, she thought groggily, struggling from the depths of sleep. She heard the sound again, and then again. It seemed to be coming from the direction of the holding pens.

The thought no sooner came to her mind than she threw the covers aside and catapulted from the bed. The animals. Dear God. Was some damn kid trying to frighten them? They spooked so easily, they might hurt themselves.

Emerging from her bedroom in hastily donned underwear, she ran full tilt into Byron. "What the hell's going on?" he said, paying no more attention to her seminudity than she did to his.

"I don't know but we'd better find out," she replied as they raced for the stairs side by side, pulling on clothes all the way. At the bottom, she only sat long enough to shove her bare feet into a pair of boots.

"Where are you going?" she cried out, seeing him head for the office. "The Suburban's out front."

"I'll need a gun," he called over his shoulder before disappearing from sight.

His words echoed in her mind as she tugged at the front door, forgetting in her panic that they had started locking it after the incident with the Peeping Tom.

The Suburban's engine had just stuttered into life when he came racing round the side of the house with a rifle in one hand and a flashlight in the other. "Move it," he shouted, leaping into the passenger seat.

The sound of firecrackers had stopped by the time they reached the holding pens. But the noises that assaulted her ears when she braked the Suburban to a stop were far more terrible.

"Shit. I thought I'd seen the last of this," Byron muttered cryptically. He yanked his door open. "Keep your headlights on so I can see what I'm doing. And stay put."

After he'd gone, Cait peered through the windshield. A thick cloud of dust obscured the scene. The banshee noises hadn't diminished. If anything, they seemed even more terrible. Good god, what had happened? She clapped her hands over her ears in a futile attempt at shutting out the sounds.

Despite the fear that pooled deep in her belly, she couldn't permit herself to cower in the car. The Outback was her idea, her responsibility. The hair on her arms stood up straight as she got out of the Suburban. A Hadean vision met her eyes when she reached the gate of the nearest holding pen.

The exotics stayed in the pens for up to a month so their condition could be carefully monitored before they were released into one of the Outback's enclosures. But one glance at these animals told Cait they wouldn't live that long. As she closed the gate behind herself, mutilated creatures hurtled past, tripping on their own entrails or staggering on broken legs.

Comanche had been sighting down his rifle, preparing to put a severely injured Arabian oryx out of its misery when he saw a shadowy figure enter the pen out the corner of his eye. The sixth sense that always let him know Cait was in the vicinity told him who it was before he could make our her features.

When a gun boomed in the adjacent pen, he realized she must have driven from the house with Neville. What the hell could the bastard be thinking, leaving her to blunder into such devastation? As she drew nearer, he saw the shell-shocked expression on her face. Good God, what must she be thinking and feeling? It was hard enough on him and he had never sentimentalized animals the way she did.

His heart constricted as he saw a huge nilgai materialize out of the pre-dawn gloom. Nilgai were usually gentle, but this one had blood on its flanks and death in its eyes. Cait stood directly in its path. Tucking the rifle in the crook of one arm, he raced to her side. As he pulled her close with his free hand, the nilgai crashed against him. Fighting for balance, he raced for the gate, not setting Cait down until they were safely on the other side.

The full length of Comanche's body pressing against her own brought Cait back to awareness. It felt so right, so inevitable that for a second she allowed herself to forget everything but the exquisite sensation of being held by him again.

"That was a close call," came the husky sound of his voice.

"For the love of God, what happened? What's going on," she cried out to be heard above the din.

"I don't know yet. But we need help. Get some of the hands over here. The vet too. And call the sheriff. Hurry, Cait, for the love of God, hurry."

Dirt and blood streaked Cait's clothes when she returned to the house an hour after dawn. She half fell out of the Suburban and stumbled to the porch. Collapsing onto the bottom step, she lowered her head onto her arms and wept.

Her dream of a luxurious safari ranch had turned into a gory nightmare. The animals in the pens had suffered unspeakable injuries, making a quick death merciful by contrast. She couldn't erase the memory of Comanche's and Byron's faces when they emerged from what had become a killing ground. Their features had been taut, their complexions grey under their tans. Worst of all had been the haunted look in their eyes.

She cared for them both in different ways and blamed herself for what they'd been through. If she hadn't been so damn determined to prove herself to her father, if she had accepted Comanche's offer to buy the ranch . . .

Lost in her own misery, she didn't hear the front door open and close. "Good heavens, *cher*," Delta said, coming down the steps and folding Cait in her arms, "I can see something terrible has happened, but please try to be quiet. You wouldn't want your father to see you like this."

Cait buried her head in Delta's bosom and clung to the older woman. "It – was – so awful," she moaned between shuddering sobs.

A stronger pair of arms circled her shoulders and Cait looked up to see her father through the blur of her tears. Despite the early hour, he was fully dressed.

"I heard that noise in the middle of the night. What happened, honey?"

Sheriff Herman Schumaker was a quiet, steady, whipcord of a man in his late forties. He had been in law enforcement all his life and took it personally when people broke the law in his jurisdiction. Automobile accidents, robberies, family disputes were his stock in trade. He thanked God every day that big city problems – murders, rapes and drug-related crimes – were still rare in Kerrville.

It was the second time in as many months that he'd been called to Pride's Passion to investigate a crime. The rustling, however, had come as no surprise. Rustling was commonplace in Kerr County. This morning had been different. He'd never seen anything like it before – and if he was very, very lucky, he never would again.

He gazed around the Pride's kitchen, an untouched cup of coffee cooling on the table in front of him. "How many animals did you lose?" he asked Cait.

"Sixty-two," she replied, her voice hoarse from the tears she'd shed. "Two dozen died outright. Byron and Comanche put the others down to end their suffering. The veterinarian told me another twenty might not survive their injuries. He's set up a temporary hospital for them in the barn."

"Do you have any idea why someone would have dynamited the holding pens?"

She shook her head. She'd been through one hell of an ordeal and, from the look in her eyes, she was near the breaking point.

"Anybody else have any ideas?" he asked, looking from Hank to Byron to Comanche.

"I told you that someone was spying on Cait the day before the cattle were rustled," Comanche replied, impatience colouring his voice.

"Has anything happened since then?"

"Not here. But what about the creep at the South Star?" Comanche replied. "Couldn't he have been the Peeping Tom?"

"I don't see how the incidents are related."

"You know your business," Comanche conceded, "but I have a feeling they involved the same man."

"Do you have a concrete reason for that feeling?"

"What if someone was out to get Cait?"

"I suppose it's possible," Herman replied, "but not likely. There's no pattern to the incidents. The pieces don't fit." Comanche was a good man, but he didn't know much about the criminal mentality. In his anxiety to protect the Prides, he was grasping at straws.

"Isn't the sale of dynamite controlled?" Byron asked.

"It's supposed to be," Herman explained. "Today or tomorrow, I'll probably get a report of explosives being stolen from a construction site."

"That still won't explain why someone would want to kill our animals," Byron said. For once, the white hunter's aplomb seemed to have deserted him.

"If we knew the answer to that, we'd have a good chance of catching the perpetrator," Herman replied.

"You make it sound bloody hopeless."

"Nothing's hopeless."

"How badly were we hurt financially?" Hank asked.

Cait had barely followed the conversation. The sound of Hank's voice forced her to concentrate on the here and now. His once ruddy skin looked like marble. His face was so gaunt that his nose jutted from it like a ship's prow. God alone knew what internal strength kept him going. He had asked her to stay on the ranch – to be with him until the end. Would he make the same request today?

"I haven't thought about it yet." She bit her lip to stay her tears. "The money is bad enough. But the poor animals . . ." Her voice trailed off. Thank God Hank hadn't seen the carnage in the holding pens. At least he had been spared that much.

"We're going to have to hire enough hands to keep a constant watch over all our animals," Comanche said. "We can't afford to lose any more."

"We can't afford to hire a bunch of new hands either." She paused long enough to draw in a shuddering breath. "There's only one thing to do." Unable to look at her companions, she kept her gaze firmly fixed on the table top. "Dad asked me to stay here to save the ranch. Instead, for whatever reason, my presence is destroying it. I don't mind the danger for myself. But I can't expose all of you, let alone the animals, to the whims of some maniac. I can't run the risk that he may come after Dad or Delta the next time. So I've decided to go back to New York."

In all the years they'd known one another, Comanche had never seen Cait so defeated. She sat hunched in her chair as if she expected another blow to rain down on her shoulders. Although she had washed her face and hands, she hadn't taken the time to change her clothes. Her pants and shirt were still spattered with dirt, blood and God alone knew what. Her hair tangled around her shoulders. Despair clouded her eyes. He wished he could take her in his arms and make her world right again.

But this wasn't the time to deal with his own emotions, not if he wanted to help Cait deal with hers. He couldn't let her give up on the Outback. His Katydid didn't belong in New York; she belonged here. Hank needed her, the ranch needed her. She had become the living embodiment of the land, just as all the other generations of Pride women had been before her.

"What about the loan?" he said softly, probing for an anchor to hold her in place. "How do you intend to pay it off if you go back to New York?"

"I'll return the unused portion. The next few years of my earnings should cover the rest." She turned to Hank, tears glistening in her eyes. "I'm so sorry, Daddy. I just don't know what else to do."

"It's all right, honey. You did your best."

Comanche knew Hank was trying to make Cait's surrender easier. But it wasn't right, not for either of them. He would never forget the pride in her voice the night she told him Hank had asked her to take over the ranch. She'd had a special glow that night. No matter how hard she worked or how tired she was, she had never lost that glow.

Until now.

Comanche took a deep breath, steeling himself for what he had to do. Although he knew he would be risking what little chance he had of winning her back, he felt certain he knew how to reach Cait. She had gone far beyond the point where sympathy would help. He had to rouse the gutsy fighter who still lurked deep inside the broken woman. And, Lord forgive him for what he was about to say, he thought he knew how to do it.

"You always were a quitter, Cait," he said in his most scathing tone. "The day you told me about the Outback, I knew you'd pull out when the going got tough."

Cait had been drooping like a wilted flower. She

straightened abruptly. "How dare you – you of all people – call me a quitter?"

"I'm not the one who's turning tail and running. Come hell or high water, I'll be here with your father while you're prancing around in front of a camera in New York."

"Now just a minute," Byron said, rising to Cait's defence.

"Just a minute yourself, you chicken shit," Comanche shot back. "The only thing you're good for is kicking some helpless drunk in the balls. I guess that makes you and Cait two of a kind. You're both scared of a real fight." His very real dislike of the white hunter gave conviction to his words. He dismissed the older man with a disdain-filled glance, then turned back to Cait. "I told you I'd buy the ranch months ago. The offer is still good."

"I'd as soon sell to the devil."

Comanche was pleased to see some colour had returned to her cheeks. "You talk a good game, Cait, you always did. But this isn't a game. You don't have the guts to go on with the Outback. So why don't you just go on upstairs and pack your bags. And while you're at it," he jerked his hand contemptuously at Byron, "you can pack his things too."

Cait's chin jutted with renewed determination. Fury fired her gaze as she stared him down. "How dare you talk to me that way? In case you've forgotten, you're just a hired hand, and hired hands come and go. You're the one who needs to pack. I want you the hell off my land! You're fired!"

"As for me, old chap," Byron chimed in, an impudent grin on his tan face, "I believe you cowboys like to settle things out behind the barn. Name the time and I'll be there."

"What's wrong with right now?" Comanche snarled.

Hank glanced from Comanche to Byron before his gaze settled on Cait. Instead of being mired in self-pity, she looked madder than hell and ready to take on the world. And she owed it all to Comanche, Hank thought. He'd been desperate to keep Cait here and utterly unable to figure a way to do it. Comanche had, though. One of these days she would thank him for it.

"Time out," he shouted into the emotionally charged atmosphere. "There will be no talk of firing or fighting while I'm alive. I know you're all tired and that you've been through a lot. That's the only reason I'm willing to ignore what's been said here this morning." He glared at Cait, Comanche and Byron in turn, playing the stern patriarch for all he was worth.

"I – he – you," Cait sputtered.

Suppressing a grin, Hank narrowed his eyes. "Now, now, Cait. Get a grip on yourself."

"I just want you to know I'm not determined to go back to New York. I was only exploring the possibility out loud."

"Have you reached a conclusion?" he asked more gently.

"No matter what Comanche says, I'm not a quitter!"

"I know that, honey."

"I was just trying to do what's best for everyone."

"I know that too."

Herman Schumaker had been quietly sipping his coffee and eating Delta's home-made buttermilk biscuits while the emotional storm raged around him. His heart went out to the beleaguered family even as his lawman's brain urged him to be on his way.

He wiped his mouth, folded his napkin and got to his feet. "I can see you folks have a lot to discuss. Thanks for the coffee and biscuits, Miss Delta. Next time I'll try to do them justice."

Bobby Rae Seeley had dressed with special care that morning. As she drove through the imposing gates of the Pride ranch, she took a moment to check her appearance in her ancient Camaro's rear-view mirror. Although she felt almost naked without them, she'd left her false eyelashes in the plastic box on her dressing table. They were part of her uniform at the café, but instinct told her they wouldn't do for a secretary – make that an executive secretary, she silently amended. Because that's what she hoped to become. The business classes she'd taken after graduating from high school, the ones her husbands had told her were a waste of time, were finally going to pay off.

She still couldn't believe her good fortune. Who would have thought Cait Pride would be her benefactor? The last time they had seen each other in the café, Cait had looked daggers in her direction. One thing for sure; she'd see to it that Cait never had call to regret her kindness. Bobby Rae intended to earn her pay from the get go. Come hell or high water, she wasn't going back to the Hill Country Café.

She drove around to the back of the house, her blue eyes widening when she saw the sheriff's patrol car. Now what can that be all about? she wondered as she parked next to it.

She smoothed her hair, got out of her car and tugged her skirt down. Hearing voices coming from the kitchen, she marched up to the door. Before she had a chance to knock, it opened.

"My goodness," Sheriff Schumaker said, "what brings you here so early?" His tone seemed friendly enough, but he didn't quite manage to hide the suspicion in his eyes.

"I'm Cait's new secretary."

His eyebrows elevated. "When did that happen?"

Even though she was fifteen years older than she'd been when he caught her playing hooky in eighth grade, he had a way of making her feel as if she was up to no good. Although she didn't owe him an explanation, she couldn't stop herself from giving one. "It happened yesterday. I gave Ralph two weeks notice but he said I could start working for the Prides right away. So here I am."

"Who's there, Herman?" she heard Comanche call out.

"It's me, sugar," she replied, pushing past the sheriff.

What next? Cait thought, watching Bobby Rae march into the kitchen as if she owned the place. She had forgotten that Kerrville's reigning sex symbol was starting work today. That Bobby Rae looked exceptionally pretty didn't improve Cait's mood. Since they last met, Bobby Rae had done something to improve her already sensational appearance. However, Cait was far too distracted to figure out what.

"Is something wrong?" Bobby Rae asked, looking around the table.

"Yes, something's wrong," Cait snapped, glaring at Comanche. Didn't she have enough on her mind without having to face his girlfriend day in and day out?

She would have said more but the telephone rang. To her surprise, Bobby Rae reacted instantly. She walked over to the phone and picked it up.

"Pride's Outback. How may I help?" she said as if she had been doing it all her life.

For a second, hearing the strange female voice, Mims wondered if she had reached the wrong number. "Is Cait Pride there?"

"May I ask who is calling?"

"Tell her it's Mims Pauling."

"One moment please. I'll see if Miss Pride is available."

"Who in the world was that?" Mims asked when Cait came on the line.

"My new secretary."

"I didn't know you planned to hire one so soon."

"It's a long story, Mims. I can't go into it right now."

"You sound terrible." There were times when Mims felt a desperate urge to mother Cait. However, it wouldn't do either of them any good. Cait needed a friend more than she needed a mother, and Mims had lost her chance at motherhood long ago. "Is something wrong?"

"Yes. But I'm not up to talking about it."

"Perhaps my news will help."

"News? Are you coming to visit sooner than you planned?"

"No. This is much better news than that. I ran into Neil Dillon at an AIDS fund raiser last night. He had a huge bandage on his hand." Mims couldn't help laughing at the memory of the wounded rock star, and what had caused his injury. "You should have seen him, Cait. He was having what you Texans call a *hissy*."

"That's your news?"

"Of course not. The point is that Neil told me his pet chimpanzee almost bit off his thumb. Remember how gaga he used to be about the animal? Well, the two of them aren't on speaking terms any more. Thanks to the chimp, he's decided to get rid of his entire menagerie." Mims paused, relishing the chance to be the bearer of good news. "I told him about the Outback and he said he'd donate the animals gratis if you made all the shipping arrangements."

"How many animals are you talking about."

"I don't have a complete list. Apparently he was well on his way to having a zoo, though. He mentioned lions, cheetahs, a couple of giraffes, a small herd of American bison, and two rhinoceroses – or is it rhinoceri?"

There was a moment of silence before Cait let out a joyous whoop. "Oh, Mims, I don't know how to thank you."

"Don't thank me. Thank the chimp."

"Are you sure Neil doesn't want a penny?"

"He's making millions. He said he can use the write-off. But he did seem to be in a hurry to get rid of them."

"When can we see them?"

"The sooner the better. They're on his farm in Bucks County. Let me know when to expect you and I'll make all the arrangements."

Cait was so stunned that she continued clutching the

telephone after she said goodbye. Bobby Rae finally took it from her hand and carefully put it back in place while Cait sleepwalked back to the table. She didn't realize she was smiling like a lunatic and crying at the same time until Comanche hurried to her side.

He put an arm around her heaving shoulders. "Are you all right, Katydid?"

Remembering the awful things he'd said to her just minutes ago, she jerked away from his touch, then turned to Byron with a triumphant smile. "We have our rhinos!"

17

Bloody amazing, the way things had turned out, Byron thought. This morning when Cait precipitously announced her intention to abandon Pride's Outback, he had found himself trying to figure out what to do with the rest of his life. This evening, as he packed for the trip to inspect Neil Dillon's animals, his future seemed assured.

First there had been Mims' astonishing phone call. Then later in the day as news of the attack on the Outback spread, local ranchers had either called or simply showed up, offering to help replace the animals the Prides had lost.

God love Texans, he thought, remembering the generous response, even from men who didn't agree with Cait's plans. From Cait to Hank to Comanche, Texans were the most hard-headed people he'd ever met. But when it came to a showdown, he sure as hell wanted a few Texans on his side.

Moving from his closet to his bed, he laid his clothing out to make certain he had enough underwear and accessories to go with every outfit. Cait had suggested he include tweeds for Bucks County and black tie in case Mims asked him to escort her to a charitable event while he was in Manhattan.

Mims. He smiled at the thought of seeing her again. Between Mims, Neil Dillon's chimp and the grizzled ranchers he'd met that day, the Outback had a new lease of life. He'd like to kiss them all, he thought, grinning to himself. He would definitely try for seconds in Mims' case.

One task remained before he went to bed. Comanche had given him no choice. His blatant continual challenge couldn't go unanswered.

Byron had never experienced so much difficulty getting along with his fellow man as he had with Comanche Killian. He'd left devoted comrades, black and white, back in Kenya. Comanche had proven to be a tough nut to crack – a pity since he rather liked the foreman.

They had a great deal in common if only Comanche could see it, a love of the land, a respect for the creatures who lived on it and a deeply ingrained work ethic that should have transcended their cultural differences. Instead, Comanche had been spoiling for a fight since that first dinner. The time had come to fulfil that need.

Shrugging with resignation, Byron closed his suitcase, left his bedroom and moved quietly down the hall past Cait's door. He fervently prayed she wouldn't hear him now, open her door and ask him where he was going. She wouldn't like the answer.

The stars were out when he left the house. He paused to take them in, thinking how different they looked from the stars over Kenya. Like his life, the constellations had been turned upside down. Only the moon remained unchanged, hanging in the winter sky like a giant pearl.

A few hundred yards away, lights burned in the old barn. Best check on the injured animals while he still could, he thought grimly. With any luck, they would survive the night. He wasn't so certain about himself.

The barn smelled of fresh hay, antiseptics and the pungent aroma given off by animals in distress. He went from stall to stall, inspecting the occupants before stopping to chat with the man on duty. Half an hour later, assured all was well, he knocked on Comanche's door.

Comanche opened it a moment later, a shabby robe belted around his waist, Trouble at his side wagging a greeting. "What are you doing here?" he demanded. "I thought you'd be in bed by now, getting your beauty sleep."

Byron ignored the jibe. He had no intention of being goaded into losing his temper. Only a fool fought angry. "This morning I mentioned something about settling things between us. Unfortunately, the time and place weren't appropriate. I'm free now."

Comanche let out a startled guffaw. "You're free now. What the hell does that mean?"

"You've been spoiling for a fight. I'm ready to oblige."

"*Not*!"

"Not what?"

"Never mind. You'd never get it. Look, I don't want to hurt you. You're supposed to leave for New York in the morning." Comanche attempted to shut the door.

To his surprise, Neville shoved his foot in the jamb.

"When I was a boy," Neville said, with the precise enunciation that always grated on Comanche's nerves, "my father taught me that a real man never starts a fight, but he never loses one once he's in it. You started this fight. I intend to finish it."

Comanche shoved the door open again, hoping the Kenyan would lose his balance. He simply danced back out of harm's way, though. Everything about Neville, including the fact that he was light on his feet, annoyed Comanche.

"This morning," Neville was saying, "I mentioned something about going out behind the barn. Under the circumstances, it's out of the question."

"What circumstances?"

"The man in the barn would undoubtedly notify Cait if he heard us brawling."

Comanche had to give the devil his due. He would have guessed Cait would the first person Nevill would want to know. With his fancy clothes and la-di-dah manner, the white hunter struck him as the sort of man who would demand sympathy for a hangnail.

Comanche thought a moment. "Give me five minutes and I'll meet you behind the tractor shed."

He dressed quickly, then locked Trouble in the house. Circling the huge shed, he was beginning to think Neville had changed his mind when he saw the white hunter silhouetted against the full moon.

The Kenyan was shadow boxing, moving quite well for a man his age, Comanche grudgingly admitted. However, shadow boxing was a far cry from fighting a living, breathing opponent. He smiled with grim anticipation, thinking how much he was going to enjoy beating the hell out of Neville.

He walked up behind him, tapped him on the shoulder and said, "May I have this dance?"

So the devil does have a sense of humor, Byron thought as he whirled around. Comanche had been so cold and withdrawn since they met, he would never have guessed. Still, the time had come to teach the insolent young pup a lesson. They wouldn't work in harmony until he had earned Comanche's respect. And work together they must because he had no intention of leaving the Outback.

"Ready when you are," he said, automatically setting his feet in a balanced stance and turning his body sideways to present the smallest target.

Comanche nodded. "We should get a couple of things straight first. No butting, no biting, no gouging, no kicking and no hitting below the waist. Agreed?"

Byron smiled. He suspected Comanche had never got over hearing how he'd unmanned that drunk in the South Star. Kicking a stranger's testes may not have been gentlemanly, but he'd needed to disable the brute without risking Cait's and Mims' safety. Under the circumstances, he suspected Comanche would have done the same.

"Agreed," he said. He began circling, his fists guarding his chest and face, his eyes locked with Comanche's, waiting for them to signal an attack.

He didn't have to wait long. Comanche rushed forward like a runaway train, a work-hardened fist aimed straight at Byron's jaw. He felt the wind of its passage even as he danced out of the way, ducking under Comanche's right to land an upper cut.

Comanche had been in a number of bar-room brawls on the rodeo circuit but he'd never felt such a blow. It sent pain ricocheting around his head. The knowledge that Byron was a skilled boxer hit him even harder. Blinking to clear his vision, he lunged forward with grim determination.

Byron danced away again and this time he landed such a solid punch on Comanche's ribs that Comanche's next breath burned like fire. He soon lost track of how often he'd been hit – or where. Every time he tried to deliver a haymaker, he paid a fearful price.

He had no hope of winning unless he got in close enough to use his size and strength to advantage. He feinted another blow and, anticipating Byron's fluid footwork, grabbed him and threw him up against the shed.

Not wanting to mark Comanche, Byron had avoided hitting him square in the face. Now, as he felt himself being lifted off his feet, he had no choice. He went for Comanche's nose and eyes with a series of lightning jabs.

Comanche pounded Byron's unprotected mid-section. Byron grunted with each impact. Comanche may not have been a trained pugilist, but he had the heart and the raw courage of a champion. Raising his arms, Byron spread his hands, then clapped them over Comanche's ears with all his might. The sudden vacuum was guaranteed to ring the foreman's chimes.

Comanche staggered back and dropped to his knees. Released from the ferocious onslaught, Byron dropped to his knees too, grateful for the respite. His breath hissing in and out of his lungs in ragged gasps, he eyed Comanche warily.

"Have you had enough?" he panted.

"Not by a damn sight!"

Comanche's lower lip felt swollen and he knew he was going to have one hell of a shiner. The blood dripping from his nose forced him to breathe through his mouth. The bastard could fight, he thought grimly. Sooner or later Neville was bound to tire. In the meantime, he set his mind on absorbing all the punishment Neville could hand out.

He staggered to his feet, Neville heaved himself up, too, and they began circling like participants in a primitive ritual, neither giving quarter nor seeking it while the stars slowly wheeled across the sky. Although the temperature fell, sweat drenched their clothes, dripping from their brows and running down their chests.

Give up, you bloody sod, give up, Byron silently implored. He had never fought a man who could take a punch like Comanche Killian. His own muscles ached, his fists felt leaden. As an amateur at Cambridge, he'd fought three-minute rounds. This battle was turning into a marathon.

The fight seemed to go on for hours although logic told him they couldn't have been going at each other that long. Blast! He was getting too old for this sort of nonsense. He threw a left jab, slipped, lost his footing and staggered into Comanche's arms.

They stood as close as lovers, breathing in greedy gulps, too exhausted to do anything but hang onto one another.

Comanche recovered first. He drove a fist into Byron's stomach. Byron automatically lowered his arms to protect his gut, leaving his face unprotected. Mistake, mistake, his mind telegraphed. Before his fists could obey his brain, Comanche hit him on the jaw so hard that he reeled back, dazed.

If Comanche had been able to follow up the blow, he would have scored a knockout. Too spent to throw another punch, he lurched toward Byron and the two of them grappled again, neither one capable of lifting their fists.

They swayed back and forth like drunks, too winded even to curse. Ever so slowly, they collapsed in a tangled heap with Comanche on top. Neither one knew how long they lay there. It might have been seconds but it felt like eternity.

"Personally, I prefer being on top," Byron gasped out.

Comanche lifted his head, and rolled off Byron. "Your virtue is safe with me."

"That's the only goddamn thing that's safe with you. I'm half dead."

"Where the hell did you learn to fight like that?"

"At college. I was the champion for my weight at Cambridge."

"Thanks for telling me."

"Better late than never."

Comanche groaned in reply. His warrior's heart urged him to get up and fight on. His body refused to obey. "What the hell do we do now?" he rasped.

"I don't know about you, but I can't move. I think you broke one of my ribs."

"Then we're even. I think you broke my nose."

Byron reached in his pants' pocket for his handkerchief. "Here," he said, passing it to Comanche.

"What the hell's that for?"

"Your nose."

Comanche took it and staunched the flow of blood. There was nothing dignified about lying on the ground, gasping like a fish out of water. He was past worrying about his dignity, though.

He stared up at the sky, his vision impeded by the swelling around his left eye. "Earlier this evening, you said something about what your father taught you. Mine taught me that any fool can make a mistake, but only a man admits to it. I've been a horse's ass since the day you arrived. I misjudged you from the get go. I apologize for it."

"Forget it. Most likely I'd have reacted the same way if a strange man intruded on my territory." Byron struggled to a sitting position and gazed at Comanche. "You look like hell."

Comanche levered himself upright. "You won't win any beauty contests yourself."

Byron produced a battered pack of Players from his shirt pocket, took one for himself and offered the pack to Comanche.

"No thanks," Comanche replied, gingerly touching his nose. "They're bad for my health."

The ludicrousness of the situation finally penetrated Comanche's brain. Here they were, not two feet apart, battered, bruised and bloodied, having their first civil conversation. He began to laugh. The fact that doing so hurt his face and chest made him laugh even harder.

Byron peered at him with obvious concern. "Are you all right?"

This from the man who'd spent the last half hour beating him to a bloody pulp? Comanche thought he'd never heard anything funnier.

Another spasm of hilarity rumbled up his chest. He grinned at Byron and Byron grinned back. "You'd better come to my place and wash up before you go back to the main house," Comanche said. "Cait would give us both hell if she knew we'd been fighting."

"Good idea. I have no desire to get on the lady's bad side. Frankly, she scares the hell out of me when she's angry."

"That makes two of us."

"I say, you wouldn't happen to have a nice warm beer?"

"No, but I do have a cold six-pack."

Half an hour later they sat at the kitchen table in companionable silence, sipping a brew while Trouble went from one to the other in an ecstasy of good feelings. The dog was a better judge of character than he had been, Comanche thought.

He felt as if his mind had been purged of a poison that had been eroding his ability to think clearly. Gazing at Byron, he finally saw him as he really was – an urbane, stalwart man with more than his share of know-how and courage. He saw something else, too, and it damn near broke his heart.

Byron Neville was more than man enough for Cait.

Falling madly in love had been the last thing on Mims' agenda when she picked Byron Neville up at the airport six days earlier. She had tried it once. The agony had exceeded the ecstasy and it had ended in disaster. Falling in love meant losing control and she'd vowed never to succumb again.

Her husbands – a male model and a performance artist with a hairy chest and a terrific tush – had happily danced to her tune. Her money and success commanded their obedience. She wouldn't have married them otherwise. They'd made passionate love until the magic wore off, then stayed married for a few more years trying desperately to get the magic back.

When it came to choosing men she had a dismal record. So what in the world was she doing in a little hole-in-the-wall coffee shop on Forty-eighth, wearing the drop-dead-sexy Mackie gown she had put on in the expectation of attending a black-tie benefit at the Waldorf and making goo-goo eyes at Byron Neville instead.

God, he was easy to look at. Although he cut quite a figure in his safari suit, he was drop-dead gorgeous in a tux. The healed cut on his left cheekbone added a certain savage aspect to his otherwise sophisticated appearance. It really turned her on.

She wanted to screw his brains out. Then she wanted to hold him in her arms and kiss away the loneliness he hid so well in the depths of his sky-blue eyes.

His voice reclaimed her attention. "I still can't believe it."

She had been so lost in her own thoughts that she had no idea what he'd been saying. "Can't believe what?"

He gazed around the luncheonette as if it were a five star restaurant. "I can't believe I'm here, in New York, in the United States of America, with the legendary Mims Pauling. It's a long way from the African bush. You've made the last week, the trip to Bucks County, the days in Manhattan, very special. I know I've told you this before, but you saved the ranch."

Was the look in his eyes affection, gratitude or lust? It pained her to realize she wouldn't settle for any of the three. Or even all of them. She wanted more from him – so much more that it frightened her.

"I'd hardly call this place special, unless you're into tacky plastic booths and tables with gum wads stuck to their undersides."

Byron's smile revealed his deep dimples. She literally went weak when he gazed at her that way. "It's not the place," he said, "it's you."

"Smooth, you're very smooth." She pasted a cynical grin on her face to match her words, using both to shield her heart.

He looked hurt. "Why won't you ever talk to me, really talk, or let me talk to you? What are you afraid of?"

"Afraid? Is that what you think I am?"

"I could spend the next hour telling you what I think you are. Surely other men have told you you're beautiful. But it's not the outside that counts. And you won't let me get close to the inside."

She made the kissable moue that had distracted so many men in the past. "You already know more about me than most of my friends."

"All you've told me are statistics I could get from any *Who's Who*. You were born and raised in the Bronx, got your bachelor's at Hunter College and your master's in business at Harvard. I'm suitably impressed. But facts and figures don't add up to a living, breathing woman. And I badly want to know the woman."

What the hell was he doing, drinking coffee until his bladder ached when he longed to tell Mims how breathtaking she looked and how very badly he wanted to make love to her? The thought of peeling her glittering gown off inch by inch made his skin go cold and his blood run hot.

Mims tore her gaze away from his. "Shouldn't we have dinner?"

"Damn it, Mims. I'm not hungry for food. I'm starving for you."

Mims could feel a flush spreading from her cheeks to the top of her breasts. "I'm flattered."

"Don't you recognize the truth when you hear it?"

"What about Cait?"

He looked baffled. "What about her?"

"Aren't you involved with her?"

"Of course I am. I work for her, and I admire her. But that's as far as it goes."

"Then you and Cait aren't . . .?"

"There is no 'me and Cait'," he declared, a wry grin making him look even more attractive. "She's a charming girl. But look at me; I'm too old for girls. I want a woman. I want you, Mims. I have since the moment I saw you at the airport in San Antonio. You'll never know how much I was hoping you would turn out to be Cait Pride." His eyes sought hers, transmitting an unmistakable message that sent a frisson of anticipation up her spine. "Now, can we get the hell out of here before I do something that will embarrass both of us?"

"And what would that be?"

Desire deepened his voice. "I don't think you want to know."

He reached for her hand and pulled her to her feet. They raced from the restaurant together, heedless of the curious stares that followed their flight. Fifteen minutes later a cab deposited them in front of the Trump Tower.

Byron gazed around, bewildered. "This isn't my hotel."

"My place was closer."

He barely had time to take in the magnificent lobby, so quickly did Mims guide him to an elevator. Although it accelerated with heart-stopping speed, it couldn't keep up with his racing desire. By the time she let him into her apartment, his erection strained against his trousers. He hadn't known such breathless excitement at the prospect of being with a woman since his youth.

"Can I get you anything?" Mims said, her husky whisper sending a sensual message to his already overloaded senses. She gestured towards the windows. "Would you like to see the view?"

"I like the view fine right here," he replied, his eyes caressing her body. She was the most glamorous creature he had ever seen, but her looks alone could not have captured his imagination. Her intelligence, her kindness, the wonderful way she had with people, those were even more mesmerizing.

"When we were in the coffee shop, I kept imagining what it would be like to peel you out of that dress."

She moved towards him with a hip-swaying walk that reminded him of a jungle cat. "You don't *peel* this sort of dress."

"We'll see about that." He grinned and pulled her close. She was so small, so delicately made, and so utterly female.

"I hope it doesn't spoil the mood, but you should know I believe in practising safe sex."

He chuckled. "A man my age shouldn't need any practice. I do believe in dressing for the occasion, though." He patted his jacket pocket. "I carry my wetsuit in here. However, I don't expect to need it for quite some time."

"What do you mean?"

"You'll just have to wait and see." Reaching behind her back, he inched her zipper down, then leaning away, lowered her dress to expose her breasts.

"You're not wearing a bra."

"You can't wear much of anything under a Mackie dress. It spoils the line."

"Bless Mr Mackie."

She trembled as he traced the curve of her mouth, then trailed his fingers down her throat, following the delicate line of her collar bones. When his fingers touched her breasts, she groaned.

"Did you know large nipples are supposed to be the sign of a passionate woman?" he asked, lowering his head to taste them. Mims' body was a *terra incognita* he intended to explore with the thoroughness of a mapmaker until he knew every inch, every delightful crevice and curve.

"Is it true of men, too?" She unknotted his tie and unbuttoned his shirt, exposing his chest.

Pleasure surged through him as her fingers found and played with his nipples. "God, I like that," he said huskily.

He lowered his arms and allowed her to strip his jacket from his shoulders. She was, he realized as she tugged his shirt from his trousers, more than a match in the erotic game of striptease he had initiated.

Now it was his turn to make a move. He lowered her zipper even more, baring her to the waist, then pulled her against his chest and plundered her mouth with his lips, tongue and teeth while his hands held her hips firmly against his manhood.

She responded with an urgency that sent his pulse racing, the thrust of her pelvis deepening his need.

"Slow down," he whispered into her ear. "We have all night, and I plan to use every minute of it pleasuring you."

"What about your pleasure?"

"They're one and the same," he murmured, releasing

the zipper a few critical inches more and tugging her dress even lower.

He drew back and ravished her with his gaze, revelling in the vision of her breasts, the inward curve of her waist, the flaring swell of her hips. His hands followed his gaze, seeking to know every round, tilt, and turn.

When he had explored his fill, he pulled the zipper down the rest of the way and let the gown fall around her feet in shimmering folds. "You're perfect, he said, his voice filled with awe.

A delicate garter belt circled her hips. Beige lace bikini panties tantalized his imagination as he tried to picture what they concealed. He gripped her deliciously round thighs, gently spread them and palmed her womanhood. God, she felt hot.

Mims thought her legs would give way at his intimate touch. She had never known such sweet torture. "My turn," she said, then opened his belt and fly to free his erection.

Keeping one hand on his shoulder for balance, she captured his penis with the other, moving her fingers up and down its velvet length. Desire raged through her and yet, she had no inclination to hasten the inevitable. She had been imagining this night since she first saw Byron.

He showed no desire to hurry either as he pulled her panties down, inch by tantalizing inch. "You're really blonde," he exclaimed in delight.

She gave him a heavy-lidded smile. "Now it's my turn. I want to see if you have that gorgeous silver hair all over."

"Help yourself." He raised his arms in surrender, standing quietly until his trousers and shorts were tangled around his ankles. He stepped out of them, picking Mims up, and carried her over to a chair. He sat down, spread his legs and positioned her on his lap, facing him.

With her legs dangling on either side of his, she was as open as a flower. He caressed her pubic fleece, then traced the intricate folds of her womanhood while her sweet musk filled his nostrils.

"I can't take much more," she said.

"Yes, you can – much, much more." Cupping her buttocks, he lifted her to her knees, pulled her closer and dipped his tongue into the heart of her femininity.

Mims felt desire gathering in her loins as Byron nipped and tongued her most intimate parts. She hadn't been with a man for a long time and never with one who took such unabashed pleasure in her body.

He made her feel things she had never felt before. He made her feel things she had forgotten. He made her feel young and beautiful again.

Perhaps, she thought before his erotic attention robbed her of the ability to think, that was the most exciting thing of all.

18

Blackjack paced his elegantly appointed senatorial office, eight steps up the Aubusson carpet and eight back. He felt as if every nerve in his body was vibrating. He ought to be in a committee meeting rehashing the defence budget. However the only budget he could think about was his own.

He needed the Nishida money – soon.

Despite his best efforts he was no nearer closing the Nishida deal than he'd been that night at Brenner's. What had seemed like an easy way to solve his financial problems six months ago had become a consummate pain in the ass. What he wouldn't give to be done with the bunch of them – Tochigi, Detweiler, Cait Pride, et al.

Tochigi's questions had grown more importunate in inverse proportion to his own failure to come up with satisfactory answers. And the real estate agent he'd employed to look for alternatives to the Pride ranch seemed as ineffectual as Detweiler.

Detweiler. He must have been out of his mind to trust a loose cannon like that with a critical job. According to Det's last telephone report, the attack on the pens had been an unqualified success. Byron Neville had left the ranch the next day. Det had all but guaranteed that Cait Pride would soon make her own hasty retreat.

After hearing Det's news, Blackjack had wasted no time putting in a call to Cait, expecting to console her with the usual bullshit – *she'd given it her best shot, it wasn't meant to be, things have a way of working out for the best.*

To his dismay, she had sounded surprisingly chipper for a woman who was looking ruin in the eye. He soon learned the cause of her optimism. Thanks to some idiot rock star's gift of his private menagerie and her fellow ranchers' generosity, Detweiler's attack on the holding pens had accomplished not a thing.

If only he could go to Kerrville and handle the situation himself, he felt certain he would find a way to accomplish his goal. However, the loss of anonymity had been the price of fame. If he headed for the Hill Country during the Senate session, reporters would trail in his wake like remoras accompanying a shark. Minor politicians would demand meetings, offering babies to kiss, gymnasiums to open, expecting him to attend boring luncheons where he'd find himself suffering through yet another greasy chicken-fried steak.

He was as much a prisoner as any jailbird, he thought, coming to a halt in front of a large window overlooking Constitution Avenue.

The street, decked out for the holidays, reminded him of how much time had passed since his first meeting with Tochigi. Six motherfucking months! Could he endure six more?

Clenching his fists with impotent rage, he turned away from the window. He had no choice. He was in too deep. The time had come for drastic action.

"Are you sorry you didn't go to New York with Byron?" Hank asked Cait, putting his lunch tray aside.

"Of course not!" Cait declared, giving him the practised smile that had adorned so many magazine covers. "I'd much rather be here with you."

His daughter was a past master at hiding her true emotions behind that glorious smile. He knew she was still upset over the horror she had seen in the holding pens the other day and smarting over what Comanche had said to her afterwards. No one could get under Cait's skin the way Comanche could.

"Won't you eat a little more?" Cait asked.

"I don't have much of an appetite today."

"Please, Dad – for me." The anxiety in her eyes made him feel worse.

"All right, I'll finish my sandwich. In return, though, I'd like you to do me a little favour."

"All you have to do is ask."

"I want you to stop treating Comanche like something you scraped off your boots."

Not on your life, Cait thought, her temper flaring. Then, realizing Hank's life was indeed on the line, she had to bite her lip to keep from bursting into tears.

"Will you do that for me?" Hank asked softly.

"I don't know if I can after the things Comanche said to me the other morning. He doesn't think I'm capable of running the Outback – he doesn't respect me."

He never has, she silently added. No matter how often she'd met his every challenge when they were kids – the risks she had taken to win his approval, the crazy things she had done in the futile hope that he would smile at her just once the way he smiled at other girls – he had never valued her at all.

Hank dutifully bit into his sandwich as a show of good faith. He washed the mouthful down with a swallow of milk, then turned his gaze back to her. "You don't get it, do you?"

"Get what?"

"If you could have seen yourself that morning, you'd know why Comanche said the things he did. He didn't want to hurt you, Cait. But you were talking about leaving. He did the only thing he could think of to make you change your mind. He made you fighting mad – and it worked. The trouble is you're still mad."

"How do you know so much about it?"

"Because I asked. Comanche would tell you if you gave him the chance."

"What about the things he said to Byron? He's been insufferable where Byron is concerned."

"I think they've worked it out."

"Are you sure?"

"If you don't believe me, talk to Comanche yourself."

Cait looked sceptical, perplexed, and most of all, intrigued. "I might just do that."

Hank smiled to himself. Cait had taken the bait. Sooner or later, she'd have to talk to Comanche. From then on, he trusted nature to take its course.

Comanche parked next to Bobby Rae's Camaro, retrieved his packages from the back of his truck and carried them into the office. He paused in the doorway and looked around, expecting to see Cait at her desk and steeling himself in anticipation of her coldness. She had barely acknowledged his existence the last few days.

Bobby Rae was by herself and so involved in her work that she seemed unaware of his entrance. Her fingers flew over the computer keyboard. She appeared as at ease in her new role as if she'd been a secretary all her life. Looked the part, too. Gone were the false eyelashes, the too tight skirts, the push-up bras and three inch heels. Bobby Rae had quietly gone about the business of reinventing herself; the pride of the Hill Country Café had metamorphosed into a top notch secretary. At least Cait couldn't find fault with him on that score.

Bobby Rae looked up from her desk, saw him and smiled. "I see you've been Christmas shopping. Just two more weeks until the big day. Do you have any plans?"

"Not really. And these," a nod of his head indicated the boxes in his arms, "are just some things for Hank. I'm not much in the mood for Christmas this year."

"This will be the first holiday I don't have to wait tables. Maybe I could fix dinner for the two of us, to thank you for getting me this job." When he hesitated, she added, "I promise not to come on to you the way I did the last time you stopped by."

The way Bobby Rae had been treating him, you'd think he was a knight in shining armour. He didn't feel very good about how he'd gone about getting her the job. Besides, he must have been crazy, thinking he could use Bobby Rae to make Cait jealous – as if Cait cared who he saw or didn't see.

He needed to level with Bobby Rae, to remove himself from the pedestal she'd put him on by telling her how he'd got her the job. And why. Christmas seemed as good a time as any to do it.

"I don't want you cooking on your day off. Why don't I make reservations for the two of us at the YO Hilton?"

"That would be very nice," Bobby Rae replied with a ladylike smile.

He smiled, thinking she had changed more than her outward appearance. The old Bobby Rae would have squealed, "Gee, swell," or words to that effect, and planted a big wet kiss on his mouth. Instead she turned back to the word processor and was quickly absorbed in her work again.

His steps were leaden as he headed for Hank's room. He envied Bobby Rae her new-found contentment. His own life had never been more unsettled. Instead of winning Cait back, he'd managed to alienate her completely. She'd probably laugh in his face if he told her he'd been motivated by love when he'd challenged her to stay on the ranch.

Love. It was supposed to be the most wonderful feeling in the world. But it was killing him.

A year ago he had been content, sure of his goals and his future. Now he couldn't look ahead and he dared not look back. Halfway to Hank's room, he paused and leaned his forehead against the wall, surrendering to a despair so deep it shook him to his very soul.

Since college, he'd seen himself as a man who was capable of accomplishing anything he set his mind to. Well, damn it, he'd set his mind, his heart, his whole being on getting Cait back. But he'd lost her for good and he had no one to blame but himself. He choked down a groan. Now he understood why Orry had given up on life after losing the woman he loved.

Comanche had no idea how long he grappled with his emotions. Some time later, he became aware of voices coming from Hank's room, Cait's lighter tones rising above Hank's baritone. God. He couldn't let her see him like this. He lifted his head and squared his shoulders.

When he joined Hank and Cait, his features gave no sign of his misery.

Seeing Comanche, Cait's heart fluttered and her stomach knotted the way they always did when he walked into a room.

Her brain, her heart and her libido had declared war on each other the day Comanche met her at the airport six months ago. Her body had been their unwilling battleground.

Could her father be right? Had she misjudged Comanche again?

She offered a tentative smile as an olive branch. "I see you've been shopping."

"I just picked up a few things for your father."

Hank looked up. "I don't need a thing, son."

Comanche set his boxes down on the bed. "To tell you the truth, these aren't gifts. I need your help."

Cait was about to say Hank was too sick to help anyone. But the expectant look in Hank's eyes silenced her.

Comanche took a tripod from a long box and set it up near Hank's chair.

Hank's brow furrowed. "You know I'll do what I can, but I'm not much good at taking pictures."

"This isn't a camera tripod," Comanche replied,

opening a second box to reveal a large telescope.

This time, Hank smiled. "I'm not much for bird-watching either."

What is he up to? Cait wondered as Comanche attached the tripod to the scope. She didn't have to wait long to find out.

Comanche carried the scope to Hank's chair and set it up so Hank could look through it by just leaning forward. "Help yourself," he said.

Hank spent a minute adjusting the sights and then rotated the scope from left to right, his ravaged features breaking into a smile.

"What do you see?" Cait asked.

"The river, the construction sites, the new animals. Why the barn is so close, I can spot a crack in the mortar." He chuckled. "By heaven, Comanche. This is wonderful. You couldn't have given me anything that pleased me more."

Comanche's taut features seemed to relax. "I'm glad you like it. But I didn't get it to please you. Every time I come in your room, I take a minute to admire the view. You can see a lot of the ranch from your window. Considering the things that have happened lately, we sure could use another pair of eyes to keep watch over the place. I can't tell you what a help it would be, if you feel up to it."

"Feel up to it? I can't think of anything I'd rather do. But if I did see something suspicious, how would I let you know? I'm not exactly mobile any more."

Comanche walked back to the bed, opened the last box and took out two walkie-talkies. "I got these at the army surplus store. You can keep one with you and I'll carry the other with me."

"You really think of everything, son." Hank's face glowed.

Cait had been sitting quietly, watching her father and Comanche interact. In some ways they seemed more like father and son than employer-employee.

A few months ago, the realization would have made her jealous.

A few months ago, she would have put her own needs ahead of Hank's.

His smile, the colour in his cheeks, told her how happy he was at having something useful to do. She knew how much he hated his growing dependence on others. The telescope had transformed him from an invalid to a man whose life had meaning and purpose.

"Can I take a look?" she asked, getting to her feet.

Grinning from ear to ear, Hank relinquished his place at the scope.

Cait peered through the sight, then drew back and gazed into Comanche's eyes. "What a terrific idea. I wish I had thought of it myself."

The warmth in her voice seemed to signal a cessation of hostilities. Instead of lifting Comanche's spirits, though, it merely deepened his despair. There had been other truces between them the last few months, other times when the merry-go-round of their relationship had started up with a cargo of hope. But each time he reached for the brass ring, the music stopped.

This time, he made up his mind not to try.

The sound of a new arrival interrupted his musing. Bobby Rae's high heels beat a tattoo on the wooden floor as she hurried into the room. "I just got a call from a truck driver in Kerrville. He wanted to know how to get here."

Cait looked askance at Comanche. "I wasn't expecting a delivery. Were you?"

An almost hysterical laugh burst from Bobby Rae. "This isn't just any old delivery. The driver said he specializes in moving live animals. He has two lions for the Outback."

"They're not due for a couple of days," Cait burst out. "Byron was supposed to be here by then."

Her heart thudded against her ribs as she thought about

transferring the lions from shipping crates to temporary cages without Byron to oversee the job.

Carroll Detweiler had been on the verge of leaving his hiding place overlooking the ranch house when he saw a delivery truck heading up the drive. The truck was prominently painted with the logo of a company that specialized in moving live animals.

He decided to stay put for the time being. The Senator had been driving him nuts, asking for news about the Outback when he didn't have any to give. Perhaps this was the break he'd been waiting for.

He shifted his aching buttocks on the winter-hard ground. Although it had become increasingly difficult to maintain his surveillance undetected, he spent the daylight hours on the ranch moving from lookout to lookout. Evenings, he made the rounds of the local bars, hoping the ever-present small town gossips would know what was happening on the Outback.

He had heard about the rock star's gift of animals.

He had heard all about the local support too. Would they be enough to offset the disasters he had engineered?

The truck came to a stop in front of the main house, the driver walked up to the porch, rang the bell and was admitted by Cait-fucking-Pride herself.

Cait and the driver came out half an hour later with the breed at their heels. The bitch and the breed got into the Suburban, the driver returned to the truck, and the two vehicles proceeded down the drive, turning off half a mile later in the direction of the holding pens.

Had the truck come to pick up animals or deliver them? He had to know.

19

"Cait, Cait," Comanche called.

Spurring Dulcinea, Cait chased the sound of his voice across a sun-splashed meadow. A Noah's ark of exotic animals grazed all around her, as placid as cows chewing their cuds. Then the deafening roar of a gun broke the bucolic serenity.

She hunched closer to Dulcinea's neck, waiting for a bullet to bury itself in her flesh. The gun boomed again and blood spurted from an eland not five feet away. Its gleaming hide turned crimson as it collapsed in horrific slow motion.

"Cait," Comanche called again, more urgently this time.

Terror wrapped its icy tendrils around her heart as a pair of powerful hands grasped her shoulders, shaking her.

"Comanche," she wailed.

"I'm here, Katydid. Wake up, honey."

Wake up? Good God, was she dreaming?

Nightmare and reality merged when she opened her eyes and saw Comanche sitting on the edge of her bed. His hands still touched her shoulders, warming her bare skin.

She sat bolt upright, heedless of her dishabille as questions tumbled from her lips. "What are you doing here? Is Hank all right? What time is it?"

"It's just past five and Hank's fine."

Comanche couldn't deny himself the chance to savour Cait's beauty. Her hair tumbled wild and free around her shoulders, her cheeks were flushed. A jolt of desire ripped through him when he realized he could see the full curve of her breasts and the dark shadow of her nipples through her sheer gown. He had no right to want her, and especially not at a time like this. But he would have given all he possessed to take her in his arms just one more time – to forget yesterday, today, and tomorrow in her bed.

"What's wrong?" she said, pushing her hair away from her face.

"The lions have escaped."

Cait's widening eyes betrayed her shock. "How could they? I checked the locks on the cages myself."

Afraid his hands might touch her of their own volition, he sprang to his feet, crossed the floor and stood by the door. "Someone broke the locks. I assigned Skip Davis to keep watch on those cages last night. I woke up an hour ago so I figured I'd spell him for a while. When I found him, he was out cold."

"Is he all right?"

"He may have a concussion. Doc Williams is on the way here to check him out. Whoever hit him wasn't worrying about the consequences."

"Do you think it was the man who attacked the pens?"

"The bastard seems to be the most likely candidate. I'd give a lot to get my hands on him."

"Why? Why would someone be so determined to hurt us?" she moaned.

"I wish to God I knew."

"What happened to the lions? Did he kill them, too?"

"No, Cait. They're gone. Skip said he checked his watch at one in the morning. He thinks another hour passed before he was knocked out."

Cait was fully awake now, her mind racing almost as fast as her pulse. "Can the lions get off the ranch?"

"No. That is, I don't think so." He paused, his emerald

eyes clouded with worry. "But then I never thought they'd get out of the cages either. Damn it. We took every precaution. We've got a small fortune invested in the animals out there – in registered cattle as well as the exotics. We can't afford to lose more of them. I'll have to go after the lions as soon as it's light."

Cait suddenly realized she was practically naked to the waist. She pulled the covers up and tucked them firmly under her arms. "What will you do if you find them?"

"That should be obvious. I'll have to kill them, Cait."

"You said it yourself, you can't afford to lose any more animals, especially not the Seattle zoo's lions. Byron will be back from New York later this mornig. I don't want you to do anything until he gets here," Cait said firmly.

No matter their differences, she couldn't bear the thought of Comanche hunting the big cats by himself, and she knew he wouldn't ask anyone else to share the danger.

"They've already been on the run for three hours. Do you really want to risk waiting six more?"

Her nerves were near the breaking point. Agitation urged her to her feet. She didn't dare get up though, not while Comanche stood in the door pinioning her with his eyes. "We need to take a few precautions in the meantime. I want you to spread the word to all the employees whose families live on the ranch. Women and children aren't to leave their homes until further notice. I'll telephone the hands who live in town and tell them what's happened. Post a man at the front gate to keep everyone but our own people out."

When he continued to stand there, staring at her so intently that she felt his gaze in the pit of her stomach, her nerves frayed completely. "What the hell are you waiting for?" she snapped.

He scowled, turned to leave, then turned back to her one last time. "You're the boss, you make the calls. I hope to God you're right on this one."

★ ★ ★

Byron thought of Mims all the way back from New York. A man could have terrific sex with a multitude of partners over his lifetime but that special connection, that unique meshing of mind and body, the feeling that here was someone who accepted you without question or qualification rarely happened.

Until it did, the love songs, the great novels, the classic films, the best art, the things you had to grasp with your heart as well as your mind, just sailed right over your head.

Although he was approaching his forty-eighth birthday, Mims made him feel as if the best part of his life lay ahead. Not that they'd made any plans or promised each other anything. Living two thousand miles apart created a whole set of problems he'd never anticipated. He could only hope absence would make her heart grow fonder. He bloody well knew it was going to have that effect on him.

He mentally ticked off the times they would be together during the next six months. Christmas, of course. Then he'd go back east to supervise personally shipping Neil Dillon's menagerie. Mims would be back in March to help finalize plans for the grand opening and back again in June for the opening itself. After that? He didn't know. Except there was going to be an "after that" for him and Mims.

Still lost in pleasurable memories, he grinned to himself as he turned the Outback's new Range Rover from the farm route onto the drive. To his surprise, the main gates were closed and one of the ranch's trucks was parked in front of them. A man he recognized as one of the cowboys who worked for Comanche, got out and hurried over.

"There's been some trouble with the lions," the man said. "Miss Pride is waiting for you up to the house."

Before Byron could ask what sort of trouble, the man opened the gates, waved Byron through and shut them again.

Byron sped up the long drive and around the back to

the office, parked next to Bobby Rae's Camaro and hurried inside. Cait, Comanche and Bobby Rae were seated at their desks. Only Bobby Rae was working.

"The chap at the gate said something about trouble with the lions. What the hell is going on?"

While Comanche explained, Byron's euphoria faded, his sweet memories of Mims blotted out by this new disaster. The Outback seemed to attract the devil's own luck, he thought, his lips thinning as he formulated a plan to recapture the escapees.

Hunting lions was always risky, even during the most carefully orchestrated safari. He had followed more animals into thick brush than he cared to remember, and had long ago learned that only fools knew no fear. Zoo lions, who had lost their respect for man, were even more dangerous than their wild counterparts.

His stomach knotted the way it always did before he took clients into the bush. For a microsecond, his first lion hunt flashed through his mind. It had ended in disaster. He couldn't let that happen today.

"Has anyone tried to track the lions?"

Comanche nodded. "I followed them to the Stone Mountain enclosure. The gate was wide open. I closed it and sent a man to make certain it stays that way. That narrows it down to two thousand acres."

"I told you not to do anything until Byron got back," Cait declared, an angry flush colouring her cheeks.

"Now, now, Cait, cool down," Byron said. "Comanche saved us some precious time. At least we know where to begin the search."

He turned to Bobby Rae. "I'll need the topographic maps the fencing crews used." While she walked over to the files, he turned back to Cait and Comanche. "As I recall, the Stone Mountain enclosure includes some of the ranch's roughest terrain. We'll have to use horses. I want a dozen mounted men to accompany us. Make sure they're the best shots on the ranch and have them bring their rifles. And I don't mean twenty-twos. Make sure they're properly armed."

"Are you going to kill the lions?" Cait asked, her voice shaking.

"Not if I can help it. I hope to tranquilize them. Have a truck and driver at the gate to transport the lions after they've been recaptured. Give me fifteen minutes to change, get my guns, and study the maps. I'll meet you out front."

He was almost to the door when he stopped in his tracks. "I say, there wouldn't happen to be any lion dogs in the neighbourhood?"

"Lion dogs?" Cait and Comanche replied in unison.

"My grandfather used to hunt lions with his ridgebacks. One of my safari clients told me he'd hunted mountain lions with dogs in the States."

"I've never heard of lion dogs in the Hill Country – just lots of coon hounds. But if you think it will help, I'll bring Trouble," Comanche said.

Byron took a moment to consider the offer. He'd have much preferred a trained lion dog, but Trouble seemed blessed with an inbred bush sense. He wasn't likely to get in the lions' way and they might need him to tree the big cats.

Two hours later, Byron let go a relieved sigh as he watched the Pride truck drive off with the first of the tranquilized lions in a large crate. The hunt had gone by numbers so far, he thought, gazing at the rugged hills of the Stone Mountain enclosure. If their luck held, both big cats would be back in their cages by the dinner hour and a dozen cowboys would someday tell their disbelieving grandchildren about the day they hunted African lions on the Outback.

He swung back up into the saddle and looked at the waiting men. "Comanche will lead off again. Miss Pride and I will follow. Stay a hundred yards behind us. Don't shoot unless the lioness tries to break through your line. But if she does, shoot to kill."

He reloaded his gun with tranquilizer darts and gestured at Comanche. "Lead on."

Comanche had proven to be a surprisingly skilled tracker, almost as good as the Kikuyus he'd used back home. The foreman quickly picked up the trail of the second lion and spurred his horse to a trot. Trouble followed at his heels, his tail wagging with excitement. When they found the first lion the huge dog had behaved as admirably as a ridgeback, keeping his distance, his ferocious bark holding the bewildered animal at bay.

They rode for another hour, moving in the direction of a box canyon. Byron wanted to urge Comanche to greater speed, but he knew it would be pointless. Tracking an animal across a broken hilly terrain of brush, scree and bedrock took time and a meticulous attention to detail.

He knew Comanche was searching for signs any but the most experienced eyes would miss – a disturbed pebble, a broken twig, a bent blade of grass, scat if they got lucky.

Although they still had a few hours of daylight, worry gnawed at him. If the remaining lioness holed up in the canyon, driving her out wouldn't be easy.

He glanced over his shoulder at the cowboys, wondering what they were thinking. They had the weather-beaten look of men who lived in close harmony with nature and had learned to accommodate themselves to its whims. But the Outback's exotics had added a new ingredient to the natural world they knew.

He'd wanted them along as insurance. So far, thank heaven, they haven't been needed. They were all brave; however, he knew from personal experience that the bravest of them might falter in the face of lethal teeth and claws.

He glanced at Cait, riding by his side as easy in the saddle as only those who have grown up on horseback can be. Her features were pinched with worry though, and her gaze never left Comanche.

The only sound came from the horses' steel-shod hooves as they approached the canyon and moved into it. The growth grew denser just a few feet beyond its mouth. Mesquite, yaupon, scrub oak and acacia crowded close, forcing the three of them to ride single file up the dry watercourse that divided the canyon's floor.

A few yards further on, Comanche raised his hand to signal a halt. He dismounted, leading his horse as he moved off again. Every few paces he dropped to his knees, his gaze searching the ground.

Byron dismounted too, walked over to Comanche and took the reins from Comanche's hand. He studied the area, not liking what he saw. The encroaching shrubbery offered too many places for a lioness to hide. "This looks bad," he said softly.

Pitching his voice low, Comanche replied, "I'd feel a lot easier if you sent Cait back with the others."

"You don't just *send* Cait anywhere, but I'll do my best."

Returning to where she sat mounted on Dulcinea, he handed the two sets of reins to her. "Take the horses back to the men and stay there. Tell them to have their rifles ready."

"I'd rather stay with you and Comanche."

"There's only room for one top gun on a lion hunt. You hired me to do the job and I intend to earn my keep. I've got enough on my mind without worrying about you."

Before she could voice any further objections he grabbed Dulcinea's bridle. Turning the mare so she faced the canyon mouth, he gave her a sharp smack. The mare broke into an easy canter with the geldings at her side.

Cait looked back just once. Then she kicked Dulcinea to greater speed, only reining the mare to a halt when she reached the waiting men.

"What's up, Miss Cait?" one of them asked.

"The lion is in the canyon. Byron wants all of you to stay here to block her escape. You're to shoot to kill if you see her." She slid from her saddle and handed all three sets of reins to the nearest man.

Consumed with anxiety, she began to pace, her boots kicking up tiny puffs of dust with each step. No matter what Byron had said about there only being room for one top gun, she was responsible for the Outback.

How could she respect herself, let alone expect her employees to, if she hid at the first sign of danger? Had she been a man, Byron would have accepted her presence as a given.

She caught up with Byron and Comanche at a place where the stream cut across a bench of pink granite. Comanche was down on both knees again, a frown creasing his brow.

"Hell," he said, looking up at Byron, "I'm sorry. I lost her trail."

Cait couldn't help noting their rapport. She'd been sceptical when Hank had told her about their new understanding. Now though, she was grateful the months of hositility were over. This was no time for them to be taking pot shots at each other.

"You don't need to apologize," Byron was saying. "You've already followed her much further than I could. It's getting late. We'll camp outside the gate and try to track her in the morning."

Comanche was still staring at the ground when a warning growl burst from Trouble's throat. The huge dog seemed to double in size as every hair on his body lifted. Before Comanche could turn to see what had roused Trouble to such fury, he felt the hair on his own neck lift in a primordial response to imminent danger.

Out of the corner of his eye, he glimpsed a tawny rocket charging out of the bushes headed straight for Cait. When had she rejoined them? A hoarse warning cry burst from his own throat. In that instant he chose to make the ultimate sacrifice, offering his life in exchange for hers.

Reacting instinctively, he threw himself at her, hoping against hope to reach her in time. He felt her soft body yield to his, heard her sharp cry as his weight crushed her to the ground. Thinking it might be his last moment on earth, he breathed in her sweet scent and nuzzled her hair, his mind already halfway to heaven as he waited to take the force of the lion's charge on his unguarded back.

For Cait the next few seconds passed in a jumbled blur of sensations. An ear-splitting roar – an anguished howl – the boom of a gun – the coppery smell of blood.

A soft moan.

A curse.

Then silence.

Through it all Comanche's body blanketed hers. When it seemed she couldn't bear his weight any longer, if lifted. She gasped, pulling air into her oxygen-starved lungs.

A moment passed before her body obeyed her brain's command to move. She rocked to her knees, then staggered to her feet, looking at the world through a dizzying haze. She sensed rather than saw Comanche by her side and reached for his support.

He ignored her unspoken plea, though. The name, "Trouble", burst from his throat in a terrible cry.

Frantic to know what had happened, Cait knuckled at her eyes. Her hands came away wet with blood – her vision cleared. Not five feet away she saw the lioness, limp now in death, her mouth drawn back in a silent snarl. Trouble was locked in the great cat's embrace. The dog moaned softly when Comanche dropped to the ground beside him.

"Good boy," Comanche said, his voice raw with emotion. He gently extricated Trouble from the lion's lethal clutch and cradled him in his own arms. "Good boy," he murmured again.

Horrified, Cait drew close enough to the mournful

tableau to see a crimson tide pouring from Touble's torn throat. The dog gazing up at Comanche with such trust and love. His white-tipped tail beat just once, then a tremor ran through his great body and his eyes glazed over. Comanche continued to cradle Trouble, rocking back and forth, his posture an ode to sorrow.

Cait felt a hand on her arm and looked up to see Byron. "I think we should leave him alone," he said so softly she had to strain to hear.

She was too racked by sorrow to resist as he gently guided her away, settling her on a boulder near the canyon's mouth. She could see the men milling in the distance, waiting for someone to tell them what to do.

"You're hurt," Byron said, pulling a handkerchief from his pocket and pressing it to her forehead.

"I am?" She felt numb.

"You must have hit your head when Comanche tackled you. Bloody hell! You're lucky to be alive."

"What happened?"

"The lion came out of the brush headed straight for you. Comanche saved your life. He must have a sixth sense for danger. I've only seen bravery like that once before. If Trouble hadn't distracted the lioness, Comanche might have been killed. By the time I could get a clear shot it was too late for the dog."

Cait felt a huge lump blossoming in her throat. "He shouldn't be alone," she said, swaying to her feet.

Byron put a supporting arm around her waist. "You're wrong, dear girl. I know you mean well. But there are times when a man needs to be by himself. I'm bloody certain this is one of them."

Comanche didn't know how long he sat rocking Trouble's lifeless body. He kept on replaying the events leading up to the dog's death, wondering what he could have done differently and blaming himself for what had happened. But for him, Trouble would still be alive. The dog had died protecting him. His only consolation was the knowledge that Cait had walked out of the canyon unharmed.

He buried his face in Trouble's body to stifle the sobs that tore up his throat. His tears shamed him. He owed Byron his thanks for making certain no one had stayed around to see them.

Concealing his emotions had been as much a part of his masculinity as the organ between his legs. He'd been raised to believe it was intrinsically wrong for a man to cry. Certainly he'd never seen Hank or Orry shed a tear.

He hadn't wept the day his mother left, hadn't once dampened a pillow over the thousand psychic wounds of childhood, hadn't expressed his sorrow when he wrote Cait that fateful letter.

On the rodeo circuit he and his peers had made it a point of honour to endure injuries in silence broken only by an occasional curse. Now he couldn't seem to stop the groans that tore up his throat. He choked on tears.

To think he'd actually accused Cait of sentimentalizing animals when here he sat, wailing over a dog, for God's sake. He knew he ought to get up off the ground, carry poor old Trouble back to his horse, get a shovel and give him a decent burial. But his fingers remained clenched in Trouble's fur, his arms locked around his neck. Bury the companion who'd been with him through all those lonely nights? How the hell was he going to manage that?

A sombre procession made its way back to the ranch. The cowboys slouched in their saddles like men who have ridden beyond bodily endurance, their normal banter replaced by mournful silence. When they reached the house, Cait left Byron to dismiss them and to answer Hank's, Delta's and Bobby Rae's questions. She needed to be alone.

Weariness tugged at her limbs as she climbed the stairs to her room. It wasn't physical weariness but rather an exhaustion of the spirit. Sadness clotted in her throat.

Despair clutched at her heart. She stripped off her clothes, put on a robe and went to the bathroom to run a tub. After it filled she sank into the steaming water, burdened by a remorse so deep that soap could never wash it away.

Everyone she loved or cared about had been jeopardized by her decision to go ahead with the Outback. She had hoped to bring joy to her father's final months and had filled them with turmoil instead. She had dreamed of saving endangered species and had seen innocent creatures suffer terrible deaths. Dozens of people had rearranged their lives to accommodate her ambition and she couldn't even promise them continued employment.

But Comanche had suffered most of all.

She had fought with him at every turn, threatened to fire him and toyed with his pride, when all the while what she really wanted was his love. And now she bore the responsibility and the blame for Trouble's death. If she had listened to Byron and stayed with the hands, Comanche would not be grieving right now.

While the water cooled, she fought to accept the fact that she couldn't undo what she had done, that she wouldn't have the wisdom to change her behaviour given a second chance.

At least the Outback hadn't been a mistake. The idea was as worthwhile now as it had been when she first conceived of it, she reminded herself. It seemed she learned of a threat to some new species every month. Although she sympathized with people whose livelihoods were endangered by the effort to save seemingly unimportant creatures such as the spotted owl, certain facts remained irrefutable.

Men could and would create new industries, new jobs. Once lost, a species could not be resurrected. If she never succeeded at anything else, she reaffirmed her vow to make the Outback a safe haven where nature had a chance to replenish itself.

She didn't realize she'd been clenching her jaws until she felt them ache. Resolution stiffened her spine. Her nemesis, the son-of-a-bitch who got his rocks off endangering her animals, wasn't going to drive them or her from her land.

An hour later, her face scrubbed clean, wearing an old pair of corduroy slacks and a cashmere sweater, she joined Byron and Delta in the kitchen. Byron was drinking a beer, looking remarkably happy considering everything that had happened.

"We were damn lucky to save one of the lions," he was telling an attentive Delta.

"Trouble wasn't so lucky," she replied. "How did Comanche take it?"

"Bad, real bad," Cait answered Delta.

Byron took one look at Cait and offered her a beer. "You look like you can use this."

She sank into a chair and took a sip.

"In all the excitement," he said, "I never had a chance to tell you about my trip. You're friend, Mims, was an incredible help. She's quite a lady."

Had there not been so much on her mind, Cait might have noted the sparkle in Byron's eyes and the lilt in his voice when he said Mims' name. She was too preoccupied though to pay it any heed.

"Do you mind if we talk about your trip later?"

"Sure. There's no hurry. Tomorrow will be soon enough."

"Where's Dad?" she asked Delta.

"In his room. He said he wanted you to stop in and say good night if you came downstairs."

"Have you all had dinner?"

"Yes, *cher*. I kept yours warm in the stove."

"Did Comanche eat with you?"

"No. The lights aren't on in his house either. I'm worried about him. You know how he loved that dog."

"I think I'll go look for him," Cait said.

"Do you want me to go with you?" Byron asked.

"Not this time. Thanks anyway."

She stopped by Hank's room on her way out of the house. Finding him asleep, she kissed him, tucked the covers around his shoulders and tiptoed from his room.

Taking an old jacket from the hall tree in the entry, she slipped outside. The coming of night had brought a cold wind that set the crepe myrtle's bare branches rattling against the house. She pulled the jacket tighter and walked to the foreman's house on the off chance that Comanche might be there.

Her heart spasmed as she opened the gate in the picket fence. If she missed Trouble's rambunctious greeting, what must Comanche be feeling? She crossed the narrow yard and the small front porch, then knocked on the door. It cracked open, admitting her to the dark house.

"Comanche?" she called out.

Although he didn't answer, she sensed his presence as she felt her way down the hall. "Comanche?" she called again, entering the parlour.

The only answer was the sigh of the wind as it curled above the eaves. The moon, shining through the lace curtains, cast chiaroscuro shadows on the floor. She saw Comanche on the sofa, his shoulders hunched as he gazed off into nothingness. He looked so alone, so defeated. Tears sheened his cheeks.

She'd never seen him that way before. A wave of compassion weakened her knees. She paused for a heartbeat, stunned by the unexpected feelings his tears evoked. They seemed to wash away all her resentment, all the years of misunderstanding, all her useless pride.

Her conscious mind finally admitted what her subconscious had known all along.

Comanche was her man. Her fate. Her future as well as her past. And he was hurting. Bad.

She walked up behind him and gently wiped away his tears, then smoothed his hair away from his brow. Then she moved around the sofa, sat down and took him in her arms. Love and longing flowed through her. Compassion too.

Byron had been right, there were times when a man needed to be by himself. There were other times though, when a man needed a woman the way a baby needs its mother's milk.

This was one of those times.

Comanche had buried Trouble at sunset down by the river at the special place he and Cait had shared. He had no idea how long he'd been sitting in the dark house.

When he heard Cait calling his name, he thought he was dreaming. He didn't answer for fear of waking up. But the woman who took him in her arms a moment later was flesh and blood. She smelled and felt just the way he remembered. He reached for her and buried his face in her breasts, a shudder running through his powerful frame.

Reacting instinctively, Cait pulled the sweater over her head and removed her bra, baring her upper body.

Comanche groaned, a primal sound of need that came from deep in his chest. Her womb spasmed in response. Then his lips and tongue found the gift she offered.

He suckled first one breast and then the other, his sorrow and grief turning to a man's passion.

Her body instantly remembered all the things she had tried so fiercely to forget – the feel of his hands as they caressed her, the hungry nip of his teeth, the taste of his mouth. He foraged at her lips like a starving man who has finally found sustenance, then feathered her closed eyes, her neck and shoulders with kisses before seeking her nipples again.

Her skin was velvet, her scent a heady musk that sent desire rippling along his nerve paths. He cupped her breasts in his hands, relishing their seductive weight, their pliant softness. He feasted at her cresting nipples while his pulse thundered in his ears.

When he reclaimed her lips he had no need for words. All the things that divided them vanished in the tumult of mutual desire. She tasted of lost sweetness and remembered passion. Desire heated his loins as he delved deep into the honeyed depths of her mouth, his tongue laving hers.

She tugged at his shirt, freed it from his jeans and ran her hands up his chest. He had taught her, long ago, that a man's nipples were almost as sensitive as a woman's. As she kissed and nibbled, he joyously surrendered his heart, his soul, the very essence of his being to the fire that burned in them both.

They sated their long unsatisfied desire on the sofa, the quiet broken only by the sounds of their passion. Resting on his elbows, he poised above her. The moment seemed to stretch into eternity as he sought to engrave her enraptured face in his memory.

"Now, please now," she begged.

Before he could reach down to guide his first thrust, he felt her hand encircle his manhood, caressing him. Aching with pleasure, he sought the soft folds between her legs and gently parted them.

Need drove him hard as the tip of his erection found her liquid heat. He entered her with one long blissful stroke that left them as surely joined as key to lock. The universe seemed centred in the fusing of their bodies.

With rapturous deliberation he pulled out like a comet escaping a galaxy, to repeat the aching joy of penetration a moment later, drawing each stroke out until he knew nothing but the feel of Cait's centre tightening around him. Then, when he could no longer endure the withholding, he poured his seed into her.

Afraid a single word would end the magic, he carried her into his bedroom and gently removed her remaining garments, driven by a hunger to possess her again, to brand her body with his kisses, to fill her.

She returned caress for caress as they climbed to new

heights of passion. This time when they reached the top, Comanche couldn't quiet the thought that had been drumming in his mind for months. If he spoke no other words this night, he had to speak these.

"I love you, Katydid," he breathed in Cait's ear.

"I love you too, hotshot," she whispered back.

He was so beautiful, with his long hair fanned across the pillow, the moon highlighting the strong planes of his face. She finally admitted why she hadn't married. *She had never found his equal*. He had been indelibly engraved on her heart long ago and no other men had erased the things he had written there.

"I used to dream this would happen," he said, breaking her reverie.

"Me, too," she replied. "God, what was the matter with the two of us? Why did it take Trouble's death to bring us together?"

A spasm of pain flickered across his face. "There are so many things I regret . . ."

She silenced him with a kiss. "I don't want to talk about regret tonight."

He pulled her down so that her head nestled in the crook of his arm and shoulder. "Months ago, I said we needed to clear the air. Now you have to hear me out. If you never believe anything else in your life, believe this. I never meant to hurt you. If I had known about the baby . . ."

"I believe you. If I've learned nothing else these last few months," she murmured almost to herself, "I've learned you can't change the past."

"It's the future that counts."

"Do you think we have one?" she asked.

"Sure, if we both want it bad enough."

"What about Bobby Rae?"

"Cait, sweetheart, I have a confession to make. I used Bobby Rae to try and make you jealous."

She couldn't help giggling. "It worked. Lord, did it

work. I wanted to kill you the day you suggested I hire her."

"Then we're even, because I felt the same way about Byron."

"There's never been anything between me and Byron, except friendship. In fact, I think he's interested in Mims."

Comanche felt as if a great weight had lifted off his soul, a disfiguring hump that he'd been carrying around for months. It had warped his vision far too long. What a self-pitying fool he'd been. "I've been wrong about a lot of things, but I'm not wrong about this. I love you Cait. I always have."

She pulled away just far enough to look into his eyes. "I used to envy you because you seemed so sure of yourself. You haven't changed."

"You're wrong, Cait. I've changed a lot. I walked away from you once because I thought I didn't deserve you. Now I'm giving you fair warning. I won't walk away again."

"I don't want you to. But I need time."

"Why? Is it me?"

"Don't be ridiculous. You're not only a terrific lover, you're the best friend I ever had."

"Is it because I'm a Killian, because my family doesn't come up to your standards?"

Cait silenced him with a burning kiss that he felt clear down to his toes. "My standards?" she said when they both paused for breath. "The shoe is really on the other foot. I've made more than my share of mistakes. You may not know it but I've been engaged before. Four times."

"Oh, I know it all right. Every time I saw your picture in a tabloid with another man, I wanted to stake him out on an ant hill the way my ancestors did."

"Then you understand why I have to be sure this is the real thing before we tell anyone."

In response, he pulled her close again, experiencing a

whole universe of pleasure as their bodies touched. "We'll do it your way for now. Just remember this. You're not alone any more. Whatever happens, we'll face it together."

He smiled to himself. Cait still had a few things to work out. The fact that her life had changed so much since her return to the ranch had to add to her uncertainty. He'd gladly give her all the time she needed because he'd meant what he said.

No power on earth could make him walk away from her again.

20

Under normal circumstances, Senator Morgan enjoyed being home for the holidays. He relished the opportunity to press Texas flesh, to renew friendships with the influential River Oaks Country Club set and cement the political bonds that kept him securely in office.

However, there was nothing normal about his present circumstances, he mused sourly as he descended the main staircase of his River Oaks mansion. The stalled Nishida deal was never far from his mind.

His expression soured as he saw the chaos in the entry hall. His wife had whipped the household into a decorating frenzy. Garlands, wreaths and ornament boxes were strewn everywhere, and an enormous Christmas tree lay on the entry hall floor. People he'd never seen before scurried back and forth on incomprehensible errands.

Although he had restructured the bulk of his debts, the strangers racing around his home represented dollars he wouldn't have until he closed the Nishida deal. It was all he could do not to thunder, "bah – humbug".

Desperate for peace and quiet, he left for Allen Center without breakfast. Half an hour later he sat at his desk, drumming his perfectly buffed nails on the mahogany surface, his thoughts even grimmer than the expression on his face.

The good old US of A had come to a sorry state when a man like him needed a man like Tochigi. Bitter gall rose up his throat as he recalled how Washington had played right into Japanese hands.

Part of the blame fell on his fellow Congressmen for approving the rules and regulations that strangled businesses, for enacting the burdensome taxes that choked off the flow of investment, for turning their backs to the junk bonds that had devoured what little cash remained.

But the worst sinners had been the Japanese, aided and abetted by an unholy alliance with those liberal, pinko bastards who got their rocks off kissing the asses of former enemies. Anyone who raised a voice against them, himself included, was labelled a racist.

The Japs had targeted certain American industries – steel, automobiles, electronics, you name it – while the powers that be looked the other way way. And now he had no choice but to cooperate too. Just yesterday, Tochigi had called again while he'd been hurrying to leave his senatorial office to catch a Houston-bound flight.

"I am most displeased, Senator," Tochigi had said after the traditional amenities were concluded. "As you no doubt recall, Nishida wishes to buy at the bottom of the market and my sources tell me Texas real estate is on the rebound."

Blackjack had heard that particular complaint half a dozen times. "Fuck your sources," he said under his breath.

Tochigi couldn't seem to accept the fact that he was doing his best to come up with a suitable ranch. Hell, the slant-eyed bastard didn't know the half of it, Blackjack thought, recalling Det's latest stunt. Releasing those lions had been more than dangerous; it had been downright stupid. If they had got off the ranch, the resulting hue and cry would have drawn the media like children to a circus.

A crimson flush coloured his cheeks as a terrible thought popped into his head. Could it be his luck had finally run out?

So many things had happened to him that would have

stopped a lesser man in his tracks. Not only had he survived, he had thrived. While he gave part of the credit to his own superior abilities, he recognized that the bitch goddess, Lady Luck, had played a role. She'd never fucked him over before. Why the hell had she started now?

The sound of the phone jolted him. Damn, he thought, his flush deepening. Couldn't anyone get anything right? He'd told his secretary he didn't want to take any calls. Jerking the receiver from its cradle, he barked, "What the hell is it?"

"I'm sorry, sir," his secretary replied with a quiver in her voice. "I know you said you weren't available. It's that realtor from Kerrville and he said you'd have my head on a platter if I didn't put him through."

Blackjack thought a moment. Milton Herbert had called him occasionally over the last few months to tout the virtues of this or that property. None of them had come near filling the bill. But what the hell, you never knew. "All right, put him on," he grudgingly agreed.

"Milton Herbert speaking," came the realtor's voice a moment later.

"What's on your mind, Herbert?"

"Are you still interested in buying an historic Hill Country ranch?"

"I told you the property isn't for me," Blackjack replied impatiently. "As for the corporation I mentioned, the answer is yes, they haven't bought anything yet."

"Do you know the Hefernans?"

Blackjack searched his memory, sorting through the thousands of Texas families he knew. At last the name clicked into place. The Hefernans owned a spread near Boerne. They had contributed to his campaigns. However, the amounts had never been large enough to merit his personal attention. "I'm familiar with the name. I'm sure you realise I'm home on holiday so I'd appreciate it if you would get to the point."

"Certainly, Senator. To make a long story short, old man Hefernan is sick. He's on the list for a heart transplant at the Medical Center in Houston."

"So?" Blackjack prodded.

"I just listed his ranch. It's thirty-five thousand acres with a terrific old house that's on the National Register of historic places."

Blackjack took a moment to consider, then said, "I don't think thirty-five thousand acres will do it."

"I didn't think so either. There is a possibility that the adjacent ranch will be coming on the market too. And it's got twenty thousand acres of prime land. I'm telling you, Senator, this dog will hunt."

Blackjack's heart reacted like a jump-started engine. Thirty-five thousand acres, he mused, with the possibility of even more. "It sounds very intriguing."

"I video-taped the Hefernan place. I'll mail the tape if you're interested."

Interested didn't come close, Blackjack thought. He wanted to see that tape . . . bad. "I'm afraid you've caught me at an awkward time," he said, sounding suitably regretful. "My calendar is jam-packed. I'll be free this afternoon and that's about it. You can send the tape to my Washington office. I should be able to review it in the next month or so." He could almost smell Herbert's anxiety as the realtor saw a dream sale slipping away.

"I could deliver the tape in person in five hours," Herbert declared right on cue. "My clients are pretty anxious."

But not half as anxious as their realtor, Blackjack thought, smiling at the way Herbert had taken the bait. "That would help a great deal. If you get here fast enough, I might even have time for a little holiday cheer afterwards."

The realtor said goodbye so quickly that his behaviour bordered on rudeness. Blackjack didn't mind, though. He had no doubt Milton Herbert would break the speed limit all the way to Houston.

He checked his watch and grinned. He had time for a leisurely lunch.

At three that afternoon Blackjack was back in his office ensconced in a deep leather chair in front of a television set, digesting the blackened snapper he had for lunch at Tony Mandola's and watching Milton Herbert's video of the Hefernan ranch.

The tape included terrific shots of lush pastures, cedar-free range, well-kept outbuildings, expensive equipment, healthy cattle and a magnificent turn-of-the-century mansion. He had to give Milton Herbert credit. Whoever he'd hired to shoot the film had done a professional job, complete with a voice-over and background music.

"Well, what do you think?" the realtor asked when the half-hour tape came to an end.

Blackjack rose, turned and gave Milton Herbert his best campaign smile. "Not bad, not bad at all."

In fact, the Hefernan ranch exceeded his expectations. If only it were bigger. "Tell me about the adjoining property."

An anxious-to-please expression rode the realtor's round face. "Like I told you earlier, it's twenty thousand acres of prime land, most of it cedar-free, with ten wells . . ."

"Never mind all that," Blackjack interrupted impatiently. "Why do you think it's going to come on the market?"

"The owners just got a divorce. They've got financial problems as well. The place is mortgaged to the hilt."

"Do you know who holds the note?"

The realtor quickly gave the name of a small Hill Country bank. Blackjack's mind began to race. His pulse accelerated. Bingo, he thought triumphantly. The bank's president was an old friend.

"If you'll excuse me for a minute, Milton," he said, using the realtor's given name for the first time, "I have to make a call."

When Blackjack invited Milton Herbert back into his office, it was all he could do to conceal his glee. The bank president had promised to begin foreclosure proceedings. Nishida was going to get a dream property at a bargain price. It was as good as a done deal.

Blackjack had been so sure that nothing better than the Pride ranch would come along. Now that it had, the pain that had sent him to a doctor thinking he had an ulcer began to fade.

He gave the realtor his most unctuous smile. "I have some news for you. However, I want your promise that it won't go any further than this room."

"You have my word, Senator."

"You'll get a call about listing the other ranch by the end of the week."

Milton Herbert's anxious look evaporated. "I told you this dog would hunt."

"I think this calls for that drink I mentioned," Blackjack said. "Why don't you meet me at the River Oaks Country Club in half an hour. Just tell them you're my guest."

Taking the bemused realtor's arm, he guided him to the door a second time and ushered him out, then returned to his desk and placed a long-distance call himself, not caring what time it was in Tokyo. In any case, Tochigi had said to call at any hour if he had something to report.

"I have very good news," he said when Tochigi came on the line.

Carroll Detweiler sat on the shabby sofa in his Fredericksburg apartment, a beer in one hand and a cigar in the other, his eyes on the television, his mind on the Outback.

Stymied by his inability to drive Cait Pride off the ranch, he had been searching for another opportunity to make her life miserable.

New animals arrived weekly. Workmen came and went as construction moved relentlessly forward. Deliveries were a daily occurrence. Surely all that activity presented any number of possibilities.

He flicked the cigar, not caring that a pile of ashes had accumulated around his feet. The place was a pit and anything he did during his occupancy couldn't make it much worse. The apartment was rented to transients on a weekly basis. It was the sort of place he favoured on an op and had its counterparts all over the world. The owners charged a little more than the market value and, in return, asked no questions.

He chugged the last of his beer down, wiped his mouth on his sleeve and had just risen to get another brew when the phone rang. Since no one else had the number, it had to be Blackjack.

"What's up?" he said, not bothering with a conventional greeting.

"Merry Christmas to you, too," Blackjack replied. "How would you like to go home for the holidays?"

Holding the receiver between chin and shoulder, Carroll Detweiler crossed the few feet from the sofa to the minuscule kitchen, took a beer from the refrigerator and popped the tab. "I wasn't expecting a Christmas vacation, if that's what you mean."

"I'm not talking about a vacation. The move will be permanent. The op is over, Det, finished. I want you to pack your gear and head on home this afternoon."

Detweiler, having just taken a swallow of beer, choked on it. He couldn't believe his ears. He'd never been shit-canned before. Blackjack was the last person he expected to stab him in the back this way. "I know things haven't turned out the way you hoped, but I have lots of ideas that ought to do the trick."

"You don't understand. Things have turned out *exactly* the way I hoped. I have no further need of your services and frankly, after your last stunt with the lions, I think it's time for you to pack it in, anyway."

The Senator's words felt like hot pincers, squeezing Carroll's brain. "If it's the money, you don't need to cover my expenses any more."

"You still don't get it, Det. Like I said, the op is over. I don't care if Cait Pride stays on that ranch until hell freezes over."

Blackjack must have hired someone else, Detweiler thought, his mouth narrowing to an ugly slash. "Look the Pride bitch isn't some kind of superwoman; she's just a stubborn cunt. I'm so close the breaking this thing wide open I can taste it. All I need is a little more time, for Chrissake."

"Shut up for a minute and listen to me, Det. The situation has changed. I don't, I repeat, *I don't* want Cait Pride bothered again. I know you've given it your best. No one could have done more. But it's over – finished. The mission is over. Go home and have yourself one hell of a holiday."

Detweiler collapsed on the sofa like a deflated balloon, then scratched his scraggly beard, a bemused expression in his eyes. "I don't get it," he finally said.

"You don't have to get it. Just do what I say."

Carroll Detweiler looked around the place that had been home the last few months. He hated breaking off an engagement when the objective was in sight, hated walking away like a fucking loser. Shit. He'd done enough of that in Nam to last a lifetime.

Besides, the Outback op had passed the point where he could think of it as just another clandestine mission. It wasn't business any more. Never really had been. It was personal. He wanted to fuck Cait Pride over, mentally, physically, emotionally, financially, any and every way he could. He wanted to ruin a Pride the way the Prides had ruined the Detweilers years ago.

"Are you there, Det?" came the sound of the Senator's voice. "Look, I have no doubt this came as a bit of a surprise, but it's really for the best."

Every officer Carroll Detweiler had ever known had said the same thing at one time or another. All for the best. Leaving Vietnam had been "all for the best", too. But he'd always prided himself on being a good soldier, and good soldiers obeyed their superiors right down the line.

"All right, sir. I'll be out of here in an hour. But I sure as hell wish I knew why you changed your mind."

"Rest assured it has nothing to do with you. You're the best, Det. Always will be." The Senator's voice sounded as warm and soothing as molten honey. "Tell you what. I'll call you in a couple of days and we'll see about getting together and hoisting a few before I go back to Washington."

Detweiler had seen Blackjack work suckers over too often not to know he was being worked over too. But the Senator was the only man on earth he'd ever looked up to. He still wanted his friendship.

"Sure thing, Senator. That would be great. I'm as good as out of here."

Detweiler put the receiver back in its cradle, absent-mindedly finished his beer, tossed the can at the trash and missed. Then he got to his feet, crossed the floor to the closet and pulled out his old army issue duffel, shambling like a bear with a pronounced limp.

Half an hour ago he'd been planning his next move, raring to be up and at 'em. Now he was painfully aware of every one of his old injuries. Shit. He felt sick. Christmas in Elgin was going to be hell.

A nerve pulsed under Blackjack's left eye as he hung up the phone. He looked blindly around his Allen Center office, not seeing the expensive furniture, the thick emerald carpet, the expansive view. It had been touch and go for a while there.

He must have been crazy, hiring a man like Detweiler for a sensitive job. Det was capable of committing the most heinous acts without turning a hair. Suddenly, an icy presentiment danced down Blackjack's spine and a cold sweat popped out on his brow.

Det knew too fucking much.

Blackjack got up and paced the floor, wondering how he could have been so stupid as to put himself in such jeopardy. Given the choice, he'd happily put a contract out on Det. Unfortunately though, Det was the only assassin-for-hire he knew. That left only one alternative. He'd have to try and buy him off.

After all, every man has a price, he reassured himself, returning to his desk. He sat down, removed his cheque-book from the centre drawer, wrote out a sizable cheque and printed MERRY XMAS – FOR A JOB WELL DONE at the bottom left-hand corner. Then he stuffed it in an envelope and scrawled Det's Elgin address across the front. That should do it.

One task remained before he headed for home. The venture capitalist who'd given Cait the loan had done so on the understanding that he couldn't lose. Either he got a hell of a return on his money or he wound up with the title to the ranch and sold it at a profit. Now that Blackjack had found another spread for Tochigi, he had to do everything in his power to assure the Outback's success. He checked his watch, then dialed Cait's number. A few minutes later her new secretary put her on the line.

"Merry Christmas, Senator," Cait said, sounding remarkably cheerful for a woman who had endured every torment Det could devise.

"And a Merry Christmas to you, my dear, and your father too. Avery tells me you've had another bit of trouble up there. I just called to see if I could help in any way."

"You've already done more than enough."

Indeed, he had, he thought, suppressing a rueful chuckle. "Nonsense, child. I've only done what your father would do for Avery if the situation were reversed. Speaking of Avery, she mentioned something about your planning a grand opening in June. I hope my name is on the invitation list."

"Right up at the very top."

"I've been thinking about it and I believe I have an idea that could give you tremendous publicity. I intend to prevail on the President to attend. He wants to be known as pro-environmental and I can't think of anyone in the private sector who is doing more for the environment than you are."

"That's very flattering, Senator. We do our best."

"Having the President attend would be a coup, wouldn't it?"

"Absolutely. Mims Pauling has been helping me line up television coverage. *Entertainment Tonight* is sending John Tesh, and Robin Leach wants to do a *Lifestyles* segment. But having the President here would attract national coverage by all three networks. Do you really think you can pull it off?"

"Of course, or I wouldn't offer. I'll mention it when I get back to Washington."

There had been a powerful disaffection with the President in conservative Republican ranks. In return for Blackjack's promise to lobby his fellow conservatives on the President's behalf, the aides would encourage the man to attend the opening. It was the sort of quid pro quo that kept the machinery of government working.

His business done, he exchanged a few more pleasantries with Cait, then hung up. Getting to his feet, he walked over to the window and looked down at the mighty city below, his expression exultant.

Lady Luck, the bitch goddess, had crawled right back into his bed.

21

It took Carroll Detweiler less than an hour to pack up and leave his Fredericksburg apartment, and another two to drive back to Elgin. He pulled up in front of his mobile home at six. A single street lamp revealed its derelict condition.

During his absence the weeds in the tiny yard had grown knee-high and some asshole had sprayed *Motherfucker* in foot-high red letters on one of the windows. Kids have no respect these days, he mused sourly as he took his duffel from the Blazer's back seat. If he ever caught the graffiti-happy little shit, he'd teach him a lesson.

When he inserted the key, the rusty lock resisted. He exerted too much pressure and the key snapped off at the shank. A series of expletives poured from his mouth as he limped around the trailer, vainly searching for an unlocked window.

Returning to the front stoop, he wrapped a handkerchief around one of his ham-sized fists and released a fraction of his anger by shattering the window in the door. Reaching through, he turned the lock, then retrieved his duffel and carried it back to what had been his mother's bedroom.

Although she had died two years earlier, he'd never changed the décor. The walls, carpet, drapes and bedspread were her favourite shade of purple. Her perfume and make-up sat on the dressing table as if in expectation of her imminent return. He still missed her.

He'd never known his father. The son-of-a-bitch had walked out before his first birthday, but Carroll had never complained because his mother had devoted her life to him, staying home and getting by on welfare so they could be together although, with her brains, she could have had any job she wanted.

He peered at himself in the grimy dressing-table mirror, wondering what she'd think if she could see him now? She would have hated the long hair that was part of his disguise. Hell, there wasn't anything she hated worse than those long-haired faggot hippies who had stayed home when he went off to Nam. He scratched at his beard, knowing she wouldn't like it either. The damn thing itched, too. He couldn't wait to shave it off.

Not bothering to unpack, he tramped down the hall to the bathroom, feeling, as he always did, like the proverbial bull in a china shop. Having just spent the last six months outdoors roaming the Pride ranch at will, the mobile home made him even more claustrophobic than usual.

Suddenly he just had to get out of there. The shave could wait. So could boarding up the broken glass in the door. Moving more quickly than he had all day, he hurried outside, climbed back into the Blazer and drove straight to the Old Tavern.

The place hadn't changed an iota in his absence, but such places never do. The neon sign still invited the weary, the poor, the disenfranchised to satisfy their thirst. He marched straight to his accustomed seat at the end of the bar and ordered a beer. The man who had been sitting on the adjacent stool took one look at him and quickly left. No one came to take his place.

Detweiler drank steadily and with purpose, hoping the icy brew would fill the emptiness inside him. But four more beers failed to improve his mood. He felt furious every time he thought about his aborted mission.

As far back as he could remember, he'd been angry

about something. Maybe he'd been born angry. In the past, though, the expectation of a new mission had helped him stay in control.

Now that hope was gone. There would be no new operation to take him far away, no escape from the knowledge that he had fucked up royally. No matter what the Senator had said, he knew he'd lost the other man's respect.

Blackjack was as likely to drive to Elgin to hoist a few brewskies as he was to resign his Senate seat, and not because Blackjack had thrown a hell of a lot of money away on the op without any return. Money didn't mean shit to a guy like the Senator. He'd been a self-made millionaire when he went off to Nam. He didn't have to serve in a poor man's war with guys like Carroll, but he had.

A fucking hero; that was the Senator.

Knowing he had failed him ate at Detweiler's brain like battery acid. Where had he gone wrong? What more could he have done?

There's no place like home, Cait thought, grinning at her own lack of originality. The living room had never looked more festive. A cosy fire blazed on the hearth, lights twinkled on the Christmas tree, evergreens draped the mantel, and a cluster of mistletoe hung over the door.

In anticipation of Mims' arrival, Comanche and Byron had helped put up the decorations last night. Ever the perfect gentleman, Byron had even managed to look in the other direction when she and Comanche made use of the mistletoe.

Byron's and Comanche's growing friendship delighted her. Byron had even started giving Comanche boxing lessons. For some reason, the two of them looked guilty as sin when they talked about it, though. Perhaps it was just one of those male bonding things.

This had the makings of the best Christmas ever, Cait

decided, her glance moving from Comanche to Mims to Byron before settling on Hank.

"Did Cait tell you Senator Morgan is going to talk to the President about attending the grand opening?" Hank was asking Mims. "Of course, he wouldn't be the first president to visit the ranch. Teddy Roosevelt hunted here with my grandfather Ulysses, and Lyndon Johnson dropped by a time or two. It's really a very historic house. One of these days Cait ought to get it added to the national registry of historic landmarks."

"That's nice," Mims replied. Clearly, she hadn't heard a word Hank said. What was the matter with her tonight? Cait mused. Perhaps she just needed some time alone with Byron. Come to think of it, she wouldn't mind having some time with Comanche herself.

She rose, yawned and stretched elaborately. "I don't know about you all," she said, looking around the room, "but I'm exhausted."

"Me, too," Hank replied, slowly getting to his feet. His cautious movements told Cait he was in pain, even though he never complained.

"How about a nightcap in your room?" Comanche asked, walking to Hank's side and putting a companionable arm around his back. Cait knew it was his way of giving Hank an arm to lean on without embarrassing him.

"I'd enjoy that, son," Hank replied.

Cait waited until they left the room before turning to Byron and Mims. "If you two will excuse me, I'm going to check on those Christmas cookies Delta's baking."

"Don't stay up on our account," Byron replied.

"I wouldn't dream of it. I'm sure you'll find some way to amuse each other. Have a pleasant evening." Cait hugged Mims, gave Byron the deliberately smarmy smile of a child who has finally figured out her parents have sex, then left the parlour.

Byron listened to Cait's footsteps fading down the hall before turning his full attention on Mims. They hadn't had a minute alone since her arrival earlier that day. Not that he expected her to fly into his arms and drag him off to bed the moment they had a chance. Still, her seeming disinterest troubled him deeply.

She had been self-absorbed and uncommunicative during lunch and had spent most of the dinner hour talking to Bobby Rae. "Have I done something to offend you?" he said into the blanket of silence swaddling the room.

She started, as if the sound of his voice had taken her by surprise. "Of course not. What would make you think something like that?"

"I can't tell you how much I've looked forward to having you here – being with you. The trouble is, you aren't really here with me. Your mind has been someplace else all day."

"I'm sorry if I've seemed to ignore you."

"I wouldn't mind so much – my ego can take the lack of attention – if you didn't look so bloody unhappy."

"But I'm not!"

He reached for her chin, tilted her head, and searched her face. "Sweet Mims, you're not a very good liar. I haven't seen a woman look the way you do since my parents died. My sister, Winifred, had an identical life-will-never-be-the-same expression in her eyes at their funeral."

"Am I that transparent?"

"Not to the others. But then, they don't care about you the way I do."

"And what way is that?"

"I've fallen in love with you," he said quietly.

Mims' matchless blue eyes widened and he could see her pulse beating in her throat. The quiet grew uncomfortably long while he waited for her to respond.

"We hardly know each other," she said at last.

"I may not know every last detail of your life but I think I know you."

That seemed to agitate her even more. She jumped to

her feet and would have left if he hadn't caught her by the arm.

"I'm not the person you think," she said, her breathy child's voice overflowing with adult pain.

Why now, Mims agonized, why did Byron have to declare himself tonight? All the way from New York, she had fantasized about seeing him again, what she would say, what he would say. She wished she could tell him she loved him too.

How could she, though, when she had kept so many things from him, things that might change the way he felt about her?

"Am I too old for you?" he burst out, getting to his feet.

The worry in his voice finally penetrated her befuddled brain. "That's ridiculous!"

"Both your husbands were younger than I am."

"Oh, Byron, they weren't half the man you are. It's not your age; it's me. Something happened today and I don't know how to handle it."

"Can you talk about it?"

She stood immobile, her eyes downcast, searching her heart and mind. "Perhaps, but not here. Let's go for a walk."

He was in the entry wearing a wool jacket when she came downstairs a few minutes later wrapped in mink. He opened the door, then followed her outside. She led the way across the porch and down the steps, moving towards the old stone barn, wondering if she had the courage to tell this very special man a truth she had kept from both her husbands.

Byron gazed at Mims' profile, wishing he could take her in his arms and kiss away all her problems. She hadn't rejected his love – hadn't accepted it either. What was it she had said? He didn't know her? Well, she didn't know him either. Perhaps it would help if he unburdened himself first.

"Evenings like this remind me of Kifaru," he said, gazing up at the sky.

"Isn't that the farm your parents used to own?"

"Yes. It was named for the black rhinos who lived there when my great-grandparents first settled on the land. *Kifaru* means rhinoceros in Kikuyu."

"Were there any rhinos at Kifaru when you were growing up?"

"Only stuffed ones. They'd been hunted out of the area long before I was born. You see, hunting was a way of life, a mark of manhood in my family. My great-grandfather, my grandfather, my father – all of them hunted. For the pot. For sport. It didn't matter. Killing animals was a big part of what made a Neville a man."

Mims didn't know why he'd chosen this time to talk about his boyhood. She was grateful for the diversion though. "You sound as if you don't approve."

He took her hand. "I don't. But I bought into the whole myth as a boy. So did my best friend, a young Masai two years my senior. Batian and I played great white hunter and Masai warrior from the day we got out of nappies. Back then hunting lion was a rite of passage among the Masai people. A Masai boy had to kill a lion before he could assume a man's responsibilities – or enjoy a man's pleasures."

"Wasn't it a bit unusual, having a black for a best friend?"

"Not in those days. Our farm was quite isolated. I grew up with Batian. His father was our headman. In any case, the year I turned twelve and Batian turned fourteen, we decided to prove how mature we were by going off to hunt lion."

"I can't believe your parents let you."

"They didn't know. We loaded our gear on a couple of horses and took off one morning while the household was asleep. We rode most of that day, set up camp at sunset and began hunting on foot at dawn. I was armed with the twenty-two my father had given me for my tenth birthday. Batian carried the traditional Masai spear and shield."

Byron's voice roughened as memories carried him back to that fateful day. "God knows what the two of us were thinking – going after lion with a twenty-two and a spear. Hell. Like all kids, it never occurred to us we might die."

He closed his eyes, the better to recall the sights, sounds and scents of an African morning on the open plains. "We came across a lone male lion around noon, a big bastard with a black mane. If we'd had any sense, we would have given him a wide berth. Years later, after I'd learned a little bushcraft, I realized he must have fought a younger male for supremacy of a pride, and lost. He had fresh wounds on his flanks, poor devil. In any case, he wasn't in the mood to put up with our nonsense."

"What happened?" she asked, her frosted breath giving form and shape to her words.

They had reached the corral fence. Byron helped her climb to a seat on the top rail and joined her. He lit a Player and inhaled deeply before picking up the narrative again. "Batian kept on moving closer to the lion, challenging him the way Masai men are taught, shaking his shield and shouting, "come here, simba, let me show you what a fierce warrior I am'. Not to be outdone, I did the same thing." He spun the unfinished cigarette off his fingertips. It arched into the night sky like a miniature missile, falling to earth inside the corral.

"When the lion charged I found out I was still very much a boy. I froze – except for my kidneys. They worked just fine. While I stood there wetting my pants, Batian took the full force of the charge on his shield like a true Masai man. He even managed to drive his spear into the lion's side."

"Did he kill it?"

"Sometimes I wake up in the middle of the night hearing Batian ask the same question. 'Did I kill the simba?' he said with his dying breath. I told him what he wanted to hear. 'Yes, brother, you are a great warrior now.' Batian asked me to take the skin back to Kifaru for his father."

"How awful for you."

He laughed harshly. "It was a hell of a lot worse for Batian. When I got home my father told me I had disgraced the Neville name. As if I didn't already know, stinking of Batian's blood and my own urine the way I did. He didn't talk to me again until the night the Mau Mau attacked Kifaru."

Byron turned to Mims and attempted a smile. However his mouth felt so dry that his lips stuck to his teeth. "By the time I left Cambridge, I almost resented Batian for dying because it had such a profound effect on my life. I went back to Africa and became a white hunter in a futile attempt at reliving that damn lion hunt and doing it right the next time." He paused to light another cigarette. "I've never told that story to anyone else."

"Why did you tell me?"

"Because I wanted you to know that no matter what's bothering you, it can't be as bad as what I did."

Had they not been seated so precariously, Mims would have thrown her arms around Byron. Instead, she settled for kissing his cheek. Any lingering doubts she may have had about him vanished. He had given her the most precious gift a man has to offer a woman, the unvarnished truth about himself.

Could she do any less?

Hank sat in front of the window in his room, wrapped in a threadbare flannel robe. He was going to need another one next winter, he thought, then grimaced as the truth reasserted itself. He wouldn't live to see next winter.

He leaned forward, put his eye to the telescope and studied the night sky. How petty his problems seemed on the stars' timetable. The trouble was, men didn't live on an eternal scale. They slogged it out hour by hour, day by day and his days were almost over. He wouldn't mind dying so much if Cait's happiness wasn't still hanging in the balance.

He was lowering the scope when a man and a woman stepped into view, holding hands as they walked towards the foreman's house. Leaning forward, he refocused the lens. His sudden smile almost erased the pain that had been etched around his mouth.

No wonder Comanche had been in such a hurry to finish that drink. Although Cait and Comanche had their backs turned, their posture told him everything he needed to know. He and Lizzie had walked that way, shoulders touching, arms circling each other's waists, years ago.

Not wanting to intrude on their privacy, he pushed the scope to the side, got up, took off his robe and laid it across the foot of the bed. The flannel sheets smelled fresh and sweet as he eased his body between them. He spent so much time in bed that Delta had taken to changing his linen twice a week. He hoped he'd be gone before they needed to be changed every day.

Now that he knew Cait and Comanche had found each other, he felt infinitely better. Once the Outback's future was assured, he'd gladly relinquish his hold on life. The land, he thought just before sleep claimed his ravaged body, everything went back to the land – all the problems, all the pain. All the joy, too.

Swallowing her apprehension, Mims reached for Byron's hand. "No one could possibly blame you for Batian's death. You were just a boy. But I was sixteen years old and I gave my baby girl up for adoption – old enough to know better." She searched his face for a response. "You don't seem surprised."

"A woman's body changes when she has a child. I saw those changes on yours the first time we made love."

"Why didn't you say something? You must have had questions."

"I trusted you to tell me about it in your own good time. Besides, nothing you said could have changed the way I felt." He paused, his expression quizzical. "There's just one thing I want to know."

Her heart knotted with apprehension. "I'll tell you if I can."

"You've been on edge since you got here. Did something happen today to remind you of the past?"

Unable to speak, she nodded.

He caught her chin in his hand, turned her face up to him and searched her eyes. "Can't you tell me what it was?"

"It was – it was meeting Cait's new secretary."

"Bobby Rae? Surely you don't think . . .?"

"Not any more. But I had to be sure. I asked Bobby Rae all about her family. Oh, God, I feel so stupid. I go through that awful mixture of hope and guilt every time I meet a young blonde woman the same age as my daughter." She shivered. "It's the worst feeling in the world."

"You're cold."

He helped her down from their uncomfortable perch. They walked in silence to the barn. Once inside, he seated her on a hay bale and put his arms around her. "I know the perfect way to warm you up," he said, nibbling at the corner of her mouth.

"Please, darling, it's my turn to talk. I won't be able to if you keep that up."

"I told you I don't care about your past. It's your future that interests me. I want to be a big part of it."

"I wish it were that simple. But it isn't."

He reached for her hand, turned it up and tenderly kissed her palm in a loving gesture of support. "You might feel better if you told me the whole story. It worked for me."

Mims searched his face, reading only love and concern written there. "When I was sixteen," she began haltingly, "I fell in love with my English teacher. I wanted to be a writer and he told me I had real talent. I was thrilled when he asked me to meet him after school so we could talk about my work."

"The bloody manipulative bastard," Byron muttered under his breath.

Mims didn't respond. She was determined to tell the whole story before she lost her nerve. "One thing led to another and the next thing I knew, we were in bed in the no-tell motel and he was telling me he wished his wife understood him the way I did. I didn't realize I'd fallen for the oldest line in the world. All I knew was I loved him. Months later, when I told him I was carrying his child, he begged me to keep it secret. He said he'd lose his job if anyone knew about us. To make a long story short, my father sent me to a Catholic home for wayward girls until the baby was born, and then he arranged an adoption through the church."

"Did you ever find out what happened to the baby?"

"I hired a detective to track her down ten years ago but he didn't find out a thing."

"Why did you wait all that time?"

Mims fought for composure. "A lot of reasons. At first I couldn't afford it. By the time I could, I told myself I didn't want to intrude on her privacy."

"Those are valid reasons," he agreed. "What made you change your mind?"

"Ten years ago one of my models told me she was pregnant and I arranged an abortion through Planned Parenthood. I didn't want her to suffer the way I had. But she went through a different kind of hell. After that I just had to try to find my daughter."

"Mims, love," he said, pulling her into his arms, "you aren't responsible for what happened when you were sixteen, any more than you're responsible for this other girl's troubles." He grasped both her shoulders and gazed into her eyes. "How many models have you worked with over the years?"

Surprised by the change of subject, she replied, "I don't know. Hundreds I suppose."

"And you do more for them than launch their careers, don't you?"

"Most of them are very young when they begin working, and very homesick." She smiled fondly, remembering the models who had spent their first weeks away from home in her apartment. How many pyjama parties had she presided over, how many late-night gab fests? "I try to fill in for the families they've left behind."

"My dear, dear Mims, has it ever occurred to you that out of the dozens of businesses you could have started with a Harvard MBA, you chose to open a modelling agency because you wanted to make up for giving up your own daughter by helping other young women?"

Suddenly Mims felt warm instead of cold. "I never thought of it quite that way."

"But it's possible, isn't it?"

"I suppose so."

"People talk about being young as if it's the most wonderful time in life but most of us carry scars from our childhood. When I came to Texas, I was determined to let go of the past. Perhaps we can do it together," he said, reaching for her.

"I'll try," Mims replied, trying not to sound sceptical, "but old habits die hard."

22

JUNE 1994

If the winter had been Comanche's season of discontent, the spring was a time of rebirth for him, for Cait and for the ranch. The exotics were thriving under Byron's stewardship. Cait had pushed the construction to successful completion. His own criollos were doing even better than he had hoped. But it was the deepening love he and Cait shared that made each new day better than the last.

He gazed across the pillow at her, wondering how a man could still be hungry for a woman he'd just made love to. It had been almost seven months since the night Cait came to him after Trouble's death, surely time enough for their passion to cool a little. Rather than satisfying his need for her, the hours they spent alone seemed to intensify it.

"Do you have any idea how happy I am at this moment?" he asked, "Or how much I love you?"

She smiled up at him, the smile that used to make his heart ache when he saw it on a magazine cover. He thanked the Lord that now that special smile was just for him.

"I think I do, but I wouldn't mind hearing it all over again."

" 'How do I love thee? Let me count the ways'," he solemnly intoned. "I love you more than Delta's pecan pie, more than a cold beer after a hot dusty ride, more than a winning poker hand, more than . . ." His voice trailed off in a rumble of laughter.

She poked an imperious finger in his chest. "Is that all?"

"Of course not, woman. Why, I even love you more than my horse." He stifled her yelp of displeasure with a kiss that left them both breathless. "The truth is, I love you more than life itself."

"That's more like it," she replied huskily.

"When I think of all the years we spent apart, being with you like this is a miracle. It's enough to make me believe someone up there is keeping an eye out for both of us. I don't ever want us to be apart again."

"We won't."

"When are you going to tell your father about us?"

She sighed, her expression growing more serious. "Do you mind waiting a little longer?"

"How long?"

"At least until after the opening."

He almost said he wasn't sure Hank would be with them then. Hank seemed to have taken a turn for the better in the April, but the first summer heat had sapped his dwindling reserves.

"Of course I can wait," he said.

"I'd better get up and go back to the house."

"Don't leave yet. Try to get a little sleep."

"All right," she replied, turning on her side and snuggling against him.

Cait came wide awake a couple of hours later, surprised to see how long she'd slept. The clock on the nightstand read four-thirty. The one that had been ticking inside her head since she got the loan told her time was running out. The first balloon payment was due in just a month. The vastness of the sum she owed weighed on her heavily.

Careful not to wake Comanche, she eased out of bed, gathered her clothes, dressed quickly and headed back to the main house, blinking at the crimson-hued sunrise.

Wasn't there some proverb about "red sky in the morning, shepherd's warning"? The closer the opening came, the more she worried about the weather – along with a thousand other things.

Thanks to a brilliant publicity campaign orchestrated by Mims, reservations had started coming in. So far, though, there weren't enough of them to assure the Outback's future. To add to her worry, a host of unforeseen expenses had eaten up her savings and Comanche's as well.

Although the travel agents' preview had been well received, the Outback's fate still hung in the balance. Her dream of a profitable safari ranch could turn into a fiscal nightmare unless the grand opening was an unqualified success. She had five more days to get ready.

She crossed the wide expanse of lawn and opened the front door with well practised stealth, feeling, as she always did, a little foolish. How many other mornings had she crept back into the house after spending part of the night in Comanche's arms?

Perhaps she was being silly, not telling her father that she and Comanche planned to marry. But she couldn't help thinking that Hank was clinging to life because he didn't want to leave her alone. If he knew the way she felt about Comanche he might just let go, and she couldn't bear the thought.

She took off her shoes and padded up the stairs and down the hall past Byron's room. The household would be stirring soon. While she showered, she ticked off the things she had to do that day. She'd always had a mind for detail. Now, though, her brain felt like an overloaded computer.

The sheriff and a member of the Secret Service were due at seven thirty to brief the staff on the security arrangements. She had an appointment with the florist at ten to finalize the centrepieces for the opening night buffet. Afterwards, the chef wanted to talk to her about making a last-minute change in their suppliers.

Just thinking about these and all the other details still to be attended to made Cait's head spin. At least she didn't have to worry about their unknown antagonist any more. Sheriff Schumaker had concluded the attacker must have been a crazed fan after all, and that he had lost interest in her after her picture stopped appearing on magazine covers.

Please God, let Herman be right, she thought as she opened her closet, pushing her designer clothes aside in favour of the jeans and shirts that had become her uniform. The last thing the Outback needed was another disaster, this time in full view of the media.

Thank God for Mims, Delta, Bobby Rae and Byron, she thought as she headed downstairs for a quick breakfast. They had more than shouldered their share of the load.

She silently added Senator Morgan's name to her list of private angels. She couldn't ignore his many contributions to the Outback, starting with the financing and ending with his asking the President to attend the opening.

She could hardly complain that affairs of state made it necessary for the Vice President and his wife to substitute. While the Vice President was a frequent target of the press, and a bit of a stiff, the media always turned out in droves wherever he went. And he was the most environmentally aware politician to hold the office. She silently blessed him for agreeing to come.

Most of all, she thanked God for Comanche.

Now she knew that what she had felt for her fiancés hadn't been love, or even a reasonable facsimile. Those relationships had been fuelled by loneliness. What she and Comanche shared was so all-encompassing that it filled every corner of her heart, mind and soul.

She could get weak-kneed just thinking about the way his eyes darkened when he was unhappy, the upward tilt at the corners of his mouth that heralded a smile. She had memorized every line of his body, his favourite foods, even his wardrobe. How proud she would be to have him by her side five days from now, greeting the Outback's guests.

One hundred and twenty of the most prominent people in the nation would join them for a three-day gala that would begin on Friday with a black-tie cocktail party and buffet. In addition to the Vice President, Senator Morgan and his wife, the Washington contingent included several Congressmen. Texas Governor, Ann Richards and various local officials had also accepted invitations.

Avery had prevailed on Maxine Messenger, Houston's all-powerful society guru, to attend along with a flock of the River Oaks country club set. When it came to celebrities, she and Mims had pulled out all the stops. The star-studded contingent would include every well-known supporter of environmental causes. Considering how politically correct all the stars were these days, the list included half of Hollywood.

While dressing, Cait mentally reviewed which guests had been assigned to which rooms, hoping none of them would be offended by the choices she had made. The Vice President would stay in the main house in the newly refurbished master suite. The other guest rooms would be occupied by the Morgans, Ann Richards and the Houston people.

The celebrities would stay in the forty newly completed bungalows that circled the dining pavilion and pool-side terrace. The architect had outdone himself when it came to carrying out the safari theme. Outside, the canvas-covered bungalows looked like tents. Inside, they were the personification of luxury, as was the magnificent glass-walled dining room overlooking the Guadalupe, presided over by a chef who had left a four-star restaurant to work at the Outback.

On her way to the kitchen, Cait stopped to look in on Hank. He was wide awake, sitting in his chair and gazing through his telescope, a cup of coffee cooling at his side, an afghan covering his legs. Delta had told her that he felt cold despite the warmth of the season.

Cait crossed the floor and kissed him on the cheek.

Startled, he turned quickly, a grimace twisting his features at the sudden movement. "I didn't hear you come in."

She bent over so she shared Hank's perspective. "How are things going out there?"

From his chair he could see a portion of the guest facilities including the pool, the terrace, the tennis courts and dining pavilion. Further off, he had a view of the enclosure bordering the Guadalupe. With the unaided eye, she could just make out a few animals down by the river. But Hank swore he could see every hair on their hides when he viewed them through the scope.

"Everything looks fine from here," he said. "You've worked wonders with the Outback. I'm so proud of you. I just wish . . ." His voice trailed off and he got a faraway look in his eyes.

He'd been doing that a lot lately and it worried her. She had the feeling he was keeping something from her. "You wish what, Dad?"

The faraway look faded. "Why, I wish you all the success in the world, Cait. You deserve it. Now get on your way. I know you have a busy day."

Cait left reluctantly. Every time she walked out of his room she had to fight off the dread that she might not see him alive again.

Despite the early hour, Delta, Bobby Rae and Mark Calhoun, the young hotelier who'd come to work in February, were already at the kitchen table having coffee when Cait walked in. Bobby Rae was wearing a severe navy linen suit, her platinum tresses pulled back into a chignon. Delta had on stylish khaki slacks and a matching blouse from a trendy local boutique. The papers spread on the table between them indicated this was no casual coffee klatsch.

The two women had changed almost as much as the ranch, Cait thought as she stood in the doorway. Delta had shown a real flare for housekeeping at an executive level and, with Mark's able guidance, had hired and trained the Outback's maids. Bobby Rae's managerial skills had developed so quickly that Cait hadn't hesitated to put her in charge of the office staff.

"Are you sure we have enough linen?" Bobby Rae was saying.

Delta rolled her eyes. "*Mais oui, cher*. We've counted them half a dozen times."

"I know you think I'm a worry wart but I just want to be sure everything goes off without a hitch." Bobby Rae cut a quick glance out the window. "Have you heard the latest weather forecast?"

"God wouldn't dare rain on Cait's parade, *cher*," Delta declared.

Byron adjusted his binoculars and took one last look at the sleek, black-maned lion. The magnificent male was resting in the sun, looking as content as if he were in the middle of the Serengeti rather than the Hill Country. His posture clearly said he was the lord of all he surveyed.

And why not, Byron thought, breaking into a smile. He had all the food he could eat and five females to keep him company. They had all come from zoos whose populations of big cats had grown too large. The male had sired cubs in the past and undoubtedly would do so again. Byron hoped to establish a healthy breeding group on the Outback. Someday Texas-bred lions might help repopulate the African plains.

To think he'd actually been concerned about getting animals when he first came to the Hill Country. After the news of Neil Dillon's gift hit the papers, offers of animals had coming pouring in from zoos, private breeders, defunct animal acts, circuses and from the public too.

He'd been dismayed to realize how many misguided souls had purchased exotics as pets only to learn you can take an animal out of the wild but you can't take the wild out of the animal. It had been a bonanza for the Outback, though. The sad thing was they couldn't take them all.

Reluctantly lowering the binoculars, he left the lion to its lordly nap, started the Range Rover, part of a fleet Cait had purchased to tour guests over the rough terrain and drove towards the enclosure's double gates.

In the last six months the ranch had been transformed into a Noah's Ark of rare, endangered and threatened species including, among others, Neil Dillon's black rhinos, reticulated giraffes and small herds of Grevy's zebras, topis, bongos, kudus, sable antelopes, lechwes, bushbucks and bongos.

The Western section of the ranch, the one designated to harbour endangered species native to Texas, was now home to small herds of bison, pronghorn and big horn sheep, as well as grey wolves, a couple of mountain lions and even a jaguar. They had plans to add a pair of Mexican wolves in the near future too. And Cait was talking about building an aviary as soon as she had the funds.

He shut the gate and reset the combination lock before opening the second gate, driving through and closing it just as carefully. He had drilled the importance of safety into every one of the Outback's employees. They had been accident-free ever since the incident with the lions and he intended to see they stayed that way.

He checked his watch before turning onto the dirt road that led to the Outback's new offices. He just had time to give Cait a briefing before they left to pick Mims up at the airport. He could hardly wait.

Last night when they talked, Mims had said she had something to tell him. But it couldn't be half as important as what he intended to say to her.

★ ★ ★

Carroll Detweiler parked the Blazer in front of the Old Tavern and slid his bulk from the front seat, being careful of his stiff knee. He didn't bother to lock the doors. Every one in Elgin knew his car. No one would fuck with it.

His irascibility had grown in direct proportion to his idleness. Since returning from the Hill Country, he'd had nothing to do but drink – and fight. He walked into the tavern and took a quick look around out of habit, giving the occupants an unfriendly glare before taking his accustomed seat at the bar.

While waiting for the bartender to deliver his beer, he idly opened a newspaper someone had left on the adjacent stool. He had grown accustomed to being left alone and was annoyed when, five minutes later, a man had the temerity to sit down beside him.

He cut a cold glance at the stranger, taking in the pale skin, the cheap clothes, the furtive expression in the watery blue eyes, the home-made tattoos that included a swastika on one bicep and a teardrop on one cheek. The man's appearance clearly identified him as an ex-con, probably one of the Aryan Brotherhood.

The stranger had been looking him over too. "How're you doin'?" he said, the words gliding out in a strangely sibilant lisp.

Not bothering to reply, Detweiler glared back until the stranger's gaze darted nervously away. Then he buried his face in the paper. After a few minutes had passed, he gave the stranger another venomous glance, hoping he'd take the hint and get lost.

When he didn't, Detweiler continued thumbing through the paper until he came to the entertainment section. A low growl burst from his throat as he saw a picture of Cait Pride standing in front of a high fence with a lioness in the background.

Her self-satisfied smile sent a burst of acid to his stomach. The headline above the picture read, VICE

PRESIDENT AND HOLLYWOOD STARS TO ATTEND GALA OPENING OF HILL COUNTRY SAFARI RANCH.

Detweiler scanned the accompanying article, cursing under his breath. Fury bubbled through his blood like molten lava as he read about Cait's success. She was on the top of the world while he was stuck in this dung-heap.

He didn't realize the ex-con had been looking over his shoulder until the man said. "I'd sure like a piece of that pussy, and I don't mean the lion."

Swivelling around, Carroll said, "Trust me, she's one cold bitch."

"You sound like you know her."

"So what if I do?" he snarled.

"Hey, chill down, man. I'm just making conversation." The stranger held out his hand. "My name's Ace Stevens. Can I buy you a beer?"

Under ordinary circumstances, Detweiler would have ignored the friendly overture. But he was so infuriated by what he'd just read that he didn't reply. Ace Stevens took his silence as agreement, snapped his fingers to get the bartender's attention and ordered two beers. "You from around here?" he asked.

Detweiler nodded.

"I just got out of the Eastham unit over Lovelady way myself." Ace sounded as proud of having been released from a prison farm as if he'd been honourably discharged by the military.

"On parole?"

Ace took a deep draught from his fresh beer. "Yeah. Hell, I'm not even supposed to be in a place like this. You don't happen to have done any time, do you?"

"I'm not that stupid."

"Stupid don't have nothing to do with it."

"What were you in for?"

"Armed robbery. But I was framed. How the hell was I

to know my friends was planning to rob a Circle K when they asked me to drive them to the store?"

"Shovel it some other direction buddy, not mine."

Most other men would have taken umbrage at Detweiler's comment but Ace just drank his beer down, then belched contentedly. "That lady friend of yours isn't the only one who knows a thing or two about dangerous animals. I could tell you some stories about raising them myself."

"Sure you could." Detweiler's voice oozed sarcasm. He'd met men like this Ace Stevens before, all show and no go.

"No, man, I mean it. We've been raising wild pigs at Eastham, using feed purchased for the domestic hog programme. Do you know anything about Russian boars?"

Carroll shrugged his disinterest.

"Ranchers imported Russian boars before they knew how dangerous they were," Stevens lectured with puffed-up importance. "Some of them got away and bred with the local stock. You don't want to mess with the wild hogs running around Texas unless you carry a big gun and you know how to shoot straight."

Carroll, who could do both, wasn't impressed. "If there are so many wild ones, why bother breeding them?"

"Most wild pigs don't get past a couple hundred pounds. The ones at Eastham are twice that size. We even had an eight hundred-pound boar who was the meanest son-of-a-bitch on four feet."

"Had or have?" Carroll asked, his interest piqued.

"I guess he's still there."

"How the hell did you get away with raising wild pigs instead of domestic ones?"

"Beats me. The programme was already set up when I got to Eastham, and you know how it is in the slammer. It don't pay to ask no questions. But I'll tell you this, I'd match that eight hundred-pound boar against a lion any day. A boar like that will attack anything that gets in its way."

The glimmer of a plan teased Carroll's brain like a feather passing over skin. "Even people?"

"Hell, yes. They've been known to kill a bull and eat it. Barbed-wire fences don't stop them either, especially if they smell food."

Carroll gave Ace what he hoped was a friendly grin. "You wouldn't be shitting me?"

"No way, man."

"What do they do with the wild hogs at Eastham?"

"Most of the time they slaughter them and give the meat to high-ranking politicians or prison officials. It's supposed to be mighty fine eating. But I heard they sell them live too. If you don't believe me, just check the paper. There's always some rancher advertising a guided Russian boar hunt. And big bastards like ours fetch a high price."

"If I wanted to buy that eight hundred-pounder, how would I go about it?"

Suddenly Ace hopped off his bar stool. "Hey, man, I don't want to get in no trouble."

Before he could move away Carroll grabbed his arm in a vicelike grip. The skin surrounding the swastika whitened. "You won't get in any trouble. And I'll make it worth your while."

"Sure, man, I can tell you're loaded just by looking at you," Ace scoffed. "Next thing, you'll tell me your name is H. Ross Perot."

It took all Detweiler's willpower not to pick the smaller man up by the scruff of the neck and shake him the way a terrier shakes a rat. "How does a thousand dollars sound to you? Half now and half when I get the boar?"

An avaricious gleam replaced the outright scepticism in Ace's eyes. "Show me the money and I'll give you a name."

23

Cait smiled to herself as she took her satin and leather confection from its padded hanger. With its suede fringe, beaded bustier and brief skirt, it was an outrageous outfit – and she adored it the minute she saw it.

She'd paid no attention to fashion since returning to the ranch and knew nothing of the cowboy-Western influence that was cutting such a wide swath through the fashion houses in Paris, Milan and New York. Too busy to shop, she had even asked Mims to buy her something special for the cocktail party. Mims had certainly taken her at her word. It didn't get much more special than this!

She slipped off her robe and began to dress for the opening cocktail party. Twelve months of hard work, of hours spent in the saddle had paid off. Her body was as fit as it had ever been.

The bustier lifted her breasts, offering them up like prize-winning melons at the Kerr County fair. The short leather skirt showed off her firm thighs. Turning from side to side in front of the cheval mirror, she felt outrageously sexy.

Thank you, Mims, she silently breathed. Picking out the dress was the least of the things she owed to Mims. If the opening was the success they both anticipated, Mims would have played a major role in making it happen.

Sitting down at her dressing table, Cait took the full complement of make-up from the top drawer where it had stayed, unused, for months. Employing every bit of artifice at her command, she applied it with a sure hand, enhancing her features while retaining the natural look she favoured.

The results were startling. The Cait Pride she had all but forgotten, the model with the enormous eyes, high cheek bones and a generous mouth reappeared as if by magic.

Byron's tuxedo had been made for him by the Saville Row tailor who'd had his measurements since Byron's university days. He threaded the diamond studs he had inherited from his father through his shirt placket, spent a couple of minutes expertly knotting his bow tie, shrugged into his jacket and shot his cuffs. Then he took a black velvet jeweller's box from the top of the highboy and slipped it into his pants pocket.

Stepping into the hall, he called Comanche's name.

"Be with you in a minute," Comanche replied.

Six months earlier, sharing the foreman's house would have been unthinkable. Today, he and Comanche were almost as close as brothers. The respect that blossomed the night of the fight had ripened into friendship. The shared sweat and pain of their sparring sessions had deepened their bond. Their mutual devotion to the Prides and the Outback bonded them even closer.

A month ago, when Cait mentioned that she needed Byron's room during the opening, Comanche had immediately asked Byron to move in with him. And then just last night, Byron had been delighted when Comanche agreed to be his best man if – no – when Mims accepted his marriage proposal. He wanted the younger man by his side as he spoke his vows.

Through the half-open bedroom door, Byron could see Comanche struggling with his bow tie. "Can I do that for you?"

Comanche came to the door and opened it wide, a wry

grin on his face. "I guess I'm not the black-tie type. Does this meet with your approval?" He held up a magnificent silver and turquoise bolo. "Hank gave it to me a couple of days ago. He told me that it had belonged to Ulysses Pride."

"It's the perfect touch. You're going to have to fend the women off, old boy."

"One woman in particular, I hope." Comanche punched Byron's shoulder lightly. "You don't need to stay here on my account. I know you're anxious to be alone with Mims while you have the chance."

Comanche waited until he heard the front door shut, then walked to the window, the bolo forgotten in his hand. He stood quietly, his expression growing wistful as he watched Byron jauntily cross the lawn to the main house. How ironic to think the white hunter had travelled halfway around the world to find the woman he wanted, while the right one for Comanche had grown up under his nose.

Mims was sitting at her dressing table, her back to the door, staring into the mirror and beyond, into the depths of her soul. She had made up her mind to stop manufacturing excuses, to do finally what her heart had been telling her to do for months. But the thought of being that vulnerable to another person caught in her throat and shivered down her spine. What would Byron say when she told him about the decision she had made?

As if in response to her silent question, he slipped into her bedroom, crossed the floor and planted a kiss on her cheek. She gasped with pleasure. "I wasn't expecting you."

"I've been wanting to do that since Cait and I picked you up at the airport."

He kissed her again and for a moment she allowed herself to forget everything but the joy of being in his arms. "We may not be alone again for days," she said, reluctantly breaking their embrace. "I have a lot to tell you."

She got up, retrieved her briefcase from the dresser, took out a thick file and held it out to him with shaking hands. It contained the contracts on her business and her condo. She hadn't expected them to sell so quickly. Now she was scared to death that Byron would resent the fact that she hadn't discussed it with him. The last thing she wanted was to make him feel trapped.

"I'd like you to read this," she said.

Instead of taking the file, he collapsed on the bed as if his legs couldn't hold him and reached into his trouser pocket. "Can it wait? There's something I want to ask you."

An unwelcome knock prevented further discussion.

"It's showtime," Cait called through the door.

Blackjack leaned forward, gazing out the limousine window with unbridled curiosity as the vehicle moved slowly along the oak-lined drive that led from the Outback's main gate to the Prides' historic mansion. His wife, daughter and son-in-law rode with him.

"Isn't it wonderful, Daddy," Avery exclaimed, one elegantly manicured finger pointing towards a herd of zebras not a hundred yards from the car. "It's just like being in a zoo. But Cait's way, we're inside and the animals are free. I know the Outback is going to be a tremendous success. I'm so grateful for everything you've done to help Cait."

"How could I refuse an old family friend? Besides, I thought Cait's plans for the ranch were admirable the first time she told me about them. The Outback does remind me of Africa," he replied, recalling the hunting trip he had taken to the Union of South Africa before apartheid and animal activists made such a journey political suicide.

Considering the way everyone in the limo was oohing and aahing, including the normally taciturn driver, Cait had a real winner on her hands. Blackjack had to give credit where credit was due. From the promotional material he'd seen – the brochures and video tapes – she had turned a dying ranch and a hare-brained scheme to save endangered species into a first-class resort.

He smiled, thinking how he had used his own God-given talents to transform his financial disaster into a win-win-win situation for everyone. At this very moment, Tochigi was undoubtedly striding the Hefernan's vast acreage in boots and chaps, playing at being John Wayne. The Nishida fee had enabled him to complete his own financial reorganization. The venture capitalist would benefit handsomely from Cait's success. Even Detweiler was ahead of the game with the bonus cheque he'd sent.

Everything had come up roses all the way around. So why did he have such an unsettled feeling in the pit of his stomach, an almost uncontrollable urge to order the driver to turn around and head back to Houston?

It had taken Carroll Detweiler the better part of the day, driving along dirt tracks and dry washes, to get the rental truck close to his objective. A couple of times he'd been sure he'd been spotted. But none of the distant riders he'd seen had turned his way. Penetrating the Outback's security, he thought, chuckling to himself, had been as easy as getting laid in Patpong.

Sweating profusely, he parked the heavily laden vehicle in a screening cluster of oaks, then took a grimy handkerchief from his shirt pocket and mopped his steaming brow. He slung his binoculars around his neck and opened the driver's door. As he got out, the vehicle shuddered and a bellow came from the rear.

The bloodcurdling sound lifted the hair on the back of Detweiler's neck. The first time he'd seen the boar at the Eastham prison farm, he'd strolled up to its steel-ringed pen to get a closer look. The animal had fixed him with a pair of malevolent red-rimmed eyes and charged the fence, moving with amazing speed considering its bulk.

Although Detweiler had faced hostile soldiers in a dozen different wars, none of them had unnerved him the way that boar had. Three days of captivity without food hadn't improved the boar's disposition.

As he limped away from the truck and its menacing cargo, he smiled to himself, thinking Cait was going to have a very hungry, very dangerous, very unexpected guest at her fancy shindig.

Thirty minutes later he limped up the crest of a small hill he had scouted a couple of weeks earlier. He gazed down, seeing the Outback's pool, terrace and dining pavilion spread out below like a picture postcard. He couldn't help admiring the layout.

A steady stream of white-jacketed waiters and waitresses were moving in and out of the kitchen with the well-ordered efficiency of army ants. A freshening breeze carried the tantalizing aroma of gourmet food as they deposited their burdens on the tables surrounding the pool.

Detweiler's lips parted in a chilling smile as he thought about the eight hundred pounds of starving ferocity that would soon follow that scent to its source.

Half a dozen men in black ties were mingling with the help. Secret Service, he thought, his practised eye detecting the almost imperceptible bulge of their shoulder holsters. While he watched, a sheriff's vehicle pulled up and parked near the tennis courts. He had no trouble identifying the man who got out as Herman Schumaker. Schumaker threaded his way through the help, stopping to speak to several of the agents. Between them, they carried a hell of a lot of fire power.

Their weapons weren't powerful enough to stop the boar with one shot. Hell, that would take an elephant gun. The animal would absorb a lot of punishment – and do a lot of damage – before it died. And the press was going to have a field day filming the carnage.

"Fucking A", he muttered under his breath. Cait Pride was going to have one hell of a time convincing anyone that the boar hadn't escaped from one of her enclosures. Her fancy opening would end in disaster, and she'd be up shit creek.

The thought was so exciting that he felt a stirring in his groin. One way or another, he was going to fuck Cait Pride over.

Hank watched as a steady stream of limousines, private cars and the Outback's own Range Rovers ferried Cait's guests to the pool-side cocktail party that began the festivities. She'd looked so beautiful when she stopped by his room half an hour ago. Her stunning appearance had been a vivid reminder of what she'd given up to devote herself to him and the ranch.

Seeing her in jeans all the time, he'd almost forgotten she'd been one of the world's most successful models. To think he'd actually been foolish enough to question her character not so very long ago. He should have put more faith in the blood of the Pride women – Elke, Reina, Philippa and his own Lizzie – flowing in Cait's veins.

Cait was his beloved Lizzie all over again, with Lizzie's beauty, kindness and intelligence mingled with his own stubborn pride.

Although his innards ached with an unrelenting agony his medication could no longer control, he leaned forward and gazed through the telescope. Soon, he thought, he'd be with Lizzie soon. But not yet – not while Cait still needed him.

Cait had told him that the Vice President would cut the ribbon that officially opened the Outback at five on the dot. Nice fellow, the Vice President, polite and well-mannered. It had been thoughtful of him to stop by and pay his respects before leaving for the cocktail party. Hank would have enjoyed the brief visit a lot more if Senator Morgan hadn't been along. No matter what Cait said to the contrary, he'd never cared for Morgan – hadn't ever voted for him either.

Through the scope, Hank could see a crowd clustering at the entrance to the pool-side terrace. The steady strobe of flash bulbs told him that the VP must have just cut the ribbon. Then, as if an unseen dam had broken, the crowd surged forward.

He moved the scope from right to left, hoping to catch a glimpse of Cait. Instead, he caught sight of something unexpected out of the corner of his eye. His curiosity aroused, he swung the scope even further to the left. A trail of dust, the sort a slow-moving car made, was rising into the sky a mile or two from the party.

What the hell was a vehicle doing over there? he fretted. The Outback had been closed to outsiders since yesterday. The hands were patrolling the ranch's perimeter and Herman Schumaker had promised that a police helicopter would make regular security overflights.

Hank had been watching over the ranch for months. Now he reached for his walkie-talkie, hoping against hope that Comanche had his with him.

Unaware of the admiring female glances coming his way, Comanche stood at the fringe of the crowd, sipping a beer and watching the party unfold as if he were viewing it on a giant television screen. Things couldn't be going better. Every one seemed to be having a good time.

Knots of people clustered around the buffet, the bar and at the edge of the terrace overlooking the Guadalupe. Across the water a steady stream of animals approached the river for their regular evening drink. Each time a new species appeared he could hear guests exclaiming with excitement.

No maatter how many times he saw the nightly parade himself, he never failed to be moved by the sight. Tonight, it was made even more splendid by the addition of the glittering crowd. This is the way it will be from now on, he reminded himself, this unique mixture of awed human beings and unconcerned animals that Cait had long ago planned for the Outback.

Her vision had come true, he thought with a surge of pride. In a few years he hoped to have his own success with the criollos. Now, though, he was more than content to share in Cait's.

He turned his thoughtful gaze back to the Crowd. The Senator was glad-handing nearby, his deep baritone voice rising about all the others. Byron moved easily from one group to another and from the way people smiled and laughed, he must be telling some of his stories. But it was Cait, surrounded by an admiring throng that included Neil Dillon and the Vice President, who caught and held his attention. She looked serenely confident – and incredibly sexy. He'd never loved or wanted her more.

"Hi, there, handsome," Bobby Rae said, walking up and taking his arm. "Isn't this some party?"

"It certainly is. Are you having a good time?"

"Are you kidding? I'm having the time of my life. The Senator just complimented me on my dress – me, Bobby Rae Seeley. Can you believe it?" Bobby Rae looked as stunned as if she'd just personally witnessed the Second Coming.

He was about to tell her that Blackjack was right, that she looked terrific and that the way Mark Calhoun was following her with his eyes, the hotelier thought so too, when the metallic sound of Hank's voice came from his walkie-talkie.

"Comanche, come in, Comanche," Hank was saying.

Startled, Comanche pulled the walkie-talkie from the pocket of his tuxedo jacket, thanking his lucky stars that he'd brought it with him even though it made an unsightly bulge in his suit.

"Are you all right, Hank?" he asked anxiously.

"I'm fine, son," Hank quickly reassured him. "But I was watching the shindig through the scope when I saw a plume of dust about a mile and a half due west of the pool. I thought you'd want to check it out."

As the crowd swirled around Cait in an ever-changing kaleidoscope of groupings, she overheard snatches of conversation. "Spectacular setting – out of Africa – wonderful idea – come back again and bring the kids – fabulous animals – boon to the environment—"

For the first time in months, she could feel the lurking tension in her neck and shoulders let go. A euphoric feeling swept over her as she realized that all the sleepless nights, the unremitting race against the clock, hadn't been in vain. The Outback was an unqualified success. They'd made it.

When she caught sight of Comanche moving purposefully towards her, her stomach spasmed the way it always did when he came into view. His tuxedo emphasized his virility rather than subjugating it. Even in this star-studded crowd, his good looks stood out. She smiled to herself, thinking how she liked him best in nothing at all.

"Where are you going in such a hurry?" she asked when he reached her side.

"Hank just called me on the walkie-talkie. He saw a trail of dust a mile or so away. I thought I'd better take a look-see."

Bobby Rae had been surprised by the abrupt way Comanche broke off their conversation without so much as a beg-your-pardon. It wasn't like him to be rude, she thought as she watched him hurry away. She frowned, wondering what she could have said to turn him off. She'd been working so hard to improve herself.

She stopped a passing waiter, helped herself to a glass of champagne and was sipping on it thoughtfully when Mims joined her.

"It's a lovely party," Mims said in that funny voice of hers. "You must be proud. Cait told me how hard you've worked to make it a success."

"That's what I get paid for." Bobby Rae finished her champagne in a single draught. "I'm sorry, Mims. I didn't mean to be rude."

"Is something wrong?"

"Comanche just cut me dead."

"I'm sure he didn't mean to. He seems quite fond of you."

"Yeah, I mean, yes, I suppose you're right. He did get a call from Hank on the walkie-talkie. Maybe that's why he ran off."

"Oh, dear, do you think Hank's worse?"

"No. He sounded just fine. He said something about seeing a trail of dust over there." Bobby Rae pointed to the west.

A little alarm began ringing in Mims' head. "Did you hear anything else?"

"No. But come to think of it, Comanche did look worried." Bobby Rae's blue eyes widened. "Good lord, you don't think . . ."

Carroll Detweiler parked the rental truck at the base of the hill he'd climbed earlier, cut the engine and took a flask from the glove compartment. Time for a quick drink before getting down to business, he thought, relishing the whisky's bite as it slid past his gullet.

He leaned back and closed his eyes, savouring the moment. He'd spent weeks imagining this day, planning every detail, rehearsing what he had to do over and over in his mind so there wouldn't be any snafus. His one regret was that he wouldn't be there to see Cait Pride's face when the Russian boar joined the party.

He took two more swigs before he screwed the top on the flask and put it away. Then he grabbed the binoculars, got out of the truck and slowly headed up the hill to make sure the party was in full swing. He had just reached the crest when he heard the whine of an approaching engine.

Tracking the sound, he saw the breed's truck skidding around the base of the knoll.

Measuring the distance back to the rental truck, he decided he still had a chance to finish the op. All he had to do was release the boar before the breed could stop him.

Comanche didn't say a word to Cait as he gunned the truck and headed due west. She was hardly dressed for a rough cross-country ride, he thought, glancing at her sidelong. Hell, she was hardly dressed at all considering the expanse of thigh revealed by that shamelessly short skirt and the way her breasts practically spilled over the top of that thing she was wearing.

Averting his gaze, he forced himself to concentrate on the job at hand. Taking one hand off the wheel, he reached back, lifted a 357 magnum rifle off the rack that bracketed the truck's rear window and handed it to Cait.

"What's that for?" she asked, her eyes widening in alarm.

"Insurance," he replied. "Herman told me a bunch of star-struck teenagers have been hanging outside the gates all day trying to get a look at some of our guests. It's possible that a few of them decided to sneak in."

"You don't need a gun to run off teenagers."

"Like I said, Cait, it's insurance. You'll find shells in the glove compartment. Do you remember how to load?"

"I remember everything you taught me," she replied.

He ignored the double entendre – and the inclination to stop the truck and make love to her then and there. First he had to get rid of the kids, or whoever had made the telltale dust trail.

Minutes later, rounding a knoll, he realized with a sinking heart that he'd badly misjudged the situation. A huge man wearing military camouflage was running headlong down the hill to their right, heading towards a truck not a hundred yards away.

His crablike gait would have been laughable on anyone

else. But this man had an almost palpable aura of menace. Comanche's vision freeze-framed as he took in every detail of the trespasser's appearance, from the military crew cut and the jagged scar on his face to his bulllike torso.

Suddenly he flashed back to the day someone had spied on him and Cait down by the river. There had been something peculiar about the tracks he'd found afterwards, something he hadn't been able to identify. He'd found the same sort of tracks near the holding pens the morning of the dynamiting and again by the lions' cages. Now he realized what made them unique. They had been made by a man with a limp.

Iron bands tightened around his chest as he looked across the seat at Cait. He should never have let her come with him. The man running down the hill had probably dynamited the pens and let the lions loose too. If so, he was dangerous. A certifiable maniac with a taste for violence.

And now Comanche had carelessly exposed Cait to that danger – that violence.

"Oh, my God, that's him," Cait cried out, as he braked the truck to a skidding stop. "That's the man who attacked me in the South Star."

"Give me the gun," he said, "and go on back for the sheriff." Comanche braked the truck to a precipitous stop.

The stranger had changed directions, veering towards them with that odd gait as Comanche vaulted from the front seat to the ground. The shock of the landing juddered up his body.

"I was hoping we'd run into each other," the stranger called out.

"Then this is your lucky day," Comanche replied, elevating the gun barrel until it pointed at the man's midsection.

Ignoring Comanche, the stranger broke into a smile.

"Well, now, look who's here. If it ain't my old sweetheart, Cait-fucking-Pride."

Comanche glanced over his shoulder in time to see Cait getting out of the truck. Of all the times for her to assert her independence. He wasn't afraid for himself, but having her with him sure as hell complicated things.

The stranger was undressing her with his eyes. "You look good enough to eat, girlie. Maybe I'll get around to it after I finish with your boyfriend."

Comanche cocked the gun. "I wouldn't count on it, you son-of-a-bitch."

The man's insolent gaze continued to crawl over Cait's body. "That's some outfit, Cait. I'm going to enjoy taking it off you."

Cait had been stunned speechless by the unexpected appearance of the man from the South Star. Now, realizing he was deliberately trying to goad Comanche into a fight jolted her from her silence. "Since you've obviously been spying on us, you must know the ranch is crawling with police, to say nothing of the Secret Service. If you leave right now, you still have a chance to get away."

"Oh, I couldn't do that," the man said in the raspy voice she'd never forgotten, "not when I went to so much trouble to get a present for you. There's an eight hundred-pound Russian boar in my truck. Seeing as how you're a local girl, you probably know all about Russian boars. This one hasn't eaten for days and he's been getting worked up, smelling the buffet." As if on cue, a bellow came from the truck.

"You aren't going anywhere. Put your hands up," Comanche said.

Any normal man, facing a powerful rifle, would have obeyed instantly. Except for his deepening smile, the stranger didn't move a muscle. "You wouldn't shoot an unarmed man. You don't have the guts for it."

For a second, Comanche's finger tightened on the trigger as he imagined the effect of the gun at such close range. It would blow a hole right through the man's middle. Could he do that to another human being?

Rage was supposed to be hot. Comanche felt like he'd taken a bath in ice water. The son-of-a-bitch was right. He couldn't shoot him in cold blood. Gesturing Cait closer, he handed her the gun.

"Sorry, Cait. I'm going to have to do this the hard way." He gave her a quick smile. "I'm going to have to earn it."

"I take your meaning," she replied steadily. Her voice roughened as she faced the stranger. "Mister, this *isn't* your lucky day. You're in for the beating of your life. I just wish I could be the one giving it to you."

A fierce, anticipatory joy sang through Comanche at her words. She understood – and approved. Although the stranger outweighed him he felt confident of his ability to beat the man – and he was going to enjoy doing it.

Never fight angry, Byron had told him. *Stay in control of your emotions and watch your opponent's eyes. They'll signal his every move.*

Byron was right, he thought, as the battle was joined. He easily sidestepped the stranger's headlong rush and landed a punishing blow to the man's midsection. A pained grunt was his reward.

Blackjack had always loved pressing the flesh, and never more so than when that flesh belonged to a celebrity who might be convinced to campaign for him in the future. Cait's cocktail party had afforded that opportunity time and again.

He should have been enjoying himself, but the prescient sense of impending disaster continued to plague him. It took considerable self-control to move from group to group and continue making the hail-fellow-well-met-small talk that is an accomplished politician's stock in trade.

He had just joined a group gathered around the internationally famous animal expert, Jim Foley, when he noticed Byron Neville and the local sheriff cutting through the crowd, their expressions grim. Now what could that be all about? With a scoundrel's inbred sense of self-preservation, Blackjack hurried after them.

He told himself he'd be a fool to borrow trouble and yet he moved even faster, propelled by the feeling that whatever had happened involved him.

They had reached the sheriff's car and were getting in when he caught up. "Where are you two going in such a hurry? Is there a problem with security?"

"Perhaps," Schumaker replied guardedly. "There's a report of a strange vehicle in the vicinity. It's probably nothing, but we're going to look into it."

"I'll go with you."

"That's hardly necessary, Senator." Byron couldn't helping wondering why the Senator seemed so agitated.

"Let me be the judge of that. I'm responsible for the Vice President being here." Without giving the two men the opportunity to object, Blackjack opened the patrol car door and climbed into the back seat.

"Very well, Senator," the sheriff said, getting behind the wheel. "But I'd like you to give me your word you'll stay in the car until I'm certain you won't be in any danger."

The motherfucker fights like a pro, Detweiler thought, struggling to breathe through his battered nose. His left eye had swollen shut and his bad leg hurt almost as much as it had the day he'd been shot. He fought on despite the pain, so intent on the battle that he was unaware of anything other than his desire to hurt his opponent – and the realization that he wasn't succeeding.

Suddenly, a commanding voice broke his fierce concentration. "Put your hands up."

Detweiler swung his head to the left, spraying blood as he sought the source of the command. The sheriff and that ball-kicking bastard, Byron Neville, appeared in his field of vision.

"Put your hands up," the sheriff repeated. This time the sight of his unholstered pistol reinforced the order.

Dazed by the sudden turn of events, Detweiler reluctantly did as he was told. Hell, he wasn't crazy enough to argue with a thirty-eight special. This wasn't supposed to be happening. It hadn't been part of the op he had planned.

He was vaguely aware of the sheriff reading him his rights. He'd heard it all a thousand times on television and couldn't quite grasp that this was real. His chest heaved, his head pounded, every part of his body hurt. He'd never been trapped by an enemy before. Who had given the op away?

The bitch, the breed and the white hunter stood off to one side, but he paid no attention to them. His entire being was focused on the man emerging from the sheriff's car. What the fuck was the Senator doing here? Could he have ratted on him? No, that didn't make any sense. Blackjack wouldn't do that to him, not in a million years.

"What's going on here?" Blackjack demanded as he joined the group clustered around Detweiler.

Although his heart flailed in his chest, he managed to keep his tone firm. "Why is this man under arrest?"

"I caught him trespassing," Comanche Killian replied.

"He's the chap who gave Cait such a hard time at the South Star," Byron added.

Had Blackjack obeyed his impulse, he would have turned tail and run and kept on running right back to the safety of River Oaks. What in the hell had got into Detweiler? Had he lost his fucking mind? Blackjack had called him off months ago.

Repressing a shiver of anxiety, Blackjack riveted Det with a murderous stare. Det has always been short on brains. But Blackjack could hardly believe he'd made so colossal a blunder.

"I really think you ought to get back in my car, Senator," the sheriff was saying. "I have reason to believe this man is dangerous. If Mr Killian is right, he's responsible for a number of attacks on the Prides."

Blackjack would have liked nothing better than to do as the sheriff suggested. But he dared not cut his losses until he knew how badly he'd been hurt. "What sort of attacks?" he asked.

"Someone has been terrorizing the Prides, killing their animals and even releasing a couple of lions."

"Why do you suspect this man?"

Schumaker looked grim. "I've seen him before. And so has Miss Cait. He assaulted her a few months ago at a local night spot."

"Shit, Senator," Detweiler burst out, "tell them why I'm here. Tell them how you hired me."

Blackjack blanched. He could see it all slipping away, everything he'd worked so hard to achieve – his fortune, his reputation, his place in society, his Senate seat.

The sheriff had turned his attention back to Detweiler. "If you're smart, you'll stop making wild accusations. Things will go easier on you if you tell the truth from the get go."

"But I am telling the truth," Carroll replied stubbornly. No way was he going to take a fall by himself. He'd be home in Elgin if the Senator hadn't made that first telephone call. "Me and the Senator go all the way back to Nam. He hired me to keep Cait Pride from opening the Outback."

Blackjack stiffened his spine. "I do know the man. He served under me in Vietnam. He's a deranged veteran."

Blackjack's mind worked at top speed as he weighed the potential danger. Could anyone connect him to Detweiler? Shit. Telephone records and that damn bonus cheque would do the job unless he could explain them away.

He spoke rapidly, authoritatively, bringing all his dignity and power to bear, riveting his listeners as he told how Detweiler had contacted him months ago, how he'd worried about his old comrade's growing mental illness, how he'd asked, then begged Detweiler to seek treatment for his mental problems, even going so far as to send him a sizable cheque to cover seeing a private psychiatrist.

Carroll Detweiler listened to Blackjack with half an ear, noting how the others were hanging on the Senator's every word. He couldn't believe his luck. The sheriff hadn't cuffed him yet. And now, Blackjack was giving him one last chance to finish the op.

Forgetting his age, his limp and his battle-weary body, Detweiler sprinted for the truck at top speed. He ignored the warning shouts behind him, the command to surrender. A bullet whipped past his head and he ignored that too.

Panting, he reached the back of the truck and worked the lock with frantic speed. With a howl of triumph, he pulled the doors open and freed the Russian boar.

It blinked in the sudden light. Its head swung from side to side. Its nostrils flared.

"Run, you motherfucker, run," Detweiler shouted, flapping his arms, "join the party."

The boar had spent four days locked in the darkness, deprived of water, starved of food, with nothing but the occasional sound of Detweiler's voice and the scent of Detweiler's body for company. Another animal might have perished during so cruel a captivity.

The boar wasn't like any other animal. It was as powerful as a bull, as clever as a monkey and as cruel as Satan.

The boar had come to hate the man who held him captive. Free at last, it paid no heed to the tantalizing aromas wafting from the other side of the hill. Detweiler's scent, the sound of his voice, swelled in the boar's brain until there wasn't room for anything else. He launched himself straight at that hated scent and sound.

Cait watched the boar's attack with speechless horror. Her breath froze in her chest as its hooves hit Detweiler in the chest. Man and animal tumbled to the ground together. Swinging its tusks like a farmer swinging a scythe, the ferocious animal reaped a terrible harvest. It opened Detweiler's stomach with the first slash, then spilled his entrails out with the second.

Comanche grabbed the rifle from Cait's lifeless hands and sighted down the barrel. "I can't shoot or I'll hit the man," he cried out.

"For the love of God, do something," Cait sobbed.

She hated and feared the man who had brought so much devastation to the Outback. But she wouldn't have wished so dreadful a death on her worst enemy.

She closed her eyes on the carnage as Comanche and the sheriff fired, again and then again.

The sounds of gunfire mingled with the screams of the man and the animal.

And then, there was silence.

Cait didn't open her eyes until she felt Comanche's arms catch her up in a protective embrace.

"It's over," he said, holding her close. "It's finally over. You're safe now."

24

For the first time in three days, the ranch house didn't reverberate with animated chatter. There were no cars in the circular drive waiting to transport guests, no staff scurrying about eager to serve. Cait had given everyone the evening off. With the first of the paying clientèle not due for ten days, the clean-up could wait until morning. At last she was free to devote herself to Hank.

She found him dozing in his favourite chair, the telescope in its accustomed place by his side. She tiptoed across the floor and gently kissed Hank's forehead. His skin felt like parchment under her lips, and he had dark circles under his eyes.

"Hi, Dad," she said, as his lids fluttered open.

"Did the last of your guests get off all right?" His smile emphasized the deep hollows in his cheeks.

She nodded, then grasped his work-worn hand, her heart overflowing with desperate love born of imminent loss. He had already outlived Doc Williams's most optimistic prognosis.

"I don't know how to thank you," she said.

"For what, sweetheart?"

"For asking me to take over the ranch, for giving me the chance to prove I was more than a pretty face, for believing in me when I didn't believe in myself. And that's just for openers."

"That's what fathers are for. I'm glad I got the chance to act like one before it was too late."

Cait stiffened. Tears she dared not shed in his presence pooled at the back of her eyes. "The opening was a smash," she said, forcing herself to concentrate on a more cheerful subject. "Half the guests made reservations to come back for longer stays. So did some of the media, and you know how jaded they are. John Tesh promised glowing coverage on *Entertainment Tonight* and the reporters from *People* magazine said we can count on a big spread. When I think what could have happened if you hadn't been looking through your telescope . . ."

"You don't need to think about it. I'm glad I was there for you. The one thing I regret about my illness is that I won't be here for you much longer."

Her throat spasmed almost shut. "How are you feeling tonight?"

"Now I know what youngsters mean about getting high. Honey, I'm so full of medication, I'm flying."

"Do you need anything?"

"Delta was here half an hour ago, asking the same question. I don't need a thing, sweetheart, except your company." He paused. "Enough about me. Have you learned anything more about that Detweiler fellow from Sheriff Schumaker."

"He stopped by earlier. Carroll Detweiler did serve with Senator Morgan in Vietnam. Avery tells me her father is devastated by what happened. He blames himself." She gave a little shrug. "Even though they did serve together, the idea is preposterous. The Senator has been wonderful to me and a good friend to the Outback. The sheriff thinks Carroll Detweiler was a crazed fan."

She shook her head in denial. "I'm not sure I agree. I just can't picture him spending much time looking at fashion magazines. Mims telephoned her office to check and there's no record of any Detweiler trying to contact me the way other fans have."

"I haven't wanted to muddy the waters but there was some serious trouble between the Detweilers and the

Prides years ago. The Detweilers came out the losers. Maybe that's why this one had it in for you."

"The Senator said Detweiler was suffering from post-traumatic stress syndrome. I guess he had a hard life. I almost feel sorry for him."

"You always did have a soft heart. This Detweiler doesn't deserve your sympathy no matter how hard he died." A pang twisted Hank's features and his complexion greyed.

Cait hated to see him hurting, trying to be brave for her sake. "How about the two of us calling it a night, Dad?"

"Not yet. We haven't had much time to talk lately."

"If you're sure you're up to it, I would love to stay a little longer. I have something to tell you."

"Good news, I hope."

She squeezed his hand, then lifted it to her lips. "The best. Comanche has asked me to marry him."

"I hope you had the good sense to accept," Hank burst out, sounding more like his old self than he had in weeks.

"I certainly did. I'm not dumb enough to let him get away a second time."

"A second time?"

"I was in love with Comanche when we were kids." She smiled to herself, thinking how lucky she was. Fate rarely gave second chances.

Hank beamed at her. "It is good news – the very best. I don't have to tell you how fond I am of Comanche. I have had my suspicions about the two of you. It's wonderful to have them confirmed, though. Have you set a date?"

"Not exactly. But I don't see any reason to wait. I'm counting on you giving me away." Cait tried to smile, but she couldn't quite pull it off. She knew she was grasping at straws, trying to give Hank a reason to hang on because she couldn't bear the thought of losing him.

Strange the way Comanche filled one part of her heart and Hank another. Taken singly, each love seemed all-encompassing, and yet she easily made room for them both. Perhaps that's what it was like when you had children, your heart expanding to fit the need. If only Hank would live long enough to see his first grandchild. Was she being selfish, clinging to him, hoping against hope to see him survive a little longer despite his pain?

The sound of Hank's voice interrupted her reverie. "I want you to promise me something."

"Anything for you."

"No matter what happens, don't change your plans. I honestly believe you and Comanche were born for one another, the way Lizzie and I were. I'd rest easier knowing the two of you were married."

"Then you should sleep like a log tonight. We're planning to get the licence tomorrow. Now, why don't you let me tuck you in?"

"I'd just as soon watch the stars for a while. You go on to bed, Lizzie."

He seemed unaware of the misnomer. It worried her, though. She could almost feel him drifting away. All her love seemed incapable of anchoring him in place. In danger of bursting into tears and fearing she might never stop once she did, she got to her feet.

"Don't stay up too late," she said, bending over to kiss him.

"Sweet dreams, honey."

She was almost to the door when she paused, turned, and ran back to his side. "I love you, Dad," she whispered in his ear.

It felt good to be back in his own room, Byron thought, even though he'd had to change the bed linen himself. What a weekend it had been! His head was still spinning from the dizzying sequence of events, the need to stick to the elaborate schedule whilst behind the scenes, the sheriff was questioning Senator Morgan about Detweiler. Thank heaven everything the Senator said checked out. It would have killed Cait if Avery's father had been implicated in the series of attacks.

Everyone involved with Outback, from the lowliest maid to the wranglers to Cait and Comanche, had surpassed themselves. Even the exotics had cooperated, always showing up at the right place at the right time as guests were driven through the enclosures in the open-roofed Range Rovers.

The real celebrities, animal behaviour experts from all over the world, had mesmerized everyone, both on the podium and off, with their discussions of endangered species and their endless fund of supporting anecdotes. And the impromptu concerts by Neil Dillon had iced an already lavish cake. Yes, he mused happily, the Outback was well and truly launched.

He stripped off the safari suit he'd worn that day, took a quick shower and put on a pair of flannel slacks and a velvet smoking jacket before slipping into the hall and knocking at Mims' door.

"Come in," she called out.

She was sitting cross-legged on her bed, wearing the tailored blue-satin pyjamas he liked so much. The colour matched her eyes and the strategic location of the pockets drew his attention to her breasts. A bottle of champagne and two glasses sat on the night stand to her left.

"I've been waiting for you," she said in the breathy little-girl voice that never failed to tug at his heart.

He gestured at the wine. "What are we celebrating?"

"The Outback's success. I'm so happy for the Prides." She looked and sounded more relaxed than she had all weekend. The opening had been hard on all of them, but his dear Mims had taken her responsibilities very much to heart. She had done a magnificent job of soothing the Senator's ruffled feathers and keeping the Detweiler incident from leaking to the press.

He uncorked the wine, filled both glasses and handed her one.

She took a sip, then gazed up at him. "I'd like to drink to something else too."

He joined her on the bed and put an arm around her shoulders. His right hand was just inches from the tantalizing swell of her breast. Had he followed his instincts, he would have made love to her then and there. But he wasn't an untutored youth, so bent on seduction that he had no time for talk. He would satisfy his own needs later. He chose to concentrate on Mims' needs now. "Anything that makes you happy makes me happy."

She pulled free of his arm and searched his face. "I hope you'll still feel like celebrating after I tell you what I've done. I wanted to talk about it before the cocktail party but there wasn't time." While she gazed at him, the frown line between her brows deepened.

"I had something on my mind too."

"Ladies first, darling. If you'll recall, I wanted to show you some legal papers. You see, I put my business and my condo on the market a couple of months ago. Considering the economy, I thought it would be a year or two before anything happened. But they both sold last week."

His heart began to pound and his throat dried. Mims was obviously making major changes in her life. Was he part of them? He was almost afraid to ask. "That sounds pretty drastic."

"It wasn't as impulsive as it seems. You and Cait are doing something meaningful with your lives. It's high time I did."

"You make it sound as if Cait and I are on some kind of crusade. But we're only doing what we care about – what's important to us. You can't live your life for other people, Mims. If you're bound and determined to make a change, do it for yourself."

The words had been bravely spoken. His heart clenched at the thought of what they implied. How would he handle it if she wanted to move so far away that they never saw each other?

"That's just what I had in mind. You know how I feel about the way AIDS has decimated the fashion industry. People are still so ignorant about the disease that it won't be long before it happens here, too. I spent a lot of time thinking about what you said at Christmas . . ."

"I said a lot of things at Christmas," he interrupted, desperate to know where she was headed, "including telling you that I love you."

"I haven't forgotten. You also talked about my letting go of the past – and I've tried. But wanting to mother everyone seems to have become a part of me."

"It's a part I love very much."

"I don't want to stop working with young people."

"You won't get any argument from me."

"I want to start an AIDS prevention and care programme in the Hill Country."

Byron's heart skipped a beat. "In Kerrville? Do you really think you could be happy in a small town after spending your whole life in New York?"

"I know it will be a big change. I've thought about little else for weeks."

"Is Cait another of your reasons for making the change now? She's going to need you after Hank dies."

"She is one of my reasons, but not the most important one." Her eyes continued to search his face. "I don't know about you, but I'm not satisfied with a long-distance relationship any more."

"Are you saying I'm the reason?"

"Do you mind? For God's sake, stop smiling and say something."

"Say something? I don't know where to begin. You're the most wonderful, generous, sexy woman in the whole world and I adore you." He reached in his pocket for the jeweller's box he'd been carrying with him since the cocktail party and realized he'd left it on the highboy in Comanche's spare bedroom.

"Blast!" he muttered.

"Blast what? Are you upset? Have I been too pushy?"

"Pushy? Not on your life. You see, darling, since picking you up at the aiport, I've been waiting for the right time to ask you to marry me. That's what I had in mind when I came to your room before the cocktail party. Frankly, I've been terrified because I didn't think you'd leave New York and I can't walk away from the Outback."

"Would you repeat that?"

"Which part?"

"The marriage part."

"I've been carrying my mother's ring around for days and now that the time is right, wouldn't you know I've left the blasted thing at Comanche's. Nevertheless," he said, getting off the bed and kneeling at her feet, "I'm determined to do this right because I never plan to do it again. Will you do me the honour of being my wife?"

"Is it a big diamond?" Mims teased.

"At least three carats. My father got it years ago from a friend who owned shares in the Kimberley mine."

She pursed her lips. "Are they flawless carats?"

"Damn near."

Mims slid off the bed, joined him on the floor and put her arms around his neck. "In that case, darling, I accept."

Hank sat back reluctantly and pushed the scope away. Watching the stars seemed to ease his suffering. Lord, he was tired of hurting. He tried to take a deep breath but a stab of pain halted the effort.

Closing his eyes, he willed himself to drift, to let go of everything. A riot of colours, greens, blues and reds burst against his lids, gradually fading to grey as he floated deeper and deeper into the darkness.

He ought to get up and join Lizzie in bed but he was just too weary. Lizzie, dear sweet Lizzie. He could hardly wait to tell her about Cait. She'd be so proud.

He could still feel the imprint of Cait's good night kiss like a blessing on his brow. Or had it been Lizzie's? He was so confused.

Suddenly he felt himself moving across a vast wilderness. At first it frightened him as he searched for, and failed to find, familiar landmarks. He hadn't planned a trip, hadn't packed. Hell. He wasn't well enough to go anywhere. Delta would skin his hide when she found out he'd left.

Darkness gobbled up the horizon behind him, an inky black that filled him with inexplicable dread. Where was he? He'd never seen a black so complete, with nary a star to guide the way. He seemed to be moving faster, heading towards a glow, an incandescent light that expanded until it filled his whole world.

Suddenly, he knew where he was going.

The Grand Canyon lay just ahead.

This time he could see the other side.

Lizzie waited there.

Cait had been anticipating Hank's death ever since Mims told her he had cancer. But all the anticipation in the world hadn't prepared her for the reality. She'd only been close to her father for a year and she would spend the rest of her life missing him, wishing she could tell him what she was doing, wondering if he would have been happy with her choices.

Grief didn't hurt all over the way she had imagined. It gnawed at her stomach so she couldn't eat, it cramped her heart so it ached with every beat, and it swelled so large in her throat that she couldn't swallow.

She had made it through the three days since Hank's death on automatic pilot, putting one foot in front of the other by route. It had got her through the funeral and now she hoped it would get her through this meeting with Hank's attorney.

"I hate to burden you at a time like this," Sandy Davis

was saying, "but I know Hank would want you to have all the facts."

Despite having a cherubic face more suited to smiles than tears, he looked as miserable as she felt. "If you'd rather I come back tomorrow or the next day . . .?"

"There's no need to go to the trouble. This afternoon is all right," Cait replied. "I know you're only looking out for my interests."

"You're a lot like your father, my dear. He liked to face problems head on too."

She was only peripherally aware of the measured cadence of his words as she gazed around Comanche's office. How many times had she seen her father and Bert McClain talking in this room when she was growing up, so deep in conversation that they were unaware of her presence, and wished Hank would pay as much attention to her?

Thinking about all the years they had wasted, of all the lost opportunities, hurt almost as much as Hank's death. If only she could go back and reclaim those lost years. Now she had a lifetime of thoughts and feelings they would never share.

Angrily, she knuckled her tears away before they could spill down her cheeks. This meeting couldn't be easy on Sandy Davis either. Hank had been one of Sandy's first cllients after Sandy graduated from law school and opened his practice in Kerrville.

"I'm sorry, Sandy" she said. "I wasn't concentrating. What were you saying about the inheritance taxes?"

Comanche stood by the fireplace in the parlour, glancing towards the hall, impatient for Cait to join them. What in the world could have been so important that Sandy Davis just had to discuss it with her today? Cait wasn't in any condition to talk business, let alone make decisions.

His chest ached as he remembered the expression on her face when she dropped the first handful of dirt on

Hank's coffin. Cait needed the support of the people who loved her. She should be here, not locked away in the old office.

He glanced across the room at Mims, Byron and Delta, knowing they had the power to alleviate her grief by sharing it. Damn it, hadn't she been through enough? He wanted her safe in his arms – today and for ever.

As he stared towards the parlour's wide entry, willing Cait to appear, he felt helpless and inadequate. All his love couldn't spare her the pain of losing Hank.

Four days ago, when they set the wedding date, she'd talked about Hank giving her away. At the time the idea has tickled him. His Katydid wasn't the sort of woman anyone *gave* away, except herself. But Hank hadn't lived long enough to walk Cait down the aisle. Now he lay next to Lizzie.

Just that morning Comanche had tried to tell Cait that Hank had what he'd wanted most, that one day the land would claim them all, that the final sleep by a loved one's side was the sweetest. But she had been too wounded to take it in.

God in heaven, what was keeping her? he thought, glancing towards the hall again. He was barely aware of Delta joining his lonely vigil by the fireplace.

"Cait will be fine. She has Hank's strength," Delta said, seeming to read his thoughts. She gestured to where Byron and Mims sat on a sofa. "Why don't you join the others."

"If you don't mind, I'd just as soon wait for Cait here."

"Of course I don't mind. It was a lovely funeral, don't you think, *cher*?" Delta's stoic face gave no hint of the devastation she must be feeling. She had been a rock, her dignity and courage never faltering. "Hank would have liked it. He didn't hold with a lot of fuss."

"You're right," Cait said, materializing in the parlour door like Banquo's ghost. "He *would* have liked it."

Comanche hurried to her side and took her icy hands in

his, willing his warmth into her. "Where's Sandy?"

"He sent his apologies. He's due in court." Although Cait held on to Comanche for dear life, she couldn't meet his eyes. Something Delta had said months ago echoed through her mind. "Everyone needs help, even a Pride."

She looked from one beloved face to another, thinking how much they had given her and the Outback. Had it all been in vain?

"Why did Sandy want to talk to you today?"

Unable to speak past the huge lump in her throat, she swallowed hard. How could she tell them what she now knew? Despite all her careful calculations, despite everyone's hard work from the youngest most inexperienced employee to Byron, Mims and Comanche, despite the successful opening and the positive attention from the media, despite the solemn promise she had made Hank to watch over Lizzie's grave, she was going to lose the ranch.

"Cait, darling," Comanche repeated urgently, "please tell me what happened."

Her lips felt stiff, her tongue frozen. It took an effort to answer. "Sandy wanted to talk about the inheritance tax. I'm afraid it's going to be much larger than we anticipated."

Relief was evident on Comanche's face. "Is that all? I was afraid something was wrong with you."

Cait couldn't repress an hysterical laugh at the irony of the situation. "You don't understand. Apparently the Outback's success has raised the ranch's value. The taxes are due in nine months. Sandy wanted to talk to me today to give me as much time as possible to raise the money. Considering how much I still owe the venture capitalist, I haven't a hope of borrowing any more." Cait's voice cracked. If Comanche hadn't been holding her hands she might have run howling from the room like a mad woman.

"How much money are you talking about?" he asked.

Appalled by the figure Sandy had mentioned, she could barely get her mouth to frame the answer. "It depends on the value of the estate. Inheritance taxes range from eighteen to fifty-five per cent. I'm afraid we're in the fifty per cent range."

Comanche let go a long low whistle. Then he pulled her into his arms. This time, however, she found no shelter there. He'd spent his life's savings on the Outback and now she could never pay him back.

Mims had been listening to the conversation with deepening concern. Cait's seemingly inexhaustible strength had given out three days ago when she walked into Hank's room early in the morning and found him dead. Mims would never forget the heartbroken wail that had echoed through the house like a banshee's cry.

Everyone needed someone to love – a parent, a husband or wife, a friend, a long-time companion, even a cherished pet. Mims felt so lucky to have found Byron. But for Cait and the Outback, it would never have happened.

She'd been wondering what she could do for Cait in return. Now, she knew.

"I had no idea your government was so greedy," Byron was saying. "I'll be happy to contribute my savings to the cause. I'm afraid they won't make much of a dent."

Mims squeezed his hands. "We haven't had a chance to talk this over yet. I think you'll approve."

"Talk what over?" he asked, his eyes never leaving Comanche and Cait.

"Give me a minute and you'll see," Mims replied, giving him a quick kiss. She let go of his hands, rose, and joined the others by the fireplace. "That is terrible news, Cait, but I think I have a solution."

"I couldn't ask you to do more than you've already done."

"I would have suggested it sooner only I knew how you felt about keeping the ranch in the family. I think I know an investor who might be interested in the Outback."

Cait rewarded her with a wan smile. "Considering our

balance sheet, he'd have to be crazy."

"Maybe *she* is a little crazy – crazy in love anyway." Mims motioned Byron to her side. "In love with Byron, with the Hill Country, with beginning a new life. I'm the investor, Cait. I haven't had a chance to tell you yet, but I sold the agency last week. How would you feel about having a partner who doesn't know a damn thing about exotics or cattle?"

This time, Cait smiled with her eyes as well as her lips. "Are you sure you want to do this?"

"Nothing could make me happier – except maybe a double wedding."

"That's more like it, *chers*," Delta said, trying to hug both couples at once.

For the next ten minutes there were so many expressions of gratitude and joy, so much laughter and tears all around, that none of them heard the doorbell until the third ring.

"One of us had better get that," Mims said.

"I'll do it," Byron offered. "I've been expecting a delivery.

He walked back into the room a few minutes later carrying a wriggling, raw-boned, red-coated puppy with a distinctive ridge of hair down its spine.

"Where in the world did that come from?" Comanche asked.

"From my sister, Winnie, in England," Byron replied, his gleeful grin making him look like a boy. "She's been raising champion ridgebacks for years. After Trouble died I wrote and asked her to send me a male pup from her next litter. I know he can't take Trouble's place, but I'm sure you'll like the breed. Why don't we call it an engagement present."

The puppy had been struggling in Byron's arms.

"I think he wants to get down," Cait said.

Byron bent over and deposited the animal on the floor. The puppy walked from one loving pair of hands to another, wriggling with ecstasy at every pat. Then he sniffed the carpet, lowered his bottom and wet the rug.

"Sorry about that," Byron said. "I think he's marking his territory."

Aren't we all, Cait thought, reaching for Comanche's hand. The four of them had a lot to talk about, but for now, she was content to exist in the magic circle of love and friendship that surrounded her.

"What do you want to call the puppy?" she said.

"Considering the mess he just made," Comanche replied, "Trouble seems appropriate."

EPILOGUE

JUNE 1995

The lioness scented the air one last time, as if to memorize the aroma of her new home before she manoeuvred her tumescent body inside the den she had prepared. It was dry, safe and secure, its depths hidden by the hill's rocky carapace.

Nature had prepared her for this moment. Although this would be her first birth, instinct told her what to do. She stretched out her tawny body, panting as a cramp rippled along her swollen abdomen. Bracing her hind legs against one wall, she tightened her stomach muscles, her lips drawn back with effort.

The spasms repeated again and again, the intervals between contractions growing shorter. At last a bloody sac emerged from between her legs. Curling around her own body, she gently nipped the sac open and began laving her first-born.

Two miles away, Cait murmured in her sleep as tension gathered in her lower back. The deepening sensation brought her fully awake. She cradled her heavy belly in her arms, sighing as the tightness receded.

She couldn't help wishing Hank had lived long enough to see his first grandchild. He would have made a wonderful grandfather, loving, opinionated, outspoken – and more often right than wrong. It would have meant so much to him, seeing a new generation of Prides born to the land.

Not that her child wouldn't be surrounded by loving adults. Mims and Byron were living in the foreman's house while they built a home of their own. If she read the signs correctly, Delta and Herman Schumaker were going to get married one of these days too. And, despite her avowal of being a dedicated businesswoman, Bobby Rae had accepted Mark Calhoun's ring.

A deep pain stabbed through Cait's lower body and she gasped in surprise. First babies were supposed to take their time coming into the world. From the strength of the contraction, this one seemed to be in a hurry. She had better wake Comanche.

The moonlight cast his features in sharp relief, emphasizing their beauty. God, how she loved him and the life they were building together.

Before she could reach out to touch him, a familiar sound came floating up the stairs. She could have sworn someone was playing Rachmaninov's *Rhapsody on a Theme of Paganini* on the old Chickering piano in the music room.

As the last notes faded, she heard a woman's joyful laughter.